THE
BIG OHHH
NIKKI ASHTON

For Jane Unwin a woman of courage and strength

CHAPTER

1

Eye contact is one of the classic signs of attraction, so if you catch someone gazing at you, let them know you're interested and available – just don't go overboard and wave manically at them as they may think the place is on fire.

Willow

A large body jostled against me, slopping half of my drink over Polly, my best friend, and I wondered again what on earth we were doing in this shithole of a bar. It was full of nubile teenage girls wearing the bare minimum and dickhead teenage boys who wanted to disrobe foresaid nubile teenage girls at the earliest opportunity.

"Why are we here?" I groaned into Polly's ear.

Polly glared at me. "Men, of course."

"Pol, they're mere boys. Look at them."

I pointed my finger around the room, stopping abruptly when I spotted a familiar face.

"Oh shit, my bloody brother is here."

Polly's head turned to where my finger was pointing. "Which one?" she almost screeched.

"Ruben," I sighed with an eye roll. "Not Declan."

My best friend had a huge crush on one half of my older, twin brothers and turned into a jelly-legged, thick-tongued idiot whenever he was around. Unfortunately for Polly, Declan was not interested in her because, and I hated to say it, my brother was extremely shallow and as Polly wasn't his 'type' i.e. five feet two, size eight with long blonde hair, she had no chance. Now if you asked my second youngest brother, Toby, what he thought about Polly, he'd probably man handle his crotch and make some sort of animal sex noise. However, at four years younger than us, Toby, in turn, had no chance with Polly, despite the fact that he was a part-time model and was, in his own words, 'a fucking hot ginge'.

"Ugh," Polly groaned, turning back to me, decidedly disinterested in my youngest brother. "Life is so unfair."

I bit back a comment about kids trawling rubbish dumps to make enough money to eat or having to walk ten miles for water and gave her a sympathetic smile. Well, it probably wasn't sympathetic, but more psychotic, because that's how talking or thinking about any of my four brothers made me feel. Add to that Polly's precious princess 'woah is me' attitude and I would quite gladly give her a slap along with the smile.

"Anyway, you didn't answer my question," I said, deciding to continue on a subject about something other than one of my brothers. "What are we doing in here? It's bloody awful."

Polly scanned the room. "Yeah, you're right," she sighed. "I heard it was getting an older crowd in here these days."

"It is. The age group used to be twelve."

"You are miserable at times." Polly rolled her eyes. "Just try and enjoy it."

I knew there was no point in arguing with her, so I twitched my cheek in the guise of a smile and took a long swig of my drink.

Almost half an hour later and we were still propped against a bare brick wall, unable to move against the crush, as we drank ridiculously priced drinks. Polly hadn't taken the hint and insisted we stay a little longer, so to entertain myself I decided to piss my little brother off and kept waving to him.

"He's quite clearly seen me." I said, throwing my arm about as though shouting for a lifeguard. "Look at him pretending he hasn't or doesn't know me."

Polly started to laugh. "Look at his face, he's bloody mortified."

There was a pure look of horror on his face, as though I'd streaked across the bar shouting 'yippee-ki-yay mother fucker'.

"He really hates you, doesn't he?" Polly stated.

I nodded and grinned. "Yep and I bloody love it."

"Wave again," Polly said on a giggle. "He's talking to a girl."

"You do it too." I gave her a nudge with my elbow and giggled.

We both started to wave frantically, laughing hysterically as we did. Finally, Ruben rudely flipped us the bird and turned his back on us. We both fell about, clutching hold of each other, the vodka making us think we were hilarious.

"Oooh shit," Polly cried, gripping hold of my forearm. "That blond guy thinks you're waving at him."

My gaze followed Polly's and I almost came on the spot. Waving back tentatively was the most gorgeous man I had ever seen.

He was tall and slim with messy hair, had a chiselled jaw and filled out his fairly tight trousers to perfection. I couldn't see the detail of his face, but the parts of him I could see were gorgeous. I was so enraptured that I continued waving like one of those lucky Chinese cats, but with my tongue hanging out. Which also meant I didn't notice that he'd waved back and had started walking towards us. It was only when Polly grabbed my arm and yanked it down that I realised he was only a couple of feet away.

"Hi," he said, giving me a knicker wetting smile. "Do I know you?"

I shook my head, silently taking him in and memorising everything about him for a spank bank session later.

"It's just that you were waving at me."

Oh shit, even his voice was sexy; smooth and rich, like melted chocolate. Now he was closer, I could see his face properly. Green eyes glinted at me when his full lips pulled into a smile that actually produced dimples.

"I-I-." I shook my head again. "Sorry, I don't know you."

"Oh, okay." He looked over his shoulder. "Was it someone else you were waving to?"

"My brother. He hates me and I was trying to embarrass him."

He laughed and when he did, I was pretty sure he'd made me pregnant. I could actually feel my milk coming in; he was that bloody good.

I glanced over at Polly; I wondered what her reaction to him was because I had a reputation for finding the weirdest of looking men attractive – apparently, I'm the only person who thinks there's something sexy about the Beast before he turns back into the Prince. I was therefore relieved to see she was equally as gob smacked as I was. Although that didn't say much, she fancied the boxer briefs off my brother and to me that was...ugh, gross.

"So, did you manage it?" Sexy Guy asked. "To embarrass your brother."

"Oh, um, yeah I think so. He turned his back on me and flipped me the finger, so I reckon it was mission accomplished."

We both laughed, although mine was a little forced because I was trying to listen to his. You know, remembering it to go along with the images for later when I was alone in bed.

"Well I'm glad about that, if you are," he finally said, as his green eyes darkened with intent.

There were a few seconds of slightly uncomfortable silence when I was convinced that he thought I was weird and would disappear, but then he shocked me.

"Listen, I'd love to buy you a drink. Is that okay?"

On instinct I looked over my shoulder, but all I saw was the wall that I was leaning against. Polly nudged me with her shoulder and in a loud voice said, "I'm off to the bog, I need a pee."

With her words came a huge wink that twisted the whole of her upper body as she did it. I let out a long sigh and wished she could learn the art of less is more at such critical times.

We watched her go and I was surprised that he turned back to me.

"So, that drink. What would you like?"

My stomach squeezed and I felt a level of excitement that I hadn't felt since I was a kid at Christmas.

"Vodka and diet coke, please."

"Great, now don't go anywhere. I'll be right back. Oh, and I'm Charlie by the way."

"Hi, I'm Willow," I replied breathily.

"Well Willow, one vodka and diet coming right up."

As I watched his exquisite arse move through the crowds, I knew I would not move one inch.

I had to be honest, I felt a certain level of guilt that I hadn't stopped talking to Charlie for almost half an hour. He made me laugh and I was interested in everything he had to say and he actually seemed to like me; at least he laughed in the right places when I said something that I thought was funny. I felt bad because Polly was most definitely the third wheel. Charlie had asked her questions and included her in the conversation, but as we moved closer and closer, our voices became quieter and quieter, and poor Polly became excluded. I could also sense that she had begun to get fidgety about being in the same place for too long. She wanted a man and there were no men around – well, apart from Charlie, and I would make sure she didn't get her claws into him.

"I'm sorry," I told her when Charlie nipped back to his friend. "But I really like him, Pol."

"It's fine." My best friend said with a huge smile. "I don't mind, in fact, I might even nip over to Zar Bar and meet up with Jasmine."

Jasmine was another old school friend who insisted that she only wore designer labels. She was a typical Abercrombitch, especially when she went out with her work colleagues, which meant that Polly and I, in our *Primark* and charity shop ensembles, didn't really fit in.

"No," I groaned. "Don't do that, she'll be with that bitch, Lulu Young."

Polly shuddered. "Her name's Louise, who the hell would name themselves after a bloody old aged pensioner from Scotland who once sang with Take That?"

"Someone who only knows about music since 2017," I mused, while I gazed over at Charlie. "What about his friend?"

I nodded over to the guy Charlie was with, aware it was a shot in the dark. He didn't look like my brother and by the looks of it was only the same height as Polly.

"Nope, too short."

Her answer was immediate, which proved that I truly did know my best friend.

She started to mess around in her bag with one hand, and her vodka clutched in the other. Finally, after much rustling and the appearance of two train tickets, one pack of chewing gum and a tampon, she produced her mobile.

"I'll text Jasmine," Polly announced, her thumbs flying over the screen. "If Lulu is with her it'll be fun."

"Really?"

"Oh yeah." she grinned; her hazel eyes twinkled. "It'll be great sport when I tell her I got the exact same handbag as hers from The Salvation Army shop for three pounds fifty."

"Brilliant, that'll make her have palpitations."

"I know." Polly's smile was evil and that was why I bloody loved her.

A few seconds later her mobile tweeted like a bird and she flicked at the screen.

"Yep, they're in Zar Bar. Will you be okay?"

I glanced over at Charlie who happened to be looking at me. He waved his arms around, as I'd been doing earlier, making me laugh.

"Yeah, I'll text you if I need you," I replied, unable to take my eyes off the tall, sexy man a few feet away.

Polly pulled me into a hug. "Take care of you."

"Take care of you," I replied in an American accent. This was our usual goodbye routine, paying homage to Kit and Viv in Pretty Woman, our favourite film since we were twelve years old.

She gave a quick wave to Charlie and then she was gone, pushing through the children standing around quaffing their brightly coloured drinks.

Charlie gave me a look of concern, said something to his friend, and then came back over to me, pointing toward the door.

"I didn't frighten Polly away, did I?"

He seemed really concerned as he looked over the masses of heads to the exit and I had to be honest, my heart sighed a little.

"No, she's gone to meet another friend." I looked at him and then over to *his* friend. "That's okay isn't it? I mean I can go with her, if you'd prefer."

"God, no." He caught hold of my elbow as if trying to stop me from leaving. "I'm glad you've stayed. My mate," He nodded toward his friend, "Bomber, he's getting off now too."

I looked over to see Bomber had knocked back his drink and had followed the same path which Polly had only a few minutes before.

"Are we really bad friends?" I asked, as I winced a little.

Charlie smiled and gave me both dimples. "I don't think so. I'm sure we'd both do the same for them."

I looked up at his kind, gentle eyes and nodded. "Yeah, I think you're right, we definitely would."

CHAPTER
2

Masturbating up to two hours before sex can help to avoid premature ejaculation - it's always a shock when it comes from nowhere.

Willow

"Ssh," I hissed as Charlie banged into the kitchen table and groaned.

"I thought you said they wouldn't mind." He pulled on my hand, turned me, and placed his other hand on my hip.

After far too many vodkas and some serious flirting, I'd thought 'what the hell' and invited Charlie back to my parents' house. I hadn't been so attracted to someone in a long time and I really didn't want to pass up the opportunity. Charlie was gorgeous and I had no doubt he'd be chatting up a different girl the following weekend, so call me fast and loose, but I was going for the one-night stand. If nothing else, it'd give me a whole lot of material for my Flickapedia page.

"They really won't," I sighed. "But they're too embarrassing for words and I'd really like to get you down to your jockeys before you realise that you need to run into the night and never stop."

Charlie grinned in the half-light that the green neon clock on the cooker gave us and lifted his hand to cup my cheek.

"They can't be that bad."

He dropped a soft kiss to my downturned lips, so sweet and romantic that I sighed with deep satisfaction – and he hadn't even touched my little man in a boat yet.

"They really are," I replied, once I'd pulled myself out of my dreamy haze. "So please stop making a noise."

He laughed quietly and nodded. "Silent as a ghost, I promise."

I lead him by the hand and sneaked past the room my mum liked to call 'the den' – she watched far too much American TV – where I knew that either Ruben or Toby would be sexing up some girl because they shared a bedroom and, as close as they were...well, ugh that's just nasty to watch your brother give a girl an orgasm. Declan and I were the lucky ones with rooms of our own, and Declan had only had his to himself for the last year since Danny, his twin, had moved in with his girlfriend, Patsy, and their dog, Nigel. So, yes, we had a pretty full house, but that's what happened when your parents procreated as if mankind depended on them.

When we reached the fourth stair up, I pointed to it and over exaggerated my step over it. Charlie's brows knitted together, and he shook his head. I opened my eyes wide to tell him silently that in no way had I exaggerated how shameful my parents were. Although they must have been doing something right because four of their five kids still lived at home.

Finally, we reached the safety of my room and when I clicked the door shut and slid across the bolt, I turned and leaned against it with a sigh of huge relief, before I reached to turn on my bedside lamp.

"Nice room," Charlie said and there was a definite smile in his voice.

"I know, it's awful, but my mother thinks she's great at interior design and I happened to mention that I'd watched Harry Potter and enjoyed it, now the little fucker has his eyes on me wherever I look."

Charlie sputtered out a laugh and picked up a plaster bust of Harry's head. "It's one way to go with a theme, I suppose."

My room was HP vomit. The wallpaper, the bedding, the lampshades, the curtains and I even had an alarm clock in the guise of Hedwig.

"She did it as a surprise when I went on holiday to Ibiza," I groaned.

Charlie's lips pursed and I knew he was desperate to laugh.

"You were clubbing in Ibiza while your mum was here creating a shrine to Harry Potter?"

"Pretty much." I moved over to my dressing table and picked up a mug that I kept make-up brushes in. "However, if you look carefully at this mug that she purchased from our local pound shop, you'll see it's actually Harry Proctor that I have a thing for."

That did it. One look at the mug and Charlie doubled over with laughter.

"Shush, you'll wake them up and then my dad will bang on the door wanting to meet you." I slapped at his arm but couldn't help laughing along with him.

"God, you're funny," Charlie sighed.

"Not me, my bloody mother."

His eyes softened as he looked at me and when his hand lifted to tuck a lock of my long dark hair behind my ear, everything turned warm and tingly and when his fingertips lingered on my neck, my stomach did a little flip too.

"You're so pretty and I really want to kiss you," he said, as he watched my tongue dart out to lick my bottom lip.

"You can if you like."

I had no idea what was wrong with me. This wasn't my first visit to the fun fair of sex, and I'd had one-night stands before, but something about Charlie made me feel nervous and a little bit virginal. He was funny and sweet as well as being hot and I really didn't want to disappoint him, because for all my head was saying it was one night and he couldn't possibly want anything more, my heart hoped that he asked to see me again. That thought in turn confused me because if it did become something more, then this wouldn't be a one night stand and I would have given up the goods on a first date and he then might think I was too easy to be someone to get serious with and...oh shit, romance was far too bloody complicated. I decided I'd concentrate on the here and now and just go with the flow.

As I inched closer, Charlie's hand slowly slid down my neck, along my arm and then landed on my bottom, all the time his gaze on me as I pushed out unsteady breaths. He then pulled me closer until my hips landed against him and I could feel the beginnings of a hard on.

Okay, so it was slightly disappointing that he didn't have full on wood. I was wearing a really cute black dress with white spots and a fairly low neckline. I also had on what I liked to think of as my 'fuck me' shoes; yellow, pointed toed stilettoes and not to mention my favourite 'Scarlett Woman' shade of lipstick.

Mentally, I pushed Charlie's half erected flagpole to one side and concentrated on the soft lips that were now kissing me and I didn't think I'd ever had such a sweet, yet hot, kiss before in my life. One hand stayed on my bum, while the other gently caressed my cheek and his tongue and lips whipped me up into a frenzy.

With soft moans, I walked him backward toward my bed, hooking my fingers into the waistband of his trousers.

"Shit," he groaned, as he fell back onto the bed. "You taste so good."

My breath sped up trying to keep in time with my heart as heat burned in the pit of my stomach and flamed its path to between my legs. Charlie pulled me down next to him and trailed a hand along my side, his fingertips whispering down to my thigh, pushing up my dress.

His lips and tongue felt incredible against mine, moving to the perfect rhythm to build up my excitement.

"Shit, Willow." he whispered reverently.

"Charlie."

"What house are you in?" he asked in between kisses.

My mind tried to think about what he was talking about, momentarily stopping me from kissing him back.

"Cause I've got something I'd love to slither in."

My breath caught as I realised what he'd said, and I pulled back suddenly wanting to cry at how corny he was. It couldn't be happening, surely someone so hot couldn't say something so ridiculous. It made my heart weep.

I opened my eyes to look at him and almost collapsed with relief when I saw a huge grin on his face as he immediately erupted into laughter.

"You bugger," I hissed, poking him in the chest.

"Sorry, but I couldn't resist it."

Charlie pulled me closer to him and wrapped his arms tightly around me. "One thing though."

"Hmm." I closed my eyes and breathed in his sexy, manly smell.

"Can we turn the light off, Harry's giving me the willies."

I groaned and rolled my eyes, only for Charlie to capture my mouth again and restart the waves of want inside of me.

Our hands roamed over each other's bodies as our pelvises seemed to be magnetised to each other. My nipples were like bullets and my knickers were soaking as Charlie's hands explored, stroked, and touched me.

I reached out my hand and rubbed the front of his trousers and felt that he was now fully erect, and my clit throbbed in time with my heart.

"Willow," he gasped as I alternated my rub with a squeeze.

I reached for the button on his trousers, popped it open and slowly pulled down his zip, as my fingers trailed down his shaft.

Charlie groaned as he thrust his hips forward, pushing himself against my hand.

"Oh fuck."

His cry was almost pained, I did a little mental skip that I was turning him on so much and then...he came in his pants.

CHAPTER
3

A rich meal eaten right before having sex can inhibit orgasms – in other words don't eat a donner kebab on the way home if you or your partner are feeling horny.

Charlie

My eyes creaked open, instantly blinded by hundreds of fucking Harry Potters staring down at me and, for a moment, I forgot where I was. After a few seconds I remembered, and turned my head to look at the sleeping body next to me. Shit, she was pretty, even with the mass of dark hair spread across the pillow and her mouth gaping open on a soft snore.

I'd really had fun with Willow the night before, she made me laugh with the stories of her job as a dentist's receptionist. I found her interesting and loved to hear her talk about her love of 70's music, romance novels, and girly films. All in all, it had been a great night.

Then I remembered and looked up at the ceiling with a silent groan.

"Fucking pathetic," I muttered, and quickly looked down at my morning wood.

I glanced over at Willow and saw that she was fully clothed, the

15

same as me, although my trousers were undone giving my cock room for its usual morning push up routine. Her dress was bunched up around her thighs and her left tit was almost hanging out, but generally we were pretty respectable, which wasn't a surprise since I'd spurted like a teenager in my damn undies.

As soon as it had happened, I wanted to smack myself in the bollocks for them being too eager, but Willow had carried on kissing me as though nothing happened. After a couple more minutes, I'd said I needed a pee but actually went to the bathroom to clean up. When I got back Willow was fast asleep, snoring much louder than she was now, so drunk and knackered, I curled up next to her.

It wasn't the first time I'd come a little too quickly, but it hadn't happened for a while. The last time had been with Tory Baker two years ago when I'd finally gone on a date with her after almost two months of chasing her. I'd explained it away as me not having been with anyone for ages, but I could tell by the look of pity in Tory's eyes that she didn't believe me. Needless to say, we hadn't had a second date, although she'd been pretty cool about it and I didn't think she'd told anyone, as we did actually get to have sex at the second attempt a little later that night.

I'd had sex with a couple of girls since, and there'd been no early release on either occasion, but then I hadn't really been in to them that much. It had been purely sex and nothing more - unlike Willow, who I wanted to see again; *badly*. There was something about her that made me feel happy and at the risk of sounding a bit pathetic, contented. I didn't feel the need to try with her, everything had come naturally - my spunk too, apparently.

Claustrophobia began to swamp me so I swung my legs and dropped my feet to the floor. I ran a hand through my hair and looked back over my shoulder at the sleeping Willow and my heart sank knowing she wouldn't want to see me again – it was Tory Baker on repeat.

I glanced at the damn ugly Hedwig clock to see it was only quarter past six, far too early to be awake on a Sunday morning. I thought about trying to go back to sleep, or maybe even sneak out and go home, but that wasn't my style, and aside from which, I wanted to try and get Willow to go on a date with me and I had more chance of that face to face.

I did know one thing; my mouth was as dry as the bottom of a bird-cage and I could definitely do with a drink of something. I pushed up from the bed, zipped myself up, padded across the room and quietly slipped the bolt across and opened the door. When I looked out the coast seemed clear, so I stepped onto the landing, trying to remember which of the closed doors the bathroom was. Nothing at all gave me a clue or reminded me which one I'd drunkenly stumbled into the night before. Desperate for a drink, I decided going down to the kitchen would be safer, at least I knew where that was and wouldn't be likely to stumble into someone's bedroom.

I made my way down the stairs, remembering about the creaking step, and went to the kitchen, my tongue desperate for the liquid that would soon be in my mouth, I was that thirsty.

When I opened the door, I was relieved to see it was empty, the only sound was that of a dripping tap – music to my ears. I took a step forward and looked at all the cream cabinets on the wall, wondering which one held the glasses or mugs for me to drink from. I opened the one nearest to me and when I saw that was full of plates, moved on to the next one. Still not what I was looking for, I'd reached for the handle of the next one when a voice behind me almost made me shit my pants – well I'd already creamed them, so it would just be my luck.

"If it's glasses that you're looking for, it's that one."

I swivelled around on my socked feet to see a tall, round bellied man with grey hair stuck out at all angles, standing in the doorway, he wore nothing but a huge smile on his face as he pointed at a cupboard.

"Morning," he said and reached his hand out to me. "I'm Ivan, Willow's dad and you must be the young man who failed to make my daughter orgasm last night."

"I-I..."

I had no fucking words for the naked man grinning at me. Firstly, he had his cock out and swinging proudly, secondly, how the hell did he know I hadn't made Willow come and thirdly...he had his cock out and swinging proudly!

"Oh, don't worry about it," he scoffed and waved a hand at me as he stalked toward me with purpose. "It can happen when you're not yet familiar with a woman's body."

"Sorry." My eyes went wide as I did a huge swallow, as if I had a whole fucking watermelon stuck in my throat.

Ivan slapped a big hand on my shoulder, and I stiffened, struck by how close his swinging cock was to my thigh.

"When it's your first time with a woman-."

"I'm not a virgin." I blurted out.

Ivan chuckled and squeezed before he dropped his hand to his side. "I know that. You wouldn't have got her making the little moans and sighs if you were."

"Were you listening at the door?" I asked, alarmed and slightly disturbed.

"No, no." He shook his head as he passed me and reached for the cupboard where he'd said the glasses were. "We have a baby monitor in there."

I stumbled back a couple of steps, as bile rose in my throat.

"What the fu-."

Ivan let out a huge roar of laughter. "I'm joking," he said, as he took a glass and moved to the sink. "I have no idea whether she was moaning and sighing, but I know I didn't hear you bring that baby home. We're in the next room and usually catch that sort of thing. The boys too, I always know when they've hit the jackpot, although our youngest seems to be struggling at the moment."

I wanted to look around and check for hidden cameras, convinced someone was playing a trick on me.

"A little tip for you." He turned on the tap, filled the glass with water, then turned and handed it to me. "Testosterone levels are highest when we first wake up, which means that the best orgasms are likely to happen first thing in the morning."

With the cold glass clutched in my hand, I tried not to look below Ivan's shoulders as he leaned against the sink, with his arms folded across his chest.

"Okay," I managed to mutter.

"So, that being the case...sorry I didn't catch your name."

"Ch-Charlie."

He winked and tapped his temple. "I'll remember, I'm usually pretty good with names. Anyway, that being the case, Charlie, I suggest you get back up those stairs and treat my daughter to something special."

I had no idea what to do or say as I stood there with the glass of water in my hand and gaped at him like an idiot.

"You know I normally charge a pretty penny for that advice." He laughed and leaned forward to punch me in the shoulder.

"Sorry?"

He dropped his head back and laughed. "I'm a sex therapist," he said. "So, you ever need any information on how to make sure my daughter is satisfied, well, you let me know. Now, I'm going to take my own advice and wake Maureen up with something special, if you know what I mean."

He winked at me again, filled another glass with water and then disappeared, leaving me in exactly the same place and position I'd been in when his swinging cock had been inches from my body.

"Did I dream that?" I whispered to myself, looking toward the door.

I then looked down at the glass in my hand and realised that it certainly hadn't been a fucking terrible dream. I'd just had sex lessons from the naked father of the girl who I'd failed to satisfy because I'd jizzed in my pants.

CHAPTER

4

Chocolate is known to contain natural feel-good chemicals which can boost your orgasm. Smear each other with chocolate and slowly lick it off – melted *Snickers* are not recommended in case of anaphylactic shock.

Willow

I smacked my lips and moved my tongue around in my mouth, desperately trying to lubricate the sawdust that seemed to be coating it. Ugh, vodka was the drink of the devil, particularly when you drank as much as I had the night before.

I knew immediately that Charlie wasn't in bed next to me but remembered waking in the very early hours with him snuggled up against my back, with an arm wrapped around my stomach. That meant he'd sneaked out at some point, probably never to be seen again, which was really disappointing. Okay, so the lack of sexual gratification hadn't been ideal, but aside from that we'd had a great night – and he was gorgeous and had drunk an awful lot of vodka too, so I wasn't going to hold one false start against him. Unfortunately, it looked as though he wasn't quite so eager.

"Fucker," I muttered as I dragged the duvet over my face. "Fucking, fuck, fuck."

"Who you talking to?" A deep, sexy voice asked.

The covers were tugged from me, and I looked up at a pair of beautiful, fern green eyes and cute dimples.

"You're still here," I gasped, struggling to push up onto my elbows. "I thought you'd gone."

Charlie shook his head and handed me a glass of water. "I went to get a drink and thought you might like one."

He lifted a glass to his own lips and took a long swig. My eyes were fixated on his Adam's apple as it bobbed with each swallow of his drink, and when a drop of water ran down his chin, I followed every inch of its path until it dropped and soaked into the cotton of his shirt.

"God, I needed that," he said, smiling at me as he lowered the glass.

I stared at him and nodded.

"So," he said and winced a little. "I kind of met your dad before."

Suddenly my power of speech returned. "Please tell me you didn't."

My stomach flipped with the dread of what my dad might have said or done. I knew that whatever it was, it would not have been good.

"What did he say?" I groaned and closed my eyes. "Tell me, no matter how bad."

I felt Charlie sit on the edge of the bed and heard him clear his throat, making my eyes flash open to see his body turned toward me.

"It was really bad wasn't it?"

Charlie's lips thinned into a straight line and his eyes looked down at the carpet. I held my breath and waited, knowing without doubt I was not going to like whatever words came out of his mouth.

"He, um, he was naked." He rubbed his forehead with three fingers and eyed me warily.

"And what else?" I asked, resigned to the fact that this would be the last time I'd probably see the gorgeous man sitting on my bed. No doubt his night with me would become a tale of hilarity that would grow in its hideousness with each telling.

"HetoldmehowtomakesureyouhadanorgasmthismorningbecauseI-didn'tgiveyouonelastnight." Charlie blurted it out in one long word without taking a breath.

As he blew out his cheeks with eyes full of fear, I flopped back against my pillows.

"*UGH!*" I cried and banged my curled fists onto the mattress. "Why me? God, I hate my damn life."

My legs started to kick up and down in time with my fists and I must have looked like a toddler having a tantrum. As I shook my head from side to side, I continued with my screams of anguish at why I'd been landed with such embarrassing parentage.

"Willow," Charlie said as he placed a hand on my thigh. "Hey, calm down. Don't get upset about it."

I stopped immediately and stared at him, with what I was sure were wild eyes. "Don't get upset. You're kidding right? You met Ivan The Fucking Terrible."

"Ivan the what?" he asked with a grin.

I waved him away. "That's what we call him when he's annoying, and my mother becomes Maureen. The point is Charlie, he's an embarrassment and now you're going to avoid me forever."

He shook his head. "No, I'm not. At least it shows he cares," he replied and stroked my leg over the duvet.

"But he was...oh shit," I groaned. "He was naked and gave you advice on sex."

I slapped my hands over my eyes and let out a strangled cry.

"You can go now if you want to," I said on a croaky whisper. "I understand."

Charlie started to laugh, and I felt the bed dip before a finger ran down the side of my face.

"Open your eyes."

His voice was soft and cajoling and almost persuaded me, but I shook my head.

"Please Willow, open them." He pulled at my hands. "Please."

23

I opened one eye and huffed out a disgruntled breath as I saw Charlie lying next to me.

"I'm not going anywhere," he said with dimples on full show. "I like you and I'd like to see you again."

"But he..." My words trailed off as I tried not to think about what trauma my darling daddy had put him through.

"It's fine. Gotta admit it was a bit disconcerting, but he wasn't expecting to see me in the kitchen, and it is his house."

"Believe me," I replied. "It wouldn't have made any difference if he'd known you were there or not, he'd have still wandered in with his meat and veg on display."

Charlie chuckled. "Well it's not an image I'll forget in a hurry, but I am really okay about it."

I scrutinised him with narrowed eyes, as I lifted my head a few inches from the pillow to get a closer look. "You can't be," I snapped. "He showed you his...oh God, I can't even say the word."

"His cock," he offered as he tried to hide the twitch of his lips.

"Ugh, no don't. It's too horrible to contemplate. Surely you think he's crazy and that you can't wait to get out of this damn house?"

"It's not the usual first meeting I've had with a girl's parents, but I can cope."

My head went back to the pillow and I sighed. "And he told you how to give me an orgasm?" I asked. "Or did I – and please let this be true – dream that?"

"No, sorry, he did offer his professional opinion."

I let out a pained groan. "He told you what his job is?"

"Yeah he did."

"And you still want to stay?" I ground out.

"Yeah I do."

I looked at him carefully and there looked to be truth in his eyes. He didn't turn away, or glance to one side, but watched me carefully.

"Okay," I finally said. "But I really can't have sex, not now I know he's awake and has actually talked about it to you."

"Is that only this morning or ever again?" Charlie asked with a grin as he pushed my hair away from my face.

"Oh, definitely only this morning. I'm used to him, so he doesn't have too much of a lasting effect on me, but sometimes it takes a little while to gather my thoughts and put the trauma behind me."

"God, you're cute." He laughed and then leaned down to kiss me – a soft, sweet kiss. "I think we're going to have fun."

I smiled against his lips. "Only not this morning."

"No," Charlie said and kissed me again, "not this morning, but most definitely soon."

CHAPTER
5

Drink lots of water and skip a trip to the toilet before sex. Research discovered that many women experience sharp, powerful orgasms as a result of the increased abdominal pressure of a full bladder – mattress protectors are fully recommended.

Willow

Charlie was in the bathroom and I was waiting nervously for him. We were going downstairs as soon as he'd finished and my whole family were down there, I'd even heard Danny's voice when I'd nipped to the loo earlier.

I supposed I could have sneaked him through the front door, but if I knew my mum, she'd already have a sniper posted on it to stop him escaping, because beyond any doubt, my dad would have already spilled the beans about me having a man in my room.

Most people found it weird that my parents were so relaxed about us having sleepovers – or evenings of gratification, as my dad liked to call them – but, when your dad is a sex therapist and your mum teaches biology to horny sixteen-year old kids, there isn't much that shocks them. They were also a pair of free spirits who quite often spoke of university days spent smoking pot and drinking cider, so while none of us kids wanted to consider it, we were pretty sure they probably had an immense amount of sexual experience and experimentation under their belts.

It wasn't only my parents I was worried about; it was the boys too. I wasn't sure if there was a collective noun for a group of brothers, but for my brothers I was pretty sure it was a 'bunch of pricks'. Individually they were all lovely – well maybe not Ruben, he really was a prick all the time – but put them together and they constantly took the piss, constantly tried to get me to lose my temper and constantly talked shit. I knew they'd act up in front of Charlie and then I'd lose it and he'd see me for the screeching harpy I actually was and never want to see me again.

"Hey," he said, as he strode confidently back into my room. "All done."

I gave him a weak smile and moved past him. "You sure you don't need to get back?" I asked as he followed me down the stairs.

"Nope. All good. Unless of course you want me to go."

I stopped three steps from the bottom and turned to face him. His smile was there but there were no dimples and he looked like a small boy who'd just had his sweets nicked. Apart from anything else, I really liked him and wanted him to stay a little longer so I'd have more time to imprint images of him into my brain, because who the hell was I kidding; there was no way he'd want to see me again.

"No," I replied with a shake of my head. "Stay for some breakfast."

"It's gone midday, Willow," he laughed.

I shrugged. "Toast tastes great at any time of the day."

"Yeah, I suppose it does."

This time his dimples appeared, and I felt my heart skip half a beat. I had to admit, it had been bloody lovely snuggled up against him in bed as we kept dozing. I'd have quite liked to give sex another go, to check out whether it was only vodka cock he'd had the night before, but knowing my dad was probably sat outside the door and taking notes to write a medical article about us, it kind of killed that mood, so sleeping and snuggling had been enough. His chest was hard and warm and the hand he rubbed up and down my arm was smooth and comforting.

"I apologise now though," I sighed. "For my family. My parents are definitely going to be Ivan The Fucking Terrible and Maureen this morning, I can feel it."

"I think I'll be fine." Charlie laughed and placed a hand on my shoulder. "I saw your dad's dick, Willow. How much more embarrassing can things get?"

I rolled my eyes and patted his hand. "You'll see."

When we got into the kitchen everyone stopped what they were doing and looked up at us, even Danny's dog, Nigel, looked up from licking his balls.

"Morning." I pulled my shoulders back and hoped no one noticed the nervous twitch in my eye.

The boys looked between me and Charlie and then back again, as though watching a tennis match.

"Hello again," Dad chimed, as he stood up and reached his hand out to Charlie. "Charlie, right?"

"Yes, that's right, hi." He shook Dad's hand and then turned to my mum. "Morning Mrs...um...morning."

Toby let out a loud laugh and slapped his palm down onto the table. "Oh, he doesn't even know your surname. What did you do, Will, roofie him?"

"Nah, she smacked him over the head and dragged him back here. You need to check your wallet mate," Declan added. "She may well have nicked it while you were knocked out."

I breathed in deeply through my nose and then let it slowly out to clear my mind and make the bad thoughts *drift away*.

"Piss off," I hissed at my elder brother and pinched his nipple.

"Ouch, that hurt."

"Good, it was meant to."

"Leave Charlie alone," Mum chimed in. "And it's a pleasure to meet you, even if Willow did force you down here."

She gave me a sympathetic smile and reached to tuck my hair

behind my ears. God love her as she tried to make out she was normal and motherly.

"I came willingly, I swear," Charlie said holding his hands up as though someone had a gun to his head – not really the way to convince my family, Charlie boy.

"Did she tell you to say that?" Ruben grunted, as he shifted up on the bench seat to make room.

Charlie laughed nervously and when Ruben nodded to the space, he glanced at me and then the bench.

"You take it," I said. "I'll make us something to eat."

Looking as though he was about to take a seat on the electric chair, Charlie slowly sidled into the space and sat down.

"Toast okay?" I asked over my shoulder.

"Perfect."

I turned to look at him and was dazzled by the beautiful smile he sent my way. It was all dimples and sparkling green eyes. It was such a pity I hadn't had sex with him, because I really needed a good orgasm and for Charlie to have given it to me would have been nice.

"So, what is it you do?" Toby asked, as he reached across the table to take a sausage from Ruben's plate.

"Oi."

Ruben tried to snatch it back, but Toby was too quick for him and practically threw it into his own mouth and chewed down on it.

"Ginger prick," Ruben grumbled, going back to the rest of his food.

"Yep and my balls and arse hair." Toby winked at Charlie. "So, carry on, tell us what you do."

"You don't have to, Charlie," I sighed. "He's being nosey."

"It's fine." He smiled and then turned to Toby. "I'm a music technician at Musica Records."

I almost dropped the loaf of bread I was holding, Ruben dropped his fork, Declan whistled, Toby's mouth dropped open and Danny carried on cleaning shit out of Nigel's eye. Mum and Dad didn't react at all but continued to watch Charlie with great interest.

"No fucking way," Toby gasped.

"Toby, watch your mouth son, eh." Dad's brow furrowed and he shook his head.

"You let us have sex, under your roof, with randoms," Toby said, quirking an eyebrow, "but I can't say fucking?"

Declan leaned further across the table, evidently more fascinated by Charlie's announcement than dad and Toby's staring contest. We all were, because Musica Records was owned by the band Dirty Riches, one of the biggest bands in the world.

"Musica Records," Declan repeated. "Shit, that's some gig you've got there."

A slight blush tinged Charlie's cheek as everyone's attention was pinned on him, even I had forgotten my hangover munchies and stood waiting to hear all about it, with the bag of the loaf of bread hanging from my fingers.

"Yeah, it's good," Charlie replied, clearing his throat. "I've worked there since I was sixteen."

"Do you see the band much?" Ruben asked, so interested in Charlie he missed the fact that Danny had nicked his last sausage and given it to Nigel.

Charlie shrugged. "Occasionally. It depends on whether they're touring or only recording. A bit more nowadays as they only do a tour every couple of years."

"'Cause they're too old," Toby said around a laugh.

"I think it's more to do with them all having kids and wanting to be home." Charlie's voice was a little tight as he defended his employers.

"They might be old," I said, "but they're still hotter than you."

Without even a glance in my direction, Toby gave me the middle finger. I should have been grateful we had company, because normally he'd jump on me and give me either a nuggy or snap my bra straps – my brothers were an absolute joy.

"Who are you talking about?" Dad asked to a series of eye rolls.

"Dirty Riches," Toby offered.

"Ooh we went to a concert of theirs once, didn't we Ivan?"

Mum moved from her spot next to Dad, by the sink, and sank into

31

the old carver chair which stood at the foot of the table, evidently more interested.

"Oh yeah." Dad joined the ensemble at the table and shoved Declan, Ruben, and Danny further up the bench seat. He pushed so far that Danny almost fell off the end.

"Shit, Dad. I almost fell off."

"Well I don't know what you're doing here," Dad said, waving him away. "You have your own house, your own food, and a bloody girl-friend you should be taking care of on a Sunday morning."

We all groaned, aware that Ivan the Fucking Terrible was about to impart some sexual advice.

"You should give her a massage, it increases the blood flow and warms the vaginal muscles, which will mean they'll perform better. Good for you." He winked. "Good for Patsy."

Charlie started to choke as he stared at my dad and Ruben pushed a glass of orange juice across the table to him with two fingers. Charlie looked down at the glass and then picked it up and took a swig.

"Thanks." he choked out as he placed the glass back on the table.

"No probs," Ruben replied. "So which bands have you worked with?"

"Was it in Glasgow we saw them?" Mum poked Dad in his arm. "Or was it in Birmingham?"

"I think it was actually Leeds, sweetie. It was the night we pinched those knickers off that woman's washing line."

"Oh yes." Mum smiled and nodded her head in recollection of such happy memories.

Ruben pinched the bridge of his nose. "So, other bands, Charlie."

"I've worked with a few big names. Alchemy Dream, Riot Invaders, James Gionetti."

My eyes widened, that was an impressive list of people.

"What exactly do you do then?" I asked as I perched on the arm of Mum's chair.

Charlie's eyes softened as he looked at me. "I make sure the recording equipment is all working and set up for the producer. I also get all the instruments ready, tune the guitars, that sort of thing. It's really not that glamorous."

"But you didn't go to Uni'." I stated.

Charlie shook his head, his gaze dropped to the table momentarily before looking back up to me. "Nope. I went to school with Rocco Mahoney and he put a word in for me when he knew his dad was looking for a general dogsbody for the place. I've learned on the job. Tom, from the band, is really good about showing me stuff. In fact, they're all big believers in people learning practically rather than going to Uni', I think it's because they are all self-taught."

"Fucking hell," Danny said. "You really do move in big circles dude."

"Why does he not get in trouble for saying fuck?" Toby asked.

"Because he's Dad's favourite," we all chimed in unison.

"And I'm Mum's," Declan then added, so we didn't forget it.

We all ignored him and turned back to Charlie.

"So, you've learned it all on the job?"

Ruben looked interested and I knew exactly what cogs were working in his dark, tousled head. He didn't want to go to university, but Mum and Dad had told him he had to take the place at Sheffield that he'd been offered. It was a business and finance degree, but Ruben was adamant he'd learn more by working.

"Yeah, pretty much," Charlie replied.

He looked at me and I saw a pleading in his eyes. He wanted me to rescue him from the questioning.

"Right," I said, as I stood up. "Riveting as this conversation is, Charlie and I need food."

As I moved past him, I felt a warm hand grab mine and give it a short squeeze. I smiled but didn't look down at him, liking the way his touch had made my heart do a little back flip.

"Well I'm off," Danny announced. "C'mon Nigel, let's go."

"I'll come with you," Toby sighed. "You can drop me off at Nick's, I left my car there last night."

"*Our car*," Ruben growled and earned himself a flick of the ear from Toby.

"We'll let you get some breakfast in peace, love," Mum said. "Come on Ivan, Declan lets go."

I heard Declan grumble and then felt a kiss on my cheek.

"See you brat-face." Danny ruffled my hair. "Nice meeting you Charlie."

"Yeah, you too." Charlie sounded a whole lot relieved that we were finally getting rid of the tribe.

Eventually, after a few minutes of dishes being dumped in the sink and cupboard doors being opened and shut, silence fell.

I turned away from the toast I was watching brown in the toaster and looked at Charlie, whose body was turned toward me.

"And that was the Dixon family," I groaned. "And I can only apologise."

He grinned and shrugged. "I've met worse."

"Really? I doubt it."

His smile dropped. "Yeah I really have."

It struck me that he looked sad and I wanted to hug away his unhappiness, but the moment I thought about it, Charlie's face broke back into a smile.

"So," he said and reached for my hand. "I'm hoping you'll say yes, but can we see each other again?"

My heart stopped. "Really?"

Charlie looked unsure but nodded. "Yeah. I really like you, Willow."

"But my family are hideous."

"No, they're really not." He pulled me closer and looked up at me. The dimples were back and his eyes were bright. "So, is that a yes or a no?"

"Yes," I said, desperate not to sound too eager. "I'd really like that."

"Great. Now, are we having that toast or not?"

I grinned and gave him a playful punch in the arm and then went back to the toast, wondering what on earth I was going to wear on our next date.

CHAPTER
6

A half glass of red wine will raise your testosterone levels and will make your reactions more intense – don't drink the red wine whilst having sex, it's likely to make a mess; see previous tip re mattress protectors.

Charlie

"So, did you shag her?" Bomber asked as he took another biscuit from the packet. "You seemed pretty cosy when I left you last night."

I'd only been home from Willow's house for about an hour, when my best friend turned up on the doorstep demanding food and drink, hence why I was dishing up three plates of spaghetti Bolognese instead of two.

"Nope. We did bits, but we didn't have sex."

I turned away from him to hide the streaks of embarrassment across my cheeks, because no one wanted their mates to find out they'd blown like a volcano as soon as the girl had touched their cock.

"Bits?"

"Yeah, bits."

"What the fuck are bits?"

"You know."

"No, I don't, tell me."

"Touching, kissing, that sort of thing."

Bomber laughed. "What, like the sort of shit we did when we were twelve?"

I groaned and gave him a disdainful look. "I didn't *touch* anyone like that when I was twelve."

"Hmm, you always were a slow starter."

I moved to the door of our small kitchen diner, choosing to ignore Bomber and leaned into the lounge.

"Johnny, grubs up."

My brother, who was busy watching some black and white film about the war, raised a hand to acknowledge me.

"Now," I growled, knowing that if I didn't, he'd continue to be engrossed in the film and his lunch would go cold.

"Okay, I'm coming." he sighed out.

I went back to the plates and placed one in front of Bomber.

"Ooh nice one." He rubbed his hands together and inhaled. "Nice and garlicky, exactly how I like it."

"You're joking right?" Johnny, my brother, complained entering the kitchen. "I've got someone coming over later, I don't want to stink of garlic."

I ignored him, put the other two plates on the table and then plonked myself on the chair next to Bomber, watching Johnny carefully as he manoeuvred his wheelchair up to the table.

"Who've you got coming over?" Bomber asked through a mouthful of food.

"Serena." Johnny scrunched his brow and looked at me. "Although she's probably going to turn around and go straight out again at this rate."

"Shut up moaning and eat," I grumbled, as I picked up my knife and fork. "Be thankful I made you something."

"Oh yeah, 'cause I can easily cook for myself."

I didn't need to look at him to know he was grinning. He may well have been in a wheelchair for the last couple of years, but my brother wasn't bitter. He revelled in the attention that it got him and the shit it helped him get away with. Of course, no one wanted him to be paralysed, including Johnny, but he didn't let it get him down. He still lived life to the full; went out with his mates, got pissed and used the wheelchair and his good looks to bag himself a different woman nearly every weekend. At twenty-one years of age, he knew he'd got years to spend in his chair, so didn't want to waste any time by being miserable.

"You can cook for yourself, so don't think I won't make you."

"Charming way to treat your crippled little brother." He winked at me and then picked up his knife and fork and started to tuck into the food – garlicky or not.

"You know your brother got off with a girl last night," Bomber offered.

"Yeah? What was she like – any good?"

I rolled my eyes at Bomber, as I wished he'd kept it to himself. I loved my brother, but he was a real piss taker and I wouldn't hear the end of it, with him quizzing me for hours no doubt.

"He's not saying. He said they did *bits*." Bomber did little air quotes and with his huge fingers it looked ridiculous; like two fat sausages waving in the air.

"What the fuck are bits?" Johnny asked before inhaling a forkful of food.

"Kissing and touching," Bomber explained.

"What are you, twelve?"

"See," Bomber cried and pointed at me. "I told you. Twelve is average age to feel a girl up."

I looked at them both and sighed. "You're so fucking wrong on every level, both of you. And for your information, no we didn't have sex."

"You think my big brother is a virgin?"

"Hmm maybe, although I remember walking in on him and Emma Woods going at it at a party once."

"Oh, okay," Johnny mused. "Maybe not."

I continued to ignore them, as I knew full well that if I said anything at all it would only encourage them, and I was right because we fell into silence while we all continued to eat.

"Lovely," Bomber finally said as he pushed his plate away. "Although it'll probably go straight through me. Mincemeat often does."

"Well make sure you go home and do it," I cried.

"Yeah," Johnny agreed. "We don't want you stinking our bathroom out. The smell of bleach and vomit from yesterday is enough to deal with thanks."

As he continued to eat, Bomber eyed me warily, aware that Johnny was on shaky ground with his choice of subject and who it was about.

"We can talk about her and the fact that she puked up again."

Johnny's tone was light and playful, and I had no idea why. I hated our mother for what she'd done to him, but he always played it down that she was the reason he was in a wheelchair.

"I'd rather we didn't," I said and pushed away my plate, no longer hungry.

Bomber snatched my half-eaten meal and tucked in while Johnny stared at me, a fork halfway to his mouth.

"What?" I asked.

He shrugged and carried on eating.

"This is good, mate," Bomber said and grinned at me. "You should maybe cook for that new bit of stuff of yours."

I groaned. "Please don't call her a bit of stuff."

"Well she's not your girlfriend, is she?" He dropped his knife and fork onto his plate. "Shit, she's not is she?"

"No, but that doesn't mean you shouldn't respect her."

"Wow, my big brother likes the pretty girl."

I rolled my eyes at Johnny and pushed away from the table, collecting any dirty dishes. I couldn't deal with his continuously upbeat frame of mind; not today. Just the mention of Teresa, our mother, had brought me down and reminded me of the shit she'd created in our lives and had turned my mood black. I didn't get how Johnny didn't hate her or insist that she leave us alone and go and find somewhere else to live.

This was his house, a bungalow he'd bought with compensation from his accident, so he had every right to tell her to fuck off, but he didn't.

We were lucky he was still able to do a lot for himself, otherwise if I couldn't be there, we'd need to employ a carer, because I certainly couldn't rely on our mum. I'd only gone out and stayed at Willow's because Teresa had been home when I left and swore that she was going to stay at home all night to make sure that Johnny managed to get himself into bed safely. Needless to say, Johnny had informed me she'd disappeared not even an hour after I had left the house. I was so pissing angry; he was a twenty-one year old guy who, despite his injuries, never worried about anything, but he was prone to infection from self-catheterising or hurting himself by falling from his chair or the bed, and I hated to think he'd been alone all night when she'd said she'd be there.

Teresa didn't give a shit about him, either of us to be fair, but Johnny should have been her priority. He'd got into a fight, protecting *her* drunken, slutty arse and it had been *her* fucking one-night stand that had pushed Johnny off a first-floor balcony and injured his spine, rendering him paralysed. Yet it never seemed to bother Johnny, because as far as he was concerned, the only person to blame was the brain dead, woman-beating, Neanderthal who'd pushed him.

"You made anything for pudding?" Bomber asked.

I wondered where he put everything. Yeah, he was a big guy, but two plates of food should be enough to finish off anyone, obviously not him.

"You may as well finish off the packet of biscuits you started about two minutes before I put your lunch out."

I knew I sounded a miserable twat, but that's what thinking about my mother did to me. Not bothering to turn around, I heard the biscuit packet rustle and knew Bomber was tucking in. After a few more minutes of washing the same dish, I felt the wheels of Johnny's chair next to my leg.

"Here you go," he said as he passed his plate to me. "And stop fucking stressing about Mum."

I looked down on him and sighed. "I just don't get it."

"Can't change anything." He shrugged. "And what was I going to do, stand by while that fucker knocked seven shades of shit out of her?"

"No, but she shouldn't have called you, she should have called the police, and she shouldn't have put herself in that position in the first place. What sane person goes back to the flat of someone who they met only an hour before, particularly when they're totally out of it and the guy looks like The Rock's uglier and meaner brother?"

"You went back to pretty girl's house last night." He gave me a stupid grin which I couldn't help but laugh at.

"Yeah, but I'm not a woman beater and she wasn't a fucking mean drunk."

"She might have been, you didn't know that."

"I did," I replied. "I spent three hours with her getting drunk and she was funny and cute."

"*Cute*," Bomber cried from the table. "Shit, you are twelve."

I flipped him the bird and turned back to my brother.

"She's really nice, Johnny. I really like her and I'm a much better judge of character than Teresa the lush."

He opened his mouth, probably to take the piss out of me, but the doorbell rang.

"Ah," he said, a gleam in his eyes. "That'll be the lovely Serena."

He manoeuvred his chair and started to wheel himself out of the kitchen.

"I hope the garlic doesn't put her off," I called after him.

He waved a hand in the air at me. "She can always suck my knob." Then he was gone.

"You know," Bomber said as his brows met in the middle. "I always wondered how...you know."

"He can have sex, Bomb. He gets an erection." I shook my head and sat back at the table, taking another biscuit.

"And does he...you know."

He made an explosion noise and the action of one with his hands.

"Have an orgasm?" I asked with a sigh.

Bomber nodded. "Yeah. I never really liked to ask."

"Well that surprises me, you're so fucking inappropriate most of the time, but yeah he can. It takes a bit longer and he has something to help."

I knew my brother wouldn't mind me telling Bomber, shit, he told anyone who would listen about his 'male vibrator that helped him go off like a rocket'.

Bomber nodded, evidently thinking hard about it. "So, he pretty much does everything we do, but spends his life being pushed around."

I could tell by the look on his face what he was thinking and dropped my forehead to the table.

"Nope, don't even say it," I muttered against the wood.

"No, not saying anything, not a word."

I looked back up and could see he was still thinking it so quickly took the last biscuit.

"I'll make a brew," Bomber said.

As he stood up the sound of Johnny's bed, banging against the adjoining wall could be heard.

"Oh Johnny, God, yes, yes, yes," Serena yelled.

Bomber looked at me and grinned.

"I guess the garlic wasn't a problem then."

We both burst into laughter and spent the next forty minutes listening to my brother doing us proud.

CHAPTER 7

The anus is an often-missed hot spot because it is crammed with sensitive nerves. A good move is a well lubricated finger gently slipped into the bottom right as climax hits - so remember the rhyme 'up your bum, surprise to come'.

Willow

"Who've we got next?" James, the dentist I worked with asked.

I looked at the computer screen and winced at my feet aching from over three hours of being on them without once being able to sit down. "Mr. Macmillan."

"Haven't we seen him before?"

"Yes, but that was ages ago, he's been going to the dentist on Dean Street for a couple of years."

"It's two years since I've seen him?"

James came and looked over my shoulder at Mr. Macmillan's record. "Shit, where the hell did that time go?"

"Um, I believe you were travelling the world, trying to find yourself." I turned and poked him playfully.

"Oh, you mean when my boyfriend dumped because I didn't dare tell my parents I was gay."

James had been deeply in love with Gareth, so when Gareth dumped him because James wouldn't tell his parents they were a couple, James took it badly and needed some time away. Thankfully, he'd come back from six months of travelling realising he didn't want to live a lie any longer and told his parents, who said they weren't surprised. Unfortunately, it was too little too late for Gareth, who had moved on.

"How was your date by the way?" I asked about the date he'd had with a guy he'd met online.

James shrugged. "Okay. He was a little boring to be honest. All he wanted to talk about was cars."

"So, you're not seeing him again?"

"No, don't think so. What about you, how was your weekend?"

I couldn't help the grin that lit up my face as I thought about Charlie and how he'd given me a sweet kiss when he'd left my house the morning before.

"I met someone on Saturday night, and he's asked me to go out with him again."

James' eyes went wide. "No way. What's he like?"

I told him all about Charlie, how he'd thought I was waving at him, how we'd talked and got drunk together and finally that he'd walked me home.

"Woah," James said. "I think you *really, really* like him."

I smiled and shrugged. "I do, but I don't want to get my hopes up. You know what my family is like, James, I moan about them often enough."

"He'll like you for you, love, even when he does meet them," he replied. "And they're not awful, they're just a little bit...well, weird."

I rolled my eyes. "Well that's the other thing, I'm nothing special and he's gorgeous." I caught sight of myself in the huge mirror we had on the wall and noticed how my tunic was getting a little tight across the middle and that my hair, which I usually spent time and effort on, was pulled back into a frizzy ponytail.

"There's nothing wrong with you." James' eyes went to my hands which was clutching my ponytail. "Well nothing that a good hair conditioning treatment wouldn't sort out."

I slapped him on the arm. "Don't be such a bitch."

"I'm not." He laughed and flung an arm around me. "I'm being your friend and it's true, your hair does need sorting out. What did you wash it with this morning, washing up liquid?"

"How rude are you?" I then took a closer look in the mirror and burst out laughing. "God, it does look shit, how the hell did I manage to get Charlie to look at me in the first place, never mind stay the night and ask me-?"

James appeared in between me and the mirror.

"You never said he'd stayed the night."

It was true, I hadn't, but if I'd told James he would have him assumed that Charlie and I had had sex and I didn't want to tell him why we hadn't. I knew it was probably a one off, we had drunk an awful lot of vodka, but I wasn't sure Charlie would want anyone knowing that he'd come in his boxers. Thinking back though, I couldn't help but smile because the lead up to that point and even after, had been lovely and sweet, yet unbelievably sexy too. Charlie knew how to get me going and I was sure when, or even if, we had sex, it was going to be awesome.

"Nothing happened," I replied. "I was too worried my parents might hear, so we just kissed and so on."

"Well kissing and so on is good, obviously good enough to make him want to stay over."

"Well, you know I'm worried about my family?"

"Yeah."

"He already met them."

I didn't miss the wince from James, and I began to worry that his words of encouragement a few minutes before had been simply to appease me.

"See, you think it's the death knell, don't you?"

James held his hands up in surrender. "I never said that. I think maybe it's a lot to meet any family on a first date."

"Yeah well it gets worse," I groaned. "He met my dad first and he was completely stark bollock naked."

James' mouth dropped open as he stared at me.

"My dad, that is," I clarified. "He found Charlie getting a drink in the kitchen, and then he met my brothers and my mum later, when we went down for breakfast."

I sagged, the happiness I felt at Charlie's desire to see me again had disappeared quicker than a seventeen-year-old boy's virginity on holiday in Magaluf.

James looked sympathetic and patted me on the shoulder. "It might not be so bad. He did ask you out again."

I dropped my face into my hands. "He's going to cancel, isn't he?"

"Not necessarily."

I looked up at James and pouted. "No, don't say anything else, I don't want to think about it."

"Okay, let's get Mr. Macmillan in instead," he said, cajoling me as though I was a small child.

I nodded and with a heavy step went to get our patient.

A few minutes later, with Mr. Macmillan reclined in the chair, James asked him to open up and started his examination.

I knew something was wrong when James remained silent as he peered into Mr. Macmillan's mouth.

"I see you've had dentures since we last saw you, Mr. Macmillan?" he said. "We thought it was a standard check-up you were having, so are you having problems with them?"

"No, I haven't," he replied with a shake of his head. "And this *is* just a check-up."

"But these are dentures."

James looked at me and gave a slight flick of his head for me to go and look. I stood next to him and looked down. I leaned in further before looking back up to James and raising my eyebrows and shrugging my shoulders.

"Um, Mr. Macmillan," James said and rubbed his chin. "These are most definitely dentures, when did you get them?"

"I'm telling you; *I* haven't had dentures." Mr. Macmillan's voice rose to a shriek as he pushed himself up from his prone position."

"But they're not your own teeth, so..." James placed both his hands on his hips and stared at the large, grey-haired man.

"I know that," Mr. Macmillan cried.

"But you said you hadn't had dentures, Mr. Macmillan." I smiled sweetly at him and leaned a little closer and surreptitiously inhaled to check for the smell of alcohol, but there was none.

"I haven't." He sat fully upright and swung his legs off the chair. "These are the wife's. We share them, I have them on a Monday, Thursday, and Friday and she has them the rest of the time."

He looked totally aggrieved that we should need to question him, and he let out a loud huff and a tsk.

"Um, Mr. Macmillan," James said, in a conciliatory tone. "We can't really examine dentures that aren't yours. They weren't made for your mouth; they were made for your wife's."

Mr. Macmillan frowned. "Well I've never heard anything so ridiculous in my life, call yourself a dentist."

"But they're not your teeth," I offered.

Mr. Macmillan looked at me as though I was the stupid one and then stood up.

"I'll be speaking to the dental board about you lot," he said and wagged a finger at us. "You mark my words."

As he slammed the door closed behind him, James and I both winced.

"Oh God," James groaned, "it's going to be one of those weeks isn't it?"

"Yeah," I replied with a grin. "I think it is."

The afternoon sped by, and it was soon time for home, but I still felt disappointed in James' reaction to the fact that Charlie had met my family. It was true that James' perception of my family came from my comments about them as he'd never met them, and I did tend to over exaggerate what they were like; but Charlie *had* seen my dad naked and he *had* been interrogated by my brothers, so it was no wonder I felt dejected. Which was why, when I was on my way home, I almost screamed when my mobile rang, and the name Dimples flashed on the screen.

"Oh shit," I gasped, as I stared down at the name that I had insisted Charlie gave himself when he'd programmed his number in.

My heart beat faster as I looked around the street, in search of some sort of divine intervention on what I should do. A normal, sane person would simply answer the bloody thing, but I was convinced his call was to cancel our date. Not that there was an actual date to cancel, we hadn't actually agreed on a where or a when.

After a few more rings, I knew I needed to be a big brave girl, I pressed at the screen.

"H-hello," I stammered, with my eyes closed against the disappointment I knew I was about to feel.

"Hey, Willow, it's me, Charlie."

His voice sounded bright enough, a little nervous thickness in his throat maybe, but okay.

"I know," I replied with a little breath to my voice in an attempt to sound sexy and flirty, just in case he was about to dump me before we'd even got started. That way he'd maybe always wonder, what if? "It said Dimples on my phone."

Charlie laughed on the other end and I felt the tension ease from me slightly.

"Oh yeah, I forgot about that."

"Hmm, you were pretty drunk when you did it."

"As were you, yet you're in mine as Willow, so what does that tell you?"

I could hear a door close in the background and I wondered if he was at work and shouldn't have been calling me.

"That you're a worse drunk than I am."

I moved over to a low wall that bordered a small row of shops near to the surgery and plonked myself down.

"Or that I'm more boring," I added.

"No way, that's not possible." This time his laugh was much louder, and a little more anxiety seeped away from my body. "There is nothing boring about you, whatsoever."

I grinned and let his words sink in, surprised at how happy one phone call from him had made me. I really couldn't remember the last time a man had made me feel like this; all giddy and girly.

"I'm glad about that." I looked down at my feet which seemed to have sprung into a little dance all of their own accord. "I'd hate to bore you to death."

"Never in a million."

"So, was there a reason you called?"

I held my breath and hoped that I hadn't been lulled into a false sense of security by his sweet flirting.

"About our date. I was thinking maybe we could go out tonight, if you're not doing anything."

The air rushed from my lungs and my feet stopped dancing and started to stamp up and down excitably.

"Yes," I replied, probably a little too quickly. "Tonight, would be great. I don't have anything planned."

Okay, so *Cosmopolitan* would have probably told me in a list of 'ten ways to hook a guy', to act cool and leave him waiting for a couple of days, but I'd experienced their advice once before and it didn't end well. *Try something new with your appearance* evidently didn't mean do a home dye job and end up with hair the colour of a soldier's combat gear, after he'd worn it for five days solid on manoeuvres in the Brecon Beacons.

"You don't? That's great."

Charlie sounded genuinely excited which transferred to me, making my heart flutter rapidly.

"I can pick you up, say eight?"

"Sounds good to me."

There was a pause and I wondered if he was grinning as manically as I was and so couldn't speak.

"Anything in particular I should wear?" I asked. "You know, swimming costume, ski wear, that sort of thing."

"No," Charlie replied around a laugh. "I thought maybe the cinema and then pizza?"

"Perfect."

"You sure? There's about three new films on, so we'd have plenty of choice."

"Honestly, Charlie, it sounds great."

It really did because I'd be close to him, next to him in the dark, and maybe he'd hold my hand, or maybe if there was a horror movie on I could suggest we watch that, because then I'd be able to snuggle into that gorgeous, hard, warm chest of his.

"Excellent, so I'll see you later."

"Okay, see you at eight." Then a thought struck me. "I'll wait at the end of the drive."

Laughter rolled down the line. "Willow, I've already met them, I know exactly what they're like."

"Okay," I sighed. "See you at eight."

He said goodbye and I left the phone to my ear until I was sure he was gone and I realised with great certainty that I already had it bad for him.

CHAPTER
8

Whenever you're on top of him, facing his feet, just as he's about to have his orgasm, grasp his toes and pull gently. It seems that the nerves in his toes are connected to the ones in his genitals, so this extra stimulation increases the intensity of his ejaculation – also it'll ensure he doesn't wear his socks to bed.

Willow

"Oh my God," I blasted, as Ruben burst into the bathroom. "Can I not have some privacy, just once?"

"I need a shit, and Mum is having a shower in her and Dad's bathroom, so..." he shrugged and indicated with a sweep of his hand that it was time I left.

"What about the toilet downstairs?" I asked as I rubbed at my hair with a towel.

"You know we're not allowed to shit in that one, now fucking hurry up."

I rolled my eyes and silently cursed my mother for forbidding anything smelly going on in the downstairs loo because it was close to the front door and the lounge. That didn't mean to say we didn't all risk it from time to time, but she had a nose like a Bloodhound and could smell even the tiniest of bowel evacuations.

I snatched my discarded clothes from the floor and like the adult that I was, flicked my tongue out at my brother.

"God, you're such a child," he complained and slammed the door behind me.

I wasn't really sure why Ruben and I didn't get on as well as the rest of us did. Maybe it was the middle and youngest child syndromes kicking in that made us both feel totally disgruntled with each other, or maybe it was because when he was fifteen I told his friends that he still wet the bed until he was eight – God, that boy could hold a grudge, but whatever his reasons, he barely tolerated me. We loved each other, of course we did, but clashed a lot.

I stomped into my bedroom, I looked down at the array of clothes that lay on the top of my bed. I had no idea what I was going to wear. There was a cute pair of ankle grazer red jeans, a pretty flowered 1940's vintage tea dress, a whole host of t-shirts and shirts, about five different skirts, and not to mention the jeans and trousers that I'd also thrown there.

"Oh God," I groaned. "This is hopeless." I slammed back out of my bedroom and went to the top of the stairs. *"Toby, I need you."*

"Do you need to shout so loud?" Ruben grunted from the other side of the bathroom door. "Some of us are trying to concentrate in here."

I rolled my eyes at the door and opened my mouth to yell for my brother again.

"What?" He appeared at the bottom of the stairs, a bowl of something clutched against his chest and a spoon halfway to his mouth.

"I need you to help me pick an outfit." I swivelled on my heels expecting him to follow.

Being a model, my brother had a great eye for clothes and what looked good and he often helped me to decide which outfit I should wear.

"Okay," he said breezily as he ambled into my room. "What are the options?"

I swept an arm out toward the bed.

Spooning *Cornflakes* into his mouth, Toby nodded and surveyed the mess of clothes.

"Where are you going and with whom?"

"Cinema, pizza and Charlie."

Toby's eyes lit up as he oohed like a gossipy old lady. "Second date, hey?"

"First, Saturday doesn't count." I tightened my towel around my chest and looked at him expectantly. "So?"

He studied the clothes, separated some out with one hand while the other held his bowl of cereal and then threw the red jeans and a short cut, white broderie anglaise, Bardot top at me.

"Those with that cute pair of white bowling shoes you've got. Put your hair up in that bow thing you do with it, red lipstick and earrings and you're good to go." Toby grinned at me and then did a little bow. "Okay, my work here is done, oh and to say thank you, put a good word in with Polly for me would ya?"

I resisted the temptation to scream no, after all he had done me a solid by picking out an outfit for me.

"I'll mention you, but you do know she's hung up on Declan."

"Yeah, I know," he replied as he drank the milk straight from the bowl and waved the spoon at me. "But wait until she sees my package in all its twenty feet square glory."

"Oh my God, you got it," I shrieked. "You got the underwear gig?"

Toby nodded. "Yep, got the call from my agent earlier."

I flung my arms around him and squeezed him tightly, avoiding the bowl. "Tobe, that's unbelievable, well done."

"Cheers," he groaned. "Now put me down and get yourself ready for your date. I have no idea what time he's picking you up, but according to Hedwig it's almost ten to seven."

"Oh shit. Go, go, go, I need to get ready."

I ushered Toby out of the door and let the panic set in.

"Wow," Charlie said, his eyes going wide. "You look amazing."

He leaned forward and kissed my cheek and I took the opportunity to sniff him, he smelled gorgeous. I couldn't tell you what of, I wasn't one of those girls who could pick out wafts of lemon and cinnamon, all I knew was that it was bloody lovely.

"You smell nice," I said as I held onto his bicep so I could take another long inhale.

"Thanks. Got to be honest, I have no idea what it is, it's my brother's."

"I didn't know you had a brother; you didn't say."

Charlie smiled and shrugged. "I guess it never came up. Johnny, he's younger."

"Oh, okay. What age?"

"Twenty-one."

"I wonder if Toby knows him. Hey, Tobe," I shouted into the lounge. "Do you know Johnny -?"

Charlie grinned. "Monroe."

"Monroe," I shouted, with a playful nudge.

Toby appeared in the doorway his hands now wrapped around a box of chocolates.

"Nope," he replied, and offered the box to Charlie. "Not the hazelnut whirls though."

"No thanks." Charlie shook his head. "Nice to see you again."

"Yeah, you too, bit of a surprise though."

"Toby," I warned. "Shut up and go back to watching whatever crap it is you're watching."

"It's last night's Love Island and it's not crap." He leaned back into the lounge. "Is it Dad?"

I groaned inwardly, half expecting my Dad to come out and embarrass me, thankfully he didn't.

"Nope, it's an extremely interesting social experiment," he shouted out to us.

Toby shrugged. "See, if Ivan the Fucking Terrible says it's good, then it must be. That man has letters after his name. Anyway, the surprise is that you actually wanted to see my sister again. She's not the easiest of people to get on with."

Toby laughed and Charlie looked distinctly uncomfortable. He obviously didn't know whether to piss me or my brother off with his response.

"Charlie, it's fine," I sighed and guided him with a hand to his elbow toward the front door. "He's messing with you. I'm one of the nicest people you'll ever meet and his most favourite sibling."

"To be fair," Toby said as he rifled through the box of chocolates, "you are. The rest of them are a bunch of wankers. You, I just about tolerate."

Charlie laughed and then saw my face and tried to hide it with a cough. "We should probably go."

"Yeah, take her and don't bring her back."

We turned to see Ruben coming down the stairs rubbing at his stomach.

"Have you been having a shit all this time?" I asked which earned me a glare.

"God," Mum shouted from the top of the stairs. "Ruben Jerome Dixon, what the hell have you been eating? That faeces smells disgusting. You could at least open the window."

"You want to take me instead?" Ruben asked Charlie. "This fucking house is hideous. Every fucker in here is fucking hideous and my life is fucking hideous."

"Ruben, language," Mum called down the stairs. "Oh hello, Charlie. How lovely to see you again."

Charlie waved a hand and at that moment I wished I was a snail so I could curl into my shell and pretend that the Dixon family didn't exist.

"Has Willow offered you a cup of tea?"

"We're on our way out," Charlie replied. "But it was great meeting you again."

"Don't forget you need to be home by eleven." Dad's voice boomed from the lounge.

Charlie's gaze swivelled to me so fast I thought his head might twist off.

"He's joking," I replied with a long exhale. "Night everyone, it's been real."

"I mean it young lady, eleven."

As Charlie and I walked up the hall, Dad's bellowing laugh could be heard.

"See," I said, and pulled at Charlie's jacket. "He was joking."

"Come back for some supper," Mum called. "I'm making beef sandwiches."

Charlie's step faltered so I pushed him in the back. "Ignore her. She'll get bored and pick on one of the boys if you do. Bye Mother."

"Bye love, and don't forget beef sandwiches and Battenberg cake, well not for Ruben anyway, he's evidently eaten enough today."

"Please go," Ruben muttered. "She'll keep going while she's got an audience."

I gave him a grin over my shoulder and was surprised to get one in return.

"Laters, you crazy kids," Toby called. "And I'll save you a seat for supper."

I rolled my eyes and reached for the door, opened it and pushed Charlie outside. When we got to the bottom of the drive, he turned to me, took my hand in his and smiled.

"I like your family," he said. "A lot."

"Really?" I looked back to the house and stared at it with my mouth open.

"Yeah, I really do."

"They don't make you wish you'd never offered to buy me a drink?" I turned back to him and gazed at his handsome face. He had a smile, his straight, white teeth showed with the tip of his tongue poked through.

"No, not at all."

He leaned forward and kissed me, it was a quick kiss on the lips, but it made my stomach flip.

"Now," he said. "Let's get going or we'll be late for the film."

He led me to a silver Golf and beeped the locks before he opened the door for me. He waited until I had my seatbelt on before he closed it and while he walked around the front of the car, I couldn't help but smile and be thankful that my brother had ignored me in a crappy bar in town.

CHAPTER
9

Having a quickie is a great way to de-stress, get your blood flowing faster and boost your endorphins, not to mention the fact that it can empower you – in other words, if you're gagging for it and he puts on the Enya CD, simply jump him and try and get a session in before the first track has even finished.

Charlie

I looked at Willow from the corner of my eye and had to hold in the laughter. Her face was an absolute picture as she watched the film play out on the big screen in front of us.

"You picked it," I said as I glanced back at the screen.

"I know but I had no idea it would be this bad." She turned to me and stared. "I thought it was a remake of a classic."

"Well obviously not."

I couldn't help it, I had to laugh. Willow had picked 'Wicker Man', because she thought, as I had, it was a remake of the old horror film, but when the main guy in the film got cursed and gradually turned to wicker, we realised we'd got it totally wrong.

"Oh no," Willow hissed as we watched the man hobble down a

road with one wicker leg and one normal one. "That's just the last straw."

"Oh shit."

I dropped my head back and laughed so loud that the one other person in there tutted in disgust.

"Wicker – straw, do you get it?" I said as I leaned into her and nuzzled my nose against her neck to smother my laughter.

God, she'd said I smelled nice, well she smelled incredible. All sweet and sugary. She looked gorgeous too and the thing she'd done with her hair; it looked like a bow on top of her head and was fantastic. In fact, every damn superlative I could think of needed to be sent her way.

I probably stayed nestled against her for too long, but I couldn't pull myself away and when she gave a little moan and stretched her neck, I really had to kiss her warm skin.

"Charlie," she said on a little gasp of air.

"Hmm?" I reached my hand and cupped her face and gently turned it so our lips could meet. "You don't really want to watch this film, do you?"

The screen flickered and reflected in her big eyes as she stared at me and shook her head.

"Good."

I kissed her slowly, both my hands cradled her head as my body angled toward hers, and it had to have been the most perfect kiss I'd ever had. Her lips were soft, her tongue gave long delicate strokes against mine and her hands clutched at my t-shirt. As I pushed closer, Willow shifted in her seat, and sent the box of popcorn that was placed between us all over the floor, but I didn't care. All I wanted and needed was her mouth on mine.

My hand moved down Willow's side, my thumb skimmed the curve of her tit and immediately I felt it swell, and as it did, my dick grew harder in my jeans. For a brief moment I worried about what had happened in her bedroom a few nights before, but somehow, I knew it wasn't going to happen again. I was as hard as steel, but there was no danger of me blowing like a geyser.

"Do you want to go somewhere else?" I asked as I kissed along her jaw.

"Your house?" she asked, breathlessly.

"My brother is home." For all Johnny didn't care if anyone could hear his sexual antics, I did.

"Practically my whole family is home," she groaned. "What about your car?"

I kissed her again, this time I let my hand rest on her tit and rubbed my thumb over her nipple. Finally, when I didn't think I had any breath left in my lungs, I pulled away.

"Okay, let's go," I gasped.

We'd practically run back to the car, even though we tried not to appear too eager, despite the fact that we were. Once inside I started it up and drove us, just about within the speed limit, to an old abandoned pub on the edge of town. The boarded-up building was surrounded by fields and I figured if we parked around the back and turned off the car headlights, no one would spot us from the road.

I screeched the car to a halt, almost doing a handbrake turn, I quickly unclipped my seat belt and made a grab for Willow, who was halfway across the centre console anyway.

"Listen," she panted out as she reached for the button of my jeans. "I don't want you to think I do this all the time, on a first, or second date, whichever way to look at it, but it's been a while and well, I really like you, just so you know."

"Don't...fucking...care," I said, in between taking her mouth in mine. "I...really...like...you...too...and...this...isn't...a....one...night... thing...for...me."

"Good, oh my God...to know."

Once my jeans had been pushed down my legs, I wasted no time as

I hastily unbuttoned Willow's and waited as my dick pointed up to the car roof, while she sat back in the passenger seat and tried to pull them off.

"Ah shit. They're stuck."

"Here," I said and beckoned her with my hand. "Give me your leg."

She did and I ripped off her shoe.

"Next one."

I did the same again and without any hesitancy, pulled her jeans off and threw them into the footwell, then I reached for her and dragged her back over to me.

When I realised she only had a thin landing strip, I had to concentrate hard not to repeat my previous mistake. Then, when her almost bare pussy and arse met my naked skin, I almost didn't give a shit about embarrassing myself again, but I thought about how fucking good it would be to be inside her and the urge to come ebbed away.

"Condom," Willow gasped as she reached between us to grab a hold of my dick.

"Shit, in my jeans."

Willow leaned back and stretched for my pocket and pulled out my wallet. "In here?"

"Yeah," I groaned. "And can you stop moving so much, the friction is...*fuck*."

"Oh God, sorry."

Willow looked at me warily and tried not to move as she opened up my wallet and flicked through the few notes inside it.

"Little pocket at the front."

She nodded and flipped open the small flap and pulled out the condom and then threw my wallet to one side, she ripped at the silver foil with her teeth, spat it out and then smoothed the latex down my begging cock.

"Wow, neat work," I said as I leaned forward to kiss her.

"I'm desperate for you to be inside me."

She raised herself up on her knees and then sank down onto me and I thought I might see stars; it was so good. She was tight and I was hard as granite, so when she started to move up and down the pleasure rushed around my body like electricity down a cable.

"Oh, oh, oh, shit," Willow groaned on an upward stroke.

"What's wrong?" I placed my hands on her hips and tried to continue the rhythm that she'd started, but I couldn't move her.

"Cramp." Her groans were strangulated, and her pretty face contorted. "I need to stretch out."

"Okay, hold on."

I reached down the side of the seat and pulled the handle, it sent the seat backward so I was lying flat. With another groan, Willow leaned forward and stretched her leg out.

"*Argh,* that hurts so much."

She began to shake her leg and must have kicked the steering wheel somehow, because the horn blared out and startled us both.

"Shit, sorry," she cried as she buried her face in my neck.

"Does it still hurt?"

I was desperate for her to move because my dick was still inside her, and it most definitely enjoyed being in a warm tight space and if I wasn't careful it might just fucking drop off to sleep.

"It's going," she puffed out.

"You think you can move?"

She gave me a lusty smile and started to move her hips in a figure eight, which caused my cock to perk right back up. We continued kissing as Willow made all the moves and it was pure bliss. After a few minutes she pushed up onto her knees again and placed her flat palms on my chest and I had to recite the seven times table in my head to make sure there wasn't a premature end to what was turning out to be a mind-blowing night.

She then reached up and pulled off her top and unhooked her bra, leaving me with the view of two perfect tits; well they were from my angle anyway.

"Give me those fucking beautiful tits," I groaned and reached up like a baby bird that needed feeding.

Willow stretched forward and down and as I was about to take a hard, pink nipple into my mouth she screamed at the top of her voice.

"Oh my God, oh shit, Charlie what the -"

She scrambled off me and back into the passenger seat, plastered herself against the door and pointed a shaky finger toward the back seat.

"What?" I cried and scrambled to sit up. "What is it? Willow, tell me."

I turned on my side, my heavy dick thudded against the seat and totally unimpressed at being interrupted let me know with a twitch. I leaned forward to see what had upset Willow and immediately felt the pain as my hand made contact with my miserable appendage.

"Fuck. Oh shit, my fucking dick."

"Charlie it's in the back seat," Willow screamed and wrapped her arms around her naked body, totally unmoved by my discomfort.

As I gingerly sat up, I winced and looked into the back seat.

"What the fuck." I shrank back and caught my dick again and more pain shot through it.

"Charlie what is it?" Willow sobbed. "Why the hell do you have it in your car? Please don't hurt me."

I looked at her, wide eyed. "What the hell...I'm not going to hurt you." I reached my hand out to her. "Willow, babe, please calm down. I have no idea what it is. It's not my damn car."

"It's not," she gasped, swiftly sitting upright and staring at me.

"No, it's Bomber's. I couldn't exactly pick you up in a damn Vauxhall Combo, could I?"

She shrugged. "I have no idea, what the hell is a Vauxhall Combo, but more to the point what the hell is that head doing on the back seat."

As Willow started to cry again, I managed to sit up and pull the condom off my now limp dick. I reached up for the light and turned to look in the back seat.

"For fuck's sake," I groaned. "I'll fucking kill him."

"W-what is it?" Willow stammered and edged herself up to peer over the top of the seat.

I reached behind for the 'severed head' and held up the life-size doll's head with the Elvis wig on it.

"Bomber's dad is an Elvis impersonator," I sighed and rubbed a hand down my face. "He keeps his wig on a doll's head to keep it straight."

Willow whimpered and reached a hand to the wig and touched it. "It looks so real."

"Yeah, well it's only a wig."

I turned the head to me and flipped it the bird before I lobbed it back onto the seat behind me.

"I'm sorry, Willow. I had no idea it was there. Are you okay?"

I reached up and thank God, she leaned forward and let me cup her cheek.

"It scared the shit out of me," she whispered.

"I can imagine, that's the last thing you expect to see in the middle of sex." I pulled her closer and kissed her mouth softly. "You want to get dressed and I'll take you home."

Her brow furrowed. "No pizza?"

"You still want to go?"

"Yeah, I'm starving. I mean I know sex is off the agenda now, but there's no need for us to go home."

I could have high-fived myself. I'd been sure she'd want to call it a night and probably never want to see me again.

"Let's go and eat then, unless you want to go back for your mum's beef sandwiches?"

The look she threw me said it all and we both got dressed. Finally, with my cock back in my boxers and Willow's gorgeous tits back under cover, I started up the car.

"Charlie," Willow said, turning in her seat to look at me.

"Yep."

"What the hell is a Vauxhall Combo?"

I groaned, shifted the car into gear, and realised that there was still a lot that Willow Dixon needed to learn about me.

CHAPTER 10

Rear entry is the best move for hitting your 'Aaah zone', but make it even better by slipping a pillow underneath your hips when you're on the bottom, it will tilt your hips forward and give him a better chance of hitting his target – be careful there's no one around who needs to park their bike.

Willow

As I waited for Polly in the café, I thought back to the night before and the disastrous attempt at sex with Charlie in his car, well Bomber's car with the bloody severed head on the back seat. It had been going well. I had started to get into a rhythm and the burn had begun to build in the pit of my stomach, even though I was the one to do all the work, which worried me a little bit, if I was being honest. I was all for equality and didn't believe in simply lying there and mentally compiling a list for the weekly grocery shop, but Charlie hadn't really made much effort. His hips hadn't moved one inch. He'd been great up until then; the point where I was ready for sex, he'd been fantastic in fact. I had almost straddled him in the cinema, but once we got naked, or semi-naked, he was the one on his back and contemplating his Fantasy Football team for the week.

Two failed attempts at sex was not good, and even though the rest of the night had been great, it had played on my mind when I'd got into bed. Obviously, I was frustrated too and had to give myself an orgasm, which was by no means as satisfying, particularly as the Battenberg cake Mum had insisted Charlie and I eat when he took me home, made me burp all night.

I took another sip of my coffee and glanced at my watch, as usual Polly was late, but luckily, I had taken half a day off so wasn't in a rush to get back to work. I picked up the menu and reread it for the tenth time, just as I finished it, Polly plonked herself down in the wooden chair opposite to me.

"Sorry I'm late, that bloody witch from accounts called me in to argue about my damn expenses for my trip to London. She tried to say I should have got the tube and not a bloody cab."

As she continued to complain, I nodded my head and listened, trying to look suitably sympathetic, with a yes or no where appropriate. Finally, she took a deep breath.

"Okay, what are we eating?"

"I'll have cheese and pickle on brown, and you'll have tuna and sweetcorn on white, as usual."

She grinned at me and waved over a waitress. "You know me so well."

After we placed our orders, Polly blew out her cheeks and pulled off her jacket. "So, spill about Charlie."

Polly had been on a course in London for a couple of days, so I hadn't had a chance to fill her in, except for a quick call on Sunday, but then her train had gone through a tunnel and we'd got cut off.

"You said he'd stayed the night, so I gather you had sex."

I shook my head. "Nope. We were too drunk and then on Sunday morning my dad kind of killed the mood."

I don't know what stopped me from telling Polly about Charlie's 'accident', because I usually told her everything. Maybe if I wasn't going to see him again, I would have, but seeing as he'd asked me on another date, I really wanted to keep that little piece of information to myself.

"Oh shit, how did he do that?" she asked.

"Charlie ran into him in the kitchen and Dad was naked." I dropped my head to the table and groaned. "It was awful, he even gave him advice on giving me a morning orgasm."

Polly's face appeared next to mine on the wood. "Did you say he gave him sex advice?" she hissed.

I sat up and narrowly missed her head. "Yep."

"Shit, no wonder you didn't do the deed. So, I take it that's it, you haven't seen him again."

"No, I went out with him last night."

Polly squealed and clapped her hands. "Tell me, tell me, tell me!"

"We went to the cinema and then pizza, oh and then had cake with the family."

She gave a loud snort of laughter, sat back in her chair and tapped a long electric blue fingernail on the table.

"You ate cake with the Dixons?"

I nodded. "Yeah, and he still asked me out again."

"Get lost," she cried and then looked around and gave an apologetic smile to everyone before turning back to me. "He didn't?"

"Yes, but the cake isn't the worst part."

I cringed thinking about the head.

"What's worse than eating cake with your family?" she asked incredulously.

I then regaled the full story and watched as my friend collapsed in hysterics. She was so amused she didn't even order her favourite chocolate brownie for pudding.

When I got home the house was quiet, which was a miracle because there was always someone knocking around. I'd at least expected

Ruben to be around seeing as he had the easiest college schedule that I'd ever heard of. Relishing the peace and quiet though I went into the kitchen and switched on the kettle for a cup of tea and noticed Dad's briefcase on the table.

He must have been home and then gone out again, but he never left his briefcase behind if he was working. Us kids had always wondered what he kept in it because it was always locked; it had been for years, since we were little. I doubted it was patient's notes, they'd be locked up or nowadays would be on his computer in his office in town, so maybe it *was* only his sandwiches.

As I waited for the kettle to boil, I leaned back against the counter and eyed the brown case suspiciously. It was weird that he was secretive about its contents, particularly when he was so open about everything else – he had wandered around naked in front of my date for God's sake, most probably without a hint of shame.

I chewed on my bottom lip and moved slowly over to the table and picked it up. It wasn't particularly heavy, but there was definitely something inside it. I gave it a shake and heard the contents move around; the quiet thud indicated that there was more than one item in there. I shook it a little and then held it in front of my face and stared at the lock.

"What are you doing?"

"For God's sake, Declan," I cried and dropped the briefcase as quickly as if it had burned my skin. "You frightened me to death."

Declan laughed and moved to stand by my side. "Staring at it won't open it you know."

"It's not only his sandwiches. There's something else in there."

Declan bent at the waist and peered at the case and shoved it with his finger. "What do you reckon it is?"

I shrugged. "Something to do with his clients?"

"His diary maybe, he's supposed to keep that locked up."

"Nah, he wouldn't leave it in there, in case it was stolen."

I bent down too, my head next to Declan's, and we both continued to stare as if we could see through the leather with some sort of super-power vision. I had no idea how long we'd been like that when the kitchen door opened.

We both jumped up and turned to see Ruben, his brows furrowed together in the middle of his forehead as he watched us.

"What the fuck are you doing?" he asked as he ran a hand through his dark hair and swaggered over to us.

"Wondering what's really in the bag," Declan replied. "And why Dad keeps it locked up."

Ruben's face broke into a smile and I realised how much I'd missed seeing it. He was a handsome boy with dark brown hair and eyes to match, but his permanent scowl tended to take away from his looks.

"Want to break into it?" he asked and wiggled his eyebrows.

Declan and I jumped back a step.

"No," I gasped. "Ivan the Fucking Terrible would kill us."

"Yeah," Declan agreed. "He'd go ballistic."

"Who's gonna tell him?"

Ruben sauntered over to the drawer next to the cooker and pulled out a knife and a metal skewer and held them up to show us.

"I can unlock it and lock it back up with these," he said with a casual one-shouldered shrug. "He'll never know."

"No!" Declan put a hand on Ruben's arm. "We shouldn't."

"You two were the ones staring at it. You've got me interested now. Come on shift out of the way."

"Rube," I said softly. "I'm not really sure about this."

He threw me his regular scowl and pushed in between us. "Stop being a pair of pussies."

Within seconds we heard the quiet click of the lock and Ruben took a step back.

"What now?" I asked.

Declan and Ruben looked at me expectantly.

"No way, I'm not doing it. You can, you're the eldest."

"No, I'm not, Danny is by two minutes."

"Well we can hardly call him and get him to come over, can we?" Ruben said and pushed me forward. "You're the only girl and dad's favourite."

"No, I'm not, Danny is."

"No, she's not, Danny is."

Declan and I grinned at each other and then turned back to see Ruben roll his eyes at us.

"Ah fuck it," he said and snatched open the leather strap that folded over the top of the case. He then pulled it open by its handles and poked his head inside. Within seconds he'd thrown the case back onto the table and turned to look at us with pure horror in his eyes.

"What is it?" Declan asked. "Someone's head or something."

I shuddered, surely, I wouldn't have to deal with two severed heads in one week.

"Nope." Ruben gave a hard swallow and put one hand on top of his head and the other flat against his stomach like he felt queasy. "Bloody dirty old bastard."

"What?" I pushed forward and looked inside the open bag. "Shit."

"Oh God, please don't tell me it's dirty photos of mum," Declan groaned.

Ruben and I both shook our heads and Ruben wiped his palms on his jeans.

"Okay, I'm going in." Declan took his turn to step forward and study what had Ruben and I so horrified.

His eyes grew wider and wider as he looked in the bag for a few seconds before he snapped it shut and pointed at it.

"Rube, lock it back up and none of us are to ever speak of this again. We don't tell Danny or Toby, particularly Toby because he's got a big mouth and will tell Dad."

He held his hand out, palm down and I slapped mine on top, then Ruben did the same.

"A promise is a promise according to the Dixon family rule," we all chanted before slapping our other hands on top

"Just one thing," Declan said, as Ruben started to lock the case with the knife.

"What?" I asked the same time as I considered whether it was too early to have a brandy.

"Why do you think Dad's got a plastic hairy fanny in his briefcase?"

CHAPTER
11

Men tend to use tongues like a mini penis. Instead give him a new mental image; Ice Cream Cone – it's not a good idea to add a flake.

Charlie

I'd had a really long twelve hour shift at work because the crack-head singer of a band recording their album couldn't remember his words, and as I wanted to move up to being a sound technician, Tom, one of my bosses and member of Dirty Riches who owned Musica Records, had suggested I work alongside the producer. Tom, particularly, had been good to me and I really didn't want to let him down, so I'd stayed until the bitter end when the singer had finally nailed a better than mediocre performance.

When I walked through the door, all I wanted to do was sink on the sofa with a can of beer and watch mindless shit on the TV, but when I saw my brother trying to tidy up Teresa's shit from his wheelchair, I almost turned back around and went out again.

"This place looks like a fucking squat," I said as I watched Johnny from the doorway. "What the hell has she been doing?"

Johnny picked up what looked like a skirt but could have been a belt and shrugged. "She was getting ready to go out."

"And she decided to do that in the lounge instead of her bedroom."

I sighed heavily and began to pick up the rest of the discarded clothes and shoes that were flung around the floor.

"She was in a good mood today. I didn't want to say anything to change that."

My brother closed his eyes momentarily and took a deep breath ready for my onslaught of abuse about our mother. I knew the arguments and sniping between me and Teresa wore him down, but I simply couldn't see his viewpoint.

She was a waste of space and time as a mother and had been since Johnny was only six years old and his dad had been killed in a motorbike accident. Pete and she weren't together at the time, because Teresa's drinking had already cocked that relationship up, but she still acted like the grief-stricken girlfriend at the funeral. She'd collapsed in the aisle at the crematorium, even though Pete was with someone else by that time. She's always been a drunk and wasn't the best homemaker or mother, but at least we were fed and reasonably clean, but once Pete left Teresa got worse. We were two neglected kids who only got a decent feed at the weekends when Johnny went to stay with Pete and I went to stay with my grandma as Pete wasn't my dad – I had no idea who my dad was and was pretty sure Teresa didn't either.

At Pete's wake she got so wasted at the pub, she forgot she'd left me and Johnny to play in the kid's area and went off with some bloke who'd known Pete from school. Thankfully, I knew my grandma's telephone number and got Pete's girlfriend, Sharon, to call her and she came and picked us up. We stayed with her for three days before Teresa realised she was missing something and found the voice message from Grandma that said she had me and Johnny. Teresa came to get us and went ballistic with Grandma, she called her every vile name she could think of, eventually dragged us home and told us we wouldn't see Grandma again; and we didn't. She died of a heart attack six weeks later, but neither Mum nor Johnny and I went to the funeral – even the loss of her mother couldn't stop Teresa from being a stubborn, drunken idiot.

I knew it wasn't Johnny's fault and didn't have the energy to argue with him, so I silently helped him to clear up Teresa's shit. Once everything was in a fairly neat pile on the end of the sofa, I picked it all up and took it to her room. It was when I saw more clothes, wet towels, empty wine bottles and beer cans which littered the floor, that I lost it and threw her pile of stuff onto the unmade bed and shouted for Johnny.

"What the fuck's wrong?" he asked as he wheeled up to the doorway and stopped on the threshold.

"It's a wonder she doesn't have rats living in here. She could have for all we know."

Johnny scrubbed a hand down his face and groaned. "I'll tell her when she gets home that she's got to tidy it up."

"No! You have to tell her to move out and get her own place that she can keep like a shit hole. This is your home, Johnny, you don't deserve to have it made a mess of like this; she's already made a damn mess of your future."

Johnny's eyes widened as he stared up at me, his hands on his wheels. "Okay, calm the fuck down and I've told you before, I'm not making her move out."

"Why the fuck not?" I threw my hands up in the air totally infuriated by him and his softly, softly approach to the woman who gave birth to us.

"She's our mum, Charlie, that's why. I don't want to be with her like she was with Grandma, because no matter what you say she still regrets that they weren't speaking."

"That's shit, there's not one ounce of regret in that woman's body. Not for being estranged from Grandma, not for being an alcoholic, and certainly not for being the crappiest mother on the planet." I walked over to him and leaned down and held onto the arms of his chair and got my face into his space. "You are in this thing because of her, don't you get that?"

Johnny nodded slowly. "Yeah, I know," he replied and sounded much more controlled than I felt. "It happened and you also have to stop blaming yourself. There's only one person to blame and it's not you or Mum."

I let go of his chair and took a step back. I drew in a deep breath and hung my head.

"I should never have dropped her call that night," I said, my voice barely above a whisper as my guilt flooded back as I remembered that night as though it were yesterday and not two years ago.

"And then you might be in this thing," Johnny cried and smacked at the side of a wheel. "Now that *would* be a fucking tragedy."

"Oh, and you being in it isn't?" I asked, my voice cracked as a pain stabbed at my chest as though a knife had been pushed inside and twisted around. Anger and grief swam through my veins at the devastation of my brother's life. Him being in a wheelchair was the greatest of tragedies as far as I was concerned, and I was partly to blame.

It was my deepest regret that I had chosen not to answer Teresa's call and had let her ring Johnny instead. I knew I would have probably handled things differently; handled her differently. I'd have dragged her drunken arse out of there and told her she'd got everything she deserved, but not Johnny, no, Johnny the hero felt as though he should defend her honour and try and fight a man twice his age and size and ended up with a spinal injury for his efforts.

"It's not as great a tragedy as if it'd been you," Johnny replied and wheeled closer to me. "I can cope with this thing, you wouldn't. You'd be miserable and depressed, and you'd hate it."

"Don't you?" I asked incredulously.

"Of course, I fucking do, but I make the best of it. I've got on with my life and use it to my advantage." He grinned up at me. "How many other paraplegics do you know get as much pussy as I do?"

"I don't know any others," I replied with the barest hint of a smile. "Which kind of makes it a shit point."

"Whatever, the point that *is* valid is the one where you would be living in a fucking black hole if this was you and I couldn't cope with *that*. I'd rather be managing and living the best life I can in my situation with a big brother who is happy and enjoying his life."

"Yeah, well that's debatable, too."

I flopped down onto the edge of Teresa's bed and scanned the room. It was sordid and filthy. Not only was the floor covered in shit, but every available surface too, and I was pretty sure I could write my name in the dust on her TV screen.

"You take care of me, Charlie," Johnny sighed. "You help to keep me going, keep me well, and I'm not sure I'd be strong enough to do that for you, so stop fucking blaming yourself and her and make the best of what we've got."

I raised my eyebrows and silently questioned his thoughts on what we had. Yes, he'd provided us with a nice bungalow in a decent part of town, we both had decent jobs and a few quid in our pockets, but we had the mother from hell and neither of us had a father figure in our lives for over fifteen years.

"We're doing okay," Johnny stressed, his voice quiet yet confident. "Forget about her and this mess, but I promise I'll speak to her about the mess, because apart from anything, I damn well hate rats."

I smiled and let out a relieved breath that we'd come through another row about Teresa without coming to blows, which was all on Johnny, who somehow always managed to remain calm when we discussed her.

"Why don't you go out and see your pretty girl?" Johnny said as he picked up a pair of boxer shorts and held them at arm's length. "Who the hell do these belong to?"

I glanced at them. "Not mine."

"No, mine neither. She must have taken them as a souvenir from some bloke."

"Unless she's had him back here."

I was suddenly glad I'd put locks on mine and Johnny's bedroom doors. They were supposed to keep Teresa away from our stuff so she couldn't sell it for booze, but if she had invited random blokes back when we weren't around, I was even gladder.

"Whatever, as long as she's being careful," he sighed and threw the boxer shorts back onto the floor. "So, why don't you go out?"

"Because I'm knackered and she's out with the guy she works with tonight."

Johnny made a strange groaning noise and stared at me.

"What?"

"You're not bothered she's out with another fella. I thought you liked her?"

"Yeah, I do. He's the dentist she works for and he's gay, so I'm fine with it."

I was fine with it, who the hell was I to dictate to any woman who she did or didn't go out with anyway, apart from which she wasn't my girlfriend – yet.

"You could join them."

"Why are you so eager to get rid of me?" I asked and pushed up from the bed. "It can't be a girl coming around because like that's ever stopped you."

Johnny shrugged. "I only want you to be happy bro, and I think your pretty girl would make you happy tonight."

I smiled wistfully. He was right, she really would. Despite being busy and thoroughly irritated by the dick head lead singer, I'd had a grin on my face all day as all I'd thought about had been Willow. There were things I needed to talk to her about, basically about my crippled brother and alcoholic mother, but once I had I was going to ask her to be my girlfriend.

She was sweet, funny, and gorgeous, so why wouldn't I want to ask her? Okay, our sex life hadn't got off to the most auspicious start, but we were new, it could often take time to get to know someone and their body. Bomber's dad's fucking Elvis head hadn't helped though.

"Give her a call at least," Johnny said, manoeuvring his chair out of Teresa's room. "I'm going to ring Si and Lucas and see if they fancy a PS night."

"You'd be okay if I went out?"

I felt a little guilty at going out again, particularly as I'd stayed out all night a few nights before. He would never admit that he needed me, and he was at work all day, but he was my little brother and it was my job to look after him, so I hated leaving him alone too often in case something happened. I hadn't been there that night; I'd chosen to stay in the pub and leave him to go and help my mother – and no the irony wasn't lost on me - so the least I could do was make sure he was okay now.

"Yes," he groaned. "Now fucking ring her. If I wasn't stuck in this thing, you'd be out of that door desperate to get your dick wet, so just do it."

"Johnny!" I hissed. "Don't talk about her like that, and for your information, you're still my brother whether you're in a chair or not."

He gave me a grin and a salute. "I hear ya, now go and see if you can join her."

As he wheeled down the hall toward the lounge, he pulled his phone out of his pocket and within seconds I could hear him talking to his best mate, Simon. Happy that he seemed happy, I went to my own clean and tidy room and hit the button for Willow's number, the one that I'd changed to say 'Pretty Girl' Johnny's nickname for her that seemed to have stuck.

When she hadn't answered after about five or six rings, I was about to end the call as I didn't want to leave a voicemail, because I had no idea what to say, but then she answered, her voice breathy and anxious.

"Hi, sorry I didn't hear it ring at first, it's so noisy in the pub and then it was a major operation to get out of the door because some woman decided to walk at two miles an hour in front of me."

I grinned and flopped down onto my bed. "Willow, it's fine."

"I know, but I didn't want you to think I was ignoring you. Are you okay?"

She sounded tentative and I wondered if maybe she was as invested in us seeing each other as I was, I hoped so anyway.

"Yeah I'm good, had a shit long day and it didn't get better when I got home."

"Oh no, what's happened?"

"Oh, nothing major, but my brother persuaded me that hearing your voice might cheer me up."

As soon as I said it, I grimaced. It sounded needy and pathetic, but when I heard a cute little giggle on the other end of the line, I relaxed.

"Well I hope it has," Willow replied. "So, what are you doing now?"

I screwed my eyes tight together and I wondered whether I should tell her why I'd called, or whether it would seem stalkerish.

"Nothing really," I heaved out, as I'd decided that to hear her voice would have to be enough.

"Sooo, how about you come and meet us. James wouldn't mind, he'd love to meet you and I'd like it if you did."

"Yes," I blurted out. "Yes, I'd love to. Where are you?"

I was pretty sure Willow gave a sigh of relief, but I wasn't really listening as I pushed myself up off my bed and thought about a quick shower.

"We're in Jacob's House, shall we wait here for you?"

Jacob's House was a pretty popular bar right in the middle of town, it was usually full of business people who went there after work, so no wonder she hadn't heard my call initially.

"Yeah, if you don't mind. I'll see you in about forty minutes."

"Great." Willow sounded excited which made me grin. "See you then."

I had never showered so quickly in all my life, and within twenty minutes was legging it into town desperate to see the girl that I hoped would soon be my girlfriend.

CHAPTER
12

Try the Three-Pointed Star position where you lie on your back with your left leg extended straight up in the air and your right leg stretched out on the floor and grab your right knee with your right hand, forming a triangle. Your partner then crouches at the bottom and enters you – if you get a cramp, try not to shout too loud.

Willow

"So, is he okay?" James asked as he grinned at me over the top of his beer bottle.

I smiled and tried not to look too excited. "He's coming to meet us, is that okay?"

I really hadn't thought it through when I'd asked Charlie to come to the pub, I should have spoken to James first, but he *had* said he wanted to meet the man who'd put a grin on my face.

"Of course, it is. I need to go soon anyway."

"You didn't say before, you're not going early because Charlie's coming, are you?"

"God no, I was going to tell you and then forgot. Honestly, I'm looking forward to meeting him."

I watched him warily, trying to see any signs that he was upset or lying, but he gave me a huge grin and poked at my shoulder.

"Shit, he must really like you Will, if he's willing to come out with you and your work colleague so soon into the relationship."

"I wasn't too keen, was I?" I chewed on my bottom lip and wondered whether I should have simply had a chat with Charlie and said I'd see him later in the week.

"Well as long as you left the Bride & Home Magazine back at the surgery, you'll be fine."

"Ha funny ha. I'm not that bad."

James tilted his head and looked at me with squinty eyes. "The veil is a bit much though, hun."

"What veil?" I put a hand to my head.

"Really?" James asked as he looked at me like I was the idiot that I was.

I rolled my eyes and huffed out a breath before I took a long sip of my drink.

"Seriously, Willow, stop worrying and wondering, he wouldn't have said yes if he didn't want to come. Now, what does he drink, I'll get us one in."

I only paused for a second before replying, "Vodka and diet, or lager. I'm not sure though what he'd prefer on a work night."

"I'll get one of each, I'm sure we can drink what he doesn't want."

James winked at me and turned toward the bar, only to have a woman who could barely stand barrel into him and spill most of her wine down his shirt.

"Oh shhhit," she slurred and wiped a hand down James' front. "So fucking shorry."

"It's fine," James said through a smile.

"Well if you wanna get me another it's good." She wobbled precariously and flashed me a glassy smile. "It's the least he can do in't it."

I opened my mouth to protest that it had been her own fault, but James shook his head to silence me.

"White wine?"

She nodded and lifted a finger, trying to point at him but evidently couldn't focus properly.

"You are a gent and if you weren't with your lovely lady here, I'd take you home and show you a *really* good time."

James coughed nervously and edged away in the direction of the bar as the woman followed him, evidently worried he'd forget her drink.

When he came back a few minutes later with three lagers and three vodkas there was no sign of her.

"How did you lose her?" I asked as I took the drinks from the tray and placed them on the high table that we were standing at.

"I gave her the wine and then she spotted some bloke who wasn't with his *lovely lady* and made a beeline for him."

"If only she knew." I laughed and looked into the crowd toward the door.

"He won't be here yet," James said, smirking. "Not unless he's superhuman; he's not, is he?"

"No, he's not, and I wasn't checking for him. I was looking to see if your lady friend was about."

"Whatever you want to tell yourself."

We carried on chatting and thankfully the drunken woman didn't reappear, but after half an hour, adrenalin buzzed around my body as Charlie walked through the door.

"Calm down," James said, with his back to the door. "He's merely a man."

"How did-."

"Your hands started shaking and your breathing quickened up, so I'm guessing he's arrived." James slowly turned and watched as Charlie, who was grinning back at me, weaved through the patrons standing around drinking.

"Wow, and what a fine man he is too. Shit, Willow, you've hit the jackpot with that one my lovely."

He turned back to me and winked, at the same time as Charlie reached our side.

"Hey," he said as he leaned in to hug me. "You sure this is okay?"

He placed a warm hand on my cheek and gave me a beautiful smile. I sighed and reached up on tiptoe to kiss him, only to be interrupted by a cough from James, in my ear. I pulled back from Charlie and giggled.

"Sorry, this is James, my boss."

"Now come on, I think you'll find you're the one that bosses me around." He offered his hand to Charlie. "Hey Charlie, great to meet you and yes this is perfectly okay. I have to go soon anyway."

Charlie shook the proffered hand and frowned. "Not on my account I hope."

"No, I'm meeting someone."

James' face reddened as he averted his eyes toward the bar.

"You never said," I gasped. "Who and where?"

"A guy I met at the gym. We're meeting at that new wine bar."

"Wow, and do you like him?"

James shrugged. "From what I know of him. He's a solicitor and is interested in art and he's three years older than me."

"That's a lot of info' for one meeting in the gym," I suggested, giving James a nudge.

"We may have gone for a coffee afterward."

"You should let Willow know when you're there though," Charlie said. "And that you've got home safely."

I turned to look at him and felt my heart melt. When I glanced at James, his face had told me he might have fallen a little bit in love with my date.

"Thanks Charlie," he said, nodding. "Good idea, I will. Now, what are you drinking, Willow wasn't sure whether you'd want vodka on a school night, so I got lager as well."

Charlie placed an arm around my shoulder, pulled me against him and kissed the side of my head. "Lager is great," he replied and took a bottle from James with his free hand. "Cheers."

We all clinked our drinks together and enjoyed chatting for another half hour, until finally James said it was time he went.

"Enjoy your date," I said as I leaned closer to kiss James' cheek. "And don't forget to let me know you're okay."

James smiled at Charlie, who had an arm draped over my shoulder, and nodded. "I will, don't worry. Nice to meet you Charlie."

Charlie removed his arm from around me to reach for James' hand and I felt sad that he was no longer touching me, so moved half a step closer to him until my hip was against his. I dropped my hand to my side and was about to rub my knuckles alongside the edge of his jeans, when a pinky finger linked with mine. My heart halted and my gaze dropped down to our connection and as it did, Charlie gave my finger a little tug. I looked up at him to be met with the most beautiful smile.

"I was saying to James, if his date works out, we should all go out for dinner sometime, what do you think?"

Charlie didn't sound too confident and when I didn't answer immediately, he nervously dragged a hand through his hair, but the only reason I hadn't answered was because my breath had gone.

"If you think-."

"That would be great," I replied and gave him the biggest smile I had. "I'd love it."

As Charlie and I gazed at each other, sharing a moment, James coughed beside us.

"Well, I'd better go."

As he turned to leave, he almost went flying as the drunken woman from earlier fell into him and landed on the floor with her arms and legs in the air as she howled with laughter while she still managed to keep a hold on her full glass of wine up above her prone body.

"Oh God, she's even more drunk now," James muttered, reaching down to help her up.

Charlie put a hand on James' bicep to stop him. "You go, I'll sort her out."

"You sure?" James asked, glancing at his phone.

"Yeah honestly, go."

As James waved goodbye and rushed off, Charlie moved over to the woman and took the wine from her hand, putting it on our table. He then leaned down and I thought he was going to help her up, but instead he pointed at her.

"Get up now," he spat out.

"Charlie," I gasped and took a step toward him.

He looked over to me and shook his head. "No Willow, she doesn't need any help, this is her regular position; flat on her back, pissed out of her head."

"W-what?"

"Willow, meet my wonderful mother, Teresa."

He waved a hand over her and then straightened up and came back to my side, folding his arms over his chest as he looked down and waited.

Finally, after she rolled backwards and forwards and with some swearing, his mum managed to pull herself up. She got up onto unsteady legs and looked around until her eyes landed on the glass of wine.

"There it is." She lurched forward and almost toppled again but caught hold of the table to stop herself.

Before she had chance to do anything, Charlie reached for the wine and emptied the contents into a tall potted palm that was standing next to us.

"Get home," he said, not looking at her, but handing me my drink. "Can we go somewhere else?" he asked.

"That was my fucking wine," his mum moaned. "Get me another."

"No." Charlie knocked back his drink and placed the empty bottle next to the wine glass that had been his mum's.

I still had a lot of drink left which I no longer wanted, so rather than leave it for Charlie's mum to drink, I emptied into the plant along with the wine.

"Charlie, I need some money."

His mum staggered forward and tried to reach a hand into his jacket pocket, but he smacked her away and then caught hold of her wrists before placing her hands on the table.

"You're not getting any money, so go home."

"Does she need a cab?" I asked and moved up beside him.

"No, it's only a twenty-minute walk and it's through busy streets, she'll be fine."

"Are you sure?"

Charlie looked down at me and his jaw tensed as he took a deep breath. "She walks home at all hours on her own, so nine o'clock on a midweek night is chicken shit to her. Honestly, she'll be fine. Now can we go?"

I let the bite in his voice go because I could understand why he was so tense and embarrassed. In fact, he must have been humiliated because I knew I would have been so early in a relationship with someone.

"Go home, Teresa," he said and leaned closer to her ear. "Sleep it off and in the morning clean up your damn room because it looks like shit."

He then grabbed my hand and practically dragged me from the bar, walking so fast that I could barely keep up with him.

Once we hit the fresh air, he pulled to a stop and took a huge inhale. I had no clue what to do, whether to comfort him or to leave him to calm down, all I knew was that the anger was practically seeping from every single one of his pores.

I was about to offer a suggestion that we go somewhere quiet, when he pulled me against his chest and wrapped his arms tightly around me. I wrapped mine around his waist under his jacket and listened to the sound of his rapidly beating heart. Every part of him was shaking with rage; aftershocks of the earthquake of his mother.

"I hate her," he whispered. "So much."

I didn't speak but hugged him tighter and slowly rubbed a hand up and down his stiff spine. As people walked past, a few glanced at us, but in the most part they jostled us on the pavement while Charlie made no attempt to move and neither did I as my touch seemed to be slowly calming him down. Finally, he let out a long sigh and buried his nose in my hair.

"I'm so sorry. I can't believe she did that."

"It's not your fault," I replied, looking up at him with my chin resting on his chest. "You did nothing wrong and she was drunk, lots of people get drunk."

He shook his head. "Not like she does, every bloody day." He looked down at me and lifted a hand to brush my hair from my face. "Can we go somewhere quiet? I think I need to tell you a few things."

"Of course, but you don't have to."

"I want to." He kissed the end of my nose. "Have you eaten?"

"No, you like Chinese food?"

"Yeah, the one on James Street is good."

"We'll go there and then we can talk."

"I hope you still want to see me afterwards." Charlie gave an empty laugh, but I could see there was no amusement in his eyes.

"Hey," I said and gave him a playful pinch on his side. "You saw my dad stark-bollock-naked, and you still wanted to see me again, so I reckon we're quits, don't you?"

"I hope so," he said on a really long sigh, "because I like you Willow, a hell of a lot."

I watched his handsome face and without his usual dimpled smile it made me feel strange, because even though I'd only known him a few days, I suddenly got the feeling that he'd hidden an awful lot of his sadness from me.

"I like you too," I replied. "Now, let's go and eat and you can fill me in on your family and I promise you, I won't judge."

I'd meant it as a joke, but the way Charlie's eyes darkened made me realise a lot of people already did judge him or had in the past.

"I hope so," he said unfolding his arms from around me. "I really hope so."

CHAPTER
13

Sex is like any other exercise. The more you do it the better you will become at it and the more you will enjoy it – although it's probably best not to do it at the gym in between your squats.

Charlie

"Are you okay?" Willow asked as she took my hand across the table.

"Yeah." I sighed heavily. "She's such a fucking embarrassment."

"To be fair, we're pretty much a pair together." Willow laughed and let go of my hand as she sat back in her chair and watched the waitress in the Chinese restaurant that we'd escaped to, place our drinks on the table. "We both have hideous parents."

"Willow, your parents are perfectly fine. Okay, your dad chatting to me while naked is an image I'll never forget, but they're good people. Whereas Teresa, well she's a drunken bitch who should have been sterilised at birth."

Willow gasped. "Charlie!"

"Well it's true. She doesn't have one redeeming feature, not one."

"She can't be that bad. You turned out okay – I think."

"Probably more by luck than judgement," I replied as I returned her smile. "My Grandma was around a lot when we were kids.

Willow picked up a prawn cracker and broke it in two before she popped half into her mouth. I watched her carefully as she chewed on it, her lips moving slightly as she dipped the other half into the small pot of sweet 'n' sour sauce on the table.

"What are you looking at?" she asked, her concentration still on scooping up the thick, orange sauce onto her cracker.

"How did you know I was?" I laughed, picked up a cracker for myself and put it into my mouth, whole.

"I felt your eyes on me and did you just put a whole one in, in one go?"

I nodded, unable to speak.

"You think I can?" she asked and took another from the plate.

I took a swig of my bottled beer and shook my head.

"No, not that one." I picked up a bigger cracker. "That one."

"That's huge," she exclaimed.

"That's what she said."

Willow's eyes grew wide and instinctively lowered to my crotch, even though it was hidden by the table and its red cloth.

"Go on then," I urged. "Put it in your mouth."

Willow started to choke and laugh at the same time and reached for the glass of water which the waitress had poured.

"You okay?" I grinned like an idiot, not one bit worried that she might choke to death in front of me.

Willow nodded and placed a hand on her chest. "Yep," she croaked. "It went down the wrong hole."

She gasped and I burst out laughing with Willow eventually joining in.

"Thanks for the save by the way," she finally said. "I was choking, and you sat there grinning."

She took another sip of water and smiled at me, her eyes shining over the rim of the glass.

"Sorry. Next time I swear I'll do the Heimlich manoeuvre on you."

"I bloody hope there isn't a next time. A nice quiet date would be lovely, what with severed heads and near death by choking."

As she sat back in her seat and fanned herself, my eyes drank her in. Tonight, her hair was in a high bun on top of her head and all I could think about was how I'd love to lick up the length of her creamy smooth neck. She looked stunning, as usual, and I had to wonder what the hell she was doing with me; a man who took her out in a borrowed car, and who had a drunken embarrassment for a mother.

"Thank you," I said, as I reached for her hand to link our fingers. "You, making me laugh has taken my mind off Teresa, and has also made me realise she's not worth getting upset about.

"At the risk of sending you back into a funk, has she always been a heavy drinker?"

"She's not a heavy drinker, Willow, she's an alcoholic and yeah for as long as I can remember, but she got worse when Johnny's dad died."

Willow followed the line of condensation on her wine glass with her finger and I could sense she was contemplating asking me more questions but wasn't sure if she should.

"I have no idea who my dad is," I offered as I took a punt on what she might want to know. "Johnny's dad, Pete, was killed in a road accident when Johnny was six and she gradually got worse from there."

"In what way?"

"Well, she left us at Pete's wake and forgot about us for three days. When I was twelve and Johnny was ten, she went on holiday with her latest boyfriend, if you could call him that, and left us with a babysitter who spent the money the guy had left for food on cheap cider and weed for her mates. Johnny and I had to eat Pot Noodles and Cornflakes for a week. And then," I sighed, "when I was sixteen, she hit me so hard with a full bottle of vodka that she broke my arm and I had to pretend at A&E that I'd slipped on some ice."

Willow slapped a hand to her mouth and her eyes went huge.

"Oh my God, Charlie."

"Yeah well, that's not the worst part," I replied as I took a deep breath and prepared to tell Willow everything.

I'd told her and she was still there, opposite me, and didn't look too horrified as we tucked into our food.

"That was not your fault," Willow whispered. "You have to know that."

I shrugged. "I wouldn't have tried to be the hero, not like Johnny, which means if I'd answered her call he wouldn't be in a wheelchair."

"But it's not your fault. Your brother chose to deal with it differently than you would've and the consequences of that were shit. The guy who pushed him is the only one who should feel guilty."

"Yeah, that's what Johnny says."

"So, what happened to him; the guy who pushed him?"

"He got sent down for a while and Johnny got a shit load of compensation, which is why I'm pretty sure Teresa is still hanging around. Actually, I know that's why she's still hanging around."

"Jeez, your life really is a box of chocolates, Forrest."

Willow swallowed a mouthful of food and looked at me with a soft, tender look in her eyes.

"Oh, by the way," she cried and waved an excited hand at me. "I looked up what a Vauxhall Combo was."

I frowned as I had no clue what she was talking about.

"You know, the reason why you took me out in your friend's car with the bloody head on the back seat," she said with a roll of her eyes.

"Oh, right." I grinned, even though my balls still felt the dull ache from that night.

"So, do you drive your brother around in it?"

"Yeah, I do. I take him to and from work and anywhere else he needs to go."

"You're his carer then, as well as working."

"Oh, shit no," I cried as I pushed my plate away. "Johnny would go ape shit if he thought he needed a carer. I mean he probably should have one to be fair, seeing as I can't always rely on Teresa to be there if I'm not, but he's too independent. He likes to do everything himself. He functions pretty well to be honest, and he thinks that having a carer means he's ready to die, or some other stupid idea like that."

I thought about my brother and how he coped, and pride filled my chest. He'd been right, if I'd been in his position, I'd have been a depressed twat.

"I'd like to meet him," Willow said as her eyes darted to the waitress who had started to clear the table next to ours. She looked uncertain, like she'd said the wrong thing.

"That would be good," I replied quickly. "In fact, we can go back there now if you'd like."

Willow's head shot up and her tongue darted out to lick her lips that still had perfect red lipstick on them. Shit, she was so bloody cute with her quirky dress sense and quick wit. I really hoped she'd want to go on more dates with me.

Tonight, she had on a bright yellow top that stopped just above the waistband of wide-legged black and white striped trousers and I kept getting a glance of the smooth skin of her stomach every time she reached or stretched for something. I tried not to stare too often because she had the ability to make me rock hard in my pants with only a glance. The problem was I didn't want her to think every date had to be about sex; not that things had gone particularly well in that department.

"It's still fairly early," I said as I glanced down at the clock on my phone, which said nine-forty-five.

"Okay, that'd be good, but..." she paused and swallowed. "I can't stay too late as I have to be up early tomorrow. We do an early morning surgery on a Wednesday."

"A quick coffee and a chat with Johnny and then I'll get you a taxi, unless you'd really prefer to do it another time."

I hoped to God that she didn't, because even though I was determined we wouldn't end up having sex – or *attempt* to have sex as tended to happen with us, it didn't mean I didn't want to kiss her for as long as I possibly could.

"Okay," Willow replied with an empathic nod of the head. "Sounds perfect."

CHAPTER
14

Forget crooners like Luther Vandross or Marvin Gaye, studies show that heavy metal and other hard rock get his pulse racing. Make sure you have a Limp Bizkit CD in your collection – let's hope it's only his biscuit that's limp.

Willow

After a lovely, gentle, twenty-minute walk with Charlie holding my hand the whole way, we reached the driveway of a white rendered bungalow with white UPVC windows and a bright red front door. The front was paved and there were neat blinds at the windows, it really was not what I expected from two single men in their twenties and an alcoholic middle-aged woman.

"It's really nice," I said as Charlie led me up the drive past a box shaped blue van, which I assumed was the Vauxhall Combo.

"Ah, so this is the Vauxhall Combo." I peered through the window and gasped with shock. "Why the hell have you got one of those beaded car seat covers? Are you really sixty years old?"

I turned to Charlie and arched a brow, waiting for him to answer. I couldn't believe how let down I felt. He may as well have come out to the pub wearing a zip up cardigan and a pair of suede Moccasins. Even my dad had better taste than that.

Charlie opened and closed his mouth slowly, evidently lost for words.

"Well?"

"I...I just...Bomber bought it as a joke and I never took it out. He thought it suited the car."

"I don't believe it," I gasped. "Your friend bought it as a bad taste joke and yet you kept it. Do you not have any pride, man?"

"I'm lazy, that's all. I swear I wouldn't have one normally, but like I said, I couldn't be arsed to take it out."

"Do you have the keys on you now?" I asked, as I held out my hand, palm upwards.

Charlie looked at it, then up to my face and back to my hand. "Seriously?" he asked as his eyes slowly lifted to mine.

"Extremely."

I thrust a hand to my hip and waited. Finally, with a sigh, Charlie reached into his pocket and pulled out a set of three keys and handed them to me. I pointed the black car key at the door and pressed, on hearing the beep I yanked the door open and thrusted my hand behind me, offering Charlie his keys back.

"Willow, I can do it."

"Nope, like you said, you're lazy and I'm afraid I can't ever get into the Vauxhall Combo while this thing is attached to the seat."

As I fiddled about trying to unhook the cover, I looked into the back quite surprised to see the amount of room there was.

"There's loads of room in the back," I called over my shoulder. "And, added bonus, no sign of a disembodied head."

"Will', come on," Charlie said with a laugh. "I'll do it."

He tugged on the back of my shirt, but I wasn't to be distracted. The damn hideous thing had to go.

"Nope, you'll leave it and leave it and next time you take me out on a date you'll turn up in the Vauxhall Combo and I'll have to get in and sit next to you while you're sitting on a bloody beaded seat cover."

"It's actually quite comfortable you know."

"*What?*" I jumped up, banging my head on the 'oh Jesus' handle. "*Argh*, shit."

Charlie's warm hand landed on the small of my back. "You okay? That sounded painful."

"I'm fine," I ground out through gritted teeth and rubbed my head. "I'm feeling a little affronted that you actually like this bloody thing."

"All I said was that it's comfy."

"Enough!" I held a hand up, even though Charlie probably couldn't see it in the dying light of the summer evening and because I was hunched over the seat of his car. "It's coming out and that's the end of it."

Finally, after much huffing and puffing, I had the seat cover off and turned to hand it to Charlie.

"Never let me see that again," I said, my tone low and serious.

Charlie grinned, dropped the seat cover and pulled me into the most wonderful of kisses. His hands cupped my face, while his thumbs gently stroked my cheeks. When he sucked on my bottom lip, I was pretty sure I made my self-induced orgasm noise – doesn't every woman make a different noise when given an orgasm by a man? Mine was definitely louder and included a couple of curse words.

"What was that for?" I whispered as my eyes fluttered open.

"For making me smile when I thought Teresa had ruined my day."

"Oh, okay."

Charlie smiled and gave me another kiss, a quick closed lip one. "Right, let's introduce you to my brother," he said as he took my hand and pulled me up the rest of the driveway before pushing his key into the door and unlocking it.

We stepped into the hall but hadn't moved one step before we heard a noise from behind a door at the end of the hallway.

"Oh, sweet Jesus, yes!"

Charlie groaned and I knew for certain that I had heard a man induced orgasm.

"And that," Charlie groaned, "is my brother."

I placed my arms around his neck and hugged him tightly, laughing so hard I nearly peed.

"I'm sorry," I spluttered as Charlie pulled away from me. "But it's so lovely not to be the only one with a barmy family."

Charlie rolled his eyes and as he grabbed my hand again, led me down the hallway and into the lounge.

"Take a seat," he said and sounded a little tentative as he leaned to peer inside another room.

Whoever, or whatever he thought might be there wasn't, because he gave a sigh of relief and pulled his phone out of his pocket and messed around with it until music started. It was Dr. Hook and I felt warm and fuzzy that he'd remembered my love of seventies music.

"Good choice," I said and gave him a cheesy thumbs up.

He took off his jacket and hung it over the back of an armchair.

"I have no idea why you like it, but you do, so..." He smiled and produced the dimples and flashed his teeth.

"Well thank you, I appreciate that you appreciate my taste in crap music."

"Okay, coffee?"

"Please."

"White, no sugar?"

I nodded and watched his perfect bum in his jeans as he retreated to the room that he'd peered into before – evidently the kitchen.

I hummed along to Sylvia's Mother as I settled back onto the sofa and looked around the room and was surprised to see it really did miss a woman's touch – despite their mum living with them. The blinds were plain grey to match the wooden floor and there were no cushions on the plain, black, leather sofa and armchair. There was nothing ornamental of any kind, not even a single photograph or picture. It was clean, fairly tidy and a little bit boring and it was quite clear it had been put together by two men. I felt sad that Charlie lived in a place devoid of any attention and vowed that if we carried on seeing each other next time I came around I'd bring a plant or some flowers.

After a few minutes of me redecorating the room in my head, Charlie joined me with our coffee and sat down next to me.

"Here you go." He handed me a mug and sat back as we heard more shouts of praise for his brother's prowess.

"So, you're the pretty girl who has my brother all cute and giggly."

Johnny winked at me as he wheeled past us on our spot on the sofa. We'd had to wait for about twenty minutes for him to finish with business and another ten while he dispatched the young lady who'd been screaming for the son of God.

Charlie had tried to drown out the noise by turning the volume of the music up but seeing as Johnny's room shared a wall with the lounge, we still got the odd snippet of what a 'fucking stud' he was.

"Cute and giggly?" I asked. "Is that right?"

I nudged Charlie and gave him an evil grin.

"Please don't listen to him, he's a dickhead at the best of times, but even more so when he's just got his rocks off. Anyway, Johnny this is Willow, Willow this is Johnny, the manwhore."

Johnny shrugged and moved his chair to face the TV. "Like the lady shouted, I'm a fucking legend." He picked up a remote from a side table and pointed it at the TV. "Cricket highlights are on."

Charlie huffed and reached for the remote. "We have a guest and for some bizarre reason she wanted to meet you."

"Well you sure about that?" Johnny asked, as he pulled the remote out of Charlie's reach, but turned the TV off anyway. "I mean, I am the better-looking brother, the one with a bigger dick and she'd never have to call a taxi if she went out with me, I can give her a lift even when I'm pissed."

I gasped and with my mouth wide open looked at Charlie.

"Sorry, he's always like this. He isn't being a knob because he has a new audience."

Johnny let out a loud burst of laughter and it wasn't long before

Charlie joined him. As I watched them, I realised how alike they were, with subtle differences. Where Charlie was fair, Johnny's hair was dark, almost black and he had brown eyes as opposed to his elder brother's beautiful jewelled green colour. They had the same strong, straight nose, full lips and cute, knicker dropping dimples and I was pretty sure if they were ever out together, they brought a room to a standstill.

"You two are terrible," I retorted and revelled in the sound of their laughter. "You need to start being nice to each other."

"Nah, not going to happen. Do you have brothers or sisters?" Johnny asked.

"She has a whole tribe of them."

"He's right, I have four brothers."

"Shit, that's a bummer. Are they likely to come on all protective and threaten my big brother, because I've got to be honest, I'm not sure I'd be much help to him in a fight?" Johnny shrugged and then pointed at the wheels of his chair. "You know what I mean?"

I couldn't help but smile at him. He was funny and chilled and didn't seem to have any hang ups about being disabled.

"No," I replied, with a giggle. "The youngest two are too interested in themselves than to worry about me and the twins, the eldest two, used to teach me how to fight and gave me all their boy secrets, so they know I can look after myself."

"Shit, Charlie." Johnny whistled. "You need to be careful you don't upset her; you might wake up one morning with an empty nut sack."

"I'll be fine," Charlie replied and gave me a sweet smile. "I don't intend on upsetting her."

Oh God, he was so lovely, and I was liking him more and more each day. In fact, I could hardly believe we'd only known each other a short time; I'd never felt so natural with someone before. I knew Charlie was embarrassed by his mum, but he hadn't let it affect us and gone all moody on me about it, like a lot of my exes would probably have done. He wasn't even phased about the fact that we sat down and ate Battenberg cake with my batty parents and brother, never mind the fact that he'd seen my dad's balls in full swing.

"He will definitely be fine," I said and smiled at Johnny.

Charlie's hand found mine and I let out a little sigh.

"Okay." Johnny's voice broke my serenity. "I think I'll make us a coffee, because all this cuteness is making me want to gag a little. You both want one?"

"Please."

"And make sure you put the milk in first," Charlie said as Johnny wheeled out of the lounge toward the kitchen.

"So, that's my brother."

"He's funny." I gave Charlie a grin and moved a little closer to him. "I'm glad we came."

"Yeah?"

I nodded. "Yes, there's always loads going on at my house, even if it's only my dad and Toby catching up on Love Island, and of course there's my mother and her bloody cake."

"I liked that cake," Charlie replied as he wrapped an arm around my neck and pulled me a little closer to him.

"Well it gave me bloody heartburn all night. I couldn't sleep."

"No, I couldn't either."

"The cake?" I asked.

"Nope." He shook his head. "Blue balls."

As my eyes widened in surprise, Johnny called from the kitchen.

"Hey, we've got cake, anyone want some?"

CHAPTER
15

According to studies, fish and beans can turn his wood to mahogany –
they can also give him bad farts.

Willow

It had been a couple of nights since my impromptu date with Charlie
and I wasn't ashamed to say that I'd missed him.

We'd texted a couple of times over the last two days, but I certainly
didn't want to appear too eager and as we'd already agreed to go out on
Saturday night there wasn't any real reason to contact him; other than
the fact that I missed him. The texts had been jokey and light, one
including a video of an old lady whose teeth fell out while she was
dancing. All nice and friendly, even though what I'd really wanted to
say had been 'I had to masturbate last night because I had a dream
about you'.

"Do you think this top goes with these trousers?" Polly asked as she
twirled from side to side in front of my bedroom mirror which bloody
well interrupted my thoughts of masturbating to images of Charlie.

We were heading into town for a few drinks and she'd got wind that
Declan was going to be out, so had arrived at my house wearing one

outfit and carrying another three, desperate for my opinion on which one would have most hope at pulling my brother.

"Yes, it looks lovely." I patted her shoulder as I walked past in my underwear, I'd still not decided on what I'd be wearing.

"Yeah but do you think Declan will like it?"

She did a full turn in time to Hot Chocolate singing Every 1's A Winner and looked at her backside in the mirror, smoothing a hand over it.

"Polly," I sighed. "We've talked about this before. As much as I love you and think you're totally gorgeous, my brother doesn't fancy you. Well, not Declan."

She gave me a serious look that furrowed her brow pretty severely.

"I've told you; Toby is too young."

"Yes, but even I have to admit, he's hot. Imagine how you'd feel walking into a bar with him, and," I said and tapped her nose with my index finger, "he's got that underwear job, so he's going to be on advertising hoardings all over the place."

"Yeah and that's when he'll dump me for some gorgeous, stick thin model."

"Ah, so you do fancy him then."

I narrowed my eyes, daring her to disagree, even though I knew she would. We'd been having this same conversation for almost a year, since Toby had realised what Declan hadn't; that my best friend was beautiful, smart and kind – she was a little bit of a pain in the arse princess at times, but generally, I loved her dearly.

"No, I don't. You know I don't. I'm simply stating a fact that if I did allow myself to become a cougar, if only for the fact that I'm getting hornier and more desperate by the day, Toby is likely to dump me as soon as he becomes famous, which sounds as though it could be soon."

I rolled my eyes and pulled an electric blue coloured Skater dress from my wardrobe and slipped it off the hanger.

"Toby isn't like that. He's actually one of the sweetest men I know."

"You're always moaning about him," Polly retorted, as she unbuttoned her top and whipped it over her head.

"He's an idiot and a pain in the neck most of the time, but he's still the sweetest of my brothers. He's extremely kind and he loves animals, now if we're were to talk about Declan. He-."

"No." Polly held her hand up to stop me talking. "I don't want to know what a slut he is, or how he never gives a girl his real phone number, or the fact that he regularly gives girls a false name. He's who I want."

"Why though?" I exclaimed as I stepped into my dress. "He's horrible to you and he's not even as good looking as Toby and why are you horny? I thought you had sex with that guy you met at the gym."

I could have sworn Polly had told me that they'd met up one night for a drink and she'd ended up having sex with him the next day in the office at the gym.

"No." She looked extremely affronted by my suggestion. "I certainly did not."

"Sorry." I shrugged. "I thought you said you did. Can you zip me up? That cami' looks great by the way."

"You like it? I love the colour." As she straightened the strap of the peacock blue camisole, Polly strutted to me and zipped up my dress before pulling my hair back from over my shoulder. "No fancy updo tonight?"

"Nah, feeling the natural look tonight. The red or yellow shoes?"

"Oh, definitely yellow. Anyway, I told you I'm saving myself for Declan, I want to be primed and ready for when he sees the light and decides he wants to ravish me."

I burst out laughing, but soon morphed my grin into a solemn line when I saw Polly's stern face.

"You sure that's a good idea?" I asked. "I mean by the time that happens your hole may well have sealed itself up as tight as Tutankhamun's tomb. There won't be no one getting in that thang gurl."

Evidently me, and my Deep South accent weren't as funny as I thought, because Polly slapped me with her bag.

Polly finally decided on her outfit and we made our way down stairs but when we reached the bottom I groaned loudly; Declan was in front of the mirror taking the opportunity to admire himself.

All my brothers were good looking, particularly Toby, but none of them actually made much of a fuss about it, Toby especially – oh, maybe except for Declan. He thought he was God's gift to womanhood and talked about it at every opportunity.

We all looked pretty similar to be honest. All of us had Dad's eyes, which were big, grey and sparkly, the boys had his square chin while I had Mum's little pointy one, and we were all blessed with her long lashes. As for our colouring, we were varying shades of brown, although I dyed my mousey brown hair to a deep chestnut colour. Toby of course was the exception and had inherited a rogue ginger gene from some-where. Dad often joked about Mum getting the gas man in to read the meter a lot, nine months before Toby was born, but there really was no getting away from the fact that Toby was most definitely from Ivan the Fucking Terrible's loins – he even farted in the same pitch as him.

"Where are you off to tonight, looking so handsome?" Polly asked in a sickly-sweet voice that I'd only ever heard before in horror films that centred on psychotic children.

Declan gave her a cursory glance through the mirror and then went back to fiddling with the collar of his slim fitting shirt.

"Polly asked you a question, you ignoramus." I stood on one foot and poked the toe of my yellow stiletto in his arse.

"Didn't realise she actually wanted an answer."

He swung around to face us, a scowl on his face as he looked us up and down.

"See you're both starring in Cinderella again tonight girls. Is it a sell out again?"

"Ooh you're hilarious, aren't you?" I replied and screwed my face up in disgust. "So where *are* you going?"

I heard Polly take a deep breath behind me and I knew I was going to have to work harder to get her off this stupid crush she had on him.

"Town."

"Want to share a cab?" I asked, because even though he was a self-centred prick at times, Declan was nothing but generous and would stump up the taxi fare.

"I suppose so, but it'll be here in..." He glanced at his watch. "Three minutes, so you'll need to be ready."

"Oh, we're ready, Declan," Polly simpered.

Declan offered her a tight smile. "Great. Mum, we're off," he called toward the lounge. "Quick, go before she comes out and offers us condoms."

Declan ushered us to the front door and pushed me a little too enthusiastically causing me to stumble on my heels.

"Okay, okay."

"Before you go..."

Too late; Mum appeared in the doorway of the lounge.

"No Mother, I don't need any condoms," Declan groaned reaching around me to open the door to freedom.

"Willow wha-."

"No, me neither," I snapped, stopping her mid-sentence.

"Polly, sweetheart. Condoms?"

I groaned as Mum held her hand up and let the condoms unfold into one long strip. I added an extra groan because I knew Polly and she loved to appear nice and sensible, and loved to please my parents, presumably so they'd like her more than me.

"Ooh please, Mrs. Dixon that would be amazing."

As she reached for the silver foil strip, Declan leaned closer to my ear.

"And that is why I will never go out with your damn friend."

"Why, because she uses condoms?" I asked, a little perturbed by his attitude to safe sex.

"No, because she's a bloody arse licker and I ain't letting anyone anywhere near my backside."

I snorted out a laugh and had to admit my brother had a point.

CHAPTER
16

When you're out in a public place, disappear for a few minutes then, when you return, hand your partner your knickers – make sure you remove any panty liners or stray pubes first.

***

Willow

As soon as the taxi pulled up outside the new gin bar in town, Declan thrust some money at the driver and pretty much legged it, shouting a 'see ya', over his shoulder at us. Polly stood and watched him; her lips pouted sullenly as her hands hung loosely at her sides.

"Rude."

"I have been telling you that for years, and at least twice a day for the last three years, since you decided that you fancied him."

I started to walk in the opposite direction to where my brother had gone, only going a few steps when I realised that Polly wasn't following me.

I swung around to see her in the exact same position, still staring after Declan.

"Are you coming?"

She looked at me over her shoulder and gave me a sad smile. "Yeah, I suppose so."

"Good, because Jasmine will be waiting."

Polly scurried after me as we made our way to the bar where we'd arranged to meet Jasmine. She was bound to be early, she always was, and she was also bound to be engrossed in her phone doing whatever social media she thought necessary in her role as an 'influencer', whatever the hell that meant.

Jasmine had never once influenced me about anything. Lovely girl that she was, she had questionable taste in everything, particularly clothes – everything she wore had to have a designer label on it and couldn't cost less than three figures, otherwise it was, and I quote 'cheap tat that should only be seen on a 9 a.m. drinker at *Wetherspoons* on laundry day'. Safe to say, Jasmine was a snob, plain and simple. Personally, I'd queued up outside *Wetherspoons* waiting for it to open for a hair of the dog on many a girls' weekend – Jasmine really didn't know what she was missing.

As Polly and I often shopped at charity shops, we had regular heated debates with her, especially when we picked something designer up for less than a tenner. It irked her pride and fried her overly materialistic brain.

I smiled to myself when we walked through the door and spotted her, as I expected, peering down at her phone and shaking her head.

"Hey," I said as I leaned in to kiss her cheek. "What you up to?"

"I'm replying to a comment on my Insta about a post I made about a charcoal face mask that I tried."

"Why are you shaking your head?" Polly asked as she took Jasmine's other proffered cheek.

"Because it bloody hurt trying to get it off and I likened it to having my VJ waxed." She looked up at us and flashed a smile that looked more like she was trying to get a piece of food out of her teeth with her tongue. "And some idiot called me a wimp."

"So how have you responded?" Polly asked.

"I told them to go and pull each of their pubes out individually with a pair of tweezers, try the face mask, and then tell me which hurt the most. I've bet them a *Kate Spade* credit card holder that the face mask hurts the most."

I furrowed my brow in confusion. "You do know that they'll lie," I offered as I glanced at what was in her glass as she was the sort of person who changed their favourite drink every week, dependent on what was on trend.

"Nope they can't," she replied airily. "I've insisted on video evidence or all bets are off."

"Who the hell would video themselves tweezering their bush?" I scoffed.

"Someone who wants a *Kate Spade* credit card holder, of course."

Jasmine's eyes went wide and her mouth dropped into a perfect, astonished, little 'o' at my apparent ignorance of credit card holders and people's desire for them.

"Well I wouldn't want one," I muttered. "What's wrong with keeping your cards in your bra like any normal person?"

Jasmine sat up straight and made a strange choking noise. "You're going to tell me that you keep your phone in there too, aren't you?"

I shrugged. "Duh."

"Oh my God, you're so...ugh, I have no words for you. Please tell me that you wear matching underwear at least.

"Well not if I'm wearing black trousers and a white top, no."

"That's acceptable, but otherwise I can't possibly believe you're a friend of mine if you mix and match willy-nilly."

Polly snorted quietly; she knew full well how much I loved to wind up Jasmine. It was my most favourite hobby and had been since we first met at high school when we were eleven years of age and I'd led her to believe that we ate fish fingers and crinkle cut chips for our Christmas lunch because my mum was Turkish so wouldn't eat turkey.

"My collars and cuffs don't match either," I added, fishing my <u>not</u> *Kate Spade* purse out of my bag.

"You mean...?" She looked at my head and then down toward my crotch. "Your VJ is not 515 Chocolate Truffle?"

I shook my head. "Nope. I'd say it's 69 House Mouse, to be honest."

Polly let out a huge roar of laughter before she slapped a hand to her mouth and earned herself a pure look of disdain from Jasmine, whose head threatened to fall off as it swivelled around on her neck so quickly.

"Are you telling me that your pubes are the same colour as the hair on your head?" I asked, bringing Jasmine's attention back to me.

She widened her eyes and gave a little 'what do you think' head shake.

"Bloody hell." I groaned.

"Really?" Polly asked.

"Yes," Jasmine snapped. "Now if you don't mind, I'm going to the loo. Aperol Spritz for me, please."

She pushed up from her stool and sashayed away, flicking her long, hot pink hair over her shoulder.

"She's weird. Why are we friends with her again?"

Polly shrugged and sat down at the high table. "I think it's for the free stuff she gives us."

I thought about the bottle of gorgeous mango and pineapple shower gel Jasmine had been asked to try and given to me.

"Oh yeah," I sighed. "That's why."

An hour later, we were in a different bar having a discussion about Charlie. I thought I'd be able to tell Jasmine about him without having to be honoured with the benefit of her advice, but evidently, I thought wrong.

"You see, seeing him as often as you have already, I do think you're lifting his expectation of your relationship," she said with a haughty tilt of her head as she swirled her straw into her drink which was the colour of my pee when I was dehydrated.

"Maybe I want him to have high expectations."

"He is gorgeous," Polly offered. "I think you're punching *way* above, to be honest."

"Oh, thanks for that. Her I'd expect that from," I said and pointed at Jasmine, "but not you. You're my friend."

"I'm your friend," Jasmine protested.

I looked at her, looked at Polly and then back to Jasmine. "I'm going to the loo, be back soon."

As I pushed through the crowd of people around us, I thought about what Jasmine had said and I was sure that the number of dates we'd had was the right thing for Charlie and me. It wasn't building up expectations because it was exactly what I wanted; a boyfriend who I saw more than one or two nights a week, depending on whether he was at a loose end or not. Jasmine might not have been ready to settle down with one man, but I was. And who thought of that phrase anyway – *settle down*. There was no settling about it. I wasn't settling for Charlie, he appeared to be the sort of man I'd hoped to meet for a long time. He was funny, sweet, and as fit as fuck, so no, settling was not the right word at all. Okay, we needed to work on the sex part, but I was sure once we managed to do it without interruption and without alcohol in our blood streams it would be awesome.

As I smiled about the possibilities of what might be to come, I turned the corner to the loos only to come face to face with Ruben. He was standing close to another guy who had his back to me, but as soon as my brother spotted me, he almost jumped a foot away from him.

"Oh hi," I said and stopped mid-stride. "Didn't know you were out tonight."

Ruben glanced warily at the other guy, who was a little taller than him and had messy blond hair.

"Yeah, last minute thing," he mumbled. "This is my sister."

The guy looked at me and thrust a hand into his pocket, before offering me his other one.

"Hi, I'm Cane."

Before I could take his hand to shake it, Ruben stepped between us.

"Who you out with?" he asked as his eyes darted everywhere but not once looked at me.

"Polly and Jasmine. Join us if you like." I grinned as I knew that would be his worst nightmare.

"No, I'm going home now."

He abruptly turned to Cane and drew in a breath. "I'll catch you later."

Cane nodded and then looked over at me before he gave me a chin dip and left. As Ruben and I watched him go, the atmosphere between my brother and me crackled with his animosity, as usual, his lips in a grim line as he watched me carefully.

"Are you spying on me?" he asked.

"No. I'm going for a pee. I am allowed, aren't I?"

"You never come here, why are you here tonight?"

"We fancied a change. What's your problem, got something to hide?" I asked as I noticed how he was almost jumping on the spot.

Then it struck me. The eagerness to get rid of Cane, his nervousness, the agitation – my brother was on drugs. That was why he was hiding in the back corridors of a bar talking to someone I'd never seen him with before. That was why he acted all shifty as soon as he saw me.

"What's going on Ruben? Who's that Cane bloke anyway?"

"Nothing," he snapped and scratched at his bicep. "And it's someone I know, so stop being so pissing nosey."

He turned around and started to walk away a hand clutched to the back of his neck.

"Ruben," I called. "Is everything okay?"

My heart began to pound as I thought about him being involved with drugs. It didn't seem like him, he rarely got steaming drunk, had never smoked and had never even wagged a day off school as far as I knew, unlike the rest of us. He was Mum and Dad's good kid, apart from his miserable demeanour.

"Fine, Willow, now piss off and leave me alone."

Then he was gone, and I was left feeling sick with worry about whether I should tell my parents that their youngest child was in trouble.

CHAPTER
17

Get right to the point and lift up your top and press your cleavage against his back – it is not recommended to do this to strangers whilst travelling on public transport.

Charlie

As I let myself into the house, I was surprised at how quiet it was. It was Friday night, Johnny usually had music blasting away as he got ready for a night out with his mates, but there was nothing, not a sound. He must have gone on an early one as he sometimes did from time to time.

"Johnny, you home?"

No one answered, but I thought I heard a thud. I held my breath and listened again but didn't hear anything. I threw my jacket over the armchair and was relieved to see the place was pretty tidy, none of Teresa's clothes or makeup were hanging about, so maybe Johnny had actually spoken to her.

I went into the kitchen to check what was available for dinner and glanced at the clock. It was still only half past six, so he had gone out *really* early which worried me because that would mean it was going to be a big session and he had his swim therapy in the morning. I, for one, didn't want to drive him around when he was hungover and potentially about to puke.

Searching through the freezer, I found a microwave lasagne and decided that would have to do. I had neither the energy nor inclination to cook anything more appetising.

I ripped open the box, and was about to throw it into the waste bin when I heard the same thud that I'd heard a few minutes before and now I was in the kitchen, I could hear it was coming from the other side of the wall – Johnny's bedroom.

I tossed the lump of iced lasagne onto the side and ran to Johnny's room and pushed open the door.

"Johnny?" I couldn't see him, but just before my eyes hit the deck, I heard him groan. "Fucking hell, you okay?"

I rushed to my brother who was face down on the floor with his leg at a strange angle, his trousers around his ankles.

"Do you think you've broken anything?" I asked, as my eyes scanned his body.

"How the hell would I know?" he groaned quietly. "I can hardly feel it, can I?"

"Fuck." I sank down on my knees and lowered my head, so it was close to Johnny's on the floor. "Okay, anywhere that you do have feeling in, does it hurt?"

"Nope," he groaned out. "Except I might have broken my nose. I fell flat on my face."

"What the hell were you doing?" I asked and hooked my phone out of my back pocket.

"Putting my trousers on, or at least trying to."

"Where's Teresa?"

I punched out the number for the emergency services, as inwardly I cursed and hated my mother. She knew she was supposed to hang around on a Friday until either I got home, or Johnny went out. Johnny finished work at lunchtime and got a lift home with his work-mate, whereas I often worked late on the night before a weekend, especially if one of the bands hadn't finished laying down their tracks

– the bosses let bands keep the studio until they finished on a Friday night at no extra cost and a lot of musicians took them up on it. That meant Teresa was supposed to be home keeping an eye on her damn son.

"She hasn't been home all afternoon," Johnny ground out. "Fuck, I think I've definitely broken my nose. Shit, what if it spoils my looks?"

I looked at my brother and sighed, wondering how the hell he kept so damn perky.

Thankfully, Johnny hadn't broken anything, not even his nose, so he was pretty happy, which was more than I could say about myself.

I was tired, hungry, and angry – so fucking angry I couldn't even describe it as hangry; it was so much more than that. While Johnny had been prodded, poked, x-rayed, and scanned, I'd tried to get hold of Teresa. She wasn't answering and because of Johnny's condition and the amount of checks he needed, I'd had a long time to wait and keep calling her, so she'd ignored a lot of damn calls which made my temper worse.

Finally, at almost one in the morning, we were able to go home as the doctors were confident Johnny hadn't done any further damage to himself.

"You know you don't have to tuck me in like a child," Johnny complained as I pulled the duvet up around his shoulders.

"Well stop acting like one and trying to do things that you know you shouldn't." I hated getting mad with him, but he'd been stupid to try and get changed without anyone around to help him.

"I get dressed on my own all the bloody time." He glared at me and pushed the duvet down to his waist.

"Yeah, but usually someone is here just in case."

"There's never been a just in case before, it was a one off so stop looking at me like I've pissed on your damn chips and then force fed them to you."

"Yeah, well even fucking pissy chips would be welcome at this point, since I haven't eaten."

I moved over to his bedside table and checked that he had everything he might need, including his catheter tube and bottle and his anti-inflammatory and muscle relaxant medication.

"It's all there, as it is every night," Johnny said with a sigh. "Stop fussing and go and get some sleep or some food, anything to sort your head out. Better still, call Willow and get her to come around for the night."

My back stiffened as I thought about her and wondered whether I was being a dick by expecting her to put up with my shit. With Teresa being so unreliable, I had to take on the responsibility of taking care of Johnny and what girl wanted to be limited to where and when they could go away because their boyfriend had to look after his brother.

Shit – boyfriend. We'd had three dates if you counted the night we met, but I could already see myself as her boyfriend; I'd been determined that I was going to ask her, but now I wasn't so sure because of my responsibilities.

"Charlie, stop over thinking it," Johnny said. "She likes you and I'll speak to Mum and tell her she's got to step up."

I spun around to face him, angry that he even thought she'd take any notice of him.

"You wouldn't have to speak to her if you got a carer. You have the money."

Johnny's jaw tensed as he ran a hand through his hair. He'd resisted having a carer ever since the accident and had always insisted that we could manage. Well the thing was, it was me who had to manage. It was me who worried about him every single minute I was away from the house, scared that even though I'd left Teresa with him she might decide to up and leave to look for booze or some bloke to shag.

"I don't want one. I'll speak to her, now go to bed or whatever it is you're going to do, but maybe don't call Willow because if she did come around, I wouldn't trust you not to fuck it up with that teenage mood you've got going on."

"As if I'd call her at this time, and I'm not in a teenage mood. I'm angry at the situation."

"What, that your brother is a cripple? Well boo-fucking-hoo Charlie, I'm the one living with the situation, not you."

I shook my head, frustrated that he couldn't see that Teresa not helping to care for him was not acceptable. His disability impacted on us all, or it should, but the woman who gave birth to him made damn sure it didn't affect her in any way. She'd even got to live in a bungalow, something that she'd always dreamed of, because of it.

"You know I don't begrudge anything I do for you, Johnny, but sometimes I need a break from the worry, because believe it or not, I fucking love you and the thought of anything else happening to you scares the shit out of me, and as our mother doesn't seem to give a toss, it's all on me."

I poked a finger, hard against my chest, and tried to steady my breathing as I looked down at my brother. I could have said so much more to him, told him so much more. How Teresa had tried to take money from his bank account when he was in the rehab centre for six months, or how she'd tried to get the bungalow put into her name, stating Johnny wasn't of sound mind – thank God the solicitor had thought to call me when Teresa turned up at his office one day, pissed off her head.

The problem was, Johnny still held hope in his heart that she'd change and become the mother that we both deserved, that he was desperate for and nothing I said was going to change his mind.

"I'm sorry," he said so quietly it was almost a whisper. "I know it's hard for you, I really do, and I swear I'll get her to take some of the slack, but please don't make me get a carer."

His gaze dropped to his chest as he rested his hand on his thigh and I knew that to him getting a carer was the beginning of the end – that was how he saw it and nothing I, or his doctors, said about that being totally incorrect would change his mind.

I nodded. "Okay. Talk to her, but one more time and *I'll* damn well get someone."

He gave me a chin dip and reached for the duvet, covering himself again.

"You comfy?" I passed him the control for the state of the art turning aid he had been given after offering to be a guinea pig for the German company that made it. Something that he'd organised himself after researching sleep aids due to a month of restless sleep when he first got home.

Johnny hung the control on the metal side of the bed and looked back up to me. "I'm good. Night bro."

"Night."

The word sounded tight and forced and I felt bad for taking my anger out on him. He didn't deserve it, there was only one person who should be on the receiving end of my anger and she was out getting pissed.

I leaned down and kissed the top of his head, expecting him to complain, but he gave me a small smile and then closed his eyes.

Once I left his room, I walked down the hall to the front door and placed my hand on the key in the lock, ready to remove it so that Teresa could get in, but after a few seconds I changed my mind. I left the key in the lock and then went to bed, not giving a shit where she found to sleep tonight, if she even came home.

CHAPTER
18

Don't rush when giving him a hand-job, going at warp speed will sometimes kill the sensation for him – maybe consider naming the Seven Dwarfs in between strokes, it may work a treat.

Willow

Charlie and I had arranged to have a few drinks and then go on to Ziggy's, but I could sense that he wasn't really into it. He was tense, distracted, and distant and as much as it made me feel pathetic, my stomach ached with worry that he was about to dump me. I watched him nurse his drink, silently, for ten minutes and then decided I'd had enough.

"Listen, Charlie, if you want to end this," I said and waved a finger between us. "Please say it and put me out of my bloody misery."

His head shot up from the depths of his lager. "What?"

"If you're worried about saying it, don't be. I get it, you don't want to see me anymore."

I reached for my bag and started to push up from the chair, but before I could even get one cheek off the wood, he put a hand on my shoulder and pushed me back down.

"Willow, what the hell are you talking about? I don't want to dump you. For one, you'd have to be my girlfriend to actually dump you and for two...well, I really like you, so why would I dump you?"

"You do?"

"Yes, you know I do."

"Do I?"

"I told you I do. I introduced you to my brother, I told you everything about my life and Teresa, do you think I'd do all of that with someone I don't like or trust?"

"But you've been quiet and distant all night. You've barely looked at me."

Charlie's face softened and he reached for my hand. "I'm sorry, I just have stuff on my mind. It's nothing to do with you at all and believe me I really, really like you."

My heart gave a sigh of relief and the knot in my stomach unraveled itself. Okay, so he didn't consider me his girlfriend, but we hadn't actually had the conversation about the state of our relationship, and we had only been seeing each other for a couple of weeks. Apparently, it was nothing like my parents' youth, because according to Mum, Dad offered her a drink in a pub, walked her home and that was it, she was his girlfriend. If only life was as simple as the olden days.

That didn't matter though. I was happy he still wanted to see me, because I liked him like I'd never liked anyone before – a lot.

"So, what's wrong?" I asked, suddenly feeling guilty about making it all about myself when he was evidently worried about something.

Charlie hissed through his teeth and pushed his pint away. "Johnny fell last night."

I slapped a hand to my mouth, feeling the worst sort of person. "Oh my God, is he okay?"

"He's fine, he went to the hospital and got checked out, nothing broken or damaged."

I rubbed a hand down his back and leaned in to kiss his cheek. "I'm so sorry, Charlie. You must have been worried sick. You should have called; we could have postponed."

He shook his head. "No, Johnny insisted that I kept our date, he's got a couple of mates going around to play poker."

"So, what's wrong?"

He looked at me and his eyes were dull and full of sadness. "We had a huge row and I locked Teresa out because she was supposed to be home when he fell. We had a deal that she doesn't go out on a Friday night until either I'm home or he goes out. You see, Johnny's normally home early on a Friday and I can often be late because of bands getting free studio time, so we agreed that she'd stick around in case he needs anything. He won't have a carer, so it's the best we can do."

"And she didn't stick to the agreement," I stated on a sigh.

"Nope. It's just another way she lets him down."

"And is she home now?"

He rolled his eyes and let out a sigh.

"Are you worried about him?"

"Yeah, I know he's probably fine, but it shook him up. He's never fallen before, not when there's no one around. He's had the odd spill out of his chair, but nothing like that. He was lucky I didn't end up pulling a real late night. It's not unheard of for me not to get home until gone midnight when studio time is being offered for free."

It was then that I noticed the dark smudges under his eyes and the slope of his shoulder. He was obviously tired and worried.

"Let's go," I said as I stood up. "We'll go back to your house."

Charlie looked up at me and tugged on my hand. "Honestly, Willow, it's fine. We were supposed to be going to Ziggy's, you don't want to go back to mine just in case my brother needs me. Anyway, like I said, he's got some mates going around."

"Ring him at least and we don't have to go to Ziggy's. I'm happy to go back now, but if you don't want to, we could have a couple more drinks and then go back."

He considered my suggestion and glanced at his phone. "Are you sure you wouldn't mind?"

"Nope, not at all."

"Okay," he sighed out. "And I promise to try and be better

company. I know it's a lot to ask of you when we've barely started seeing each other, but he's my brother and-."

"Charlie," I said as I leaned down to kiss his cheek. "It's fine, honestly."

I went to move away, but he captured my chin in his hand and gave me the softest of kisses sending a pulse of electricity through the whole of my body.

"Now," he said, "where do you fancy going next."

When we got back to Charlie's house, a taxi had pulled away from the curb and Johnny was watching from the doorway.

"You finished your game?" Charlie called as he led me up the driveway, our fingers linked together.

As we passed the Vauxhall Combo, I glanced in through the window to double check the awful beaded car seat cover hadn't made a reappearance.

"Yeah, I lost a decent wedge and Aaron won big time. He took money off all three of us."

Charlie pulled me in front of him as we waited for Johnny to wheel himself back inside. Once he started to make his way down the hall, Charlie tapped my bum to urge me inside.

He'd cheered up a lot after he'd told me what was wrong, but I knew that suggesting we went home early had taken a huge weight off his shoulders.

"Drink?" he asked as he followed me into the lounge.

"Do you have any wine?" I asked tentatively, not sure if they kept alcohol out of the house because of their mum.

"Yeah, Teresa keeps a stash in the shed that she doesn't think we know about."

"Like we keep a stash of beer in a mini fridge in Charlie's wardrobe that she definitely doesn't know about."

The two brothers laughed, and as Charlie went off to get the drinks, Johnny yawned and stretched.

"Shit, I'm knackered."

"I heard you had a late-night last night."

He rolled his eyes. "Yeah, I was lucky not to break my nose."

"Well what a tragedy that would be." I laughed and kicked off my shoes, feeling totally at ease in their home.

"It would have. Imagine it spoiling my good looks."

It was then my turn to do the eye roll.

"Here you go," Charlie said and handed me a glass as he turned to Johnny. "You want a beer?"

"No thanks, I'm going to bed. I need some kip after last night. Anyway, it'll give you two some alone time."

Johnny winked at us and started to wheel himself out of the lounge, reaching out to poke my knee.

"Don't wear him out."

"Fuck off to bed, dickhead," Charlie growled and dropped down onto the sofa next to me. "You need any help?"

Johnny didn't answer but flipped Charlie off and wheeled himself out.

"You not having a beer?" I asked, as Johnny closed the door behind him.

"Nah, don't feel like it."

He looked at me with a twinkle in his eye and I knew exactly what he was considering, and I was most definitely on board with that.

I put my glass down on the floor and pretty much pounced on him.

"Oh my God, I really need this," he moaned against my lips. "Kissing you makes me forget all the crap."

"Good." I gasped, as his hand slid under my top and he pinched my nipple over my bra.

"Shit, sorry did that hurt."

My mouth covered his hungrily, not wanting to talk, but to kiss and taste him. As the blood pounded in my head, my hunger for Charlie increased and my lips enticed him to open up so that my tongue could explore his mouth.

"Willow."

"Hmm." I continued my assault on him, still not wanting to chat.

"So, bloody hot."

He started to rub and knead my left boob and weirdly thoughts of a cottage loaf flitted through my head, but pushing the idea of crusty bread away, I reached down to his crotch where I could feel his rock-hard cock, pushing against the fabric of his trousers.

"*Fuck.*"

Charlie's hand that wasn't treating my boob like a hand pump, moved down my side and pushed up my skirt, with a finger skimming the edge of my thong, so close to where I was desperate for him. My coochie was hungry and throbbing, desperate for some attention from Charlie, so when he pushed the lace to one side, I let out a sigh of pure contentment.

He immediately began to rub at my clit but was doing it so fast I wondered whether he'd end up with blisters – or at the very least friction burns. I wanted him to slow down and go gently so I pulled my hips back slightly, trying to lessen the contact, but Charlie was a real trooper and evidently believed if you kept rubbing that stick, you'd get a spark sooner or later.

I was wet, no doubt about it, but his fervent fingers weren't doing much to bring my big 'O' home. Not wanting to make him feel uncomfortable, I decided to go with it and try and rid my mind of images of loaves of bread and Boy Scouts trying to start a fire.

After a few more minutes of heated kisses, I moved my hands up to the button of his trousers and popped it open before I slowly pulled down the zip and slipped my hand inside. I was surprised to find he didn't have any undies on but didn't pause to think about it before I wrapped my fingers around his smooth, hard, cock.

"So good," he whispered as he lowered his mouth down to my neck, sucking on it.

His suck was hard, but unlike his boob grabbing, it was fucking good and I felt myself get a little wetter and started to pump him.

His cock felt so good, that my mouth started to water at the thought of taking a lick of his cock and giving it a nip with my teeth before I wrapped my lips around it.

With a little force, I pushed Charlie onto his back, sat back on my heels and stared down at him as his big, beautiful cock poked out through his trousers.

I licked my lips and breathed in and out slowly, which I knew made my boobs look fantastic and then bent down to take him in my mouth.

"Come on in love," a voice slurred behind us. "I'll get us a dri-."

Charlie shot up and banged his head against my chin, and scrambled to get off the sofa. As I straddled him, I was unceremoniously dumped on the floor and landed with a bang on my arse.

"What the hell?" Charlie cried, pushing up to his feet.

"Oh my God, really Charlie."

I pushed myself to sit up and saw his mum and a short, dark-haired guy were watching us from just inside the doorway. The guy, to be fair, had a hand in front of his eyes, but Teresa was staring at Charlie and pointing at him.

"Put that away."

Charlie grabbed at the zip and before I could warn him, he yanked it up and almost immediately screamed out in pain.

"Shit."

I scrambled to my feet, using the sofa for leverage and stumbled toward him.

"Oh my God, Charlie, are you okay?"

I cupped his face that was screwed into a grimace of agony.

"Fucking Christ, *shit*."

I looked down and shrieked; the skin was actually trapped in the zip and I felt a little faint.

"Shit, shit, shit," Charlie cried, and looked down at it. "Oh shit."

He then looked up to me, his eyes pleading for help as sweat started to form on his brow.

"Willow, please."

"What shall I do?" I cried, looking at Teresa, who was puffing on a cigarette, and then back to Charlie, my hands hovering over the trapped cock.

"Yank it down," Teresa said, swaying a little.

"Oh, I feel funny."

Thud.

I looked to see Teresa's date had flaked out and was lying at our feet.

"It really hurts." Charlie hissed and pushed the heel of his hand against his forehead. "I can't take this, fuck."

"I've told you, just yank it down."

Teresa moved to Charlie with her hands outstretched and I didn't hesitate in smacking them away. For one I didn't think 'yanking' the zip was the best action, and for two, no twenty-five-year-old man wanted their mum touching their appendage, especially when she had a lit cigarette hanging out of her mouth.

"No! Don't do that. It could make it worse." I looked up at Charlie and wanted to cry for him, his face was still screwed up with pain. "I think you're going to have to go to A&E."

He shook his head vigorously. "Nope. No way. Not a fucking chance. You can do it, Willow, please."

I looked down at his cock which was going a very funny shade of purple and grimaced. It had been such a beautiful cock. It was a tragedy that it was meeting such a sorry demise. I would remember it fondly.

"Please Willow, do something." Charlie's voice was a little high pitched and when I looked up at him the colour had totally drained from his face.

"Hang on, let me call my mum."

"What?" he cried. "No way. Oh shit, I feel sick."

I reached for my bag and fished around for my phone and as I pulled it out, Johnny wheeled into the room wearing only a pair of cotton pajama bottoms.

"What the hell is going on?" he asked. "I was about to get into bed."

"Your brother has his dick caught in his zip," Teresa said, bending down a little unsteadily to study her date.

"No way. Fucking hell, Charlie. Let's see."

"Piss off," Charlie groaned, pulling his shirt down over his cock. "Will, please don't call your mum."

With a start I remembered I was supposed to be doing exactly that and dialled her number.

"Hello love," she answered within two rings.

"Mum, I need your help. Please don't question me about it, just give me the answer."

"Ooh are you on Who Wants to be a Millionaire, love. You never said."

"No," I sighed, impatiently. "We have a situation and as a teacher of sixteen-year-old boys, I figure you'll know what to do."

"Oh, okay." She sounded hesitant. "You're not *with* a sixteen-year-old boy, are you?"

"God no. That's weird. I'm with Charlie."

"Please, Will, I feel sick."

I turned to see Charlie was indeed very grey and very sweaty.

"Shit, that looks like you might need surgery," Johnny added, not really helping the situation.

"I've told him to bloody yank it down." Teresa bent back down. "Are you okay now love, bit faint, were you?"

Johnny turned to see who his mum was talking to.

"Shit bro, I think you've killed him with your dick," he laughed, pointing at the man on the floor.

"Listen Mum," I said, turning away from the devastation. "How do you free a penis from a zip?"

"What?"

"I know you heard me, Maureen," I snapped in annoyance. "So please tell me what to do."

"I think Charlie's got his winky caught in his zip. You know Ivan, like in that film you like, the one about Mary...you know the girl with sperm in her hair-."

"Maureen! You can tell Dad when we've finished on the phone. Give me the answer please, he's in agony."

"No, don't let her tell your dad," Charlie groaned behind me.

"You want to sit down bro? You look like you might faint along with him in a minute."

"I'm fine thanks, a cup of sweet tea would be nice," Teresa's date replied.

"Mother, please." I implored her. "He's in real pain."

"Oil. Baby or vegetable. Smother it on really thick and pull the zip down gently. If the skin is broken put antiseptic cream on it and maybe get him to go and get a tetanus injection."

"Thank you. And if you ever mention this to the boys, or me or Charlie ever again, I will take a hit out on you, is that understood?"

"Oh, you are dramatic, but yes, it's understood."

"Not even a knowing look from either you or Ivan."

"Okay, okay."

"Thank you," I sighed and ended the call before turning back to Charlie who was looking down at his cock in despair. "Have you got baby oil?"

"I have," Johnny answered. "It's in my room." Without another word, he whizzed off.

"You okay?" I asked, stooping to look up at Charlie, whose head was still dropped as he looked at the damage.

"I feel a little sick, but I'll be fine." He gave me a small, sad smile and lifted a hand to run a finger down my cheek. "I'm so sorry."

"Hey, you've nothing to be sorry for."

"Yeah, right."

His shoulders slumped in defeat and if I hadn't thought it might cause him excruciating pain, I'd have given him a hug.

A couple of seconds later, Johnny came back with a large bottle of baby oil on his knee. He stopped and passed it to me.

"You want me to do it?" I asked.

"Well I'm not and *she* certainly isn't."

He nodded toward Teresa who was emptying the ash from her cigarette into her hand.

"Please, Will," Charlie said breathlessly. "Just do it before I puke."

I nodded, flipped open the lid and slathered my hands in oil.

"Err Willow, I think you're supposed to put it on the dick and the zip," Johnny said, with a throat clearing cough.

"Oh yes. Sorry."

I squeezed oil along the zip and onto the trapped skin, there was so much of it that it was dripping down the sides and onto the floor.

"Okay, try pulling the zip down now...slowly," I urged.

Charlie took a deep breath and gently edged it down. When he sucked in a breath, I squeezed some more oil on. He looked up at me through his lashes and started again. Finally, after lowering it slowly, inch by inch, his beautiful cock was free.

We all let out a huge breath of relief, Charlie's being the loudest, as if he'd defused an unexploded bomb.

"Fuck," he groaned. "That was..."

"Fucking gross," Johnny finished for him. "I never want to see that again. Either your dick or your dick caught in a zip. That skin was stretched to the max."

"Yeah I do know," Charlie huffed out as he carefully tucked himself into his trousers.

"Is the skin broken?" I asked. "Mum says you need antiseptic cream on it if it is."

He turned his back to us and lowered his head to take a look. "Nope, it's fine. A little bit bruised."

"You want arnica on that," Teresa's date offered. "Will help with bruising and swelling."

Johnny gave me the side-eye and then shook his head.

"Well much as I'd love to be introduced to my new step-dad and discuss how we stop Charlie's dick from swelling to the size and colour of an aubergine, I need to sleep."

"Night Johnny and thanks." I handed him the oil and gave him a small smile.

"Yeah night, and if you want my advice bro, wear some damn underwear in the future."

"Yeah," Charlie groaned, walking a little gingerly toward his brother. "I will. You sure you don't need my help."

Johnny held up a hand. "I got it covered, that's what the damn electric hoist is for, so stop fussing."

I looked to Teresa who was helping the man up from the floor with one hand, while she still held her cigarette ash with the other.

"Come on Dean, we'll go into the kitchen."

I guessed she was actually going to take him into the shed for the secret stash of wine.

"You want me to call you a taxi?" Charlie asked, grimacing.

"I could stay."

God, I really wanted to stay. He looked so sad that I wanted to be there for him.

"I don't think-."

"A little cuddle will be fine. If you're okay with that?"

A beautiful smile lit up his face and our latest failed sexual experience didn't matter. I was sure next time would be much better...hopefully.

CHAPTER 19

The blood vessel-like seam on the underside of his penis that runs from just below the shaft to halfway down the scrotum is his scream seam. Massaging it will directly massage his urethra, a super sensitive tube that is capable of registering intense pleasure - maybe wear a raincoat in case of a surprise evacuation.

Charlie

When I woke up, I was roasting hot and there was a warm, soft arse against the small of my back. It was then I remembered the nightmare of the dick situation the night before.

I groaned quietly, before I pulled at the waistband of my boxers and looked down at the damage. It didn't look too bad, thank God, but it was definitely tender and throbbing a little – and not in a good way. I was only glad there hadn't been blood, I'd heard horror stories about men losing pints of blood and even having to have their dicks operated on, so things could have been much worse.

I looked over my shoulder to see Willow was still fast asleep and making funny little purring noises from the back of her throat. It sounded really weird, but she looked cute, all curled up with one hand under her face and the other cupping her tit, which I was getting a pretty good view of as my sports vest she was wearing was far too big for her. As I looked at her, I thought about having my hands on her fantastic tits and felt myself getting hard, but my poor fella couldn't muster up the energy and soon flopped to snuggle back under the waistband of my boxers. He was probably still traumatised, I knew I was.

Yawning, I stretched and glanced at my phone which was charging on the set of drawers next to my bed. It was still pretty early, and I didn't want to wake Willow, so I settled back down to get some more sleep.

"Morning." Willow surprised me, her voice raspy with sleep.

"Morning, sorry did I wake you. I was trying not to."

Gingerly, I turned onto my other side to find Willow doing the same so that we were facing each other.

"You sleep okay?" she asked, with a huge yawn in my face.

"Not bad. I think those painkillers helped. I daren't even ask Teresa where she got them from."

"It was good that she had them, and nice of her to bring them in to you." She smiled and moved a little closer.

I rolled my eyes. "It'll take a lot more than a couple of painkillers to make her mother of the year."

"I suppose so, but at least she knocked this time."

Willow giggled and although I tried not to, I couldn't help but laugh too. We'd been getting into bed when Teresa knocked on the door offering some pain relief. I was a little wary of taking them at first, but she'd offered, so I took them instead of the paracetamol from the bathroom cabinet. I'd zonked within ten minutes of swallowing them and had a pretty restful sleep.

"How is it feeling?" Willow nodded in the general direction of my dick.

"Well I've checked it out and there's no major damage, but it aches a bit, like it went a few rounds with Tyson Fury, and he managed to get a couple of punches in, but not enough to knock it out."

"So, it's still active then?"

The smirk on her face told me she wanted to start where we painfully left off the night before and I hated that it was going to have to be a no.

"Not that you'd notice. I thought about getting my hands on your beautiful tits before and while it made a valiant effort, it wasn't happening."

"You were thinking about my boobs?" Now she had a full-on grin. "Nice."

"Yeah, it was." I sighed, giving her cleavage another quick glance. "But thinking is all I'll be doing for today at least."

"We could talk instead," she offered, looking a little unsure.

I frowned, wondering why she'd said that, we talked quite a lot, or so I thought.

"Do you think I've neglected the getting to know you part?" I asked as I brushed her hair from her eyes. "I'm sorry if you do."

"God, no." She caught my wrist with her hand and gave it a gentle squeeze. "Not at all. I just...well, I could do with your advice about something."

"Me?"

"Yes, as someone with a younger brother, you might be able to help. Also, I'm sure you're very wise, even if you are stupid enough to trap your cock in your zip."

I burst out laughing and pulled Willow to me, only to wince when her knee very gently brushed against my boxers.

"Oh shit, I'm sorry," she said, moving away from me.

"No, don't move, just keep your knees away from the goods." I huffed out a breath, feeling the tenderness of my dick. "Okay, so what advice is it you'd like, hey?"

I kissed the end of Willow's nose being careful to not get too close as her expressive silver eyes looked up at me with hesitancy.

"I can't give you my wisdom if you don't tell me, can I?"

She rubbed at her nose and then let out a long breath. "I think my youngest brother might be taking drugs."

"Woah, okay." I raised my brows. I didn't know her brother, but I was getting to know Willow and she was a pretty straight to the point person as far as I could tell, so if she thought that he was involved in something dodgy maybe she was right. "And what makes you think that?"

"I caught him looking shifty in the corridor at Carrington's. He was talking to another guy, about his age, but when he spotted me, he moved away and pretty much sent the guy packing."

"That doesn't mean it was drugs. He might have been surprised to see you. Didn't you say he ignores you when you're out?"

"Well yeah, but..."

"But what?" I asked as I watched concern and worry mask her face.

"It was more than that. They both looked...well, shifty. I have no clue what to do. Do I ask him? Do I tell my parents?"

I shook my head. "Don't worry your parents before you need to, before you have the full facts. Maybe speak to – Ruben is your youngest brother, isn't he?"

She nodded, smiled and cupped her small hand against my cheek. I wasn't sure why, but she was looking at me as if I was a damn superhero.

"Well, maybe speak to Ruben first and see if you can get him to open up. If your relationship is on dodgy ground already you don't want to make it worse by telling your mum and dad if there's nothing going on."

"I don't know what else it could be?" she groaned as she buried her head in the pillow.

"Hey, come on," I said, stroking a hand down her hair. "It could be nothing more than him not wanting you to meet his friends, or the guy might be dodgy, and he doesn't want you getting to know him. To be honest, it's probably more likely he doesn't want you in his business."

Willow looked up at me and contemplated what I'd said. "You think so?"

"Only he knows at this point what was going on, all I'm saying is, don't jump to conclusions and if it is drugs *then* you tell your parents and get him the help he needs."

A bright smile spread across her face and the worry went from her eyes. "You see, cock disaster aside, you are very wise."

"I know."

As I moved to kiss her, Willow gave another huge yawn in my face.

"Ooh sorry, morning breath," she groaned, slapping a hand over her mouth.

"Hmm, I've smelled fresher, I've got to be honest."

We both laughed and then yawned at exactly the same time.

"How about we get a couple more hours sleep?" I picked up my phone and looked at the time. "It's still only seven-thirty and it's Sunday morning, so unless you have to be somewhere..."

"Nope. More..." she yawned again, "sleep sounds good. Turn on your side away from me."

"Why, is my morning breath that bad too?"

"No," she said, as she smacked my chest playfully. "Mine's gross, but I want to cuddle and with the state of your thing down there, you can't spoon me, so I'll be the big spoon on this occasion."

God, I really liked this girl. She was so straight and natural and didn't care about the shit that was going on in my life, or the fact that I had an out of action dick.

"Sounds good to me." I gave her a soft kiss and then turned over.

Willow took a couple of minutes to get herself comfy, and her wriggling around next to my arse didn't help the dick situation. I willed it to get hard, but it was most definitely on strike while it was injured, but when Willow settled and linked her fingers with mine, resting on my hip, I was more than satisfied.

"Night-night," she whispered and dropped a kiss to my shoulder blade.

It might have been girly, and I would never admit to anyone, especially my brother, but I felt butterflies take flight in the pit of my stomach and it was the best feeling ever.

I lifted our joined hands to my lips and kissed the back of Willow's and then kept a tight hold of it against my chest for the extra three hours that we slept.

CHAPTER 20

You can have a quickie without leaving your table at a restaurant. If the tablecloth is long, just use your big toe to masturbate each other – moral of the story, wash your feet before you go out to dinner.

Willow

"Charlie," I giggled down the phone. "I'm fine, it's midday on a Sunday and nothing is going to happen to me."

"Your taxi driver might be dangerous," he replied with a laugh.

I looked at the little, bald man, who was probably half my body weight, driving the car and grinned.

"I think I'm safe, so go and do whatever it is you need to do."

"I want to be sure you get home okay. I wish you'd have let me drive you."

I knew he was pouting; I could hear it in his voice.

"You have to take Johnny to his swimming physio, so the last thing you needed was to drive me home."

"It'd have taken twenty minutes at most."

"And twenty back, making it forty, not forgetting the snogging time we'd have needed before I got out of your car."

I couldn't help but grin and feel a little bit warm and fuzzy all over.

Besides the sex, which we hadn't managed particularly successfully yet, things were going well between us. The morning snuggles had been lovely, especially as he held my hand the whole time. We'd only woken when we had because Johnny had barged in bawling at Charlie, saying we needed to get up because he had his physio at the pool in an hour and didn't want to be late.

"Oh yeah, can't forget to add on the snogging time," Charlie said, his tone low and seductive.

As I allowed my head to think of things that made my heart flip, the taxi pulled to a stop at the end of our driveway.

"I'm home," I sighed and almost asked the driver to go around the block, so I could continue my conversation with Charlie. "Hold on a sec."

The driver pressed the button of his fare meter and turned to me in his seat.

"That's seven-seventy please."

I handed him a tenner and waved away the change before I got out of the taxi.

"I'm back," I said as I started to walk up the drive.

"You've paid almost eight quid for a taxi." Charlie growled down my ear.

"Well ten actually, I let him keep the change."

"I could have driven you," he sighed. "And you'd have got a snog at the end of it, I bet the taxi driver didn't offer you that."

"No because that would have been almost like prostitution, me paying for a service with sex." I stopped walking and looked down at the drive and kicked at a pebble while I grinned like a stupid idiot.

"I'm on board with that, although I'm not sure I agree with it with the taxi driver, but next time you want to pay me with sex, that's fine."

I continued to smile, but at the mention of us having sex, the joy left me. I really wanted to have great sex with him, but I was beginning to think it wasn't going to happen. I knew it was quite soon for me to have sex with someone, particularly as we were only dating, but bearing in mind he'd started out as a one-night stand, the four-date rule seemed a little redundant.

I then remembered the 'one-night stand' and how that had been disastrous in the sex department too, and my happiness ebbed away a little bit more.

"Maybe we should consider it then," I replied, the flirtation gone from my voice. "Anyway, you need to go, and I'd better get inside and let my parents know I'm still alive."

"Didn't you tell them where you were last night?" he asked, sounding concerned. "*Willow.*"

"I did, I sent them both a text, so stop worrying. I was joking, honestly."

"I hope so because I don't want to piss your mum and dad off."

"Why?" I asked as I furrowed my brows together.

"Because I don't." He sounded serious but didn't elaborate. "Okay, well I'd better go, and I'll call you tomorrow."

My heart sank, hoping he might want to chat later, but I couldn't be greedy and at least he hadn't used the word 'sometime' as the timescale for being in touch.

"Okay, speak to you tomorrow. Bye."

"Bye."

When I was sure he'd gone, I slipped my phone into my bag and made my way up the rest of the drive. As I was about to put my key into the lock, Toby appeared at my side with a huge tub of popcorn, the contents of which was being shovelled into his mouth.

"You just getting home from last night too?" I asked and looked at him over my shoulder as I opened the door.

"No, cinema." As his mouth was full of food a piece of popcorn hit my cheek.

"Ugh, you're so gross." I wiped a hand along my face and walked into the hall. "What did you go and see?"

I hung my jacket and bag over the bannister to take upstairs later and waited for Toby to finish off another mouthful of popcorn.

"Nothing," he finally said. "I only went to buy the popcorn. It's so much nicer than that bagged shit you get at the supermarket."

"You mean you walked all the way to the cinema only to buy popcorn?"

I knew he'd had to have walked because Mum and Dad's cars were on the drive. Declan's wasn't and neither was Toby and Ruben's shared car, and I didn't have one, preferring to save my money and borrow Mum's instead.

"No, don't be stupid, I got a taxi," he replied and looked at *me* as if *I* was the idiot.

I thought about saying something, but decided against it, it was Toby after all and why should I be surprised about anything that he did.

"Where've you been anyway?" he asked as he pushed past me where I lingered by the mirror assessing my dishevelled appearance. "Or do I need to ask? Been with *Charlie,* have you?"

The way he said Charlie's name, like an eight-year-old child would, made me smile.

"Maybe."

"Ooh it's getting serious if you're already having sleep overs." Toby winked at me and then shoved more popcorn into his mouth.

I simply smiled, not sure if we were getting serious but I also didn't want to say, 'it wasn't what it seemed like', because neither Charlie nor I seemed to mind that it was *exactly* what it seemed like.

"Who's home anyway?" I asked as I grabbed a hairband from my wrist and swept my hair into a messy bun.

"Only Ivan the Fucking Terrible and Maureen," Toby replied as he offered me the tub of popcorn.

I took a handful. "Where's Ruben?" I asked as I thought again about what I'd seen in the bar.

"He went out about ten this morning, said he was going to meet some mates for a game of snooker or something."

"At *ten* on a Sunday morning?"

I started to eat the popcorn as worry for my youngest brother reared its head again. Snooker halls weren't open that early, surely.

Toby shrugged and started to walk toward the lounge door, and I wondered whether I should go against Charlie's advice and tell my parents my worries about Ruben; my head was totally messed up about the situation. Deciding not to make any hasty decisions, I followed Toby and as he pushed open the door, I found myself covered in popcorn as he threw it into the air with a loud scream.

"What the hell-"

"No," he cried. "That's disgusting."

I looked over his shoulder to get a great view of Ivan the Fucking Terrible's bare arse and Maureen's legs, adorned in a pair of pop socks, wrapped around him.

My parents were having sex.

Ugh.

My. Parents. Were. Having. Sex.

On the family sofa at lunchtime, on a Sunday.

"Oh my God, that's just..." I made a gagging sound and promptly turned around, only to be pushed to one side by Toby.

"Let me get past," he cried. "I need to go and bleach my eyes."

"Oh, don't be so ridiculous," I heard my dad say behind me. "It's perfectly natural."

"Not on the bloody sofa in the middle of the afternoon, when any of your *five* children could walk in," I practically screamed, as I pulled popcorn from my bun.

"We got carried away, didn't we Ivan? We thought Toby would be a while and assumed you wouldn't be back until later, as you were with your boyfriend."

"Yeah, you know what assumed did, don't you Mother? It makes an ass out of you and me, and that's one bloody ass I didn't want to see."

"Willow, make it stop," Toby cried as he came out of the kitchen with a wet paper towel over his eyes.

"Oh, stop being so stupid," Dad said, right next to my shoulder.

I closed my eyes and shuddered. "Please tell me you have clothes on, and you are not standing behind me naked."

"Of course, I have clothes on, we were only having a quickie."

I then heard his zip go up and shuddered again.

"You and your boyfriend must have quickies, surely."

My sexually frustrated self couldn't take much more and I seriously wished I had a time machine and I could go back to being snuggled up with Charlie in his bed.

"No, we bloody don't and he's not my bloody boyfriend."

"Willow, help me," Toby cried, melodramatically sliding down the wall with his paper towel still over his eyes.

"Oh, for God's sake, stop being so pathetic," I hissed, accidently on purpose kicking his leg as I stepped over him. "I'm going to my room, call me when lunch is ready."

"Will do love," Mum called, as though we hadn't just found her on her back with her legs in the air and Dad nestled between them. "It's pork today."

"*Argh.*" I screamed as I flounced up the stairs, my bag and jacket dragged behind me. "I bloody hate this family."

CHAPTER
21

The beauty of the clitoris is that it doesn't need to have any rest and relaxation after climaxing. As long as it gets stimulation, you'll keep on coming. Apparently one woman who took part in a study had a staggering 134 climaxes in a row – how the hell did she have time to do the ironing?

Willow

At Mum's request, we were all around the lunch table, despite the fact that two of her children were traumatised, and I had no idea where to look. If I looked at her, I could see her legs wrapped around Ivan the Fucking Terrible's back and if I looked at him, well, all I could see was his bloody arse pumping away. There were definite drawbacks to having parents who worked in 'sex'.

The other problem I had was, Ruben. He'd arrived back in time for lunch looking...happy. Something I hadn't seen him look for a long time; so, he had to be high. He sat opposite me at the table, which made it easy for me to check him out, or it would have been had he not had his head down, shovelling Mum's pork roast into his gob. When he finally took a breather, I leaned across the table to check out his eyes, I wanted to see if his pupils were bigger than they should have been – or was that smaller? I had no clue, but I'd know if he was on drugs, I'd see it in his eyes somehow.

"What the hell are you doing?" Ruben asked, as he pushed a hand against my forehead.

I quickly sat back and gasped; I hadn't realised how close I'd evidently got to check him out.

"I'm...well, I'm...checking you've eaten all your sprouts," I replied, like it was the big fat lie that it actually was.

He pulled his brows together and looked down at his plate which was almost empty bar a roast potato that I knew he was saving until last.

"What does it look like, or were you trying to see if they were actually in my mouth? Weirdo."

"Stop bickering you two," Dad grumbled as he tried to chew on a piece of crackling. "It's Sunday, the day of peace and tranquillity."

"And shagging apparently," Toby offered.

"Ugh, do you have to," I groaned. "It hadn't crossed my mind for at least five minutes, now you've brought it all back again."

"What are you talking about?" Declan asked, as he sat back in his chair and rubbed his stomach.

"We caught Maureen and Ivan doing the nasty," Toby explained. "It burned my eyes, Dec. I'm not sure I'll ever be the same again."

"Nor me," I said and held up my hand.

"Oh, stop being so dramatic. How do you think your dad and I managed to have five children?"

"Ugh. Yuck," Ruben said, as he pushed his unfinished spud away.

"There's nothing wrong with two people having sex. It's the most natural thing in the world and because your mum and I are over fifty it doesn't mean we can't experience a happy and fulfilling sex life. Studies say-."

"No," I cried. "Please don't talk shop, and let's change the subject."

The last thing I needed was to hear about how studies showed couples who had a lot of good sex were the ones who were happiest and had the longest lasting relationships, especially as I wasn't getting any with my hot new...whatever he was.

"Personally, I think the fact our parents are still having sex is pretty awesome." Declan smiled at them both as Ruben, Toby, and I all made gagging sounds.

"What are you after?" Toby asked. "Want letting off with your rent this week or do you need to borrow Dad's car 'cause there's something wrong with yours? Come on what is it?"

"There's nothing," Declan said, and gave Toby a narrow-eyed glare, which proved there obviously was.

"Declan knows he doesn't need to butter me up for anything." Mum smiled at him all gooey eyed.

"Because he's your favourite." we all chimed together, even Dad.

"So, what do you want?" Dad asked Declan.

He tried to look affronted, but as we stared at him expectantly, he soon huffed out a sigh.

"Okay, but it's only a loan. Work have messed up my bonus and the lads and I are going to book our trip to Vegas tomorrow after work and I don't have the deposit."

"I thought you were some big shot marketing salesman who earned megabucks?" Ruben asked.

"And?"

"Well if you earn so much money every month why don't you have the deposit saved up?"

"Ooh, ooh, I know that one," Toby cried as he excitedly jumped up and down in his chair. "It's because of all the shit clothes he buys."

"Oi, there's nothing wrong with my clothes."

Ruben, Toby, and I all burst out laughing and stared at his awful *Gucci* t-shirt with two black panther's heads on it, which I knew cost him over three hundred quid, the too-tight jeans and the *Nike* trainers which were the same puce yellow as his t-shirt.

"How much do you need?" Dad asked as he evidently felt the need to change the subject.

"Five hundred?" Declan looked at Mum as he gave the figure because he knew if he batted his eyelashes at her she'd say yes.

"Five hundred for a deposit?" Dad groaned. "Where the hell are you staying, the bloody Bellagio?"

Declan winced and shifted back in his chair.

Dad shook his head and picked his half-chewed crackling back up. "I'll get it for you in the morning, you'll have to come and pick it up from my office if you need it before tomorrow night."

"Thanks Dad," Declan sighed. "And I'll pay you back as soon as they sort my bonus out. The stupid admin girl forgot to put it through, although she says I was late putting the sales forms in, but I wasn't."

"Okay, okay." Dad replied as he chewed. "I've said I'll lend it to you. I don't need a sob story to go with it. Now, Maureen, what's for pudding?"

As Mum and Toby cleared away the plates, I watched Ruben as he messed around on his phone. He read something on it, presumably a text message, and frowned before quickly typing a response, his thumbs moving at lightning speed. I wondered if they were quicker than usual and it was the drugs that had made them so fast, but I couldn't say I'd watched him text often enough to notice.

As Mum was placing apple crumble and cream in front of us, the dining room door opened and Danny, Patsy, and Nigel walked in.

"Ooh you could smell the crumble, couldn't you?" Mum pulled Patsy into her arms and kissed her on the cheek.

Patsy then moved around the table, giving us all a hug, an especially tighter one for Ruben who was her favourite of all of us. Ruben gave her a bright smile and something akin to jealousy soured in my stomach. He was my little brother, yet never looked at me like that, even though we'd always been close when he was a kid. I took him everywhere with me until I was around fifteen or sixteen and then boys and drinking cider with my mates down by the river became more important. As I watched him pat Nigel on the head, I wondered if his animosity toward me was my fault and whether he felt as though I'd abandoned him in some way.

"Hey, Willow," Patsy said as she pulled up a chair beside me. "I hear there's a new fella on the scene."

I glared at Danny and then turned back to his gorgeous girlfriend with her thick, waist length, scarlet coloured hair and rolled my eyes.

"He's got a big gob, but yes there is. His name's Charlie Monroe and it's early days."

"I know that name," Patsy said, as she pursed her lips which were the same colour as her hair. "Does he have a brother in a wheelchair?"

I nodded. "Yeah, how do you know him?" My question was filled with dread, because I wasn't sure what I'd do if she said he was a well-known douche, or she'd been out with him herself – ugh imagine that, it'd be tantamount to having sex with my brother by proxy.

"I have a friend who works with him, his brother I mean, they're both accountant managers at Oxygas. She's always going on about how fit Johnny and Charlie Monroe are and that they should shoot a calendar."

I grinned, feeling pretty proud that I'd bagged myself a potential model – well in Patsy's friend's eyes anyway.

"She's only dating him, you know," Mum chimed in. "I don't understand why you can't just be boyfriend and girlfriend. All the kids at school are the same. All this dating, it's because of programmes like that bloody *Love Island* that you two watch," she said, as she wagged a finger at Dad and Toby. "They only *date* on there."

"Dating basically means shagging, Mum," Danny said as he helped himself to my apple crumble.

"Or not, as the case may be." Dad gave me a sympathetic smile and reached for my hand and patted it. "Was it the zip incident love, or is it something else?"

"What zip incident?" Toby asked.

"Oh he-."

"Mum! No! I will have you taken out."

She grinned and ironically mimed zipping her lips.

"You know, if you do need my help, I'd be more than willing."

My eyes went as wide as Frisbees as I pulled in a sharp breath.

"No, I don't, thank you very much. I don't *need* or *want* it."

"I'm only saying, you don't have the glow of a young woman enjoying good sex with her virulent new *date*."

"Well maybe they're taking it slowly," Patsy offered and nudged me with her shoulder.

"Or maybe he doesn't find her attractive," Ruben muttered.

"Or maybe I don't want you lot knowing my business."

"Yeah, but we're your family," Danny said as he continued to tuck into my bloody pudding. "Anyway, I'm here to invite you all to a party at ours next Saturday. I don't want to, but you're my family so..."

"Ooh lovely-."

"No, not you and Dad, Mum."

"Danny!"

"What? They're not invited, Pats. You know we've talked about this."

"You could be a bit nicer about it." Patsy threw him a stare that said he was in trouble when she got him home.

"It's fine," Dad responded.

"Only because he's your favourite," I ground out as I snatched my pudding back from my brother and tipped my diet coke over it.

"God, you're so childish," Danny said and then reached for Ruben's untouched crumble, as he was distracted by texting again.

"Anyway, back to you and Charlie, love," Mum said chirpily. "Why isn't he your boyfriend?"

"'Cause he's her 'not getting fucked buddy', by the sounds of it."

"Toby, your language is terrible. Ivan, tell him."

"Toby your language is terrible. *Do* you want my advice or help?"

"No Dad," I cried as I pushed up from the table. "Leave me alone."

I stormed out of the dining room to a chorus of 'ooh', slammed the door behind me and stomped toward the stairs.

"Willow." Dad's voice was soft and coaxing behind me. "What's wrong love? Is it your sex life, because I can help you know?"

"Oh my God," I said through gritted teeth. "Just leave me alone."

"But-."

I swung around to face him.

"God, if you want someone's business to interfere with, interfere with Ruben's. He's the one taking bloody drugs, not me."

As soon as the words were out of my mouth, I knew I'd done the wrong thing. Dad looked stricken as he stared at me and gripped hold of the bannister.

"W-what?"

"Forget I said anything."

It was a pathetic attempt to take back the words I'd already said, but I didn't know what else to do, or say. Dad looked desolate, a look that I'd never seen him have before.

"No, Willow, you said your brother was taking drugs. Is it true or are you saying that because I've pissed you off?"

"Dad-."

"Willow, please tell me. I need to know if my son needs help."

His shoulders sloped and he closed his eyes against the pain that he was obviously feeling.

"I don't know for sure," I sighed. "I caught him hanging around with some dodgy looking guy near the toilets in a bar and when he spotted me, well, he looked shifty."

"So, what makes you think its drugs?" Dad shook his head in disbelief.

Now I'd said it out loud, I wondered whether I believed it myself. When I'd told Charlie, I'd been so sure, but now looking at Dad and the worry etched on his face, I knew I should have got more proof before shooting my mouth off.

"That and his bloody moods all the time," I continued. "It seemed to make sense, but I don't have any other proof. I can try and-."

"No, Willow," Dad said quietly, putting a hand on top of mine. "It's not your problem. Thank you for looking out for him, but I've got it from here."

"What are you going to do, Dad?"

He shrugged. "I'll speak to your mum and we'll decide how to approach it."

"I might have got it all wrong."

He gave me a small smile. "Let's hope so, love. Let's hope so."

With that he turned and went back to the dining room where I could hear laughter and I wished once again that I had a time machine.

CHAPTER
22

When in a 69 position, keep pace together by putting on some music with a strong, steady beat – I always find Agadoo by Black Lace does the trick.

Charlie

"Morning, Charlie," Deke Johnson, the producer I was helping out, called to me. "We all set up?"

"Hey, Deke. Yeah, I just need to finish setting Jimmy's drums up in the isolation booth, but otherwise all done."

A popular Indie band, Devil's Doorbell, were recording their latest album and Deke Johnson was a huge name to be producing for them. He was the producer of some of Dirty Riches' best albums, and having him on board generally guaranteed a hit, so the fact that I was working with him was astonishing.

Jake and Skins from Dirty Riches had visited the studio the day before and both of them had told me to make the most of the opportunity and learn as much as I could, because if production was something I wanted to go into, they'd help me every step of the way – and people asked why I'd worked here since I was sixteen.

"You have a good weekend?" Deke asked as he shrugged off his battered leather jacket.

I thought about Johnny's fall and my dick trapped in my zip and groaned.

"Not the best, got to be honest."

"What, no golden moments at all?" Deke sat down at the mixing console.

I thought of Willow, snuggled in my bed and smiled. "Yeah, there was. I'm dating an amazing girl, so seeing her was pretty special."

"Dating? What is this dating shit, my kids tell me the same thing and I have no fucking clue what that means?"

I smiled. "It's what we young kids do these days, Deke."

He shook his head in obvious disgust. "Stupid idea. If she's so amazing, ask her to be your damn girlfriend."

He was right, I knew he was, and I'd been going to do it, despite the fact I'd only known her for a couple of weeks. What was the point in waiting when I already knew how much I liked her? She'd already experienced my damn mother and still seemed to want to keep on seeing me, so yes, I wanted to ask her to be my girlfriend.

"I think that, maybe you oldies had the best ideas, Deke," I said and grinned at him.

"Yeah and maybe we oldies know what we're talking about. Now, less talking and more working. The band will be here in about ten minutes and we have a lot to do."

"Okay," I replied, moving toward the door, "so how many sugars do you want in your coffee?"

We'd had a great morning as the band had managed to lay down the bed track *and* the vocals of the first song for the album. They'd worked hard, but Deke wasn't one to let them slack anyway, so I'd been the one to suggest we stop for lunch.

The band had decided to nip out and grab something, whereas I chose to use the subsidised café that we'd recently had installed at the studios. When I walked in, I noticed how quiet it was, considering all the studios were being used. I looked at my phone and realised we were pretty late for lunch which would account for the lack of people. It also meant that I was unlikely to be able to get a proper lunch.

"Hey, Maggie, what've you got left?" I asked the sweet, middle-aged lady who worked the counter.

"Not much I'm afraid, love. Chef has gone, so it's a jacket potato or sandwich I'm afraid. Unless she's left something in the fridge. Want me to check?"

She gave me a dazzling smile that creased the corner of her eyes and it struck me, as it did most days, how great it would have been to have a mum like Maggie.

"Whatever is easiest for you," I replied, as I picked a bottle of water from the cooler.

"Anything for you." She leaned forward and pinched my cheek. "It's those bloody dimples."

I rolled my eyes. "A sandwich would be great. Cheese and ham, please."

"Okay love, I'll sort it for you. You go and sit down."

Taking my pick of the tables, I pulled out a chair with my back to the door and flopped down onto it. I had forty minutes to kill, so decided to check out some social media.

As soon as I turned my phone on it pinged with a message.

Pretty Girl: I know you're busy today but need to tell you this. I'm totally embarrassed but I walked to work with my skirt tucked into my knickers. An old lady on a motorised scooter beeped at me and actually shouted 'put your drawers away, love'. No idea what she meant until James pointed them out when I got into work. OMG I'm such a dick!

· · ·

I tried to keep my laughter quiet, but it wasn't long before Maggie was looking up from making my sandwich and watching me.

"What's tickled you?" she asked.

"A text from the girl I'm seeing."

Maggie nodded and picked up the plate with my sandwich on it. "Means a lot when someone can make you laugh. My Tony makes my sides ache with laughter sometimes."

Her eyes twinkled as she placed the plate in front of me.

"You been married long, Maggie?"

"Thirty-one years. Got married at twenty-one and while it's not been perfect, we've been very happy."

"Wow, twenty-one?"

I had still felt like a kid at twenty-one, never mind getting married.

"Yep. You married young in those days though, love, you didn't really live together first. Marriage doesn't seem to be so important now." She gave me another warm smile, patted my shoulder and went back behind the counter to carry on whatever she'd been doing before I came in.

I smiled and sent a text back to Willow.

Me: And what size and colour were the knickers? I need to know for visuals when I get a break later.

I put my phone down on the table not expecting a reply, because I knew she'd be in surgery, but at least when she did eventually read it, she'd know I'd been thinking of her. Thoughts of her brought a smile to my face and I decided I'd ask her out on another date when I got home.

"Hi."

The soft, sultry voice grabbed my attention and when I looked up, I was surprised to see Viv Cator, the drummer for Legal Breakup, who were recording in one of the smaller studios. I'd done some set up for them before and they were a pretty decent bunch, inviting me out for a drink with them on their last day of recording – and now they were back.

"Was pretty disappointed not to see you in the studio this morning," she said as she ran her tongue along the edge of her teeth. "Patrick is great, but he's not you."

"I'm working with Deke Johnson and Devil's Doorbell," I replied, feeling proud to be able to say it and trying to ignore the way she was looking at me – like she was a spider and I was a big juicy fly.

"Devil's Doorbell? Wow."

Her eyes went wide and she looked suitably impressed, and I had to admit that I liked that I'd managed to make her a little awe-struck; I had an ego just like everyone else.

"So, you're going up in the world." Smiling, Viv moved a hand to my shoulder and gave it a squeeze. "That's great, hon."

I moved back a little, trying to create some distance between us, because she'd maneuvered herself so that her crotch, in tight leather trousers, was in my eye line which made me feel uncomfortable.

"Yes, it's been great. Deke has shown me loads already."

"I heard he's good."

She tilted her head on one side and let her eyes graze over me and her scrutiny made me feel a little awkward. I could flirt with the best of people, but there was something about Viv that felt a little predatory and it didn't sit well with me.

"Yeah he is." I flashed her a smile and then shifted my chair, so that I was turned back to the table.

When I picked up my sandwich and took a bite, I hoped she'd take the hint, but was shocked when her head appeared in front of me and she took a bite too.

"Hmm, nice," she said, as she wiped at the corner of her lips. "Tastes good."

"Err, I'm sorry but I'd rather you didn't." I looked back at the sandwich and threw it onto the plate. "Hey Maggie. I need to get back, so is it okay if I take this to go?"

Maggie looked up from filling the counter chiller with cakes and smiled. "No problem, love. Make sure you bring the plate back when you're next in."

I nodded and pushed back my chair. "Well, I'll get back. Great seeing you Viv."

Her smile faltered and she put out a hand to touch my arm, but I quickly stood and shifted to one side, avoiding her touch.

"You fancy a drink sometime?" Viv asked, evidently not getting that she was being brushed off.

"I don't think so," I replied. "Thanks anyway."

"Why?"

She looked petulant with her lips pursed and hands on her hips.

"Well, because I have a girlfriend."

It wasn't totally untrue. I had Willow and she was my friend, and I wanted us to be exclusive. I *wanted* her to be my girlfriend.

Viv shrugged. "And?"

"Well unless she's invited, which I doubt, I don't think it would be right to go out for a drink with you."

"She wouldn't need to know," she said, adding a tinkling laugh that grated on my ears.

"But I would. I wouldn't like her going out for a drink with another man, so I don't think it's fair for me to go out with you."

I also wanted to add, I also think you're a little too pushy to be even remotely attractive, but she was a client and I wasn't totally sure she wouldn't try and twist things.

"You do know how big we're going to be, don't you?"

"Well I've heard you, and you're good, yeah."

Viv tilted her head and grinned. "*I* could get you a job on our tour," she said with assurance, as if doing me a favour. "The tour that's going to make us massive, bigger than fucking Devil's Doorbell."

That was a matter of opinion. Legal Breakup were nowhere near as good as Devil's Doorbell. They weren't as gifted musically, wrote pretty mediocre songs and didn't work hard enough.

"Well, I'm happy here thanks." I moved to walk past her, not wishing to waste another minute of my lunch break on her.

"Let me take your number, in case I can change your mind." Her hand landed on my chest and long, thin fingers worked their way in between the buttons of my shirt.

I slapped my hand down on hers and then picked it up and pulled it away from me.

"Like I said, Viv. I have a girlfriend who I care about a lot. I don't want to risk what I have with her and to be honest, she's the only woman I see."

Her intake of breath was inaudible, but I saw how her shoulders straightened and her lips parted. This was definitely a woman who didn't usually feel rejection.

"Your loss." Viv curled her lip and moved to let me pass. "Don't forget where I am though hon, when it all goes to shit with your girlfriend."

"It won't," I said confidently. "This one is a keeper."

And I meant every word.

When I slipped out of the café into the corridor, my phone beeped in my pocket. I pulled it out and saw a text from Willow.

Pretty Girl: Pink lace and pretty small – or maybe that's cos my arse is so big??? BTW my brother is having a house party on Saturday if you fancy going with me.

Shit every single thing she did or said made me smile.

Me: Yep I have a visual for the whole afternoon not only on my break. Thank you, Lord. Also, there's nothing wrong with your arse...

Her bum wasn't tiny, she was right, but fuck it was sexy. Adjusting my jeans, I continued texting.

. . .

Me: ...Party sounds good. Look forward to it xx

Yep, I'd put kisses at the end, but sod it, I didn't give a shit. Most men did end texts to their girlfriends with kisses. Something that I was going to talk to her about as soon as I could. As I thought about it, another text came in.

Pretty Girl: That's great. I'll let you know time etc. Enjoy the rest of your day x

The text had come back pretty quickly, so she hadn't had to think about it and so the kiss on the end must have been done naturally. Okay there was only one to my two, but it was a kiss and...what the fuck was I doing thinking about kisses on a text – I was turning into a damn teenage girl. I sent one more text before I turned my phone off and slipped it into my pocket and going back to work. It was only when I got back to the studio that I realised I'd forgotten my sandwich.

Me: I will and you. Oh, and I'll call you tonight about maybe going out tomorrow. Not sure I can wait until Saturday to see you xxxx

CHAPTER
23

Standing is best used for quickies, but make it better by turning around, leaning over and lifting one leg sideways. Once he's inside, you can close your legs slightly, so he doesn't pop out – this is also known as the dog having a pee position.

Charlie

I was a grown, twenty-five year old man who had conversed and worked with one of the biggest rock bands in the world, had laughed and joked with some of the best producers in the music industry, yet the thought of being in a room with all four of Willow's brothers made me want to shit my pants. They all seemed to be great guys, but I was worried they were going to give me shit about their sister.

Danny had been nice enough to invite Johnny too, but as he couldn't make it, Bomber had decided he'd take his place. Willow had assured me all the way to Danny and Patsy's house it would be fine, that neither Danny nor Patsy would mind, but I still kept glaring at him for his damn cheek.

"Hi." Willow called as we let ourselves in through the kitchen.

There were a few people in the kitchen fixing themselves drinks or standing around chatting. Through the doorway I could see the lounge had been converted into a temporary dancefloor. The music was pumping loud, a little too much bass in my professional opinion, but there was a good vibe going on by the look of the number of people in there.

"Hey. Finally," The guy I recognised as Danny, said, as he pulled Willow in for a hug. "I expected you ages ago."

"Why?" she asked as she scrunched up her nose.

"I wanted you to make that nasty cocktail you make. You know the one with the rum."

"Rude Boy?"

"Yeah, that's it. Can you make some?"

Willow folded her arms over her chest. "And what would the magic bloody word be, rude boy?"

Danny rolled his eyes. "Please."

"Okay, but me, Charlie, and Bomber get first dibs on it."

Danny nodded and led her by the elbow toward one of the counters where there were at least four bottles of rum, a jar of coffee and a load of cans of something, which when I looked closer,

saw it was Irish Stout.

"Shit," I muttered to Bomber. "Rum and stout? That sounds gross."

He rubbed his hands together. "I can't wait."

"Right," Danny said as he rejoined us. "What can I get you both until the Rude Boy is ready? Oh, and I'll get the first one, but after that you're on your own."

Bomber and I both thrust carrier bags of booze at him.

"Oh, and this is Bomber by the way. Johnny already had plans to go to a friend's wedding, so this rude wanker decided to invite himself along."

Bomber elbowed me in the side and held out a hand for Danny.

"Hiya mate, pleased to meet you and thanks for inviting me."

Danny laughed and slapped Bomber on the back. "No problem, the more the merrier."

He took the bags from us, laid it all out on the table with the rest of the booze and then looked over his shoulder. "A lager each?"

"Yeah please," I replied and walked toward him. "Seriously though, thanks for inviting us."

"Like I said, the more the merrier. I'll introduce you to Patsy in a minute, but she's gone to check on Nigel. We put him in our room out of the way."

"Oh yeah, good idea, you don't want him getting trodden on."

"That your kid?" Bomber asked, as he took a proffered can from Danny.

"Nope, my dog. He'd be fine, but someone would be bound to leave a door open and he's stupid enough to wander out."

"What sort of dog is he?"

"I have no clue. We went to the dog pound for a Chihuahua for Patsy and came back with him. I think his mother was a bit of whore because honestly, I can see about five different breeds in him. He was found in a cardboard box next to some bins behind a restaurant."

"Danny, you do know only one dog can have impregnated his mother, don't you?" Willow called without looking up from her cocktail making.

"Yes, Willow, I am aware," he replied with a sigh. "It was a joke and get on making that drink. I've been bigging it up with everyone."

"Where'd you learn to make that?" I asked as I moved to Willow's side to watch her pour a can of stout into a huge bucket.

"Tigger from Birmingham." She turned and grinned at me and it struck me how damn cute she looked, especially as tonight's hairstyle was two little buns on the top of her head, making her look like a cute teddy bear.

"You look gorgeous," I said on instinct.

She blushed a little and then leaned forward and gave me a closed lip kiss. "Thank you, now go away, you're distracting me from my art."

Taking a deep contented breath, I moved in closer and gave her a long, lingering kiss before taking Bomber to try and sort out the bass on the music.

"She looks beautiful," Toby shouted into my ear as we watched Willow and Polly try to teach Bomber some dance.

"I take it you mean Polly, although I've got to say your sister is rocking those leather leggings."

As Willow shimmied her shoulders, her loose-fitting t-shirt fell off her shoulder, revealing creamy, smooth skin which got me thinking about what I'd like to do to her if we were alone. My eyes moved down past her ample arse, down her long legs and to the high neon pink ankle boots which were the same colour as her top and lipstick. She was so damn sexy, and I knew I was mad if I didn't ask her to be my girlfriend soon.

"Yes, I mean Polly," Toby scoffed and punched me in the arm. "As much as I love my sister and agree she has great genes, admitting that she's beautiful would be slightly weird."

The look of disgust on his face made me laugh. I'd had a chat to all her brothers throughout the night and each one was great, even Ruben was laughing and joking with me, but I think I liked Toby the most. Even though he was a model, obviously good looking and had almost every woman in the house fawning over him, he was chilled and totally unaffected, and I liked that about him.

"She still not succumbing to your charms then?" I asked. "Willow did tell me that you had a thing for her."

He sighed heavily and shook his head. "Nope. I'm going to have to pull out the big guns soon."

"And what are they?" I asked as an amused smile twitched at my lips.

"It. What is it."

"Okay, so what is *it*?"

He pointed to his dick.

"It's fucking huge man, but I really wanted to keep it a surprise for our first night together."

I bit on my lip, trying not to laugh because he looked so damn serious about the whole thing.

"What if you don't get a first night?"

"Exactly," Toby replied and slapped my back. "So, she needs to know what the possibilities are. The problem is, Willow made me promise to keep it in my boxers, well if I wore any."

I winced and instinctively put a hand to my dick, wondering whether I should warn Toby of the consequences of going commando.

"So," Toby continued. "That's where you come in."

"Me?"

"Yeah, you could persuade Willow to let me free the anaconda."

I should not have taken a sip of my lager at that exact moment because I almost choked.

"Your...*anaconda*?"

"Yep, but what I call it is inconsequential," he said rapidly. "I just need Willow's permission to get it out and show Polly."

"You can't show her! What are you going to do, slap it on the table and say 'look at this'?"

"Not what I had in mind, but it'd work."

As Toby contemplated my idea, which was the worst fucking idea ever, I decided to nip to the toilet and hopefully give him time to come to the realisation that he needed to rethink things.

"I'll be back," I said as I put my glass down. "Don't get the anaconda out just yet."

I laughed to myself and made my way through the party to the stairs and up to the bathroom. I'd already been up once and as Danny had put a picture on the door of a woman stood up peeing in a urinal, there was no forgetting which door I needed.

I went inside, slipped the lock and sighed with relief as I peed for what seemed like ages, giving me time to look at the pictures on the wall above the toilet. They were of all Willow's brothers, except Danny, some of Willow and some of another girl, who had a varying range of hairstyles from short, spiky and black, to long, wavy and pink – I guessed from meeting Patsy and seeing her pillar box red hair that the girl in the pictures must be her sister, Dolly, who she'd told me was currently travelling with her boyfriend.

I smiled, seeing the humour in having a gallery of their siblings in the toilet and wished that Johnny and I had as many photos of each other as Danny and Patsy had. I wished we'd had the same sort of childhood that they'd all appeared to have, but maybe the photographs and the memories came hand in hand with happiness and that was something we hadn't experienced much of growing up.

I flushed and then moved over to wash my hands and above the sink where two black and white pictures, one of Joanna Lumley as Patsy and one of John Travolta as Danny Zuko and I laughed out loud. Shit, I wanted what these two appeared to have and I was pretty sure if things kept going in the right direction, I'd want them with Willow. I'd never been so hooked on a girl in such a short space of time and while it was a little bit scary, it was exciting, too, thinking about the possibilities of a future with someone like her.

I opened the door and started to make my way back downstairs, when I heard someone talking in one of the bedrooms directly in front of me. The door was slightly open, and I could see through the gap that it was Ruben. He didn't see me because he had his head down and was dragging his hand through his hair and stamping his foot.

"No," he hissed. "I told you, you can't come here, it's too risky... fine...I don't know, the usual amount."

I realised I'd stopped walking and was eavesdropping when I shouldn't have been, so darted past the room as quietly as I could and made my way back downstairs.

When I got back into the lounge, Willow was bouncing around as she pumped her hands in the air and shook her head. She looked so full of joy I guessed it was seventies music that was playing as I didn't recognise it. She caught my eye and waved as she lost herself in the music.

"Dance with me," she cried. "It's Crazy Horses by The Osmonds."

I laughed and shook my head. "I'm fine babe, you go for it."

She rolled her eyes and waved a hand at me. "Spoilsport, but I'll get you later."

"Okay, I'll save you a dance."

When the chorus kicked in, her dancing got wilder and I decided to retrieve my drink and find Bomber, with what I'd heard Ruben saying playing on my mind. I wasn't sure I should tell Willow; there wasn't much to tell, and it wasn't really my business. It worried me though that Willow was right, and he was mixed up in something he shouldn't be. I picked up my drink from where I'd left it, and noticed that Bomber was sitting in a corner. He was propped up against the wall, fast asleep and had a blue, plastic fish slice poking out of the neck of his t-shirt.

"What's Bomber doing?" I asked Polly, who was gazing at Declan.

She startled and turned her head to me. "Oh, teaching him The Chameleon took it out of him, I was using the fish slice to keep him in time, so he stole it from me." She laughed, but her eyes quickly went back to Declan, who was now snogging the face off a small, blonde haired girl.

"You should give Toby a chance," I suggested and nudged her with my shoulder.

She flashed me a smile and rolled her eyes. "Please don't tell me he's been bending your ear too. He's too young."

"He's only four years younger, isn't he?"

"Four years is a lot," she protested. "Anyway, he's going to be a famous model and won't be around for much longer."

"He comes across as a pretty loyal guy though, Polly, and he's chased you for long enough from what Willow told me. I'm guessing he wouldn't risk losing you if he did manage to persuade you to give him a chance."

She looked at me thoughtfully as she chewed on her lip, but then quickly shook her head and looked back at Declan, who now had the girl's legs wrapped around his waist as their kiss was becoming a little less PG than it had been before.

"I'm going to go," she sighed. "I'm too drunk and too bloody emotional and will end up making a fool of myself."

"Don't go," I said, as I looked to where Willow was dancing and tried to catch her eye. "And how are you getting home."

She held up her phone to show me a taxi app. "I can have one here in five minutes."

I glanced over at Willow, who luckily was looking at us, so I beckoned her over.

"Hey, what's up?" she asked breathlessly.

"Polly is going home." I indicated to Declan with my eyes and Willow sighed.

"Don't go because of him," she said, pulling Polly into a hug. "Come and dance with me."

"It's not only that," Polly replied. "I'm too drunk and I've got to go to my cousin's baby's christening tomorrow with Mum and Dad, so I don't want to be too knackered or too hung over."

"You sure?"

"Yes, honestly." She pulled Willow into a hug. "Take care of you."

"Take care of you."

I looked at them quizzically and wondered what the American accent was all about.

"Pretty Woman," they chorused together without me even having to say anything.

"Right," I replied, still having no clue as I followed Willow to walk outside with Polly and wait for her taxi.

I peeled my eyes open and groaned at the thudding inside my head. We'd partied until the real early hours and hadn't stopped drinking until the place was dry. It was almost four in the morning when Willow finally stopped dancing, dragged me onto the sofa with her, and covered us with a duvet that Danny had brought downstairs. That was where we'd stayed, snuggled up against each other.

Willow's back was turned to me, and her arse was pushed against me and I remembered almost falling off at one point, which was why I had one foot on the floor. I smiled to myself recalling what a great night it had been. It'd been nice to kick back, knowing that Johnny was okay as he was staying over with his best mate, Simon, who was someone I trusted would make sure that my brother was safe. It had been Johnny who'd suggested it, knowing I wouldn't enjoy the party if I was worrying about Teresa being home when he got back from the wedding reception that he'd gone to.

As I looked up at the ceiling, I was aware of something weird going on around my crotch, something a little unpleasant. I bolted upright, which physically hurt, and saw Nigel licking my jeans over my dick.

"What the fuck!" I cried, trying to push the scruffy black and brown dog away without the risk of getting myself bitten. "What the hell are you doing?"

"Charlie?" Willow groaned beside me.

"Nigel, fuck off," I cried and pushed his head.

"Nigel!" Willow sat up and gave him a shove. "Go away, you naughty boy. You wankers, get out here now."

"What's going on?" I asked and stared at Willow with wide eyes.

"Those brothers of mine are a bunch of pricks. *Get out here now!*"

One by one the Dixon brothers appeared from the kitchen, all laughing and clutching their sides.

"You vile people," Willow said as she caught a cloth that Danny threw at her. She handed it to me. "Wipe your dick love, those idiots smeared dog food over it."

"You bastards." My head shot to them all as they stood in a line as tears of laughter rolled down Declan and Ruben's faces.

I grabbed the cloth and started to wipe away the remaining dog food from my crotch as I looked up at Willow, who now looked less like a cute teddy bear and more like a ragged doll that was usually strapped to the front of a dustbin truck. She had joined in the laughter and was bent over at the waist with her hands clutched at her sides.

"Very funny," I said, unable to help the twitch of a grin on my own lips. I pointed at all the brothers and then threw the cloth at them and watched it land in the middle of Declan's chest. "I'll get you all back one day."

"Oh shit, that's so funny," Willow gasped. "Sorry Charlie, but it is."

"And don't think I won't get you back too, because I will." I leaned over and kissed her cheek, avoiding her mouth. "Morning."

"Morning," she sighed and fluttered her eyelashes at me, or she would have if they hadn't been matted together with sleep.

"Ah, sorry mate," Toby said. "We couldn't resist it. Your junk was there on display and you were dead to the world. It had to be done."

"Yeah sorry, Charlie," Danny offered. "At least you didn't get a stonker."

"Oh my God," Willow groaned. "That's bloody gross."

She stretched her arms and yawned, and then tapped my leg.

"Let me get up and I'll run to the cafe at the end of the road and get us all coffee and pastries. You all want some?" she asked her brothers as she scrambled off the sofa.

Everyone agreed it was a great idea and she took orders, including one for Patsy who was apparently in the shower. I offered her money, which she declined, but didn't offer to go with her. This was one time I wasn't going to be the caring and respectful gentleman my grandma had told me I should be.

When the door slammed behind her, we all burst out laughing.

"Well," I said as I laughed hard. "I wonder if anyone will tell her she's got glasses and a moustache drawn on her face."

CHAPTER
24

Instead of licking when giving oral, hum. You'll both experience an incredible orgasm – I refer again to Agadoo by Black Lace.

Willow

The silence was absolutely sublime. Not one noise could be heard around the house. No one coughing, no one talking and no one farting. I was alone and basking in the peace. Declan was on a stag weekend, Toby on a modelling job in the Scottish Highlands, and Ruben had been forced into a weekend at our Auntie Rosemary's in Brighton with Mum and Dad.

I did feel a little guilty about Ruben, if the truth be told, because if I hadn't put the idea of him taking drugs into Mum and Dad's heads, they wouldn't have made him go with them. Unfortunately for Ruben, he may well be eighteen, but Dad still had the ability to rule the roost and my little brother was given no choice. Obviously he argued about why they couldn't make him go, but Dad said he wanted him to visit the university while they were there to rule it off his list if necessary – which was something else Ruben was adamant about i.e. not even going to Uni', it simply made the argument louder and more intense. Needless to say, the parents won that battle with Ruben determined to win the war.

I pushed my guilty thoughts from my head and thought about the night ahead. I'd had a lovely relaxing bath, shaved every area that had a hair follicle, apart from my head, and creamed every inch of my skin until it was soft and smooth and smelled of coconut. Now I was waiting for Charlie to arrive.

We'd seen each other a couple of times during the week, once for lunch and once for another more successful trip to the cinema but as he had to pick Johnny up from somewhere on the way home, we didn't even attempt to try car sex again. At least we'd have had more room as Charlie had picked me up in the Vauxhall Combo, but to be honest, I didn't mind. When I'd held his hand and he'd kissed my neck in the cinema, it had been lovely – just enough to make me feel squidgy inside, but not too much to get me all hot and horny.

Tonight, though, was going to be different. He was going to stay over because Johnny had a couple of mates staying with him and I was so excited, convinced this was going to be *our* night.

Finally, after wearing a furrow in the carpet, the doorbell rang, and thousands of butterflies took flight in my stomach. I quickly checked my appearance in the mirror above the fire and then dashed to the door.

"Hey," I said breathlessly as I swung it open.

"Hi."

Charlie gave me his best dimpled smile and stepped forward and cupped my face with one hand as he took my mouth with his in a hot, sexy kiss. His hips pushed forward and I immediately felt his dick was hard – a huge surprise. He dropped his bag to the floor, his other hand came up to rest on my hip and he pushed me back against the wall, as his soft lips and sweet tongue made me soar.

"Oh wow," I gasped, when he finally let me go.

"Yeah well, I've kind of missed you this week."

"You saw me on Tuesday for lunch and Thursday at the cinema," I giggled and reached up to brush his hair from his eyes.

"Yeah but it was all a little bit teenage date, when actually what I really wanted to do was far more grown up." His hand moved down to my bum and gave it a gentle squeeze. "I'm so looking forward to having some time with you."

"Yes," I sighed. "Me too."

I kissed him this time, and made sure my hips were pushed forward as far as they could be while I held on to his biceps – I was exhilarated by the feel of him through the thin cotton of my pretty retro summer dress.

"Come on, I've cooked you some dinner."

Charlie's eyebrows rose. "Really? What're we having?"

I chewed on my lip, a little nervous, but I hoped he'd like it. "Well it's nothing fancy. Johnny told me what your favourite meal was, so it's only sausage and mash."

His eyes went wide and the green orbs twinkled. "Peas and gravy too?"

I nodded and puffed out my chest, very proud of myself.

"Oh shit, Willow, you are incredible."

Before I had chance to stop him, he rushed past me down the hall to the kitchen and by the time I got there, he was sitting at the table with a knife and fork in his hand.

"I was going to lay the dining room table," I said as I laughed at the sight of him.

Charlie dropped the cutlery, pulled me onto his knee and kissed below my ear. "Here is fine." He then placed a soft kiss on my shoulder. "Thank you."

"What for?" I asked as I craned my neck to give him better access, as I had my hair in a fishtail plait over the opposite shoulder.

"Making an effort to find out what my favourite meal was and for going to the effort of making it. Oh, and for wearing this dress, you look beautiful."

He ran a hand down my side and leaned in for a soft kiss. One that warmed me from my toes right up to the tips of my ears.

"You look pretty handsome yourself," I eventually replied as I looked down at his dark blue jeans and slim fitting shirt with a green and grey small flower print.

"Honestly, I got Johnny to come shopping with me. I needed some help to steer me away from my usual plain t-shirt and faded jeans combo."

"That's your style, and it suits you, so don't ever apologise for it."

"Yeah," he said as he pulled the top of my dress forward and peeked down it. "And you always look gorgeous."

"You talking to me or my boobs?" I could feel he was hard again, so I was pretty sure the decision not to wear a bra had been a good one.

"Both," he replied giving me the dimples. "Now, feed me, woman."

———

"I still haven't forgiven you for laughing at the dog food incident," Charlie said as he rubbed a hand up my bare leg which was draped over his lap.

We'd finished our food a half hour before and were in the lounge listening to an old 70's compilation album of my dad's on his ancient stereo, which I thought was still in good nick, but Charlie said the treble had gone on it, whatever that meant. All I knew was that Marc Bolan currently singing 20th Century Boy sounded awesome.

"We're equal matey," I scolded and wagged a finger at him. "You let me go outside knowing they'd drawn on my face. I honestly thought the guy behind the counter at the café fancied me, the way he stared at me."

"Probably did," he replied as his hand went higher. "Wouldn't blame him."

As Charlie's strong, dexterous fingers crept up my thigh, his phone on the side table next to me chirped that a text had arrived.

"You want to look at that?" I asked as I twisted to pick up the phone.

"Better had, in case it's about Johnny."

As I picked up the phone, the preview pane was quite clear to see and while I wasn't normally the jealous type and Charlie had given no reason for me to be jealous, what I was reading was something I definitely wasn't going to accept.

"Okay, I think you need to explain what that is all about."

My heart thudded and my stomach swirled as I threw the phone at him. I pulled my legs away and dropped my feet to the floor as I stared at him. I was fuming and evidently looked scary if the fear on Charlie's face was anything to go by.

"And who the hell is Viv?"

Charlie looked at the phone and I had to admit he looked surprised as he read the full message. The only part I'd seen had been 'Hi Charlie, it's Viv, I'm desperate to come. Can I sit on your face?' which was bad enough, so I hoped that there wasn't much more than that.

"Fucking hell," he cursed and started to text back. "I have no idea how she got my number, Will, I swear to you."

"So, who is she?" I snapped as I crossed my arms over my chest and tried to dampen down the anger, before I exploded.

He paused texting and looked up at me. "She's a drummer in one of the bands who are working at the studio. She came on to me last week, but I told her I wasn't interested because I had a girlfriend."

His head dropped back to his phone and I couldn't help but smile that he'd called me his girlfriend – even though he hadn't even asked me yet. I was still angry though, wondering whether he actually liked her, or had led her on in some way.

"Here, look."

He thrust his phone at me to read the text message he'd sent.

Me: I have no idea how you got my number, but whoever gave it to you shouldn't have. I'm really sorry Viv, but I did tell you I'm not interested and don't appreciate getting texts of that tone when I'm with my girlfriend. Please don't text me again.

· · ·

I looked up slowly and shook my head. Okay, so he'd didn't appear to have led her on from his text back, but it wasn't exactly the tone of text that I'd have used had the roles been reversed.

"Please don't text me again. What sort of response is that to someone who's sending you unacceptable text messages?"

"Why, what do you want me to say?" he asked and took the phone from my hands to look down at it.

"Piss off would be a start."

"She's a client. I can't do that; I'd get the sack. She may well have got the wrong number anyway."

"Err she put 'Hi Charlie', so if she's desperate for another Charlie to chow down on her then it's a huge bloody coincidence."

Charlie's lips twitched and I knew he was desperate to laugh, not that I could see anything to laugh about.

"It's not funny."

"No, but you saying chow down about oral sex is." He let out a laugh and then slapped a hand over his mouth. "Sorry."

"You sure you're not interested in her?" I asked as a little doubt gnawed at me.

"Fuck no. Like I told her, we have something I would never want to risk."

He didn't look as though he was lying. He looked me straight in the eye and didn't fidget in any way.

"And you told her I was your girlfriend?"

He narrowed his eyes and groaned. "Yeah, I was kind of going to talk to you about that tonight."

"Were you?"

"Yeah, I was going to ask you...you know, if you would be my girlfriend."

My attempt to act annoyed was difficult when all I wanted to do was jump up and down and punch the air, but I was still pissed off about Viv and her bloody hungry fanny.

"Would that have been before or after we had sex?" I asked as I tried to string it out a little longer.

Charlie grinned and pulled me to straddle his lap. "Before, during, and after if you like."

As he pushed his hips forward, I felt his dick, hard against his jeans again and was surprised, considering all I was doing was sitting there. Admittedly my boobs, which he loved, were pushing against his chest and my bum, which he also seemed to like immensely, was safely ensconced in his big hands.

"Have you actually been hard all evening?" I asked with a grin. "Or am I just that sexy?"

"You are sexy," he replied as he kissed down my neck, "but I must admit your sausage and mash did it for me. I can't stop thinking about them."

"Really?"

I gasped as he pulled down the front of my dress and slowly licked around my nipple, before taking it into his mouth and sucking on it. It was the perfect intensity. Not too hard that it hurt, but not so soft I could barely feel it. The relief I felt was immense, particularly after the way he'd gone at my boobs and clit on the night of the dick in zip incident.

"Yeah," he whispered against my heated skin. "You though, you are the sexiest woman I've ever met and if I'm truly honest it's actually you that's had me hard all night. From the minute you opened that front door, I wanted to bury myself in you and get these pretty little nipples in my mouth."

He then took my other nipple in his mouth and as adeptly as before, sucked on it. The pleasure was powerful, and I dropped my head back, moaning with a need for more. Obviously understanding my want, he slipped his hands up my skirt and pushed them inside my lace boy shorts, squeezing the cheeks of my bum gently, and once again it was perfect.

"Charlie," I whispered as I pushed my hips forward.

"Tell me what you want, Willow."

"I need your fingers."

His mouth was on my neck as he kissed and licked along it and moved one of his hands from my bum and tickled it over my thigh before he slipped a finger inside my shorts and up through my wetness to my clit. As he rubbed it gently and swirled his finger around it, the throb began, and I started to breathe heavily. It was sublime, and I knew that he was going to make me come.

"Will you be my girlfriend?" he whispered against my ear.

"Oh God, yes," I breathed out, my body feeling electrified.

As he moved his mouth back to my nipple, Charlie slipped his finger inside of me and started to pump and as I picked up his rhythm, he added another and then...his phone started to ring in his pocket right next to where my VJ was being pleasured.

"Ignore it," I said as I tried to regain my concentration. "It'll stop."

Charlie muttered a curse and then started to pump his fingers faster and he sucked my nipple harder. All the pleasure I'd been feeling started to fall away and I closed my eyes and held my breath as I tried to chase the orgasm that had been so close, but the big "O" had well and truly left my body.

As I wriggled trying to get the feels back, Charlie increased his speed even more as his phone started to ring again. I wasn't sure how it was possible, but it sounded more insistent this time. He stilled momentarily and then sucked so hard on my nipple it made me squeal.

"Shit, I'm so sorry," he said. "I just..." He dropped his forehead to mine and groaned as his phone continued ringing.

"Answer it," I said and tried not to sound like a petulant child. "I can't concentrate while it keeps going off."

I scrambled off his knee and pulled the top of my dress back up as I flounced back onto the sofa. Charlie pushed his hand into his pocket and gave me an apologetic smile that took me all my time to return it.

"Yeah," he answered without even looking at who the caller was.

If it was bloody *Viv,* I was pretty sure I'd end up throwing the bloody phone against the wall and then stamping on it, but when I looked at Charlie and his face went white, I knew it wasn't her. He pushed up from the chair and took two paces before half-turning back to me.

"Okay," he said to the caller with a shaky voice. "I'll be there in about twenty minutes. Keep him warm and call the doctor's number on the board in the kitchen. Thanks Dean. I'll see you as soon as I can."

Charlie ended the call and ran a shaky hand down his face.

"What's wrong?" I asked as I stood up and went to him.

"Johnny's got a fever but says he's cold. I'm sorry but I need to go. If he gets pneumonia..." His voice trailed off as he looked around the room.

"Is he likely to?" I asked as I watched him carefully.

"Probably not, but it's dangerous for him. We have to be sure it's not an infection from him self-catheterising. An infection is more dangerous for...actually you know what, Willow, I'm sorry I need to go. Do you know where I put my car keys?"

"Should you drive, you've had a beer?"

"Only had two and we ate all that food."

"Yes but-."

"Willow, where the hell are my keys," he cried. "I'll be fine, I swear."

I knew he was worried and probably hadn't meant to snap, but it still stung a little. I tried not to let it bother me as I went out into the hall and found his keys on the shelf by the front door. I turned around to take them to him, but he was already behind me, picking up his duffle bag.

"Shall I come with you?" I asked as I reached for my own keys.

"No," he answered immediately. "I may have to take him to the hospital or sit up with him. It wouldn't be any fun for you."

"I want to be there to support you," I offered.

He gave me a brief smile and then a quick kiss to the cheek. "I'll call you when I can. Okay?"

I nodded and stepped aside to let him pass. As he opened the front door, he turned back to me again.

"I am sorry, Will. I really am and I'll ring you as soon as I have some news." He reached for my hand, gave it a quick squeeze and then was gone.

As I watched him pull away all I wanted to do was cry. I knew it hadn't been his fault, but our perfect night had been ruined yet again and what made it worse was that it was my first night as his girlfriend.

CHAPTER
25

Heat up the action by re-enacting those steamy love scenes from films such as 9 ½ Weeks. Take it in turns to blindfold each other and feed and drip food over every orifice – only include the ears if they've been cleaned of all wax.

Charlie

As I closed the door on the doctor, I heaved a sigh of relief. Johnny had nothing more than a virus. Yes, we had to be careful he didn't develop something more serious, such as pneumonia, but it wasn't an infection which was a huge positive. Johnny was particularly glad because if he got an infection from self-catheterising it would be likely he'd keep getting them and then the doctors would recommend a permanent catheter which was something he was desperate to avoid.

I was grateful that Dean and Si, Johnny's mates, had noticed quite quickly that he was looking flush and then acted so quickly. They'd got him into bed and checked his temperature before calling me but when it went up that was when they knew I should probably get home.

I'd made sure to drive carefully coming back, because although I knew I was safe to drive, I was also worried that two beers might have taken me over the drink driving limit. Once I got through the door though, I knew I'd been irresponsible and should have got a taxi, but I was too worried to wait. I vowed I wouldn't risk it ever again, but my brother was the most important person in my life, and I couldn't stand the thought of not being there for him.

"Charlie."

Johnny's croaky voice surprised me because I'd left him asleep only a few minutes before. I rubbed at my chest and made my way down the hall to his room which was in darkness.

"What's up?" I asked as I moved to the side of his bed and rested my forearms on the rail.

"Sorry I fucked up your night. I know you were looking forward to it."

"It's fine, there'll be other nights."

I smiled and forced myself not to pull his duvet further up his shoulders – he hated people fussing around him.

"Yeah but, you seemed really excited. Like it was going to be a big night. You weren't going to ask her to marry you, were you?"

"No," I scoffed, not wanting to tell him I had asked her to be my girlfriend though.

I closed my eyes against the thought of how the night had gone down. It had got off to such a great start and then Viv's text and Dean's call had ambushed everything. That wasn't Johnny's fault though and he shouldn't feel bad about it.

"Was she okay about you leaving?"

Huh, was she okay about me leaving? She was a fucking trooper and had sucked it up and accepted it and then I'd snapped at her and told her I didn't want her with me, when really, I should have jumped at the chance to have her support.

"She was fine. Willow's pretty chill, so there were no dramas."

"Well that's good. I think I'm going to get some sleep now."

He pulled his duvet up, right above his ears, where I wanted it to be and closed his eyes.

"The switch for your bed is on this side." I said and got a small nod from him. "Night."

I left the room and quietly pulled the door, leaving it open just a crack in case he needed me in the night. Once I was in my own room, I fired off a couple of text messages.

Me: Teresa not sure if you even care but Johnny isn't well. He has a virus. Know you hadn't planned to come home tonight but if you do be quiet – he needs his sleep.

With a sigh I wondered why I'd bothered, I then typed out the next one to Willow.

Me: Hi Will, really sorry about tonight and for snapping at you. I get panic stricken when anything happens to him. I'll make it up to you, I swear. I don't know when he'll be well enough for me to leave, so will keep you informed. And just so you know, your boyfriend thinks his girlfriend is amazing x

I read it twice, wondering whether the last sentence was too soppy, but I really *did* think she was amazing, so quickly hit send hoping it would go some way to apologising for the way I'd shot out of there.

I had started to undress for bed and had only got my jeans off when I heard my phone go. Reaching for it, I couldn't help but feel relief when I saw it was Willow.

Pretty Girl: There's no need to be sorry, Johnny is your priority and we can do it again some other time and I totally understand your worry. Let me know how he's feeling and if there's anything I can do; you know, maybe sit with him if you need to go out or even get you some shopping. Anything at all xx

. . .

My heart sank a little when I noticed she hadn't mentioned the sentence about me finding her amazing and I worried that maybe she'd changed her mind about being my girlfriend. I wouldn't blame her with the amount of false starts and drama that we'd had in only three weeks of seeing each other. I knew it wasn't the ideal way to start a relationship, but Johnny had to come first, and I hoped she didn't give up on us too soon.

I was in bed and almost asleep when my text went again. I sighed with frustration thinking if it was Viv again, I would definitely tell her to piss off, but when I picked up my phone, I noticed it was Willow. I sat up quickly, worried that something was wrong remembering that she was alone in the house.

Pretty Girl: Sorry, I got distracted by Polly calling me. She's now having a sleep over btw. She's not much of a substitute for you in the cuddling stakes and she hogs the bed, but she'll do. I wanted to say your girlfriend thinks her boyfriend is amazing too <3 xx

I hadn't realised how worried I'd been until I'd read her text, the relief felt enormous. I was so glad she still wanted to be my girlfriend and that she realised how I had to put Johnny first. I couldn't be with someone who didn't respect that, and I really wanted to be with her. So, with a huge grin on my sleepy face, I sent her one last text.

Me: Don't let her snuggle too much, I'm already jealous. Night-night, get some sleep and speak to you tomorrow xx

CHAPTER
26

Carry a quickie sex kit with you such as, condoms, scarves or handcuffs and lubrication – perhaps don't include electrical tape in case you get stopped by the police and they think you're off to kidnap someone.

Willow

A second pair of shoes were thrown across my room with a curse, almost taking the Hedwig clock out. I was in a foul mood and had decided to take it out on my wardrobe and the score was currently Willow – 0, Wardrobe – 2; the two being the boxes which had fallen on my head and the leather belt buckle which had hit me in the ear making it throb.

The reasons for me being the bitch from hell was my period and my boyfriend. One was present in my life and the other one wasn't and as my boyfriend hadn't actually managed to come other than in his pants, it wasn't hard to work out which one was hanging around.

I'd woken up with the usual dull ache in my back and cramps in my stomach and by the time I'd practically crawled to the bathroom I was in agony. Thankfully, we had a quiet day at the surgery, and I was able to moan to my heart's content and swallow painkillers as if they were peanut M&M's. At one point, James actually yelled at me to either stop moaning or go home, but when I burst into tears he couldn't retract the statement quickly enough, so when it got to three-thirty and I asked Zoe, one of the other nurses to stand in for me for the last couple of hours, I know I heard him sigh and mumble 'thank the fucking Lord'.

Needless to say, I was not happy to hear music booming through the lounge window when I got home. All I wanted to do was to curl up in my bed and go to sleep – forget about my period pains and forget that Charlie hadn't called in two days and all I'd had was a sodding text that said 'Johnny still not too good. Hope you're okay' with one bloody kiss at the end of it. Well if that was him 'keeping me informed', he was shit at it. In the end, Toby's music was so loud, I decided to tackle my wardrobe instead of getting into bed and feeling sorry for myself.

"Ugh," I ground out as I tried to extract an intricately strapped dress from a broken coat hanger. "Sod off."

The dress and hanger joined the shoes over in the 'what the hell was I thinking' pile.

"What the hell is your problem?" Ruben appeared at my bedroom door, rubbing at his eyes. "I'm trying to sleep, and now numb nuts has turned his music off, all I can hear is you swearing and throwing things around, so shut the fuck up."

"What have you been doing that you need to sleep at five in the afternoon?" I asked, immediately thinking he'd been taking some sort of drugs to keep him awake at night.

"I didn't sleep much last night and we had really late nights at Auntie Rosemary's. Anyway, what's it got to do with you?"

"Plenty, if you're doing something stupid."

Ruben curled his top lip. "What does that mean? I'm trying to sleep, what's so *stupid* about that?"

"It's why you need to sleep is what's stupid," I replied, getting up from kneeling next to my wardrobe. "Tell me what you've been doing."

"I told you. We had late nights and I didn't sleep much last night."

"What were you doing on your late nights?" I took a step closer to him and peered into his eyes.

"You're being weird, why do you keep staring at me? Do you need glasses?"

"No. Just answer the question, Ruben."

"Playing cards and talking, if it's any business of yours. What did you think, I'd been out clubbing with Maureen and Ivan the Fucking Terrible?"

"I don't believe you," I snapped as I thrust my hands to my hips.

"What, that I didn't go clubbing with Mum and Dad? Shit, what do you take me for?"

"I don't know Ruben, and no I didn't mean that. I want to know why you were so bloody cagey when I saw you near the toilets at Carrington's."

His brow furrowed and then he shook his head. "You really can't keep out of my business, can you?"

"Tell me."

"It's nothing to do with you, Willow, so stop fucking prying." Ruben leaned his top half closer to me, pointing a finger in my face. "I'm tired because I played cards with my family until late every night and couldn't sleep because I drank too much coffee and ate too much damn Chinese food last night, so if I want to sleep at five in the afternoon, I will."

"So, you haven't been taking anything that might keep you awake?" I asked as I tilted my chin in defiance.

"What, apart from coffee?"

Ruben dropped his hands to his sides and stared at me. I had come so far; I knew I might as well come right out and ask him.

"Are you taking drugs? Was that guy you were with your dealer?"

Ruben's mouth dropped open and he shook his head in disbelief.

"I think you're the one on drugs. That's what you think, that I'd be stupid enough to do drugs? Do you even know me at all?" He scratched his head and turned toward the door. He only took two steps before he turned back again. "I can't believe you'd even think that of me, Willow."

I had to admit, he looked hurt and if it didn't mean keeping him safe, I'd have felt awful for raising it with him.

"I just think-."

"Hang on," he cried. "That's why Mum and Dad made me go with them wasn't it. You told them you think I'm a druggie, didn't you?"

I felt my face heat up at being caught out, but I still wasn't sorry.

"They needed to know. We love you Ruben and don't want you falling into something that you can't get out of."

"I'm not taking damn drugs," he yelled. "You had no right to tell them that. You have no proof and that's because I'm not taking anything I shouldn't."

"But you looked cagey and twitchy and it was more than me being in your business. You wanted me away from you and he looked dodgy as hell."

"That doesn't make either of us coke heads."

"Ah!" I cried. "I never said coke, so that's what you're doing is it."

"No!" Ruben stamped his foot and looked up at the ceiling. "I'm not taking drugs, why can't you get it into your head."

"So what Ruben, why look so damn suspicious hanging around a corridor with a dodgy looking guy?"

"Because he's my damn boyfriend, Willow," he yelled, inches from my face. "I'm gay, okay."

His words were spat at me and his chest heaved as a whole host of emotions crossed his face – anger, fear and maybe relief.

"Gay?" My voice was small as the word came out as a question.

Ruben let out a long exhale. "Yes, Willow. I'm gay. Satisfied now?"

He flopped down onto the edge of my bed and rested his forearms on his knees, he looked down at the floor strewn with clothes.

"Why haven't you told us?" I asked as I sat next to him and put a hand on his back. "You surely don't think we'd be ashamed, or even care, do you?"

His head shot up and narrow eyes glared at me. "No, I know you'd all be fine with it."

"So, what is it?" I pulled him closer, feeling heartbroken that he would feel the need to keep his sexuality secret from us. *"You're* not ashamed, are you?"

"No," he replied, but sounded a little hesitant.

"Ruben, surely not." I felt his shoulders tense and squeezed him tighter against my side.

"No, not really. I'm not, it's the boys all have this reputation of being great with women and we're all supposed to be good looking, able to have any girl we want but..."

"You can have any boy you want, so what?"

He looked up at me and gave me the first proper smile I'd had from him in ages. It made my heart crack and the pain pierced my chest. I'd missed the twinkle in his eyes and the feel of his love. I'd missed my little brother.

"I'm not ashamed, I swear," he said and rested his dark, tousled head on my shoulder.

"So why keep it from us then?" I asked as I took his hand in both of mine.

"You are part of this family, aren't you?" he replied on a laugh. "You do know how it works?"

"Yeah, well there is that."

We both laughed quietly and sighed at exactly the same time.

"Seriously though," Ruben said. "I wanted something for me for a while. Something that I didn't have to share, or that Maureen and Ivan the Fucking Terrible would feel the need to discuss or impart their wisdom about."

Then something struck me. "So, what about the girls in the den? All those times I've come home and either you or Toby have got someone in there."

He shrugged. "I did think I was bisexual at one time, but I think that was me denying it, so I did bring a couple of girls back. I actually had a boy in there once." He grinned and winked at me and I suddenly saw the old Ruben, the cheeky, funny and happy, Ruben.

"No way."

He nodded. "Oh yeah, but it was too scary sneaking him out in the morning."

"You are being careful, aren't you?"

"Yes, of course I am." He rolled his eyes and then snuggled closer to me. "So, no need to hand out the condoms, Maureen."

"Oi you." I smacked at his arm. "I'm nothing like Maureen. Hey, is that why you've been off with me, because I'm like our mother?"

"God no," he replied, screwing up his nose. "You get on my nerves generally." He grinned again and wrapped an arm around me. "Truthfully, I was jealous of you. I knew if you were in my position, you'd tell everyone and then give them some snarky remark and get on with it. You wouldn't get pissed off with the questions and if you did, you'd just tell them to piss off."

"Oh, and you wouldn't do that?" I laughed. "You and I are very alike Ruben, we're both sarcastic and mean when we want to be."

"I guess," he replied and raised a brow. "You're the one I'm closest to, or was, and it's true you always hurt the one you love most. I also knew if you and I were close again you'd figure it out and then the whole damn pack would know, and I wasn't ready for it, so I thought it was better to keep you at arm's length."

I sighed and sagged with relief. "It wasn't because I told your mates you wet the bed until you were eight, or that I stopped taking you everywhere with me when you were about ten?"

"Nah, although I'm still going to get you back for the bed wetting thing. Wait until you get married, I'm going to offer to do a speech." He gave me an evil grin and laughed. "I suppose I should tell everyone else then."

I shrugged. "It's up to you. I would, but it's your decision. You know they'll support you and you also know they'll ask loads of questions and Maureen will try and give you hundreds of condoms while Ivan the Fucking Terrible will offer you advice on how to keep your sex life interesting."

Ruben rolled his eyes. "Yep, can't wait. So, you think my boyfriend is dodgy then?"

"Not really," I replied with a grimace. "I think it was more the situation. He's very good looking by the way."

"Of course he is. I'm a hottie, I'm not going to attract anyone else but a good-looking guy."

"Well your ego is still huge, that's for sure." I kissed his cheek and hugged him tightly. "I'll come with you when you tell everyone."

"That'd be good. I'll WhatsApp them all, get them together tonight and get it over and done with."

"It's probably best."

"Yeah." Ruben pulled away from my arms and stood up to leave, but when he got to the bedroom door he stopped and turned back around. "Oh, and Will."

"Yeah?" I asked, giving him a huge smile.

"Your boyfriend is pretty hot too."

I picked up a flip flop and threw it at him, but he was too quick for me.

Five minutes later a message came to the family WhatsApp group.

Ruben

Hey suckers, get yourselves into the dining room at 8pm tonight. Something I need to talk about.

Maureen

Do I need to bring cake and condoms?

CHAPTER 27

Try having sex on a car bonnet, lying back with your legs spread wide and your partner between them – be sure to leave your car park ticket in full view in case the Car Park Warden wants to check it while you're in full swing.

Willow

"Honestly, Rube, it'll be fine."

Ruben worked his jaw backwards and forwards, he looked at me with steely eyes, as if he didn't give a shit either way. I knew him better than that though, I knew he was nervous about telling the rest of the family his news.

"You do know everyone will support you, don't you?"

"Yeah I know," he said and let out a shaky breath. "But I really don't want all the questions."

"We agreed, you'll tell them to piss off."

Ruben gave me a small nod of his head and a smile and pushed open the door of the dining room. It was as if there was about to be a board meeting. Dad was sat at the head of the table, with a pad and pen in front of him and the rest of the Dixon's were seated along the sides, all waiting with their hands clasped together on the table.

"Remind me again what job I've applied for?" Ruben hissed at me through the side of his mouth.

I chuckled softly and guided him to a chair with a hand to his back.

"What's occurring?" Toby asked, looking up and down the table. "What've we all been summoned for?"

"Yeah," Danny said as he scratched at his chest. "What's so urgent I had to cut football practice short?"

Dad cleared his throat and announced, "I think your brother has something important that he needs our support with. Remember though, Ruben, we all love you and will help you in any way we can."

Ruben shot me a look and then turned back to the eager faces around the table.

"Contrary to what Willow might have you believe, I'm not on drugs."

Dad looked at Mum, who sagged back into her seat shaking her head.

"You don't have to deny it any longer," she replied. "We're not going to judge; we're going to help."

"He's being honest, Mum," I said as I reached for Ruben's hand under the table. "He isn't on drugs."

"So, what is it then?" Dad asked and pushed his pad and pen to one side.

"Don't tell me, you've got some girl pregnant." Declan tutted and gave Ruben a 'did I not teach you anything' kind of look.

Ruben and I gave each other wide eyes at the irony of Declan's thoughts.

"So, tell us," Toby said. "What's the big secret?"

Ruben glanced at me and then straightened his shoulders.

"I..."

"Go on Rube," I whispered. "It'll be fine."

I may have sounded confident, but my stomach was in knots for him. This was a big thing he was going to tell them, and he was the most private of the lot of us, yet I knew what the consequences of giving up his secret would be. I almost wanted to blurt it out for him.

He was my little brother and even though we hadn't been close for a long time, my need to protect him was still there.

"Rube, you're not dying, are you?" Toby asked, as worry marred his handsome features.

"Shit no," Ruben cried. "I'm...oh shit...I'm gay."

Mum and Dad let out a collective sigh of relief, I giggled nervously, Toby sat with his mouth open, Danny nodded sagely, and Declan stared at Ruben.

Ruben turned to look at me tentatively and licked his lips before he turned back to the rest of the members of our family still at the table.

"So, Willow was right, I was hiding something, but it wasn't drugs."

"But I've seen you with girls," Toby said with a frown.

Ruben exhaled and shrugged. "I was confused?" he said, as a question.

"Really? Because Tiffany Jackson didn't sound like you were confused when we were at Gucci Reid's party." His face was a picture of shock at evidently being privy to things none of us had ever been.

"What can I say, I've got skills." Ruben shrugged again.

"Who the fuck calls their kid, Gucci," Danny moaned.

"It's not unusual for young people to feel confused about their sexuality," Dad said with his therapist voice. "Often-."

"I'm not confused any more, Dad," Ruben interrupted him. "I know now I like boys, I'm definitely gay, I *was* then, but at the time part of me felt it was what was expected of me." He looked at Toby, Danny, and Declan. "I was a Dixon boy; I was expected to follow in your foot-steps...and not only by people outside the family."

"Shit, Rube," Danny sighed. "No one ever wanted to pressure you into something you didn't want to do. You could have told us, and we'd have laid off the efforts of hooking you up with girls or introducing you to them."

"Yeah," Toby cried. "We'd have found you some hot guys instead."

Ruben muttered 'exactly' under his breath.

It was then that Declan got up and almost toppled his chair over as he stormed out of the room and slammed the door behind him.

"The absolute wanker," I hissed and pushed up off my chair to follow him.

"Willow." Dad's voice boomed. "Stay put. Declan is not our priority, giving Ruben our support is."

Dad's face told me he wouldn't take no for an answer, so as anger punched at my chest, I slipped back onto the chair and grabbed Ruben's hand again.

"Ruben, son, continue."

Ruben nodded and licked his lips again.

"You trying to hook me up with people is one of the main reasons why I didn't tell anyone. Don't get me wrong, I'm not ashamed, or scared of what you'll think, but being gay makes me different than the rest of you and I didn't want to become the family 'case study'."

He didn't look at Dad, but I was pretty sure that particular comment was aimed at him.

"We-we wouldn't," Dad stammered, as he evidently understood too. "Okay, I wouldn't."

"Dad, you would. Which is why I'm also going to say this, to all of you. I don't want you asking me loads of questions, or checking if I've met anyone or," he gave Mum a wide-eyed stare, "asking me if I need condoms every time I go out. I'm a grown man, I know how to be safe and the same as I don't want to know how you get Patsy to scream your bloody name, I don't want to tell you how I get my boyfriend to scream mine either."

Danny looked a little shamefaced and nodded.

"I ask you all if you need condoms," Mum said, her first words for a while.

"Yeah and we *all* find it annoying," Toby offered.

Mum let out a sigh. "Well when you've seen as many teenage pregnancies and STD's as I have and how it can ruin the lives of young people who have so much potential, you'd offer you condoms every time you went out too."

Mum had been a family planning officer for years before she went back to University to get her teaching degree, so with that and having ten years teaching experience behind her, I understood why she always had a lorry load of prophylactics in the house – I agreed with Toby though, it was annoying.

"So, apart from the obvious, which we've established I'm not telling you," Ruben said. "Does anyone have any questions?"

Everyone looked at each other and Dad scribbled something into his notebook but remained silent. Mum then put her hand up.

"Yes, Mum," Ruben said, sounding like Mum probably did during class.

"Are you happy?"

Ruben's shoulders sagged a little and he smiled. "Yeah Mum, I am."

"Tell them about Cane," I whispered.

"Oh, you mean that dodgy looking guy?" Ruben whispered back with a grin.

"Yes, and okay, I got it wrong."

"What are you whispering about?" Mum asked. "Is there something bad that we should know?"

"No Mum," Ruben groaned. "As usual Willow is sticking her nose in."

I kicked him lightly under the table. "Who is it that helped you 'come out'," I said, doing speech marks around the phrase with my fingers.

Ruben rolled his eyes and turned back to the family. "I'm seeing someone at the moment. His name is Cane, he's twenty and lives in Manchester. He's not out to his family, so that's all I'm telling you about him."

Mum couldn't help herself and clapped her little hands with glee. "Have you been seeing him long? Is he handsome?"

"Yeah he is." I offered.

"When did you meet him?" Toby asked me, his face etched with a frown of perplexity. "Why has she met him, and I haven't?"

"I thought he was dealing drugs," I replied. "They were looking dodgy around the toilets in a bar."

Mum tutted. "Toilets? Really, Ruben, you have a perfectly good den here for that sort of thing."

"No Maureen," Ruben cried. "Nothing like that. We were talking about his parents and how bigoted they are." He gave a soft smile in the direction of Mum and Dad. "They're not like you two."

"Shit, thank God for that," Danny muttered. "You don't need weird in-laws as well as parents."

"Thank you, Ruben, for appreciating us," Dad replied giving Danny the side-eye. "Even if your brother doesn't."

"So, is it serious?" Toby asked.

Ruben shrugged. "I don't know. We've only been seeing each other a couple of months and like I said, he hasn't come out or anything."

"Is it your first relationship?" Dad asked.

"Ivan, we said..." Mum warned.

"It's fine, Mum, and no it isn't."

All of us sat up to attention at that. He'd told me he'd sneaked a boy into the house, but I wasn't sure I'd believed him, I thought it was just bravado.

"I was seeing a guy from school for a while, right before we went into sixth form, but it didn't work out."

Mum clasped a hand to her chest. "Did he break your heart?"

Ruben exhaled and shook his head and dropped his gaze to the table. "No, I broke his. We don't speak any longer, which is sad, but you can't stay with someone only because they're a nice person if you don't have an attraction for them."

My eyes widened in surprise as I wondered how the hell he'd become so sensible and wise with the four of us as his elder siblings, not to mention Maureen and Ivan the Fucking Terrible as his parents?

"Well," Dad said, as he stood up. "I'm a very proud man. Proud that you finally felt you could tell us Ruben, and proud that we, as a family, are supportive enough that you can be who you want to be. It must be very difficult for your friend Cane, and please tell him he's welcome here any time."

He moved around the table until he was in front of Ruben and leaned down to hug him tightly. Ruben closed his eyes and even though he was surrounded by Dad's big frame, I could see him sag with relief. We all stood and moved toward Ruben and hovered around him to give our own hugs.

"There is one member of the family that needs to pull his head out of his arse," Danny said. "I'm going to-."

He didn't say anything more because at that precise moment Declan came into the room. His eyes were red rimmed, and I have never felt more like punching him. How dare he cry simply because our brother was gay?

"You really are-."

Declan held his hand up to quieten me, which made me even angrier.

"Hold on for a second before you go shouting your mouth off," he said sternly. "Because it's not what it looked like."

"Yeah and that's what Mrs. Chivers said when her husband came home early."

Our heads all shot to Toby who grinned and then ducked his head.

"Sorry, it slipped out."

"Tobias Nathanial Dixon," Mum gasped. "I think you and I need to have words about that statement you just made about our neighbour."

Ruben laughed and mouthed 'busted' at Toby, while the rest of us gaped in silence.

"Anyway," Dad said. He looked confused and turned back to Declan. "You had something to say."

Dec nodded and took a step toward Ruben. "I'm not ashamed or sad that you're gay, Rube. I left because I'm ashamed and sad that you felt you had to keep it from us because of the pressure you felt from everyone. As the eldest," he said and waved a finger between him and Danny, "that's on us and I'm sorry about that. You seem pretty chill about it all, but if you weren't you wouldn't have had anyone to talk to and that upsets me."

"Yeah things must be bad for you to tell Willow first," Danny scoffed.

Ruben shrugged a shoulder. "It just came out really. I didn't tell her on purpose, we barely speak."

"Yeah, well that's changing," I scolded him. "No more pretending you hate me."

He grinned at me cheekily. "Who said I was pretending?"

"Whatever," Declan continued. "That was why I left. Not because of you and who you choose to sleep with, that is not an issue and never would be because I love you and always will."

Emotion pricked at the back of my throat as Declan pulled Ruben into a hug and clapped his arms tightly around him. I'd never seen Declan show such tenderness or empathy to anyone. Even Mum only got kisses from him on high days and holidays.

"Dec," I groaned as I felt the tears start to build.

"I'm sorry, Rube."

"Dec, shut up," Ruben replied. "We're all as bad as one another and maybe I'm too precious about my privacy."

"No," Mum said as she ran a hand down his hair. "You should have as much privacy as you want, you all should. Your dad and I won't interfere and question you all, and I will try to stop offering you all condoms, although-."

"Maureen," Danny groaned. "No. Let's go and get a cup of tea instead."

Mum laughed and nodded. "Okay, oh and I defrosted a lovely fruit cake that I pinched from the home economics room before the holidays."

As everyone followed Mum out, Toby pulled Ruben into a neck hug and Danny and Declan laughed about the fact that we would be eating stolen goods, which left only Dad and I in the dining room. I was about to follow them when Dad caught my arm.

"It was a good thing you did, Willow," he said and cupped my face with his big hand. "I doubt he'd have had the nerve to tell us if it wasn't for you. Although, drugs? Really?"

"Sorry," I groaned. "I got it totally wrong. I'm glad he finally realised that we are all actually here for him."

"Yeah," Dad sighed and looked through the window into the garden. "Your mum and I really should let you live your lives."

I didn't reply because me agreeing wouldn't exactly add to the warm, loving vibe we had currently going on.

"So," he said, as he followed me out. "Charlie didn't stay over in the end at the weekend."

"No," I said tightly. "He had an emergency."

"Ah right. Nothing too serious I hope."

"Ivan," I warned.

"What? That's not interfering, that's me being caring." he protested.

I rolled my eyes and took a deep breath before continuing.

"His brother is disabled and so he has to take care of him quite a bit," I replied. "And Saturday night his brother wasn't well, so he had to go."

"Oh no, that's awful. I didn't realise his brother was disabled."

"Yeah, he fell from a balcony and damaged his spine, so he's in a wheelchair."

Dad shook his head. "It must be difficult for him to juggle everything then; his brother, his job, and you."

I hated feeling it, but the fact that Dad had put me last on the list made me feel a little jealous, which was awful because I'd only been in Charlie's life for three weeks, so it was quite right that I came down the pecking order of his priorities, but I really liked him and wanted to spend more time with him.

"Yeah, it is," I sighed and gave my dad a barely there smile.

"You know Willow," he said as he tapped my shoulder with his pen. "There are things you can do if you don't have much time together."

Oh no, he was about to 'therapy' me, I knew it.

"Dad."

"Hear me out. A quickie can often be just as satisfying, if not more, than a long sex session with lots of foreplay or-."

"*Ivan.*"

I wanted him to shut up because I was annoyed and as per usual when he pissed me off, he had quickly gone from being Dad to Ivan.

"If you're sex life isn't what it should be, it's probably because he has the constant worry of his brother. You simply need some time away, just you two."

"*Ivan.*"

"Or, I tell you what is tremendously sexy if you don't get much time together, phone sex."

I huffed and stormed away, Ivan the Fucking Terrible trailing behind me.

"Honestly, it's very erotic and-."

"*Mum,*" I called as I walked away. "Tell Ivan, he's interfering again."

"I could give you a book on it..."

CHAPTER
28

Stroking gently through underwear can be very sexy and a huge turn on – but don't give your partner a wedgie, it'll kill the mood.

Charlie

I flopped back on my bed and pinched the bridge of my nose, entirely pissed off that I hadn't seen or spoken to Willow in almost four days. Johnny had been pretty sick with the cold virus that he'd got so I'd even taken a few days holiday from work to look after him.

Finally, though, he seemed to be feeling a lot better and had even managed to eat something today, which was a bonus. He was currently in bed watching a film, so I decided to leave him to it and maybe give Willow a call. I knew she'd be home because she finished early on a Wednesday as they did an early morning surgery.

When I picked up my phone, nerves started to get the better of me. I had no idea whether she was pissed at me for bailing on her on Saturday night, or even if we were still a thing. For all I knew she might have been so pissed off with me and the fact that I snapped at her, she may well have dumped me and was waiting for me to call so she could tell me.

I hoped I was wrong as I punched at my phone and called her

number. It rang for a while and right when I was expecting voicemail to kick in, she answered it.

"Hey, you," she said, with a bright tone. "How's Johnny?"

I closed my eyes and breathed out slowly as relief seeped through me that she seemed okay and not mad.

"He's much better today. It was some sort of cold virus, but we have to be careful in case it turns into pneumonia, because in paraplegics that can then turn to sepsis."

"God," she gasped. "I didn't realise. You only think of the things they're not able to do, not that a normal cold can be life threatening."

"I think sometimes I'm too cautious, but infection is always a worry, so the fact that it's a virus was okay. I wanted to be sure it didn't get worse, so I'm sorry I've not been in touch."

I heard her let out a sigh and my stomach churned, not seeing her face gave me no indication of whether it was of relief or resignation and I wondered whether this was when she would dump me.

"Charlie, listen, you don't have to apologise to me. I totally understand," she said. "That's why I didn't call you, because I knew you'd be busy taking care of Johnny."

"Yeah, but the way I bailed on Saturday night after you'd gone to such a big effort to cook for me. It wasn't acceptable."

"It was fine, honestly, it was only sausage and mash, nothing too difficult."

She giggled softly and as my shoulders relaxed, I realised how much I'd needed to hear from her and hear her laugh.

"No, Willow, it meant a lot. I wasn't particularly pleasant to you when I left either."

"You were worried about your brother; you were bound to feel anxious and tetchy. All I ask is one thing."

"What's that?" I asked with a smile as I knew that there would be a little furrow between her eyebrows.

"Let me help you in the future. Let me be there for you. I could have come to the hospital with you, or even stayed at the house and got stuff ready for when you got home." She let out a short laugh.

"I've no idea what stuff I'd need to get ready, but I'd like to be able to."

I ran a hand through my already messy hair and took a deep breath before letting it out very slowly.

"You're not dumping me then?"

"What?" she cried. "God no, what sort of girlfr- person would I be if did that?"

I chuckled quietly. "You can say girlfriend, Willow. I did ask you after all."

"I-I wasn't sure you meant it, or even remembered."

"Of course, I remember." I sat up sharply and dropped my feet to the floor. "Why would you think I didn't mean it, or that I'd forget?"

"I don't know," she replied tentatively. "You've had so much on and..."

"Willow, I meant it *and* I remember it. Not sure I remember you saying yes though." I was smiling and hoped that she heard the humour in my tone. I didn't want my first conversation with her in a few days to be stressy.

"I'm pretty sure I said yes." She sounded a little lighter now and the relief was massive.

"Oh yeah. I think I do remember now. Your exact words were 'oh God yes'."

Willow started laughing and the sound went straight to my dick, which once again had been rudely interrupted the last time I'd seen her.

"Was that supposed to be me?" she asked. "Because if it was, it was a bloody shit impression."

"I thought it was pretty good."

I felt much happier as I put my legs back up on the bed, shuffled toward the headboard, and adjusted my pillows behind me, put one hand behind my head and got comfy for a long talk with my girlfriend.

Shit, I was a damn wet pussy, but I really liked the sound of that word - girlfriend.

"Okay, Johnny is in bed watching a film, which no doubt he'll fall asleep halfway through, which means I have a couple of hours free, so talk to me. What've you been up to?" I asked.

"Not much really. Although we did discover what's being going on with Ruben."

"You did? Was it what you thought?" I asked and hoped to God it wasn't.

"No. He did tell me that I could tell you and Polly, but no one is to ask him any questions about it." She sighed heavily and I wondered if she was rolling her eyes, which she tended to do a lot when talking about one of her brothers.

"I don't really know him well enough yet to ask him anything."

"I know, but that's what he said. None of us are allowed either."

"Okay," I wondered what the hell it could be.

"He's gay," Willow said with a matter of fact. "The guy I saw him with was his boyfriend."

I had no idea why he'd felt the need to keep it such a big secret. It wasn't like people judged others about their sexuality these days, particularly Willow's family who, from what I could gather, were pretty open and chilled about everything. They all seemed pretty supportive of each other from the little I knew.

"Did he think you'd all be mad or something?"

"No, he's just really private, but he did say he felt he had the Dixon boys' reputation to uphold. Stupid idiot," she grumbled.

I thought about Johnny and how he'd always seemed pretty confident in himself and had never really looked to impress me, at least I didn't think so anyway. If anything, I was the one who looked up to him and his capability to accept his disability like a fucking warrior.

"I guess if that's how he feels."

"Yeah, I suppose. I guess I feel sad that he didn't feel he could tell us without there being a load of fuss about it or us wanting to know all the details."

"Well I'm happy it wasn't drugs, although," I said a little warily, "I was beginning to think you were right."

"You were? How come?"

Willow sounded worried and I wondered whether I should have kept my mouth shut, but it was too late now, so I told her about the conversation I'd heard Ruben having on the phone at Danny and Patsy's party.

"Now we know though, I'm guessing he was arranging to meet his boyfriend."

It did sound logical and I hoped Willow thought so too, I didn't want her getting more ideas about her brother and drugs. Thankfully she agreed with me.

"Oh God, poor Ruben having to sneak off to call his boyfriend."

"Well," I said as I got myself comfier. "I know how he feels, I've had to sneak off and call my girlfriend."

Willow giggled and once more it went straight to my crotch. I had no idea what it was about the way she laughed, but it was fucking sexy and definitely woke my dick up.

"I've fucking missed you," I admitted.

"Really?" Willow asked but sounded a little unsure.

"Yeah, I can't believe how much."

The line was quiet for a short pause and I wondered if I'd said the wrong thing, but then Willow cleared her throat.

"I missed you too. A lot."

"Yeah?" I asked as I felt my heart thud in my chest.

"Yep."

I slid down to lie on the bed. "What have you missed about me the most?"

"Well," she replied. "Apart from your beautiful smile and dimples, and your sexy bum, I've missed talking to you. I've missed you making me laugh."

Fuck I really liked this girl.

"What else?" I asked and moved my hand from behind my head and snaked it down to the waistband on my sweatpants.

"I've missed kissing you."

Willow's voice was soft and gentle, but I could hear her move around and then a door close.

"Where are you, Will?"

"My room. I've just closed and locked the door." Something else opened and closed and Willow laughed. "And I've put Hedwig in a drawer too."

"Why?" I asked tentatively, with hope that my thoughts were along the right lines.

"Because I'm not sure I can concentrate with his beady little eyes watching me."

"Watching you do what?"

My heartbeat started to increase, and my dick got harder, and I knew that if I was wrong, I was going to have to cut the call short and throw one off. Simply listening to her voice, her laugh, and contemplating what I thought she was about to do had me rock hard.

"Have phone sex with you," she almost purred. "You're going to talk dirty to me while I touch myself and we're going to tell each other exactly what to do and then we're both going to come really hard."

Fuck me, this was exactly what I needed, and I couldn't think of anyone better to do it with than Willow.

"So, Charlie," she said seductively. "What do you want me to do?"

I closed my eyes and imagined her in front of me, naked except for a pair of those bright coloured, ridiculously high, pointed shoes that she always wore. Her nipples were hard and tight, and her trim waist curved into her wide hips and lovely plump arse that she was lifting in the air for me to get a better view of.

"Take off your clothes."

"All of them?" she asked with a little giggle.

"Yeah. Everything. Throw them on the floor. Hang on, what's on your feet?"

She took in a breath and groaned. "My slippers."

"Take them off and put a pair of those fuck me shoes on that you've got. The yellow pair."

As I heard Willow move around, I kept the image of her in my head and while I waited, imaginary Charlie slapped her bare arse once, just to remind her that I was there.

Finally, she spoke again. "What now?"

"Now, I want you suck two of your fingers and then circle your left nipple with them," I breathed out and pushed my hand into my sweatpants and boxers. "What do you want me to do?"

Willow was silent for a second or two and then on a shaky breath said, "What are *you* wearing?"

"Sweatpants and a t-shirt," I replied, as vivid pictures of Willow's nipples buzzed around in my head.

"Take off your t-shirt and..." She paused to breathe heavily. "And push your sweats and boxers down to your thighs."

"You want me to take them off?" I asked, my chest moving up and down rapidly.

"No, just to your thighs."

I quickly did as Willow had asked, not wanting to waste a second and then snatched my phone back up from the bed and put it on loud-speaker.

"What now?" she asked with unsteady breaths.

I looked down at my dick and groaned quietly as it bobbed on my stomach, lying next to the thin trail of hair that led down to it. My balls were aching for release, but I didn't want to rush it, I wanted to take the pace that Willow set for me so that we would come together.

"With one hand, trail your fingers between your beautiful tits," I replied, desperately trying not grab my dick and start pumping. "With the other, pinch your right nipple."

My mind's eye watched her do it and she looked fucking beautiful. Her head was back, and her mouth parted on a gasp as the whisper of her own fingers set her body on fire.

"When you reach your pubes, I want you to trail your fingers across from one hip to the other. I want you to tease yourself, but don't you dare touch until I tell you to."

"Hmm hmm," she murmured her acceptance and all I could hear then was heavy breathing on the line for a few seconds. "Charlie," she finally gasped. "I want you to cup your balls and squeeze them gently."

I hesitated, scared of being too excited and causing myself pain, but when I heard Willow moan, I was desperate to be there with her.

"Is your pussy bare, Will?" I asked on a deep groan as my hand covered my balls. "Tell me what you did to be ready for me."

"I waxed it," she replied. "I left a thin strip."

"What else?"

"It's wet and I can see my juices on my lips."

"Fuuuck," I groaned, my head dropped back as I swallowed hard.

"S-s-shit," she stammered. "Charlie what do I need to do now?"

She sounded frantic, as though she'd die if she didn't touch herself soon, but I was loving the anticipation of it. This was foreplay like I'd never experienced before, and it was fucking blowing my mind.

"Run two fingers along your slit and tell me exactly how wet it is."

I heard a little mewl and the need inside my bollocks was too much, so I squeezed them hard, enjoying the pain it caused.

"How fucking wet, Willow?" I demanded and screwed my eyes up tight.

"Really wet, Charlie." She sounded emotional, as though she might burst into tears. "My fingers are covered."

"What shall I do?" I asked as I looked down at my dick as pre-cum glistened on my head.

"Oh shit," she panted. "Grab your cock and run your thumb over the end but keep hold of your balls with the other hand."

I did as I was told and felt the tug of pleasure in the pit of my stomach as images of Willow, skimming her fingers through her juices almost persuaded me to start to pump my dick.

"Will," I groaned. "Put two fingers inside yourself and pump them in and out."

"Slow or quick?"

"Really slow, babe. Make sure you coat them with your wetness."

"Oh, shit Charlie, I need to come."

"Yeah," I gasped. "Me too, but we're going to take our time."

"I can't," she protested. "Charlie, make me come now."

"Tell me what you want me to do?" I asked, desperate to join in but to also take her mind off the need to orgasm. "What now?"

"I want you to pump your cock, Charlie. Really fast and hard. I want you to imagine you're fucking me. Tell me how you're fucking me, Charlie."

"*Shit.*" As I began to jack off, my balls tightened, and my heartbeat increased tenfold. "I'm fucking you from behind, with that fucking incredible arse of yours in the air. My hands are grasping your hips with my fingers digging into your flesh."

"And what am I doing?" she panted. "What do I need to do?"

"You're rubbing your clit, circling it with your fingers that are dripping in your juices. While you do that your other hand is pulling at your nipple because the pleasure is too much and you need some pain to balance it out."

"How fast am I rubbing my clit?"

Willow's last word was delivered on almost a yell and I knew we were both ready.

"Fast, Will', really fast. As fast as I'm pumping my dick into you."

"Harder Charlie, harder," she cried.

I tugged at my shaft, images of Willow and what she was doing flashed in front of my eyes. I was holding onto her tight, possibly too tight, my fingertips leaving marks on her skin. One of her shoes fell off with the movement and fell to the floor from the bed and when I felt my orgasm was almost there, I went harder and faster, the headboard banging against the wall.

"Charlie," Willow cried down the line. "I'm...oh shit."

As her fingers circled quicker and her gorgeous tits jiggled with the force of me drilling into her from behind, I blew my load and screamed her name.

"*Willow.*"

Trying to get my breath back, I listened carefully to the phone lying on my bed and all I could hear was a similar sound to my own; heavy breathing and someone gasping for air.

"Babe, you okay?" I asked between breaths.

"Yeah...you?"

"Fucking hell, that was fantastic."

I broke out a huge, self-satisfied smile, as my eyes closed suddenly feeling tired.

"Oh my God, Charlie," Willow whispered down the line. "That was the best thing ever. I thought I was going to explode."

"I'm so glad you suggested it. You really did miss me, didn't you?"

"Yeah, I really did," she replied, her voice all sweet and sleepy. "But I understand why."

I exhaled. "I know you do, and I really appreciate that."

She sighed and then said, "I better go. I kind of need to clean up."

"Yeah me too." I looked down at the cum on my stomach and grinned. "I'm a bit of a mess."

"Nice," she joked. "So, let me know how Johnny is doing and I'll call you tomorrow, is that okay?"

"More than okay," I breathed out and wished that she was with me to cuddle up to and enjoy our post orgasmic bliss together. "I've taken the week off, so will be home all day, so call me any time."

"Okay. Bye and speak tomorrow."

"Yeah," I whispered. "You definitely will."

Once the line went dead, I yawned, grabbed a tissue from my chest of drawers and after cleaning myself up and pulling my sweats and boxers back up, rolled onto my side and slept for a whole hour dreaming about a pretty girl with the most perfect arse in the world.

CHAPTER 29

Try something new like sweeping everything away from the kitchen table, lie on your back at the edge and extend your legs straight up with your hands under your buttocks to elevate your pelvis when your partner enters you – ensure your parents have finished their dinner first.

Charlie

"You knew I wanted to go out tonight," I hissed, as Teresa fluffed up her stringy brown hair, as she stared in the mirror and pouted.

"I thought you said you were out tomorrow night."

She stopped primping and looked over her shoulder at me, twitching her lips into a half smile, so that the smoker's lines at the side of her mouth deepened.

"You know I didn't."

She knew exactly what I'd said that morning when she'd finally got out of bed and helped herself to my cup of tea. I hadn't seen Willow in almost a week, and she'd asked me to meet her and Polly at the pub later. At first, I'd said no, but then decided to surprise her as Johnny was much better. I figured that the least Teresa could do would be to stay around in case he needed anything while I was out.

"He'll be fine anyway," she scoffed and turned back to the mirror.

I had no doubt he probably would for the few hours that I'd be out, and I knew I was being too overprotective, but he'd recently had a bad virus and I wouldn't risk the chance that he might fall ill again and no one being around to help him.

"He has a phone too," Teresa offered. "He can call you if he needs you."

"Oh, like he did when he fell, when you were supposed to be here."

Teresa tutted and it took all my self-control not to slam the damn mirror over her head. Don't get me wrong, I hated violence, particularly against women but my dearest mother was someone I could quite easily make an exception for.

"He's a grown man, so leave him be instead of bloody fussing over him all the damn time," Teresa spat out impatiently. "Where's my bag?"

"I have no idea, and I'm not fussing over him. He's a paraplegic who's had a virus, does it not register with you how dangerous that could have been?

She shrugged and picked up a cushion and then another before she flung them to one side.

"Of course, it does, but he's fine, so like I said, stop fussing."

"I can't help but fuss," I cried and clutched at my hair. "He's my brother, of course I'm going to worry, and he's your damn son so why don't you?"

Teresa didn't answer, but continued the search for her bag, muttering to herself as she searched everywhere in the lounge. I was pretty sure I'd seen it on the table in the kitchen, but I'd be fucked if I was going to tell her that.

"Are you even listening to me?" I asked and grabbed hold of her shoulder to spin her to face me.

"What?"

"You. Are you listening to what I'm saying?"

"What are you saying, because it sounds like bloody white noise to me? Now leave me alone while I find my bag."

"*No,*" I bellowed, my voice echoing around the lounge. "I won't. You need to step up and take care of your son, *because he not my fucking responsibility.*"

I hadn't meant to shout so loud, or grab her hairbrush and throw it, but I was at my wits end with her. She was spoiled and selfish and didn't give two shits about anyone except herself.

"Well he's not mine," she spat back. "He's big enough to look after himself, you're being a bloody martyr."

"No, I'm not, I care about him and so should you. He shouldn't be left alone, and I want to go and see my girlfriend because I haven't seen her all week because I've been looking after *him.*"

I knew as soon as I saw Teresa's eyes go wide that Johnny was behind me and had heard every word. My skin went cold and dread thundered in my chest as I slowly turned around to speak to him.

"You know what," he said through gritted teeth. "Both of you go out, I don't need either of you staying with me. I'm perfectly capable of looking after myself."

"Johnny-."

"No Charlie, I don't want to fucking hear it. All I want is for you both to fuck off and leave me alone."

"Johnny, please." I reached out a hand toward his shoulder, but he batted it away.

"Fuck off and don't touch me. Go out with Willow, and you," he said turning to Teresa. "Go out with whichever sleaze ball it is you're seeing this week."

Teresa didn't take any persuading; she was out of there faster than I'd ever seen her move before. I looked at Johnny and let out a sigh. Yes, he was much better, but he still looked pale and I wasn't comfortable leaving him alone, even for an hour.

"Go on," he urged, moving his chair to one side.

"I'm not going out and leaving you," I replied stoically. "I'll call Willow."

"I don't want you here, Charlie, because God forbid you feel fucking responsible for me."

"You know I didn't mean it like that." I moved toward him and held out a conciliatory hand, but he spun his wheelchair around, and moved toward the kitchen.

"Just fuck off, Charlie, and leave me alone. I don't want to be anyone's fucking problem."

I dropped my head and sighed, wishing that I'd kept my stupid mouth shut. I hated that my brother felt as though he was a burden. He wasn't, not one bit, but I wanted a break to go and see my girlfriend. All I needed was one night where I wasn't worrying about him. I wanted my mother to give a shit about her son who was in a wheelchair because of her.

After Johnny went back to his room with a can of beer, I ended up on the sofa watching some crap dating show. I had no idea why I was putting myself through it, it was painful seeing the lengths people would go to for a date. On this show the contestants were stripped naked and let someone from the opposite sex pull their body to pieces, hoping they'd be picked based on the shape of their knob or the neatness of their pubic hair.

I was almost considering painting the walls and watching them dry when my phone buzzed on the floor next to me. Turning the volume down on the TV, I reached down for my mobile and noticed straight away it was Willow.

"Hi," I said and felt my mood lift. "You okay?"

"Charlie." Simply from saying my name I could hear the anxiety in her voice and dread washed over me as I lowered my feet to the floor. "I'm so sorry but your mum is in here and she's kicking off with some bloke who she reckons stole her drink."

"Shit," I growled, stood up and moved toward the hall. "Where are you?"

"Dracos, the new gin bar. I'm so sorry, but I didn't know what to do. I tried to calm her down but-."

"Will, no don't go near her." Fear struck me as I remembered what happened last time someone who I cared about went to her rescue. "Seriously keep away from her, I'll be there in about ten or fifteen minutes."

"You sure you don't want me to go over. She's going crazy."

I opened the door to my room and shoved my feet into a pair of trainers and grabbed the keys for the car.

"No babe, please don't."

"Okay," she said hesitantly. "I'll ring you if she leaves."

I closed my eyes and pinched the bridge of my nose. "She won't. She has an audience; she'll stay as long as they do. I'll see you soon."

As I ended the call a red mist took over and I kicked the waste bin next to my dressing table across the room. Why was she so damn intent on ruining both mine and Johnny's lives?

"Fuck!" I cursed and stamped my foot as I swept everything off the top of the chest of drawers. A bottle of aftershave, my Bluetooth speaker, and a pile of change clattered against the wall.

"What the hell's wrong?"

I turned to see Johnny in the doorway. He was wearing his glasses which made me think he'd been surfing the internet, probably for a new place to live away from me and Teresa after our argument before.

"Teresa," I said as I edged past him out of my room.

"What the hell has she done now? I assume she has done something, as you've just fucking decimated a perfectly good speaker."

I looked over my shoulder to see my speaker on the floor with its guts spilled out.

"She's causing a scene in Dracos. Willow called to tell me."

As I moved down the hall, I could hear the rubber of Johnny's wheels squeaking on the tiled floor behind me.

"I'll be as quick as I can," I said and pulled open the front door.

"I'm coming," he said.

I stopped and turned to face him as he reached up for a jacket from the coat peg.

"No." I put a hand on the arm of his chair, leaning into his space. "Not happening."

"I'm coming," he retorted, staring at me with a steely gaze. "I'm sick of being treated like a fucking cripple who can't do anything. Believe it or not big brother, I'm an adult, almost fully fucking functioning except for a pair of dodgy legs. She's my damn nightmare too, so I'm coming."

He jutted out his chin, daring me to say no, and I knew if I didn't take him, he'd wheel himself there.

"Stay there until I get the ramp out."

"Don't you dare fucking leave me, Charlie."

"I won't," I snapped. "So, shut up and let me get the ramp sorted."

A little over ten minutes later, we parked outside Dracos and I locked up the car.

"At least we got the blue badge," Johnny said as he wheeled himself the two feet to the entrance of the bar. "We could have ended up parking miles away otherwise. This disabled lark has its benefits."

I shook my head and wondered, not for the first time, what actually went through his head at times. As I followed him into the bar, with its rough wooden floors and bare light bulbs hanging from the ceiling by plaited wires, I scanned the room. It wasn't a huge place, but there were lots of alcoves and dark corners, but it didn't take me long to spot Teresa – to be honest, I heard her ear-piercing screech first.

Teresa was stood with her back to a wall as a female police officer tried to reason with her by the looks of it. I could have told her not to bother, once Teresa was on one, it took a lot to bring her down to the level of a normal human being. Standing to one side of her was Willow and her friend Polly. Willow had her hands resting on her head and was talking animatedly to a male officer, while Polly's head moved from left to right between Willow and Teresa. She looked like she was watching a tennis match, not the hideous sight of my mother screeching like a drunken banshee.

I tapped Johnny on the shoulder and pointed in the direction he needed to go and as he wheeled through the crowd, it parted for him like the damn red sea for Moses.

When we reached them, Willow spotted me straight away and excused herself from the copper.

"Charlie," she sighed and pulled me into her arms. "I'm so sorry for calling you, but I thought you'd want to know. The police are talking about arresting her if she doesn't calm down or leave." As she pulled away from me, she noticed Johnny. "Hey, Johnny."

"Hey, Willow," he replied, his eyes on our mum. "What started it?"

Willow shrugged. "It appears it was over a drink. I don't think she'd seen me, or even remembered me to be honest, but I saw her come in. She was with a man and another woman and they were getting a bit lairy but nothing too bad, just noisy really. Then the couple left and within minutes she started shouting at some guy who was in here with his mates, saying he'd nicked her drink. One of them said something to her and she..." Willow looked at us both in turn and then made a hand gesture like an explosion. "She lost it."

"Who called the feds?" Johnny asked, moving a little closer to Teresa.

"Not sure, the manager I think, but him and the guys she was arguing with disappeared as soon as the police turned up."

"Yeah, that'll be right," my brother muttered. "Don't want to get their own fucking hands dirty."

I was about to argue that he did the right thing, getting the coppers to come in and sort her out, but realised it was pointless. Johnny always tried to see the best side of Teresa – like the fact he didn't think it was her fault he was in a damn wheelchair, so I kept my thoughts to myself.

"What's the copper say?" I asked Willow as I linked my fingers with hers.

"I tried to tell him you were on your way, but he said she's causing a disturbance and needs to be ejected from the building and arresting her might be the only option."

I sighed heavily and nodded.

"Okay, I'll speak to him. Johnny see if you can get her to shut her damn mouth for a few minutes."

Johnny grunted in agreement and wheeled himself over to Teresa who was now pointing a finger at the female officer.

"This is Teresa's son," Willow explained to the cop who had just finished talking on his radio.

The cop flashed me a smile. "Evening sir, I'm PC Strong and as you can see your mother is causing a disturbance and if she doesn't pack it in, I'll have her arrested."

I wanted to tell him to go ahead, but I knew that Johnny wouldn't like that. He'd want us to do everything we could to get her out of there and back home.

"My brother is going to try and talk to her." I nodded toward Johnny who was now in between Teresa and the officer and had a hand on Teresa's shoulder. Even though he was in a wheelchair, Teresa wasn't much taller than him. She was a slight woman, with piercing blue eyes which over time had been dulled by alcohol. I vaguely remembered her having curves at one time, but her body was now thin and fragile, and it was anyone's guess how she managed to sink as much booze as she did without regularly passing out.

"Doesn't look like he's having much look," Willow said, her face strained with discomfort.

"Listen," I said. "Why don't you and Polly get off, go to another bar."

"No." She shook her head vigorously. "I'm not leaving you."

Polly then took a step toward us. "Is there anything we can do?" she asked.

"I think it best you leave it to us, miss," PC Strong advised. "I'm sorry sir, but your girlfriend is right, I don't think your brother is having much luck."

The anger I was feeling was in danger of causing me to do something stupid, like throw Teresa over my shoulder and dump her in the street and when I looked over and saw the sadness in my brother's eyes, I knew I had to end it.

"Give me a second."

I started to march toward them, but before I'd even had chance to take two strides, Teresa had leaned across Johnny and made a lunge for the female cop.

"Oh shit," Polly groaned.

"Teresa!" I yelled, as I made a grab for her.

As I did, Johnny wheeled backwards almost knocking over PC Strong who had decided to aid his colleague. Teresa swayed on her feet and dodged my outstretched hand but fell into the female officer who quickly had her hands behind her back.

"Johnny, you okay?" I asked, as Teresa was dragged from in front of him.

"Yeah." He looked shell shocked as he wheeled around to watch our mum being forced out of the bar.

"Do you want to go to the station?" Willow asked as she appeared at my side. "I can come with you if you do."

I shook my head, my eyes still pinned to the embarrassing scene of the woman who'd given birth to me being arrested.

"No."

"No," Johnny snapped. "We're not going anywhere. Let her fucking rot in there for all I care."

I looked down at him to see he was staring at her. His eyes firmly on Teresa until the two cops had bundled her through the door.

As soon as she was gone, the quiet murmurings of everyone in the bar suddenly got louder and as quick as a finger click, the scene was forgotten, and they all carried on drinking.

Johnny turned to me and frowned. "I think maybe I've reached your limit with her, bro."

"Really?"

"Yeah. She's out of control and I wouldn't see it. I'll speak to her about moving out and I'll see about a carer too."

My mouth dropped open, not sure what to say. I'd been on at him for ages to employ someone but he'd flatly refused.

"It won't be a bad thing," I replied, placing a hand on his shoulder. "I promise."

He gave me a single nod and then started to wheel himself toward the bar.

"Right, I need a fucking drink, anyone else?"

Willow's eyes were guarded as she looked at Johnny and then me. "Is he okay?" she mouthed silently.

I shrugged and went back to watching him. He was holding his hand out to Polly and when she extended hers, he took it and kissed the back of it. Johnny then pulled her closer, whispering something in her ear which made her giggle. As Johnny grinned up at Polly a feeling of ease seeped through my veins. It was his usual happy grin and I knew he was totally at peace with what he needed to do, and it blew me away *again* at how damn levelheaded and accepting he was.

I swallowed back the emotion as a small, warm hand slid into mine and gave it a squeeze. Willow smiled at me and laid her head on my shoulder.

"Are you okay?" she asked.

I looked down at her and sighed, so damn glad I'd met her. "Yeah," I replied. "Now I'm with you, I am."

Her eyes lifted and she gave me a beautiful smile, as Polly's girlish giggle rang out once more and I knew that this was the girl I was probably going to fall in love with.

CHAPTER
30

In the heat of passion, changing your breathing pattern can help increase an orgasm's impact; the faster you breathe the more excited you get. Consider keeping an inhaler with you at all times.

Willow

"Why the hell are we doing this, again?" I asked Charlie, who had my hand firmly in his as we followed Ruben toward the pub.

He looked down and dropped a kiss to my temple. "Because you're a lovely sister who wanted to help her brother."

"How is it helping him though?" I hissed. "He's more chilled about coming out than anybody. He doesn't need to talk to James and now I feel bad, like I'm introducing the trainee gay guy to the professional gay guy. I feel awful." I groaned and looked up at the sky. "It's no wonder he couldn't stand the sight of me."

"You can stop talking about me, you know," Ruben called over his shoulder.

I didn't want us to go back to how we'd been, barely talking, and I hated that me interfering in his life might do that. I'd thought that he might like to talk to James and get some perspective on what it had been like for him coming out, and how *he'd* told *his* friends and family.

Okay, so none of us had been nonplussed by Ruben's news, but he had admitted to me that he still hadn't told his friends and was a little wary about it, but had planned a *PS* night at our house for them all and was going to tell them all together. Thinking about that, I realised he had this. He didn't need me sticking my big fat oar in.

"Ruben, wait."

I pulled up and waited for my brother to turn around.

"What?" he asked, walking back to us.

"You don't have to do this. It was a stupid idea. You don't need anyone to help steer you through the waters of homosexuality and I was being condescending to think you did."

Ruben raised his brows and laid a hand on my shoulder. "Listen, I know you were only trying to help. It's not your fault you've stereotyped every gay man as being scared and naïve, I'm only glad you didn't buy me some leather hot pants and get me a place on a float at Gay Pride."

Charlie burst out a laugh as I stared up at Ruben with my mouth open.

"I would never-."

"I'm joking," Ruben replied with a grin. "I know this comes from a good place, Willow, so stop stressing. But one thing."

"What?"

"Do not try and fix me up with your boss. I have Cane and I'm happy with the way things are going, okay. Anyway, James is like..." he paused and grimaced. "Thirty or something, ugh that would be so wrong."

I nodded with a smile and instinctively pulled him in for a hug and gave him a tight squeeze. I think he was about to tap out when Charlie cleared his throat.

"Erm guys, we're kind of blocking the pavement here."

I let my little brother free. "If you want to go, I'll explain to James."

Ruben shook his head. "Nah, it's fine. I'm thirsty and as the first two rounds are on you, I'm not going anywhere."

He then turned and strode away, leaving Charlie and I to follow.

"How's things with your mum?" I asked Charlie when we were alone at the table.

"Johnny told her, well we both did, that we want her out, but she turned on the waterworks and my big-hearted brother gave her a month to find somewhere." He shook his head, his lips turned down into a grimace. "I'd have said tough luck, but it's his house, so he gets the final say."

"Did they charge her?"

"Nope. Wish they had, but once she'd sobered up, she gave them a sob story about her poor boy being in a wheelchair and how she worried all the time about him."

"They told you that?" I was shocked, I expected she'd have at least been done for drunk and disorderly.

"No, that's the excuse she always comes up with when she's in trouble – pretty much works every time. Anyway," Charlie sighed. "I don't want to talk about her. How do you think this is going?"

He nodded toward the bar and my gaze followed his to where Ruben and James chatted together. I'd been right, Ruben really didn't need any help and if anything, he'd been the one giving James information. He'd told him about a couple of groups, particularly Stonewall, a support group who'd helped Cane when he'd wanted advice about how to try and tell his parents and when James had told Ruben he didn't go out much, but relied on dating apps to meet people, my brother had offered to take him on a night out and introduce him to some of the best bars.

"He's totally sorted isn't he," I replied with a smile.

"Yeah, he is. I can't believe he's only just told you all. You'd think he'd been out for ages."

We continued watching as James listened intently to whatever Ruben was telling him.

"He told me his boyfriend hasn't told his parents yet," Charlie added. "That could cause some issues between them if they have to continue sneaking around."

"I know, but Ruben said Cane might move out of his hometown and more into the city, that way his parents are less likely to find out. I think Ruben wishes he'd tell them though."

"Have you met Cane yet, apart from your assignation near the toilets?" Charlie grinned and took a swig from his beer bottle.

"Listen, it looked dodgy to me, I didn't know, did I? And to answer your question, no, but he's coming for lunch next Sunday."

Charlie's eyes went wide and he almost choked on his beer.

"I know," I groaned. "Poor guy. He has no idea what he's letting himself in for. I'm surprised at Ruben for even considering it, especially if he's serious about him."

"Oh, so does that mean you're not serious about me?"

Charlie had a smirk on his lips, so I knew he was joking, but he did have a point.

"You're different," I replied as I smacked at his arm. "You *were* only meant to be a one-night stand, but I didn't bank on my magnetic charm and personality and now, well of course now I can't get rid of you. Don't forget, you also saw my dad's knackers so you're practically one of the family."

"I was going to be a one-night stand, eh?" He placed his bottle on the table and leaned back to study me. "I didn't know that."

I felt my cheeks burn at the realisation of what I'd said. "I don't make a habit of it, and to be fair, I did think you'd be a bit of a love 'em and leave 'em type."

"Why?" he asked and looked totally affronted by my accusation.

"Well, because look at you," I sighed. "You're gorgeous and could get any girl you wanted to, so why would you want more than one night. Would you choose plain cauliflower when you could have cauliflower cheese, no you wouldn't."

"Hang on," Charlie said with a shake of his head as he shifted in his seat to sit sideways on to me. "Are you likening yourself to plain cauliflower?"

I thought about it. "Yeah, I suppose."

Suddenly I was engulfed by his strong arms and pulled against his tight chest. He smelled delicious and was all hard and chiselled, yet safe, comfortable, and warm at the same time. I couldn't help but breathe him in to make sure he was real.

"There is nothing plain cauliflower about you," he whispered against my ear. "Everything about you is most definitely *not* plain or cauliflowery."

My stomach went funny and I felt all girly as Charlie squeezed me tight.

"Oh God," I breathed out on a sigh. "I really like you."

"Good, because I really like you too and don't ever think of yourself as anything less than cauliflower cheese, okay?"

I nodded against his neck and took another sniff for good measure before a loud voice rudely interrupted our moment.

"You never said you were coming in here," Polly cried from somewhere behind me.

Reluctantly I pulled away from Charlie and turned to see my best friend standing arm in arm with Jasmine, who was dressed head to toe in what I thought was Ted Baker – which surprised me as she thought TB was the poor man's designer clothing and often screwed her nose up at it. Times must be hard, I thought, either that or she'd had a bump on the head.

"I didn't realise I had to tell you," I replied with a grin. "And who do we have here? Surely that isn't the lovely Jasmine Mellor dressed in Mr Baker?"

Polly snorted while Jasmine shifted from foot to foot and looked decidedly uncomfortable.

"You said no one we knew would be in here," she hissed to Polly.
Polly shrugged.

"So?" I asked as I waved a hand up and down. "Explain."

"I am an influencer you know," she snapped. "And sometimes as an influencer we have to promote things we wouldn't normally consider."

"Unless the price is right," I offered.

"Maybe. Anyway, I find this little outfit quite pleasant." She stuck her nose in the air and turned to Polly. "I'll have a brandy sour please, as it's your round."

"Anyone else?" Polly asked.

"Let me," Charlie said and pushed up from the seat. "What would you like, Polly?"

"Honestly, I'll go," she argued.

Charlie was adamant and moved to her as he put a hand on her shoulder. "No, I'd like to, so what are you having?"

"I'll have a vodka and diet coke please, if you insist."

"Same again, babe?" Charlie asked me.

Before I had time to answer, Jasmine held her hand up. "Excuse me, do you not think it would be good manners to introduce me?"

I rolled my eyes as I knew for a fact she knew who Charlie was. Okay, I probably should have formally introduced them, but I was so caught up in my wind up of Jasmine it hadn't entered my head.

"Jasmine this is Charlie, Charlie, Jasmine."

"Hey, nice to meet you," Charlie said as he flashed her a smile.

Jasmine slowly scrutinised him, from his feet right up to the top of his head. I knew because I could see her eyes moving inch by inch.

"And lovely to meet you too," she practically purred.

Polly looked at me with saucer like eyes and mouthed 'what a slut', while I had to force myself not to get up and pee on Charlie's leg to mark my territory.

"Same again, please," I snapped, unable to take my eyes from Jasmine, who in turn had fixed her stair on my boyfriend.

I glanced over to gauge his reaction to her and under her scrutiny, Charlie's face had morphed into something that looked like he could be having the most difficult shit ever as he scratched behind his ear.

"Right," he mumbled. "I'll be right back."

As soon as he'd gone, Polly came and flopped down on the bench seat next to me, while Jasmine pulled out the chair that Ruben had been using.

"You never said he was that gorgeous," Jasmine gasped and opened up her hideous handbag that was pink and shaped like an elephant. "I mean, he's totally hot."

She then pulled out what I recognised as a Louboutin lipstick and, without a mirror, perfectly applied more bright pink to her lips.

"Yes, I know," I stated knocking back the last of my drink.

Polly must have sensed I was a little tense because she laid a comforting hand on my knee, but it did little to calm me down. I'd been here before with Jasmine, when she'd taken a fancy to a guy that I liked or was dating. She'd flutter her eyelashes, stick out her boobs and do the very best to avert their concentration from me to her. I'd said it before, and I'd say it again – why the hell was I friends with her?

"I'm a little surprised," Jasmine said as she pushed up her tits until they almost spilled out of the silk cami top she was wearing with a matching skirt. "He's not your usual type."

"What's her usual type?" Polly asked.

Jasmine looked me up and down and then glanced over at the bar. "Oh, I see Ruben is here too," she announced. "And who is that he's talking to?"

"James, my boss, so go on," I ground out. "What's my usual type?"

"Well," she studied me with her head on one side and then smiled. "Not *that* gorgeous."

I felt like a damn bull about to storm a matador as steam practically pumped out of my flaring nostrils and I stamped a foot on the floor. She could be so damn rude yet appeared to have no compunction to tone it down. She'd always been the same, but when you're eleven years old and starting high school the need to create your own little pack is far more important than realising a member of that pack is actually a total bitch and that when you're twenty-four you'll wonder why you're even friends with her.

"I think you're very well suited," Polly added, ever the peace maker. "And the way you were wrapped around each other when we came in, I'd say he's mad about you. Now Jasmine, why don't you tell Willow how you tried to get Gucci to let you promote their latest handbag and they said no. What was the phrase they used 'lacking in public recognition'?"

Ruben and James had joined us back at the table and as we discussed whether to go and get a curry later, Toby and his friend Maxwell entered the pub.

"Hi Polly," Toby said before acknowledging anyone else. "How're you doing?"

"Hi Toby, hi Maxwell," I said as I waved at them, to let my brother know I did actually exist.

"Oh hiya," Toby said, his eyes only flicked to me before they went back to gaze at Polly.

Maxwell didn't even bother peeling his eyes from Jasmine but simply held his hand up and then cupped his balls in his tight trouser that he was wearing with loafers and no socks, the thought of which made me shiver.

"All those crusty pieces of sweat inside his shoes must be gross," I groaned to Polly.

"And the fact that he's staring at our friend and holding his bollocks isn't?"

I shrugged. "I have four brothers, your point is?"

"Would you like a drink, Polly?" Toby asked and fluttered his long lashes that were far too long for any male.

"I'll have one," I said as I held up my glass.

"I can get them," James offered.

"No, let Toby," Ruben added. "He hardly ever buys a round."

"I'm asking Polly," Toby said with a frown. "Oh hey, Charlie. Nice to see you again."

"Hi Toby, good to see you too." Charlie leaned into me. "You want another, I'll get you one."

"No, it's my turn," I said. "I only wanted to see if I could distract him, but evidently he has it as bad for her as ever."

"I think that Maxwell guy has gone into a coma," Charlie said with a laugh. "He hasn't moved a muscle since he came in here. He's transfixed by Jasmine."

I turned my head sharply. "How do you feel about that?" I snapped.

His brow furrowed. "What, that he's in a coma? I'm a little worried, but I'm sure he'll snap out of it eventually if we all talk to him and play him Westlife CD's."

I couldn't help but grin at him but bit my lip to stop the belly laugh I wanted to give.

"No, the fact that he's transfixed by Jasmine."

I knew I was probably being pathetic, but I'd actually lost one boyfriend who said he didn't think it was fair to keep seeing me when he was evidently attracted to other women i.e. Jasmine. He didn't actually go out with her, or even ask her on a date, but she'd pushed her tits out and flirted enough to give him doubts. I probably should have stopped being her friend then, but a day later she offered to take Polly and me on a spa weekend as long as we took lots of pictures for social media with us holding a particular brand of haemorrhoid cream. Once the spa weekend was over the situation with William, my ex, didn't seem so important compared to all the free stuff I would get from her – you never knew when you'd get piles.

"Like I said," Charlie replied. "I'm sure he'll come out of it if we all talk to him and play Westlife CDs."

I nudged him with my shoulder and rolled my eyes. "Seriously, do you find her attractive?"

Charlie turned and looked at Jasmine who was busy on her phone, and then turned back to me. "Nope. She's pretty enough, but she's vacuous, shallow, and competitive."

My mouth dropped open. "Wow, you're good, you've only known her twenty minutes. I've known her thirteen years and she still manages to surprise me every day with new and vile attributes. And what do you mean, she's competitive?"

"She thinks she's in competition with you," he said with a shrug.

"You don't need designer clothes or bright pink hair to stand out. Look at you in that dress, you look amazing and I bet you found it in a charity shop, didn't you?"

I looked down at the sixties mini dress I'd found in a vintage store and the flat ballet pumps that I'd bought from a jumble sale that Mum's school had organised.

"Well it's vintage, not charity shop, but it did only cost me thirty quid, but the shoes were only fifty pence."

"There you go." Charlie leaned forward and gave me a closed mouth kiss. "And believe me, she doesn't want me, or even fancy me, she doesn't want you to have a boyfriend when she doesn't. I could be one of the Hanson brothers before they grew into their looks and she'd still flirt with me. So, to answer the question you didn't ask – no, you've nothing to be worried about. I don't fancy her. I only have eyes for you."

"Is that the Boyz II Men version or the classic version of 1975 by Art Garfunkel?"

Charlie looked shocked. "Art Garfunkel of course, what else?" he whispered against my mouth.

As I kissed him slowly, we heard cat calls and whistles behind us, until I decided I really should pull away. As I did, Jasmine reached for Charlie's hand and took it in hers.

"Has anyone ever told you that you look like that model, Matthew Noszka?"

"No, can't say they have," Charlie replied, prising his hand away from Jasmine's.

"Hey, Jasmine," I cried. "I meant to tell you, those shoes you've got on, well they have them in Cut Price Shoes, for only thirteen-ninety-nine."

Jasmine's eyes dropped to her designer shoes and then shot back up to me. "*No!*"

"Yeah," I replied and nodded enthusiastically with a huge grin. "In three different colours."

She went a strange shade of green and stood up. "I need to go to the ladies."

"Okay, see you in a bit."

"Where's she going?" Maxwell asked, his puppy dog eyes following Jasmine's path.

"Ladies," I replied. "She's got a terrible bad stomach and she didn't want anyone to know but she's just farted and followed through. I think she said it was all up her back, so she may be a while."

Maxwell's face was a picture as his mouth dropped open. "Really?"

I nodded and tried to look despondent. "Yeah and unfortunately it happens a lot. She really has no control over it, especially in the middle of sex."

Charlie snorted next to me and then quickly picked up his bottle of beer to take a drink, while nudging me.

"Tobe," Maxwell said and turned back to my brother. "I reckon we should get off somewhere else, what do you reckon?"

"Hey," Ruben cried, with a huge grin on his face. "Jasmine won't be long. Why don't you ask her to go with you?"

"Yeah," Toby added excitedly. "You could come too, Polly."

My heart sank as I expected him to be disappointed, but Polly surprised me.

"Okay," she said with a sigh. "But only because I want to go somewhere that I can dance."

"Yeah, yep, okay," Toby said, as he almost bounced on his toes. "We can do that, can't we Maxwell?"

At that very second Jasmine returned and stood next to Polly and, with classic comedy timing that I could never had hoped for, sprayed perfume on and around herself. "What's happening?" she asked.

"You and Polly are coming with me and Maxwell," Toby said. "We're going to go to Ziggy's so Polly can dance. It'll be like a foursome."

"No, it won't," Polly snapped at the same time as Maxwell.

"Okay," Jasmine replied and fluffed up her hair. "As long as we can go for a curry afterwards. I could do with a good blowout."

It was that point that Maxwell practically sprinted out of the bar.

CHAPTER
31

Tobacco constricts the circulation of blood and may lower the sex drive hormone. A study reveals that quitters had more orgasms afterwards than they did when they smoked. - the lesson being, ladies quit chewing tobacco, not only will you have more orgasms, but your old spittoon will make a lovely flowerpot.

Charlie

I don't know what had persuaded me to say yes to have Sunday dinner with Willow's family, but I had and was about to knock on the front door feeling nervous yet excited about the prospect of the evening ahead. Eccentric and crazy they may be, but the Dixons were also fun and great to be around, however, it was still a big deal being asked to dinner and so it was only natural to be nervous. Apparently, Ruben's boyfriend Cane had chickened out – sorry, he'd forgotten he had other plans, so it looked like I would be the only specimen on show tonight.

Actually, I lied. I did know what had persuaded me to say yes. It was her – Willow. I was totally gone for her, almost to the point of drawing a heart with our initials in it on every available surface. She was all I could think about, which when you're supposed to be concentrating on learning from one of the best music producers in the business, could be very distracting. A couple of days earlier, Deke had asked me what I thought about turning the volume of the drums up above the guitars on one of Devil's Doorbell's songs. I had no clue what he was talking about, because I'd been thinking of whether it was too early in our relationship to suggest Willow and I went away for a weekend – once Johnny had a carer in place.

Teresa still hadn't left, and Johnny didn't seem to be pushing it, but he had registered with an agency to find someone to help. The problem was, he'd hated every one of the four people that they'd sent for interviews so far. I called them interviews very loosely. He hadn't let me sit in on them and the longest had lasted a mere fifteen minutes and I was pretty sure that was only because the woman brought her pug with her and Johnny was a damn sucker for dogs. When she'd trailed back through the lounge and given me a dirty look, I guessed it didn't matter how much Johnny liked her little Douggie, she hadn't got the job and my brother had evidently upset her.

I was busy thinking about Johnny, when the door burst open and a frazzled looking Willow faced me. Her hair was in two plaits and she was wearing a pair of dungarees with a striped t-shirt and she looked fucking cute. Looking at her though, I couldn't help but think of the Pippy Longstocking books Mrs. Jefferson, my old primary school teacher, had read to us for the last half hour of each day. I'd hated them at the time, but Willow in the guise of her was pretty sexy.

"I'm so sorry," she huffed and opened the door wider to let me in. "My brother is being a dick."

I leaned in for a quick kiss and then raised my brows in question.

"He thinks it's funny that he's compiled a questionnaire for you to fill in."

"A questionnaire?"

"Yeah about your suitability to by my boyfriend."

"So, me not kicking off at them for smothering my cock with dog food wasn't my initiation ceremony?"

"No. Apparently, that was merely a 'bit of fun'." She did quotation marks with her fingers and flared her nostrils in time with each waggle.

Her face in a pissed off grimace, Willow reached up on tiptoe to give me another kiss. "Hi."

"Hi," I replied as I ran a finger down her cheek. "And don't worry about the questionnaire. I feel pretty confident that I'll pass with flying colours."

"You haven't seen the questions yet," she sighed out. "The first one is about your bank balance."

I burst out a laugh and pulled Willow closer, giving her a hug. "I think I'll need to lie about that one. Which brother has done it anyway; Toby?"

"No, Declan, would you believe. The one who is a miserable troll most of the time. You should have seen him, Charlie; he was almost pissing himself laughing as he wrote it. He's printed it out and actually asked Mum about using her laminator, until he realised you wouldn't be able to write on it if he did." She gave a groan and shook her head. "He is so getting shit whenever he brings a girl home, *if* it ever happens. Anyway, come on in, the fam is waiting in the lounge, oh and ignore the fact that Toby is wearing a monocle and sucking on an unlit pipe."

I leaned back and examined her face to see if she was joking, but there was nothing but sadness in her eyes which only made me laugh again.

———

Dinner had been cleared away and everyone was sat back and having a chat around the table, some seventies Fleetwood Mac was playing in the background, my arm was resting across the back of Willow's chair, as my thumb rhythmically rubbed her shoulder and I didn't think I had ever felt so relaxed.

"I only want to leave this mortal coil knowing all my children are happy," Maureen sighed, looking at Declan with worry in her eyes.

"Being married, engaged, or even going steady as you call it, won't make me happier," Declan groaned. "Now, me having sex with lots of different girls definitely would."

As Declan and the boys laughed, Willow groaned.

"You're such a pig." She looked at each of her four brothers in turn. "In fact, you all are. The only gentleman at this table is Charlie."

I started to cough as I knew that if she could have read my mind when she was bent over to pet Nigel, Danny's dog, I would not now be called a gentleman. I could see right down her top and copped a glimpse of the beautiful globes of her tits, thus thoughts of my dick shoved between them had invaded my head.

"He's being a gentleman now," Toby said, "but you wait until you've been going out a bit longer. He'll start farting, belching, and scratching his nads at the table."

"Toby is right, Willow," Patsy chipped in. "Danny was polite, well-mannered, and sweet for a couple of months, now he does all those things."

Danny grinned at Patsy and leaned in for a kiss, which lasted a little too long for it to be comfortable. To me anyway, no one else seemed to care.

"I worry you're going to get some STD." Maureen turned to Declan again. "And what about the respect for those poor girls, do you actually have any?"

"I respect them a lot," he replied. "Especially when they're su-."

"Declan," Ivan growled. "I think we get the picture."

All five of the Dixon offspring giggled like little kids, while Maureen gave them a look only a mother could give – well, unless it was my mother.

"Anyway, changing the subject," Danny said. "Why the hell were you wearing a monocle and smoking a pipe, Tobe?"

"I've been asked to do a clothing campaign for a company that sells tweed jackets and they're going to shoot it in the reading room of the British Library."

"And?"

"Well I wanted to get into the right frame of mind. You know, get into character."

"When have you ever known anyone to smoke a pipe in a library?" Willow asked.

Toby shrugged and started to bang a beat on the table in time to the song in the background, which I think was called Tusk.

"Exactly," Willow replied. "And who the hell even wears a monocle these days?"

"Ah leave him alone," Maureen said as she brushed the hair from Toby's eyes. "He's an artist and who knows why he does the stupid things he does?"

"He's a piss artist, but that's about it," Declan added.

Toby grabbed his sides and pretended to laugh and then quickly pulled his face back to deadpan. "You need new material big brother, that joke is centuries old *and* shit."

Declan flipped him the finger which earned him another mother look from Maureen.

"I think this is all degenerating into the usual Dixon crap talk, so I propose we play a game of Monopoly. You in Charlie?" Ivan asked.

Before I had time to answer, Willow was up out of her chair and had pulled me with her.

"No sorry, we're going up to my room. Charlie likes to nap after a large meal, don't you?"

"Yeah?" I answered as a question.

"Oh, is that what they call it," Ruben muttered as he leaned on the back two legs of his chair and reached over to the bookcase, pulling a Monopoly game from the bottom shelf.

"It's true," Willow protested. "As if we'd be able to do anything else after Mum's mammoth feast."

Maureen smiled widely and sat up taller and straightened her shoulders.

"It was pretty mammoth wasn't it?"

Patsy patted Maureen's hand and then started to move glasses and mugs to make a space for Ruben to put the board out. While everyone busied themselves picking a piece to play with, Willow dragged me from the dining room and up the stairs.

"You don't like Monopoly then?" I asked as she closed the door on her little slice of Harry Potter heaven.

"Not when Danny is playing, no. He's cutthroat. You know, once he wouldn't speak to Toby for a week because he wouldn't sell him Park Lane but then sold it to Ruben who then won because he had one more property than Danny. We only finished then because we'd been playing for five hours and it was almost one in the morning, otherwise Danny wanted to carry on until one of them was bankrupt."

"That was the only way they could be separated, by one property?"

"Yeah," she sighed and jumped onto the bed. "Same money, same total value of their property, everything. He's never let Toby forget it, so I'm pretty sure there'll be bloodshed at some point during the game."

"I'm glad we ducked out then," I replied as I kicked off my shoes and bounced onto the bed next to her.

Once I was comfy, I pulled Willow into my side and kissed her temple. "I've really enjoyed myself tonight, thanks for inviting me."

"I didn't, my mum did, I was all for not telling you and maybe keeping you for a bit longer."

She rolled her eyes and then grinned at me, she looked so damn beautiful, I couldn't help but drop my mouth to hers and take it in a long, deep, kiss.

Willow's hands moved to my hair, her fingers threaded through it and tugged it as my lips and tongue became more insistent. With my hand on her perfectly plump arse, I dragged her closer so that our hips and groins touched and as soon as we were, my dick sprang to life. The ache in my balls was instantaneous and intense as I rolled us so that Willow was underneath me. Immediately she opened her legs and let me settle between them as she wrapped them around my waist. We fitted together perfectly and caught a mutual rhythm as we started to grind and steal the breath from each other's lungs with our kisses.

My hands moved to the strap of her dungarees and blindly tried to unfasten the strange button and hook fastening. I wasn't sure I'd have been able to do it with my eyes open and both hands on the job, but it was even more difficult with my full concentration on the kisses I was giving her. Finally, after me pushing and pulling at the button, Willow moved her hands from my hair and took over. Once both straps were undone, she urged me to lift up so she could push the dungarees down to her waist.

As soon as her hands continued to exact the pleasurable pain of pulling my hair, I pushed one of mine up her top and cupped her tit and brushed the hard nipple with my thumb. Willow gave a little moan and I paused as I wondered whether I'd hurt her, but when she thrust her hips up sharply, I realised she wanted me to get on with it.

I moved down her body and dragged the soft denim of her dunga-rees with me as I did so, and pulled them over her hips and down her legs. Willow kicked them onto the floor and grinned down at me as she lay there in a red and white striped t-shirt and a pair of knickers that said 'Sunday' on them above a picture of a roast dinner.

"Nice knickers."

"I know, I thought you'd like them. I wore them especially for you."

She looked perfect, with her plaits spread out on the pillow, her nipples hard and pushing against her top and her long, tanned legs spread apart. If angels wore striped tops and picture knickers then Willow Dixon was most definitely one.

"You're so beautiful," I whispered and leaned down to take her plump bottom lip and drag it slowly between my teeth. "You're all I can think of every fucking day."

"Oh my God, you say some of the nicest things," she replied breathily.

Her hand lifted to cup my cheek and she licked her lips; the tip of her pink tongue ran smoothly along them as she enticed me and made my dick harden even more.

"I need you to fuck me, Charlie."

I didn't need any other invitation, and nothing would have stopped me at that point. I pulled my t-shirt over my head at the same time as Willow got rid of hers and we threw them together to one side. Both of us were grinning as we then got rid of the rest of our clothes and under-wear until we were both naked. My dick was hard and at full mast as

Willow placed her arms above her head and placed one foot on the bed, so her leg was bent at the knee. She'd gone from angel to porn mag centrefold within minutes and while I loved every single one of the looks that she was able to pull off, at that very moment porn mag centrefold was my particular favourite, especially when she lowered one of her hands and started to play with her own nipple.

"Fuck," I ground out and wondered how I'd got so lucky to have met her.

She was like no other girl I'd ever been with. She was sexy and confident about her sexiness which only made her...well, sexier.

As I lowered myself over her, a thought struck me, and I groaned. "I haven't got any condoms," I said through gritted teeth. "I'm sorry."

Willow pushed up onto her elbows and instead of kneeing me in the bollocks as I'd expected, she nodded toward Hedgwig who was staring at us, enjoying the show.

"Top drawer," she said with a grin. "My mum is a biology teacher for teenagers don't forget."

With a deep sense of relief, I leaned across and pulled open the drawer.

"Shit, does she have shares in latex or something?"

Inside there were various boxes stating different sizes, plus dozens of loose ones in their own silver packet.

"It's her *thing*. Now grab a box of large and get on with it."

I looked down at her and smiled. "Large, eh?"

"Yes," she replied a little huffily. "You know you are."

With pride, I reached for the appropriate box, flicked it open and pulled out a condom. I had it out of the packet and on my dick within seconds.

I immediately dropped back down over Willow and braced myself on my hands and dropped my head to kiss her. Her hands went to my back, fingertips dug into my muscles, while her legs once more came back around my waist, her heels pushed into my arse and urged me forward.

Our kiss was almost feral as we used lips, tongue, and teeth and I knew that if I didn't get inside her quickly, I'd probably come in the condom without even going near her – at least it was better than my boxers, but I tried to push that memory right to the back of my mind.

I pushed her legs further apart with my knee and then dropped to one forearm, while my other hand still braced against the pillow next to her head. Willow's mouth searched for mine and one of her hands from my back moved to my head, pushing it, as if to eliminate every inch of space between us.

When she thrust her hips forward, I pushed inside her, not able to wait any longer. The feel of her walls wrapped around my cock was insane, it was perfect, and it was mind-blowing. I paused to take in the gorgeous sight below me and then started to pump. I tried to take it slowly and relish the electricity that pulsed through my veins, but it was too good, she *felt* too good and the need to let loose and chase my orgasm was too great.

"Willow," I groaned. "You're so fucking perfect."

Willow wiggled beneath me and then picked the rhythm back up, and pushed as I pulled and pulled as I pushed. Everything around me disappeared and the only thing I could hear and see was the beautiful woman I was inside. She didn't speak though, the only sound she was omitting was her breathing.

All too soon, I felt the heavy pull in the pit of my stomach and as much as I wanted to delay the gratification and to relish in her body for longer, I couldn't.

"*Fuck.*"

I snapped my hips forward twice and I was done. My veins felt like cables carrying electricity around my body and every single part of me became electrified and in danger of combusting.

As my chest heaved with exertion, I flopped onto my back and laid one arm over my eyes while the other flopped onto Willow's bare stomach that was barely even moving. In fact, I couldn't even hear her breathing. Shit, had I killed her with my dick. Johnny had joked about it on that fatal night of the zip incident, but he wouldn't be laughing if I actually had dicked my girlfriend to death.

I sat up sharply and looked down at her, only for my heart to sink. Don't get me wrong, I was glad she wasn't dead, but there was something much worse wrong. She was staring up at the ceiling chewing on her bottom lip and I instinctively knew what had been fucking awesome for me hadn't been the best for her.

"Shit, you didn't come, did you?"

I ran my knuckles down her face and groaned inwardly – she hadn't even broken sweat. My heart stuttered as I thought of how selfish I'd been, but I could put it right, I knew I could.

"Let me sort that out," I said and tried to sound playful.

I got off the bed and pulled a tissue from a box on the dressing table to wrap the condom in and once I'd thrown it into the waste bin, I turned back to Willow. She looked beautiful and desperate to satisfy her, I got back onto the bed. I dropped a kiss on her stomach and let my fingers whisper up the inside of her leg. She shivered beneath my touch which triggered the relief that seeped into my chest. I pushed out my tongue and licked a path up her leg and along her pubic bone and then moved my fingers to her pussy. She was wet, which was a good sign, but as I coated my fingers and then rubbed them around her clit I heard it, the almost imperceptible sound of a sigh and it wasn't one of those 'oh God, that's so good' sighs, it was most definitely an 'I'm not really into this' sigh.

I wasn't the sort of man to give up easily, but I knew that this was one brick wall I'd be banging my head against for a while. Willow's body was stiff, her breathing steadier than that of a corpse, and she was more absent than the sun on a bank holiday in England.

"What's wrong?" I asked and rested my chin on her thigh.

"Nothing, I'm fine."

Shit I was in real trouble if she was *fine*. I sat up and pulled her to join me.

"Willow, you need to tell me. I'm not a mind reader, but even I can see the words 'I'm pissed off' are in your head. So, tell me."

She looked at me with her expressive silver eyes and what I saw made me wish I could take the words 'so tell me' back. She looked fucking sad and empty. If I didn't know better, she looked like she was about to dump my arse. I had to be wrong though, because we'd been good before I'd been inside her. Everything that lead up to the sex had been fun and we'd acted like any normal couple and then-. Shit, that was when it hit me.

She hated the sex.

"Fuck." I closed my eyes and dropped my head back and blew out an exasperated breath.

"Charlie," she whispered and placed a warm hand on my arm. "It's not...I just...I."

"Willow, it's okay," I said as I looked down and gave her a small smile. "I get it. It wasn't good for you and I was only thinking of myself. It was so fucking good and I got carried away."

"And that's fine, honestly. It's not always going to be good is it?"

There was that damn good word again.

"That's the problem though, isn't it Willow," I bit out as I pushed myself off the bed. "It's never been good between us, has it?"

She gasped and shuffled on the bed to face me as I reached down for my boxers.

"The phone sex we had was incredible," she cried and lowered her feet to the floor and pushed her knees together, as if in that moment I'd want to cop a look at her pussy!

My eyes widened and I stopped with my boxers halfway up my thighs.

"The phone sex," I repeated as I pulled my boxers the rest of the way up. "Not the time in the car, not at my house on the sofa?"

"Well, no not really," she replied with surprise. "They were hardly epic, were they? I mean there was a severed head and a broken dick that kind of spoiled things."

Phew, at least she hadn't mentioned the premature ejaculation on our first night. She had a point though, the best sex we'd had was the session when we weren't even in the same fucking house, never mind room.

"And the one time we actually managed to finish without incident,"

I said as I waved a hand at the crumpled duvet, "wasn't any good for you, well go fucking me, what a damn stud."

She quickly pushed off the bed, came to me and wrapped her slim arms around me.

"Charlie don't be like that. You know how sexy I think you are, and how much you turn me on."

"Yeah, I'm not too good at sealing the deal it seems, well not unless I'm about twenty fucking streets away."

I moved away from her and reached for the rest of my clothes and silently pulled them on, full of self-pity. My ego wasn't bruised, it was fucking annihilated and was on the ground sobbing and screaming for life support.

"You know, my dad thinks that maybe you're too stressed about Johnny, you know worrying about him being on his own and you're rushing to-."

"Your dad thinks what?" I roared and took a step backward. "You told your fucking dad?"

Willow's face crumpled into a pained grimace as she made a grab for her top which was hung on the corner of the chest of drawers.

"He kind of guessed," she said almost in a whisper.

"How the hell do you guess that sort of thing, unless someone drops one huge bloody hint?"

"I swear Charlie, it's not like I went to him for help. He asked why you hadn't stayed over when you were supposed to, so I told him about Johnny and he put two and two together. He is a sex therapist; he sees things that someone with an untrained eye wouldn't."

I shook my head in disbelief. "Oh, like the fact that his daughter is walking around totally dissatisfied. What happened, Will, did you have to ask him for more batteries for your vibrator."

She stopped and pulled on her knickers and glared at me. "No and don't be so fucking coarse."

"Really?" I asked incredulously. "That's coarse but your dad walking around stark bollock naked is perfectly normal?"

"I knew it," she spat. "You did lie when you said you were okay with it."

"In what world would anyone not be weirded out about it? Oh yeah I know, a world where a twenty-four-year-old woman tells her dad she's fucking sexually frustrated."

I slipped my t-shirt on, picked up my socks and pulled them on before shoving my feet into my shoes and then made my way toward the door.

"Charlie," she pleaded. "Don't go. I didn't."

I almost turned around but knew if I did her pretty face and those damn plaits would entice me to stay, but I was too angry to deal with the shitfest of my sex life at that point. I felt totally degraded and betrayed by the one person who I was beginning to think I could rely on. The one person who I was beginning to lean on, the person who I knew would always make a shitty day better.

"I'll see you," I managed to say before I opened the door and almost ran down the stairs.

As I got to the bottom, Ivan was walking up the hall from the kitchen.

"Hey Charlie, you're not leaving, are you?"

"Yeah, sorry Mr. Dixon, I need to go."

As I put my hand on the door handle, I heard Willow stomp down the stairs behind me.

"*Charlie.*"

"Are you two still having problems finding alone time," Ivan said. "You know, I can help."

As I flung the door open and pushed through it, the last thing I heard was Willow practically screaming.

"Go to hell, Ivan, you've ruined my life."

Yeah well, she needed to walk a mile in my fucking shoes to know how that felt.

CHAPTER
32

Skip lunch and have a nooner instead. Testosterone levels in adult males rise and fall in 24-hour cycles and tend to peak shortly before midday - if you're both in McDonald's having lunch with the kids, it might be a better idea to wait until you get home.

Charlie

My mood was as fucking black as the devil's heart and I didn't care who knew it, or who I took it out on. I was furious that my girlfriend had blabbed to her dad about our sex life and the fact that I hadn't yet managed to get her off, oh unless it was over the phone. What the hell had possessed her? I was embarrassed enough that I hadn't done my job properly but for her to then let that fucking little nugget slip, well I had to get out of there, and I hadn't spoken to her since.

Okay, so I was being a little bitch about it and ignoring her calls and texts for the last twenty-four hours was pathetic and childish, but I needed to calm down.

I had my pride and a man's sexual prowess was something that the male of the species was extremely protective of. I could have put Willow's lack of orgasm on Sunday down to a one off, I could have put it right, made up for it, but to know that she'd already had concerns made me feel like shit.

I knew sex wasn't everything, but it was a huge fucking chunk of what made a successful relationship, particularly when the relationship was so fresh. We should have been banging each other like rabbits, but instead we'd had a handful of unsuccessful attempts.

"What the fuck is your problem?" Johnny said as he wheeled himself into the kitchen. "You're banging and slamming around in here is louder than a jungle stampede."

I chose not to answer and shoved past him and reached inside a cupboard for a couple of plates.

"So, you're not going to tell me then?"

"Nope."

"I'm guessing it's something to do with Willow by the look on your face since you got home last night."

"Don't want to discuss it and I don't recall suggesting we partake in a game of twenty questions."

"For fuck's sake, are you on your period or something?" Johnny shook his head and took a glass from the draining board and filled it with water from the tap.

"Said I don't want to talk about it."

"Well, whatever you have or haven't done to upset her, you need to fix it. She's too fucking good to let go."

"Who said I've done anything wrong?" I asked as he wheeled himself to the table, waiting for his dinner to be served up.

He looked at me nonplussed. "Because you're a man, and we all know it doesn't matter who starts the fight or whoever is in the wrong, it's always the man who takes the blame and apologises."

"Yeah well," I replied and laughed emptily. "This is most definitely on her."

I knew ultimately it was probably my fault, after all I'd been the one who lacked in the delivery of orgasms, but she should not have, never even considered, telling her damn dad about it.

"You should still apologise."

Johnny took a sip of his water and looked at me expectantly.

"Not happening."

My brother sighed and rolled his eyes. "You apologise for getting mad and not understanding that whatever she did was coming from a good place."

"What if she cheated on me?" I asked as I dished up the curry I'd made.

"No way. I can't see Willow doing that, she's too fucking nice."

He watched me carefully to check if there was any semblance of the truth in my words.

"I knew it," he cried. "No way would she cheat on you, so what's the deal?"

I slammed a plate in front of him and then crossed my arms over my chest. "If I tell you and you even twitch a lip into a smile, I'll tip you out of that chair in the middle of town and leave you there."

"Shit, that bad?" Johnny's eyes were wide in shock as he looked up at me.

"Yeah," I replied with a sigh. "That fucking bad."

***

"Fucking hell," Johnny groaned as I told him everything while we ate our homemade curry.

"I know." I rubbed a hand over my face and let out a strangled groan. "I feel totally humiliated."

Johnny studied me and then pushed his empty plate away. "You want my opinion?"

"Not sure I do, but I know I'm going to get it anyway, so..."

I waved a hand for him to continue.

"I think her dad has a point. I think you need some alone time, so I have a proposition."

"Johnny if this involves you and those twins you know, the answer is, forget it."

His brows knitted together momentarily and then his face broke into a smile of remembrance.

"Oh yeah, those two." He gave a quick shake of the head. "No, it's not about them, it's about you and well, Mum, I suppose."

"How the hell does us talking about Teresa solve my problem? I can't think of anything better to deflate a hard on than talking about her, Willow, and sex in the same sentence. It's fucking horrific to be honest."

Johnny laughed and then screwed up his face. "Yep, gross. No, I was thinking you should maybe take Willow away for the night and I'll get-."

"No, you're supposed to be getting rid of her, not trying to prove her reliability."

"Let's get her to do this one thing and then we'll talk again about asking her to leave. It would mean you can go away for a night and I'll have someone to shout for if I need anything."

"You actually trust her?" I asked, totally perplexed at the idea. "And there's also the fact she's supposed to be looking for somewhere else to live. If she thinks we're trusting her, she'll never look."

There was something about the way Johnny tightened his grip on the arms of his chair, and his gaze turned soft that made my heart sink.

"You've told her she can stay, haven't you?"

Johnny lifted his chin and nodded. "She's our mother, she needs us."

"And what about us fucking needing her, but her never being around. You know when we were little kids and needed food and clothing, oh and heating. Have you forgotten the times we huddled together in that bed with the grimy sheets and duvet because we were so cold? Or what about when she went off on her binges without feeding us and we had to eat dry bread or shitty *Ryvita* because that was all there was?"

"Charlie," he sighed. "It was fucking years ago, so let it drop because it's eating you up inside and it's not healthy. Concentrate on sorting things out with Willow and I'll sort Mum out."

"Yeah but you won't, you'll let her carry on walking all over you, like she always does."

"Yeah well," Johnny said, pushing away from the table. "At least she *can* walk."

"Johnny," I called after him. "Don't do that, don't make a fucking joke about it."

"Jokes are better than reality big brother, and if I can let *that* go, you can let a few fucking crackers and some skanky bedding go. Now get on the damn internet and book a night away for you and Willow, or I will, and you know that whatever I book will be above a nightclub and next door to a brothel."

"I don't know-."

"Just fucking do it, Charlie."

He then disappeared and left me alone to think about his words and to realise there was a lot of truth in what he'd said. I couldn't let everything go with Teresa, but I could put things right with Willow. Yes, I was still angry, but most of that anger was actually pride and if I had only looked past it, I'd have known things hadn't been perfect in the sex department, and should have done something to put it right. I should have realised that having sex with her while her whole family were downstairs wasn't the best way to send her to the fucking stars. It didn't matter how chilled they were about sex as a family, it wasn't the best way to show your new girlfriend a good time. Neither was the back of a damn borrowed car and neither was the sofa of the house I shared with my brother and alcoholic mother. I'd been an idiot and didn't deserve someone as beautiful and as good as Willow.

Mentally kicking myself in the balls, I reached for the laptop and opened it up, determined to find somewhere nice for me to wine and dine my gorgeous girlfriend and hopefully give her the night of her life.

CHAPTER
33

Clenching your buttocks and your upper thigh muscles helps increase the blood flow to your entire pelvic area, creating greater lubrication and sensation. - it's so much cheaper than joining a gym too.

Willow

I walked across the park on the way home from work worried that it had been two days since Charlie had stormed out of my bedroom, out of the house, and seemingly out of my life and I was miserable. I'd left numerous voicemails and sent a similar amount of text messages, but had no response, not even a 'we're over' reply and all I'd been able to do was mope around and play 'The Sound of Bread' on repeat.

I knew I liked him but hadn't realised how much until the prospect of not seeing him again had hit me. We didn't see each other every day, but we did send daily texts or had quick calls during the day, to have no contact at all was akin to my *Netflix* subscription being taken away, only worse.

As for Ivan the Fucking Terrible, I was barely speaking to him, even though he hadn't really done anything wrong. I'd been the one to let it drop to Charlie that the phone sex had been my dad's idea. I should have kept my stupid, big gob shut. The problem was, I agreed with

Ivan, we needed some quality time where Charlie wasn't worrying about his brother or his mother and I wasn't expecting half my family to be waiting outside the door ready with some lame joke or jibe.

Yes, I was worried that it was the time where we were supposed to have the best sex ever and weren't, but it wasn't like Charlie couldn't get me horny, he really could, it was the final outcome that wasn't the best it could be and I truly believed if we had some time alone that would be different. I had to believe that, because I liked him so much and while sex shouldn't be the most important part of a relationship, it *was* important. If things between Charlie and I were going to go further, we really didn't need something that big coming between us.

As I had that thought I started to giggle to myself, because there was no doubt that Charlie was big and I really didn't mind 'that' coming between us. He wasn't so big it was uncomfortable, but big enough that I bet he was never scared to walk naked around the men's changing rooms, even in the middle of winter. He was bigger than any of my past lovers anyway.

I started to giggle again, 'lovers', it made me sound like a middle-aged woman whose husband was too old to service her, so she had secret lovers. Then it struck me that Charlie may now be classed as a past lover and my heart felt heavy.

"Hey."

My head shot up and the heart that had only moments before felt heavy, suddenly sprang to life. Charlie was standing in front of me and was holding a bunch of flowers. Not some huge, over the top bouquet, but the most gorgeous bunch of hand tied wildflowers, the prettiest things I had ever seen.

"Hi," I replied and slammed a hand against my stomach.

"These are for you." He held them out to me and there was a small, shy smile on his face.

"I'm sorry," I blurted out as I took the flowers. "I swear to you, I didn't tell him anything. He was being...well, Ivan the Fucking Terrible. He was doing what he does best, sticking his nose into his kid's business."

Charlie took a deep breath and I thought he might turn around and leave, but he shook his head and took a step closer to me.

"No, I think he was right, and I also think I was being a stupid, pig headed man letting my pride get in the way." He looked down at the floor and rubbed a hand across the back of his neck, looking totally dejected. "So, sorry."

"Charlie, you've nothing to be sorry about," I said and reached out a hand to place on his bicep. "It's only circumstances. We haven't really had anywhere to go to be alone."

He looked up at me and his green eyes flashed with regret. "Yeah, most twenty-five-year-old men have a place of their own, not still sharing with their brother and mother."

"Like I said; circumstances." I moved my hand from his arm to cup the side of his face. "And most twenty-four-year-old women don't have four idiot brothers and two interfering parents, but I do, so I think I've said this before, we're pretty suited."

Now he smiled at me. It was small and barely moved his lips, but it was definitely a smile. "I want to ask you something actually," he said.

"Okay."

I dropped my hand, but as soon as I did, Charlie took it in his and linked our fingers together. "I was wondering if you'd like to come away with me on Saturday night."

He chewed on his lip, looking nervous, but I had no idea why because there was no question of what my answer would be.

"Oh my God. That would be brilliant. Where to?"

"Really?" he asked. "You want to go?"

"Yes of course I do. Why wouldn't I?"

"Because I was a dick and stormed out on you and have ignored you for two days." he laughed and shook his head. "Like I said, I was a dick."

"I thought you'd dumped me," I confessed with a rush of breath. "I was considering coming around to your house and camping on the doorstep until you'd see me."

As though a tonne weight had been removed from him, Charlie's shoulders relaxed, and he blew out his cheeks.

"No way, I was angry I'll admit, but I never even thought about dumping you." He pulled me closer, squashing the flowers between us as he wound his arms around my waist. "I missed you so fucking much."

"Me too," I whispered as I stood on my tiptoe to drop a kiss to his lips. "Don't ever ignore me again if you're mad at me, talk to me and tell me how angry you are."

Charlie nodded and rested his forehead against mine. "I will, I promise."

"So, where are we going?" I asked excitedly at the thought of a whole night away without any interruptions.

"Nothing fancy," he said as he squeezed my waist. "It was a little short notice, but I got a really nice hotel just outside of Manchester and thought we could go and have a few cocktails in the evening before..."

His voice trailed off and I giggled.

"Before the main event?" I asked.

A deep groan came from the back of his throat and I felt his body stiffen. "Got to say, Will, I'm a bit nervous about that. Last time wasn't my greatest moment was it?"

I felt awful and wished I hadn't made a joke about it, but I didn't want it to become a huge issue between us.

"Charlie," I whispered. "You have to know how sexy you are, and how much you turn me on."

He shrugged but didn't speak.

"Seriously, you do," I urged. "And I know it'll be great; we'll be alone and no chance of being interrupted." Then a thought struck me. "What about Johnny, are you okay leaving him?"

Charlie rolled his eyes. "Yeah, well that's another story."

"You sure you're okay about this?" I asked. "Because we don't have to go away."

He shook his head. "No, I want to take my girlfriend to a nice hotel for the night. I want my full attention to be on her alone, and I want to prove to her that I can make her come when I'm in the same room."

His grin was cheeky and sexy and when he pulled me closer to kiss me, which pretty much decimated my flowers, I had no doubt that he was right.

CHAPTER 34

To prevent yourself gagging while giving him a blow job, hold the base of his penis as you suck. That way you control how deep he goes. - unless of course, your gag reflex muscle is right next to your stomach like a horse.

Charlie

As we drove up the pebbled drive of the hotel, I couldn't help but feel nervous. Two reasons; one, I hoped that it was as good as it looked on the website and two, well I hoped that I actually managed to give my girlfriend an orgasm after the last fail.

"Oh God, Charlie," Willow squealed and bounced in her seat. "It's gorgeous."

She turned to me and grabbed my knee to give it a squeeze.

"I wanted to take you somewhere nice."

"Well this is more than nice," she gasped. "It's gorgeous."

As I pulled into a parking space, I looked up at the beautiful white, double-fronted, Georgian hotel. A few steps led up to the duck egg blue front door and either side of that were flower beds, filled with wild-flowers sweeping down to the sides of the steps, before flowing down to the bright green lawn in front of it. I don't think I'd stayed anywhere as nice; certainly not as a kid. The only time we'd ever gone on holiday had been two nights in a leaky caravan in Wales, and that was only because Teresa had hooked up with some bloke who worked the funfairs and he'd moved on from our home town at the end of a rainy bank holiday weekend. Johnny and I had shared the small bedroom but had heard everything Teresa and her new boyfriend had got up to each night. Thankfully, he'd caught her nicking money from under his mattress, so after two days we were on our way back home.

"Thank you, so much." Willow leaned across to kiss my cheek and her hand gave my leg another squeeze.

"My pleasure," I replied and totally meant it. It really was a pleasure to make this girl smile. She was beautiful anyway, but when she smiled, fuck, the whole room lit up and if I was told I'd lose my sight, my biggest regret would be not being able to see that sunshine ever again.

I unbuckled my seatbelt and then opened the door and looked over my shoulder at Willow whose gaze was still on the hotel.

"You ready to see if it's as good inside?" I asked.

As she clapped and bounced in her seat, I guessed that she was.

***

"Oh Charlie," Willow gasped as she grabbed my hand. "It's beyond beautiful. How comfy does that sofa look?"

I looked over at the huge pale green sofa which hugged the wall under a row of three windows and nodded, although I had to be honest, my main thought was Willow bent over it.

"Sir, can I help you?"

The man dressed in a black suit and pinstriped waistcoat gave us a broad, genuine smile.

"Yes please, I have a room booked for the name Monroe."

As the man, whose name badge said he was called Geoff, looked at the computer, Willow sidled up beside me and linked her fingers with mine.

"Do we have to pretend we're married?" she whispered.

I felt her shoulders shake as she laughed, so I tugged on her hand.

I bent a little to be level with her ear. "Yeah," I whispered. "They think it's our honeymoon so know not to disturb us, even if the place is on fire."

This time her shoulders shuddered, and I heard a little moan and was hopeful the night was going to go well.

"I'm so sorry," Geoff said and gave us an apologetic smile. "Your room isn't quite ready, so could I offer you a drink with our compliments from the bar?"

"Yes, that's fine," I agreed and looked down at Willow. "You happy with that?"

She nodded enthusiastically.

"Excellent. Leave your bags here and I'll get Brian to take them up for you and if you go through there," Geoff pointed to some double doors at the end of the reception area, "Bev will serve you."

I was able to give Geoff a quick thank you before Willow tugged me toward the bar.

"I feel decadent," she said. "I'm going to have a cocktail."

"Okay, I may join you. What're you going to have?"

Willow pushed open the door and paused as she looked up at me with narrowed eyes. "Hmm, maybe a Rude Boy."

"Remind me what a Rude Boy is again?"

"Rum, Irish Stout, coffee, and nutmeg." She grinned and rubbed her stomach. "Gorgeous."

"Oh yeah, the one that sounds like a dessert and by the look of her," I said and nodded toward the lady who I assumed was Bev. "I'm not sure she'll have the ability."

Willow followed my gaze and snorted out a laugh. A small, round woman with her chin in her hands leaned against the bar and she looked as though she'd just been told she had to go on a ten-mile hike, in high heels. Her face was crumpled and sad and I would bet that if she had a dog it was a bulldog.

"Oh my God," Willow whispered. "She looks like she might cry."

I shrugged and led her to the bar. "Hi," I said brightly. "Our room isn't ready, so Geoff suggested we come and get a drink."

Bev slowly lifted her head and looked me up and down, finally stopped at my eyes and she let out a long sigh of what sounded like desperation.

"What do you want?" she asked a little begrudgingly.

"I'll have a pint of lager and my girlfriend would like a cocktail please."

She sighed again. "Which lager?"

I looked at the pumps and pointed. "*Peroni*, please."

"*Peroni's* off."

"Oh, okay." I looked again. "*Bud*, then."

"*Bud's* off as well."

I heard Willow snort beside me and nudged her with my elbow and then smiled at Bev. "*Carling?*"

"That's off too," she said morosely as she scratched her head.

I took a deep breath and forced out another smile, this one though wasn't nearly as wide.

"Maybe if you told me what's on?"

Willow cleared her throat and I knew by the way her shoulders shook that she was about to burst out into laughter.

"We've got *Peroni* and *Bud* in bottles," Bev replied.

Not able to hold it in any longer, Willow snorted and buried her face in the back of my arm, her whole body shook.

"I'll have a *Peroni* then, please," I ground out.

Bev sighed again and turned to look in the fridge. It was then that I noticed her black cardigan was on inside out but chose not to bring it to Willow's attention that Bev was evidently a size eighteen and shopped at M&S, according to her label.

"I'll have to go down to the cellar," she grumbled and slammed the fridge door closed. "I won't be long."

I felt Willow peek out from behind me and watch as our friendly barmaid shuffled from behind the bar in her sensible shoes with her podgy feet spilled out over the top.

"Shit," Willow hissed. "She's hilarious. Why didn't she tell you they'd only got bottles?"

"I've no idea, but I think I was right about you not getting your Rude Boy."

"Oh no," she replied and shook her head while she looked at me with wide, excited eyes. "I'm asking for it. I want to see how she copes."

"You're mean," I laughed and pulled her to me to kiss her forehead. "She might just break down at the thought."

"I could offer to give her a lesson on how to make it, I suppose."

I wrapped my arms around her shoulders and pulled her to my chest. "You never did tell me the story of how you know about them."

"It's not that interesting really. Polly and I were on holiday in Jamaica and it rained for three days so Tigger, the barman, showed us. By the end of the second day we were recreating scenes from Tom Cruise's film, Cocktail. The hotel manager almost threw us out though because we'd smashed so many bottles of spirits, but Tigger covered for us and said there'd been a mini earthquake and couldn't understand how no one else had felt it. He was brilliant and I've never tasted any as good as his. He made the best I've ever tasted, and I've had a mixologist in London make me one."

"What the fuck's a mixologist?"

"What a posh cocktail maker likes to be called."

"I have a better name for them," I offered.

"What?" Willow's chin rested on my chest as she grinned up at me, as if she already knew my answer.

"Twat."

We both started to laugh and were only alerted to Bev's return by the noise of a bottle being slammed onto the bar.

"A bottle of *Bud*," she announced.

There was indeed one bottle on the bar, only the one as well. I looked to see if she'd bought any more up with her, but it appeared that we would only get the one drink.

"What else?" she asked as her voice cracked as if I'd given her some bad news.

"A cocktail?" My response was a question because for all Willow wanted to see what Bev was made of, I wasn't sure I wanted to have to deal with her if she broke down.

She pushed a small menu toward me. "They're on there."

I passed it to Willow and leaned in to whisper in her ear. "I don't think the Rude Boy is a good idea, babe. I think she might cry."

As Bev whimpered, Willow gasped and nodded.

"Ooh what do you recommend?" she asked Bev, brightly.

"What?" Bev screwed up her eyes and tilted her head to one side as she examined Willow.

"Which cocktail do you recommend?" Willow almost sounded like she was cajoling an errant child and it was my turn to swallow back a laugh.

Bev shrugged. "No idea, I only drink bitter."

Unable to hold back my laughter, I started to fake a cough as I tried to disguise it.

Willow took a step forward and rested her forearms on the bar, studied the cocktail menu again. Evidently tired of the wait, Bev turned around and started to shift some bottles around. I wondered if she'd decided on a cocktail and gathered the ingredients together, but she produced a duster from her skirt pocket and started to rub it over them and the shelf. I nudged Willow who shrugged and mouthed, 'What shall I have?'

I decided to take matters into my own hands. "Which cocktail can you make best, Bev?"

She turned slowly, cloth in hand and stared me up and down.

"What?"

"Which cocktail can you make best?" I repeated as I tried not to lose the fake smile from my face.

With another sigh from her repertoire, she threw the duster onto the bar and moved closer, leaning into Willow and me.

"Rum and coke, vodka and coke or gin and tonic," she hissed.

Willow side-eyed me and took a step back.

"I'll have a vodka and coke then please," she replied, a little tentatively.

"We're out of vodka."

"Oh my God," Willow cried as she wiped the tears at her eyes. "I thought she was going to knife me when I asked for diet coke."

We were at dinner and laughing about our run in with Bev the Barmaid earlier and how we'd never been so scared to ask for a drink before. As we thought, we'd only had one drink, but by the time we'd finished our first one the room was ready and Geoff told us we had thirty minutes until dinner was served. That put paid to my idea of me giving Willow a much-deserved orgasm, considering we'd been advised we had to be prompt as Chef liked to serve everyone early and at the same time because he liked to leave for home before it got too dark. It was at that point I realised why the price for such a beautiful hotel had been very reasonable – it was shit. I had apologised profusely to Willow the whole time we freshened up, but she'd waved my worries away, as she convinced me it all added to it and Bev had been hilarious so an early dinner meant we could spend more time in the bar with her. It meant more time to ensure that I gave her a good time in the bedroom, which had to be said was gorgeous and luxurious. Thick, plush curtains at the windows, a huge comfy bed that was so soft you were almost enveloped by it, and the best hotel bathroom I'd ever seen with a large, claw foot tub by the window that overlooked the fields which surrounded the hotel and a double headed shower big enough for both of us; something I planned on taking advantage of later.

To be fair, the food had been delicious so far, both of us had crab cakes to start and opted for lamb in a red wine juice for our main course. It was actually called a jus on the menu, but to me it was fucking juice or gravy – who thought these twatty names up anyway?

"Apart from Brutal Bev, are you enjoying yourself?" I asked.

"I really am," she replied as her eyes softened when she looked at me over the top of the candle. "Thank you so much, Charlie."

"Told you, it's my pleasure." I cleared my throat and put down my cutlery. "I am sorry I was such a dick the other day, Will. I just..."

"It's forgotten about." She leaned across the table and took my hand in hers. "I'm sorry too that my dad felt the need to interfere."

I shook my head. "He wasn't interfering, he was simply doing his job."

Willow rolled her eyes. "Whatever, I really don't want him to 'do his job', with us ever again." She gasped and her mouth dropped into a perfect 'O'. "Not that he'll need to, it was a one off, I know it was."

I laughed quietly. "I think we need to forget about the other night, start afresh and both of us stop worrying about what might happen."

"You're worried?" Willow frowned and shifted forward in her seat.

"A little bit," I admitted.

"Well don't." Her mouth drew into a thin line of consternation. "Now, let's enjoy our dinner and think about what exotic cocktails we can ask Bev to make later."

As I watched her continue to eat and give little moans of appreciation, I felt my heart stutter and my stomach do a somersault. She was so fucking beautiful and if I didn't cock things up, I knew we could have something great long-term. I wanted something that would last with her because she was everything that I'd ever imagined my ideal woman to be. The feelings I had for her had come hard and fast; more each day. It was becoming more and more difficult to imagine a life without her in it.

"Will," I whispered to gain her attention.

"Hmm," she replied and glanced up at me with a mouthful of food.

"I want you to know how much I like you. You make me so damn happy and I can't believe that I actually met someone like you, someone who makes me smile every day. I don't think I ever believed in fate before, but how can I not when an unplanned night out gave me you."

Willow's eyes shone; her features soft as she gazed at me. She was silent for the longest time and I was beginning to wonder whether I'd said the wrong thing, whether it was too much too soon, even though there was so much more I could have said.

"If I've said the wrong thing-."

"No, you haven't," she breathed out. "And I think I've eaten enough. I'm ready for bed now."

She pushed her plate away, threw down her napkin and pushed her chair back. "You ready?"

I nodded and as the adrenalin started to pump through my veins, I swallowed the last of my wine and followed her out of the restaurant

CHAPTER
35

It might not sound romantic, but plan for sex. It can be a useful tip if you're always busy and builds up the anticipation knowing what is to come – perhaps you shouldn't put it in your work diary though, we all have one of those nosey colleagues who likes to check what you're doing at the weekend.

Willow

As I left the dining room in a rush, I could feel the heat from Charlie at my back. His hand lay lightly on my bum as he gently guided me through the tables.

"Was your dinner okay, sir, madam?" The head waiter hovered by the doorway, craning to look at our table where our unfinished meals were.

"It was lovely," Charlie replied. "Willow has a headache coming on."

"I bloody hope not," I muttered and felt a nudge in the back from Charlie.

"Oh no, if there is anything at all we can get you, I can send it up to the room."

"No, it's fine, I think I can sort her out."

I bit down on my bottom lip to stop me laughing out loud and tried to morph my face into one that looked as if I might have a headache.

"Well, I hope you feel better in the morning."

"Oh, she will," Charlie promised, and I totally believed him.

This was going to be it, this was going to be the best sex of my life, I knew it. Charlie was going to show me what a stud he actually was by giving me numerous orgasms, all of which would actually shake the bones in my body.

As we reached the lifts, Charlie pulled me into his arms and began kissing me. One of his arms held me close to his body, while the other reached out to punch at the button to call the lift.

"I'm going to make this so fucking good for you," he said against my mouth. "You're going to come screaming my name and the whole of this damn hotel is going to know that you belong to me."

OH. MY. GOD.

I think I came there and then.

Charlie's kiss deepened as his hand slipped to my bum and gave it the most wonderful squeeze that sent an electric shock from my buttock straight to my vajajay.

At the point where I considered climbing him, the lift arrived, and we pulled apart to see two older ladies get out. They looked Charlie over appreciatively and then both gave me a huge smile. I couldn't help but grin back, give them a thumbs up and mouth silently, 'I know'. As he chuckled himself, Charlie pulled me into the lift and immediately pushed me against the wall where he continued his onslaught of my mouth.

The way he kissed slowly up my neck and along my jawline told me that tonight he was definitely going to take his time with me and deliver everything that his touch and kisses promised. Thankfully, even though we were on the top floor, it was only three flights up, so pretty quickly the lift juddered to a halt and the door slid open.

"I can't wait to get you into that bed," he groaned as he gave me a quick kiss to the lips before we walked out of the lift. "I'm going to fucking worship you, exactly how you should be worshiped; very slowly and for a very long time."

I let out a little moan and started to drag him down the corridor toward our room. Charlie already had the keycard in his hand and was about to flash it when his phone started to shrill in his pocket. It wasn't his usual ring tone, but something that sounded like a brass band playing.

He paused, his hand midair and I could see he was holding his breath. It stopped ringing and I thought he'd let out a sigh of relief, but he didn't, he stayed stock still, waiting. Right on cue it rang again and stopped and then started again. On the third ring, Charlie cursed and pulled it from his pocket.

"Yeah, it's Charlie...fuck...when...okay, thanks Vera...where is he... okay, I'll go straight there...thanks again."

He stabbed at his phone to end the call and banged his forehead against it three times, each one followed by a 'fuck'.

"Charlie, what's wrong? Who was that?"

He let out a deep sigh and turned to me, disappointment, regret, and anger all painted across his beautiful features. He lifted a hand and cupped my cheek before he let it snake around to the back of my head and laced his fingers in my hair.

"I'm so fucking sorry," he groaned as he pulled me into his chest. "We have to go home."

I pulled back to look up at him as fear made my stomach roll over. "Why, what's happened?"

"That was our neighbour, Vera. She knows to call me if there are any problems and I know it's urgent if she calls three times, it's something we came up with so that Johnny doesn't feel as though he's being checked up on."

Shit, that explained why he waited.

"So, what is it?" I reached up and held his face in both my hands to force his gaze on me. "It's okay, we'll sort it, what's happened?"

"Johnny, he wanted to give Teresa a fucking chance and I told him she'd cock up, but he wouldn't have it, he said she'd be fine. I fucking hate her, Will. She ruins everything and now she's put him in danger again, *isn't it enough he's fucking crippled because of her?*"

His chest heaved with the exertion of his emotion and his eyes were dark and angry as his hold on me tightened.

"Oh my God, what is it, what's she done?"

"She fell asleep with a lit cigarette dangling from her fingers and set fire to her coat which was on the floor, it caught the armchair she was in."

I felt the colour drain from my face as I pulled the key from Charlie's hand. "Is she okay?" I asked as I let us into the room.

"Don't care." Charlie's tone was harsh and when he moved alongside me and picked his bag up, I could see how his complexion had turned red with rage. He slammed his bag onto the bed and then moved toward the wardrobe where we'd hung the few clothes, we'd brought with us. "She can be a shrivelled up piece of charcoaled flesh for all I care."

"Charlie!"

"No Will, she promised she would take care of him. One fucking night was all I asked for."

"And Johnny, he's okay?"

Charlie sighed and I heard a thump so turned around from packing everything from the dressing table to see him resting his head on the mahogany door of the wardrobe.

"Charlie, he is okay, isn't he?"

"Yeah, he's fine. He put the fire out with the extinguisher we have in the hall, but because of him being disabled our fire alarm is rigged up to the fire station, so they ended up coming out, which is how Vera found out. Apparently, the fire brigade doesn't think he should be sleeping there with the stench of smoke, but he's insisted. He told Vera not to call me but as Teresa decided she did want an overnight stay in hospital, he's on his own and Vera doesn't think he should stay there with the smell either."

"So, he doesn't know we're going back?" I asked as I moved to him and placed a hand on his back.

Charlie looked over his shoulder at me and gave me a sad smile. "Nope, but I can't leave him, Willow."

"God no, and I wouldn't expect you to. We'll go back and get you both sorted. You can stay at ours if you like. Mum can make a bed up for Johnny in the den."

Charlie didn't answer but nodded and went back to taking his clothes from their hangers.

We had been in the Vauxhall Combo for almost twenty minutes and Charlie hadn't said a word. In fact, the only thing he had said since we'd left our room was a quick thank you to Brian who took our bags out to the car. The atmosphere was cold and icy, not something I was used to with him. I got that he was angry with Teresa, but it wasn't doing him any good building up such vitriolic hatred inside him. It wasn't that I hadn't tried to make conversation, I had, but had received one word answers each time.

"Can I put some music on?" I asked because I hated the silence more and more with each minute that passed.

"Yeah, sure." He nodded toward his phone on the centre console and then pressed the media button on the audio system.

As I picked up his phone, I glanced at him from the corner of my eye, but his jaw was still rigid, and his knuckles were still white from gripping the steering wheel. I decided not to attempt any further conversation and went to his music app and scrolled through. When I came across a playlist called 'Willow', I couldn't help but smile. I turned the screen toward him and was about to make a comment about it, but he let out a long sigh and then blasted his horn at a car which had pulled in front of us.

Instead, my eyes went back to his phone and I opened up the playlist to see what was on it and I wanted to kiss him when I saw that it was all seventies music; cheesy seventies music at that. They weren't all from the same year either, or the same album, so the fact that he'd taken the time to find the songs and put them all together, for me, gave me huge butterflies in my stomach.

Once I pressed the buttons, I sat back and waited for the first song to sound out and hoped that when he realised what I'd picked to play, Charlie would realise how much I appreciated it and him.

When Andrew Gold's 'Never Let Her Slip Away' started, I couldn't help but hope that each song, although cheesy, actually meant something to him. That they somehow reminded him of me.

I sang along to each song and did it at the top of my voice. Not in an attempt to get a response from him, but because each song he'd picked brought me joy and was one of my favourites. At one point I caught Charlie watching me, but he didn't laugh or smile. He wasn't angry either, he simply looked sad.

As we drove into Rickeby, I realised that we were going to my house, yet I knew Charlie was desperate to get home to Johnny.

"Are we not going to yours first?" I asked as I did a half-turn in my seat.

"No, I'm taking you home."

"But I thought you and Johnny were going to stay, are you going to get him after you've dropped me off, because you don't have to."

He didn't speak but drew in a deep breath and suddenly I felt sick, because he was getting prepared to say something. He was going to tell me something that I wouldn't like. I knew it deep in my bones, every nerve in my body knew it and more importantly my heart knew it.

My pulse sped up and my hands began to shake as the car rolled up to the pavement outside my parents' house and Charlie turned off the ignition.

"Don't say it, Charlie," I whispered, not sure whether it was to myself or to him.

"Will," he whispered and my name almost sounded like a plea.

"No," I said as I shook my head. "You're not saying it. I'm getting out of the car; you're going to go home, get Johnny and come back here, where my mum will treat you like a pair of her long-lost sons. That's what's going to happen."

I unbuckled my seatbelt and moved to open the door.

"This isn't fair on you." He reached for me and grabbed my hand.

"I tell you what wouldn't be fair on me, Charlie, is if you finished this because you have some stupid idea that I'm pissed off that we've had to come home, or that you have to put your brother first, because neither of those things are true. And, if you actually think they are, then you have a really low opinion of me."

"I don't think those things, which is why we have to stop seeing each other. You're so great about all my fucking shit and it's not going to get any easier, and I can't do that to you."

As I watched his lips move, my hands started to shake, and my stomach twisted as I felt nausea rise with each of his words.

"I like you too much Willow to have half a fucking relationship with you because I have a drunk as a mother and a brother who needs me."

"It wouldn't be half a relationship, because I'd support you every step of the way. What we have is great and I know it's going to keep getting better and better, and I don't care if you can't always give me one hundred percent, because I like you a lot, so much, that would be enough for me."

Charlie shook his head and kissed the back of my hand. "No Willow, that would never be good enough for you, not as far as I'm concerned. You deserve to be given everything, the whole fucking world and I can't give that to you. I hate it and hate myself a little bit more each time I have to let you down."

"It's been a couple of times," I scoffed. "Hardly major is it."

"A couple of times and we're only just starting out, what happens when it's a couple of times a week and we're *six months* down the line and you hate me for it too. I can't-."

"I won't, I would never hate you for taking care of your brother."

Charlie's face looked pained as he placed my hand back on my knee, pulled his away, and sat back in his seat.

"You would," he said quietly. "And I don't think I'd be able to take that, it's bad enough having to end this now, so one, two, six more months, it'd be hell."

"Charlie, please don't," I begged and tugged at the tight bun in my hair, pulling some of it loose. "Sleep on it and if you feel the same tomorrow…"

I knew I sounded pathetic as I pleaded like an idiot, but I also knew deep within me and deep within him, he didn't really want to do this. Everything had been perfect at the hotel until his neighbour had called. He kissed me so deeply I could feel it in my soul, he'd told me that he was going to worship me slowly. There was no way that this had been his plan.

"Nothing will change, Will. I'm sorry, but I want you to be happy and being with me and dealing with my baggage won't let that happen."

I really didn't want to cry, I tried so hard to suck the tears back in, but when I felt them slowly creeping down my cheeks there wasn't a damn thing that I could do about it.

"I will never, ever forget you." he whispered and leaned across to kiss me gently on the lips.

As he went to move away, I grabbed his face and kissed him hard, not wanting to let him go or feel his lips on me for a last time.

"I hate your mother," I said against his mouth as salty tears dropped to my lips. "And so you know, you're making the biggest mistake of your life."

He gave a low laugh and stroked his knuckles down my cheek. "Oh God, I know that, I promise you." He kissed me again, this time it was a little harder but just as short. "Take care, Will."

Charlie then pulled back and cleared his throat as he turned his gaze to the road ahead. I reached over to the back seat and grabbed my overnight bag as I thought of the new underwear I'd bought and not used, and as The Bay City Rollers sang Bye Bye Baby, I got out of the car and closed the door quietly behind me as I stood with my back to it until I heard it pull away.

CHAPTER 36

Don't be afraid to be vocal during sex. Men love nothing more than to hear that their partner is enjoying themselves – you should keep it quiet however, if you're on the sofa and the kids are watching Peppa Pig.

Charlie

When I pulled up on the driveway of the house, I felt as though my lungs were far too big for my chest. The tightness was uncomfortable, and I felt like I needed to puke. I'd let the best thing to ever happen to me go. I'd told her we couldn't be together and yet she was the one who I'd started to need to keep me sane with my fucked-up mother issues.

I dropped my head to the steering wheel and took a deep breath and let it out slowly through my nose. My pulse raced and fought with the anger which built up inside me. If I didn't get them both under control, I knew as soon as I went inside the house, I'd take it out on Johnny, and this wasn't his fault. No, the fault all lay at Teresa's feet. I'd lost the one girl I thought I could build something with because she, my mother, was a waste of space drunk who thought of no one but herself.

My throat felt raw at fighting back the emotion, my head was pounding and all I wanted to do was get into bed and disappear under the covers until my chest didn't hurt so much, but I needed to see how much damage she'd caused. I needed to check that my brother was okay.

I pulled my bag from the back seat and then locked up the car, before I slowly trailed up to the front door and pushed my key into the lock. As soon as I went inside the clawing smell of smoke hit me and yet Vera had said it had only been a small fire. Even so, I was sure that there was some cleaning up to be done.

When I pushed open the door, I was surprised to see Teresa on her hands and knees cleaning up the mess as Johnny watched over her, his arms crossed firmly over his chest, his mouth turned down into a grimace.

"I should be in the hospital," Teresa croaked.

"Yeah well they checked you out and said you were fine, so hard luck."

She gave an affected cough, but Johnny didn't flinch. I, on the other hand, felt my resentment at her rise another notch.

"Well you really fucked up this time, didn't you?"

Johnny and Teresa both turned their heads to face me and as soon as his gaze landed on mine, my brother let out an exasperated sigh.

"Who told you?"

"Vera." I dropped my bag on the floor and took a couple of steps forward to get a better look at the destruction Teresa had caused.

"She had no right," Johnny groaned. "It's all fine, so get back in the car and back to the hotel." He moved his body to look behind me. "Where's Willow?"

The pain spiked in my chest again as I thought about how I'd left Willow outside her house.

"We're finished." I wasn't sure how I managed to get the words out as my mouth was dry and my tongue felt thicker than usual.

"Fuck off," Johnny cried. "She didn't finish with you because you had to come home – which you didn't have to do, by the way."

I shook my head and looked down at Teresa who was still on her knees, dull eyes stared at me with nothing behind them, nothing to say and no feelings.

"I ended it, thought it was better for her, considering I can't be relied upon."

"Don't be such a fucking idiot," Johnny cried as he threw his arms up into the air. "From what I know of her she wouldn't care that you feel as though you have responsibilities, which you fucking don't. I'm fine, I told you I'll get a carer."

"I've told him too," Teresa said, her eyes still on me. "He treats you like a kid."

"Oh yeah, 'cause that would suit you fine, wouldn't it," I scoffed. "If I didn't care about Johnny then I wouldn't give a shit that you don't give a shit. That'd let you off the hook wouldn't it. Leave you free to carry on drinking yourself to death and making a show of yourself in town. Well hard luck, Teresa," I snapped. "I do fucking care. He's my brother and I love him, more than I can say for you."

"I love him," she said and struggled to her feet.

"I meant it's more than I can say for the feelings I have *for* you."

"Charlie!"

"No Johnny. It's about time she realised that I have zero feelings about her, and if it wasn't for the fact that you were in this house at the time, I wouldn't have been bothered if it had burned to the ground."

As Teresa stood fully, I took another step closer to her. My heart pounded in time with my head, the emotion I was desperate to hold back brimmed at the precipice and about to overflow to mix with the anger.

"Charlie, you don't mean that." Johnny reached a hand up and placed it on my arm which was hanging by my side.

I swallowed hard and shook my head. "I've never meant something more in my whole life. I hate you for every time we were hungry as kids, for each moment that we were scared shitless hiding in our bedroom because of some of the pieces of shit you brought back to the house. I hate you for always putting yourself and booze before us and I hate you for what you let happen to my brother. My brother who I should have been there to protect." My voice broke and the tears I had tried so hard to stem began to slowly crawl down my cheeks. "He's my little brother and because of you and how you are, I didn't answer your call but instead he went and -."

"Charlie, no," Johnny said, his voice scratchy as he grabbed my wrist. "Enough. This won't change anything, and you are not to fucking blame."

"No, she is," I said, my cry engulfed with a sigh as my shaky finger pointed at Teresa. "She's to blame for me not being there, but I'm also at fault for not being a better person and going to her."

My chest heaved as the tears flowed and when Johnny wrapped his arms around my waist, I practically collapsed against him. Both of us sobbed as we let out all the hurt and pain that we'd felt almost from the minute we'd been born to a woman who didn't deserve to be called a mother.

"I tried to be a good parent," Teresa said, which caused me to pull abruptly away from Johnny.

I sniffed and shook my head before I let out an empty laugh. "Sorry, I'm sure I heard you say you tried to be a good parent."

"I did, but you both were so headstrong, little brats, the pair of you. You have no idea what it's like being a single mother."

Johnny gave a low growl. "You drove dad away with your drinking, and you were only on your own with Charlie for a year or so, and then you had Grandma to help you, but you fucked that relationship up as well."

Teresa floundered as she looked between me and Johnny, while her hands rubbed up and down her arms.

"Yeah, exactly." He looked down at the remnants of her coat on the scorched floor and the armchair where the leather was melted, and he sighed. "You know, this place is the nicest home we've ever had and we have it because Charlie and I work hard to make it that way, and because you let your latest hook up push me over a fucking balcony, yet you think you're entitled to be here because you gave birth to us-."

"I didn't let him," Teresa cried, her eyes going wide.

Johnny took a deep breath. "He had me pinned against the balcony and threatened to push me over unless you gave him back the money and the watch that you'd stolen from next to his bed."

My stomach felt like it dropped a hundred miles as I looked at Johnny and then Teresa.

"W-what?" I stammered as I felt bile rise in my throat.

Johnny turned to me with resignation in his eyes. "She'd taken some stuff from him and he wanted it back. Even though he had me pinned against the balcony and he was as high as a fucking kite, she still denied she'd taken it, but," he said and turned to Teresa, "I knew she had it. I could see it in her eyes. I begged her, fucking *begged* her to give it back, but she kept denying it. He gave her one last chance, pushing me backwards and holding onto my t-shirt but when she denied it again, he pushed me over."

My legs almost buckled as the words my brother had said sunk into my brain. She'd stood by and let some psycho hurt one of her kids, all for some cash and a watch. The idea of it was like a punch to the stomach, I had to bend over and rest my hands on my knees as I gulped in air.

"It wasn't that simple," Teresa said tentatively. "I-I-."

"Shut the fuck up and get out," I screamed, still bent over. "Get your fucking stuff and get out of this house in five minutes or I'll fucking throw you out and burn your crap."

I pulled myself up to face her and wondered if there might be some remorse in her eyes but all I could see was fear – fear of how she was going to manage without me or Johnny to sponge from.

"You've got five minutes, Teresa," I warned.

"Johnny?"

"No, Teresa. I'm done with you. You could have killed me last night, and you've made our lives hell for years. Enough is enough. Like Charlie said, you have five minutes."

We both stared her down until eventually she moved past us and nudged me with her shoulder as she did.

"Why didn't you tell me?" I whispered.

Johnny shrugged. "I knew you'd go mad and kick her out and I kind of needed her."

My chest tingled and my mouth slackened as I stared at him.

"She was my mum, and she may have been a shit one and she may have been partly to blame, but I was scared, Charlie. I was fucking petrified and, like a big kid, I needed my mum."

I rested a hand on his head and pulled him against my stomach as I wished with everything I had, I could turn back time and take that damn call.

"I'm so sorry bro," Johnny said as he pulled his head back to look up at me.

I let him go and sat down on the sofa so that we were at eye level.

"You have nothing to be sorry for. I'm sorry I didn't pick up her call that night. I'm sorry I didn't have the bravery to tell a teacher when we were kids, or beg Grandma to take us in. I'm sorry for so fucking much, Johnny."

"You were a kid too; it wasn't on you to make sure we were safe."

I didn't answer, because I had no words to give him. I knew how I felt about it and it was and would always tear me up inside.

After a few seconds of silence, Johnny grabbed my arm. "You can't end things with Willow. Don't let Teresa spoil that for you too."

I shook my head. "Whether you like it or not, you're my priority and this with Teresa won't end here. She won't give up so easily and I can't expect Willow to have to go through all that."

"Why? She's your girlfriend, who I'm pretty sure is mad about you, so of course she would."

I let out a sigh. "I know she would, without any complaint, but she deserves more than that. I don't know, maybe in a couple of months when we know Teresa is definitely out of our lives, maybe then I'll see if she'd like to meet up again."

I said the words, but I didn't believe them. I knew in a couple of months Willow would be with someone else. A woman like her wouldn't stay single for long. I only hoped whomever she was with made her happy and got to see that smile that lit up the whole fucking world.

CHAPTER
37

Studies show only 30% of women orgasm during intercourse because women really need stimulation to the clitoris. The best touch being one that moves around it. – it's time to tell your partner to stop pressing it like a doorbell or you'll never get off.

Willow

"Come on," Polly cajoled. "It'll be fun."

It was her attempt to get me to go out into town with her and have a few drinks. It was Saturday night after all and a bank holiday weekend, so who knew what fun and japes were to be had.

"No, I've told you three times so fuck off."

"Well, you're a positive ray of sunshine, aren't you?" Polly sighed and snatched a magazine up from the floor next to the sofa where I'd been lying for almost a week, when I wasn't at work of course. As for work, well James was pissed off with me too and by Wednesday had asked Zoe to be his nurse and had pushed me out to do a stock take and a deep clean of some of the equipment – so he was a tosser as well.

"Did you know," Polly said as she peered over the top of the magazine, "that forty percent of men are turned on by the natural smell of your nether regions? Ugh." She pulled a face. "I know a girl at work who only showers once a week, can you imagine the natural smell of her nether regions?"

"It's cod for tea love, are you staying Polly?"

Even I couldn't stop the laughter that burst through my melancholy as Maureen bustled into the room.

"Excellent timing, Mum," I said through a laugh.

"Ooh you seem better; it must be Polly having a good influence on you. I've told her Polly, lying around here and eating chocolate isn't going to change anything except her waistline. She needs to get out there and get over him."

She stooped down to pick up my empty chocolate wrappers and then lifted my legs to remove some empty crisp packets that I was lying on.

"Thanks, Mum," I groaned. "You've just reminded me why I'm so miserable and now my heart hurts again."

She sighed heavily and hit me across the head with the empty crisp packets. "Stop being so dramatic. I've told you, give him a few weeks and when he's calmed down about everything that happened, I'm sure he'll call you."

"Really? What do you think, Pol?"

She tilted her head and put a thumb and finger to her chin as though she was thinking hard. "Well, have I changed my mind from the last thirty times you asked me...hmm, no. I've told you exactly the same as your mum, who gives excellent advice by the way, Mrs. Dixon."

Ugh, she was such a damn creep and she'd already been invited to stay for tea, so it was entirely unnecessary.

"I agree he'll call soon. He felt he let you down and didn't want to do it again, which in my opinion is very admirable – stupid but admirable."

"Exactly," Mum chimed in. "Now go and get a shower and pick out an outfit because you're going out with Polly tonight."

Polly grinned at me. "She does give good advice and you should listen to her."

"Ugh, fine," I groaned. "But I am not getting drunk."

"I think I might love him, Pol," I slurred as my best friend looked at me like a mother might look at her child when it's being a little shit, but she thinks it's cute.

"I'm sure you do, poppet," she replied as she went cross-eyed as she looked down at the straw in her glass.

"Do you think he might love me, just a teeny-weeny bit?" I held up my thumb and finger measuring the minutest of distance.

Polly shrugged and carried on slurping.

"What's that mean?" I copied the shrug and turned down my lips, making it much more of a Gallic gesture than Polly's.

"It means..." she shrugged again.

"Yes, but what does..." I did my impression of a Frenchman again, "mean?"

"I don't know."

"What, you don't know what it means, or you don't know if he might be in love with me?"

Polly shrugged again and despite how drunk I was I'd had enough of her shenanigans.

"Oh, suit yourself."

We were silent for a few minutes while I tried to think of something to talk about. It wasn't normally so awkward between us, but I only had Charlie on my mind, so he was all I wanted to talk about, and I had a feeling that Polly was all Charlied out for one night. That thought then made me giggle, as I thought of Polly snorting Charlie. I knew I shouldn't laugh, it was totally illegal, but we'd tried it once when we were both at college and had hated it. To be fair we had no clue what we were doing, and it had made me sneeze and send snot spraying all over Polly, who then wanted to puke, but coughed which sent it all over both of our tops. When I got home, Mum had asked why I had talcum powder all over me and I almost wet myself with the fear of being caught out. When I tried to feign surprise, she pulled me to her by my top and then stuck her nose against it. I screamed as I thought my mother was going to be high as a kite and pushed her away before I shouted for Dad to call an ambulance. Mum shook her head and called me a stupid idiot, one for taking it and two for actually having spent good money on a baggy of Johnson's Talc. When I took a quick whiff of my top, she was right. It wasn't something we ever tried again, in any case I was grounded for three months and had my phone and laptop taken away in the evening as well. It could have been worse, Polly had to work in her grandad's bakery every weekend for no pay, so for three months everyone thought she had thrush because she stunk of yeast.

"Erm, Willow," Polly hissed and brought me back from my reverie.

"What?" I asked, as I felt a slight rise of nausea. "Why do you look like you've been slapped across the face."

"No reason, I just think we should go. It's late and you didn't want to get drunk."

I frowned as I studied her carefully. She looked panic stricken. "What's going on?"

"Nothing."

The fact that her eyes flashed behind me didn't escape my notice. It was quick, but I'd been friends with her for years, I knew her every move.

"Polly?" She dropped her head into her hands and groaned. "*Polly, tell me now.*"

"Charlie's over there."

I felt the colour drain from my face and sobriety sweep over me. "I feel sick."

"Let's go," Polly said. "We don't have to stay and speak to him, unless you want to."

I remained silent and shook my head.

"Okay. Let's go."

"How does he look?" I asked and pushed a hand against my stomach.

Her eyes flashed again, and I knew that there was something wrong. I had no idea why, what evil being possessed me, but I slowly turned around to see him, the man who I missed more than I ever would imagine.

As soon as my gaze landed on him, the gasp was out of my mouth and the tears ran down my cheeks. The nausea rose again only this time I got the awful watery feeling in my mouth.

"I need to go." I ran for the toilet and just about got there in time to empty my stomach into it.

I had known it would be hard to see him for the first time, but I hadn't expected it to be that hard and have that much of an effect on me; but then again, I hadn't expected him to have a pretty blonde draped all over him.

CHAPTER
38

Being exposed to 15 minutes of sunlight will release the feel-good chemical, serotonin, making it easier to orgasm - when you're on the beach go and have a quickie, tell the kids there are sharks in the sea to stop them going into the water while you're gone.

Charlie

I moaned and put a hand to my head, trying to remember what I'd had to drink the night before and when a warm body shifted next to me and threw an arm over my stomach, I knew whatever it had been had been far too much. I wondered what the time was as I reached for my phone, where it usually was, but it wasn't there, so God knew where I'd left it. I'd have to find it later but at that moment I needed to get out of the bedroom.

Full of regret, I picked the arm up, slipped from under it and then placed it back on the bed. I snagged up a pair of sweatpants to pull on over my jockeys and sneaked out.

When I got into the kitchen Johnny was already there, with a huge grin on his face that was asking to be knocked off.

"What?" I asked as I scratched at my bare chest.

"You and your friend didn't half make some noise last night. You had a fair bit to drink."

"Ugh, don't. The thought makes me want to puke." I sat down at the table and pulled the teapot toward me and filled up a mug and added more than my usual one sugar. "Where's Simon?"

"Gone home," Johnny replied. "Said he needed some sleep because you two woke him up last night with your noise. He also said Teresa's old bed is shit."

His jaw tightened as he mentioned Teresa. I knew Johnny felt uncomfortable about what had happened that night, but deep down he also knew it was the right thing to do. Unbelievably, we hadn't heard from Teresa in the week since we'd thrown her out. Johnny had got word from the son of a cousin of my Grandma's that she was currently staying with the guy she'd been seeing, but how long that would last was anyone's guess. We had no idea who the guy was, it may well have been the one who fainted on our living room floor but knowing Teresa there'd probably been another couple since him.

"We should probably get that room cleaned up and decorated." I took a big gulp of tea and already started to feel a little better as the warm liquid washed down. "Maybe get a new bed, what do you think?"

Johnny nodded and wheeled his chair over to the toaster. "Yeah, let's do it next pay day. Get it done and then we can think about the night carer as well."

I noticed his back stiffen as he said the words and felt bad for him. He really didn't want a carer of any kind, but a night carer to Johnny was nothing more than a babysitter. We had to sort something out though, because after everything that had gone on with Willow, I knew I couldn't keep on taking all the responsibility. Tom Davies, one of my bosses, had asked me if I'd like to go and do some music production courses alongside learning on the job. It'd mean being away for a week or more and I didn't want to let the opportunity pass me by, so we needed to put plans in place and if that meant a night carer then that's what it would be.

"Did you have a good night then?" Johnny asked as he turned back to me with a plate full of toast.

"What do you think?" I grimaced and took the plate from Johnny as he manoeuvred himself up to the table.

"You're being a fucking idiot. You should call her and tell her you're sorry you were a prick and have hated every damn minute without her."

"It's not that simple, and like I told you she deserves better. It won't be long before Teresa is back and the shit hits the fan again, or you piss the new carer off and I have look after you more." I grinned as I made the last sentence which earned me a pinch to the nipple. "Oww, that fucking hurt."

"Good, you deserved it." Johnny grinned back and then winked at me. "So, what are you going to do about your guest?"

I groaned and dropped my head. "Fuck knows."

"Well you better think about it because I hear some dainty foot-steps coming this way."

Right on cue a figure appeared in the doorway.

"You got a cup of tea for me?" Bomber asked as he walked to the table while he scratched his balls. "Your brother hogs the fucking duvet by the way."

"You could have slept on the sofa," I replied and pushed a mug of tea toward him.

"You were the one who said we could share a bed." Bomber eyed me warily. "There wasn't a reason for that was there?"

I rolled my eyes while Johnny burst out laughing.

"No fucking way. I was pissed and felt sorry for you without any blankets."

Bomber took a piece of toast and then grabbed the butter. "What happened to the blonde? The one all over you in Zar Bar?"

I shuddered, as I remembered how she'd draped herself around me and then tried to put her hand down my jeans. I'd had to really fight her off and, in the end, had been pretty nasty and told her to fuck off. I didn't want anyone's hands other than Willow's down there. Not now and the way I was currently feeling, not ever. She was gorgeous and funny and was going to be hard to get over.

"I finally got rid of her," I replied. "If that had been the other way around, I'd be on a charge for sexual harassment this morning."

"When the only person you really want to sexually harass is Pretty Girl." Johnny said as he lightly tapped on the wooden table three times with his knuckle as if to force the point home.

"She was in Zar Bar last night," Bomber said as he poured himself a cup of tea.

My stomach flipped and my heart sank as I thought about her being there and not seeing her. Shit, I'd missed her and even a glance of her last night might have helped ease the continuous pain in my chest.

"Who was she with?" I asked as I swallowed to get some moisture back in my mouth.

"Her mate, the fit one, Polly."

"No one else?" I wasn't sure I wanted to hear the answer, but I needed to know. I needed to know if my pretty girl had moved on already.

"Nope. Just Polly. Anymore toast?"

Bomber pushed away from the table and moved to the bread bin taking out two more slices and putting them in the toaster. Johnny looked at me and frowned before he scratched his ear.

"Christ, fucking call her," he hissed.

I really wanted to say I would, that I'd call her right away, but I knew it wasn't fair to her. I loved my brother, I really did, and would never tell him, but he was a big responsibility and I needed to be there for him whether he liked it or not. How could I expect Willow to put up with that; broken dates, me being late or us not being able to go out at all, never mind not being able to decide to go away for a weekend without weeks of planning. Not to mention the shame of having Teresa hanging around and causing problems.

"Charlie, you're a fucking prick. I'm doing what you asked, I'm getting a carer, I've even said I'll get one for the night too, even though it's nothing more than a fucking babysitter. Teresa isn't coming back, so stop worrying about it, and anyway, even if she does it won't change how Willow thinks about you."

"Johnny, I'm not having this conversation again. I'm not calling her."

"Well more fucking fool you," he hissed. "You love her and you're punishing yourself for something that wasn't your damn fault."

"I never said I loved her," I cried and then looked over to Bomber who had finished making his toast and had his eyes on me and my brother with as much interest as if he was watching the latest Avengers film.

"And?" I asked him.

"Just listening and waiting to give you my point of view."

"Did I ask you for it?" I shook my head and ripped at my toast with my teeth.

"Nope, but I agree with Johnny, if you did want to know."

"That I should call her? Because like I said, I'm not."

"No," Bomber said with a mouthful of toast. "At the risk of sounding like a fucking pussy; that you love her."

"Shit," Johnny groaned and rubbed a hand over his face. "We're going to be plaiting each other's hair and waxing Bombers nads while talking about Real Housewives next."

"But he does love her, and he should call her."

I slammed my mug down and threw the remainder of my toast back onto the plate before I pushed my chair back and scraped it along the tiled floor.

"I'm not fucking calling her, and I don't fucking lo...ah fuck this, I'm going for a shower and then back to bed for the rest of the day. You two fuckers can...fuck off."

I stormed out and as I paced through the lounge heard my brother and my idiot best friend laughing like a pair of imbeciles.

CHAPTER
39

To add some excitement to your relationship, consider having sex in the car. A good position is facing him with your knees pushed against your chest and your feet on the seat or hooked over the neck rest - one tip, this isn't recommended when you're in a traffic jam as other drivers may get distracted.

Willow

I looked at my mobile again, wanting to make sure I'd read it correctly.

Charlie: Can we talk? Over at my house at 7?

When it had arrived earlier in the day, I'd swallowed down the butterflies that were trying to fly out of my mouth, and quickly responded with a simple 'Yes. OK'. A huge part of me had wanted to say no, ask your new blonde bint instead, but at that moment I hadn't been able to say anything else but yes.

I'd told Polly I thought I was in love with him, but there was no doubt about it, I knew after only one month I was in love with Charlie Monroe. My thoughts had been constantly on him, every single one being a wish and a hope that he'd change his mind. Admittedly, seeing him with the blonde had literally made me sick, that and the booze, but I still wanted to believe it had been nothing and that they weren't together. The thought of her hanging off his arm was bad enough, but to think he might have kissed her or even had sex with her gave me heartburn and I was far too bloody young for that.

Throughout the afternoon, I'd contemplated calling Polly and telling her about the text message, but I was afraid that she might insist I tell him to piss off. She'd been gutted for me when we'd seen him in Zar Bar, and I think if I'd asked her to, she'd have gone over and given him a mouthful on my behalf. Not that he really deserved it. We weren't together any longer, so he was entitled to have whomever he wanted draped over him.

So, instead of telling anyone, I'd kept the text all to myself and was at Charlie's house worried that I was doing the right thing. Once I knocked on the door, I knew I couldn't turn back and if it all turned to shit, well at least I wouldn't have to explain it to anyone else.

It felt as though the wait had been ages, but it might only have been seconds, when the door swung open and I was faced with Charlie. Beautiful, sweet, Charlie who looked as though he'd just woken up with his messy bed hair and tired eyes. He did not look like a man who had expected a visitor at – I glanced at the phone still in my hand – six, fifty-eight, precisely.

"Willow?" he gasped as he ran a hand down his chest.

"Well, yeah." Then a thought struck me. "I've not disturbed you, have I? You don't have a visitor or anything?"

He frowned and shook his head. "No, I was having a kip. Catching up on some sleep."

Oh my God, she'd stayed with him last night and they'd had lots of sex and now he was exhausted.

I felt myself pouting and ready to run but decided to wait and see what he had to say first. Find out why he'd wanted to see me.

"Come in anyway."

He stood aside for me to pass and when I did, I almost moaned with appreciation. He smelled gorgeous and I could have stayed there all night sniffing him.

"Go through, I'm not sure where Johnny is but he might be in there."

I gave him a small smile and moved down the hallway to the lounge where I expected to see Johnny grinning at me from his wheelchair, but the room was empty. As I walked in, I noticed the faint smell of smoke and spotted black scorch marks on the floor. The leather armchair that had once been there was gone and in its place was a wing back chair covered in a grey and black checked fabric.

"I like the new chair," I said as I looked over my shoulder to Charlie, who'd followed me in.

"Yeah the leather one was a bit of a mess; you know with the fire." He dropped his gaze and I noticed his cheeks were tinged with pink and could only guess he was thinking how one small fire had sent a lot of things to shit.

"Not too much damage though?"

"No," he replied his gaze back on mine. "We were lucky that we have a fire extinguisher and that Johnny was home, otherwise who knows what would have happened. Although to be honest, we'd all be a lot better off if Teresa had gone up in smoke."

"Charlie," I gasped.

He shrugged and walked past me toward the kitchen and stopped at the doorway. "I can't help the way I feel, Willow. I know I sound harsh saying it, but I have nothing to thank that woman for, but everything to hate her for."

He looked into the kitchen and frowned.

"What's wrong?" I asked as I moved to him.

"I have no idea where Johnny is, he wasn't in his room when I came to let you in, but he didn't say he was going out."

He then looked a little surprised and took a couple of steps into the kitchen and picked up a note which was propped up on the table. I wasn't sure what I should do, hang back or follow him in, so while he read the note I stayed where I was and watched him carefully as his back stiffened and he let out a series of curses.

"Charlie?"

He turned to me and crumpled the paper into his fist. "Did you get a text or a call asking you to come here?"

My heart dropped as instantly I knew what he was going to say.

"Yeah, a text, but it wasn't from you, was it?" I took a deep breath and tried to hold back the tears as realisation kicked in that he hadn't asked me here to beg for forgiveness. "I can go, it's fine."

Charlie lunged forward and grabbed my elbow and dropped the screwed-up piece of paper in the process.

"No, stay. I'd like to talk, I've...well, I've missed you."

My heart gave a tiny little jump. Simply because he'd missed me though didn't mean that he wanted to get back together. As far as I was aware, he still had the same issues in his life that he'd had a week ago.

"Okay," I said quietly. "But who sent me the text if you didn't? Was it Johnny?"

"I'm guessing so by the note he left." He stooped down, picked it up and smoothed it out before passing it to me.

'You should be getting a visitor at 7, don't be a dick and talk to her. Bomber has taken me to his for the night, where his mother THE NURSE *lives, so guess what dick head, I'll be fine. There's a cottage pie in the fridge – no I didn't make it, I sent Bomber out earlier while you were sleeping your mood off, although I'm hoping you'll be too busy to eat. DON'T call me and have fucking fun.*

Johnny

p.s. your phone is back in the bread bin where you left it last night when you and Bomber were throwing darts at pictures of Teresa.

I smiled and looked up at Charlie, who was staring at me warily, his arms folded across his chest and his hands tucked under his armpits.

"You brought Bomber back here last night?" I asked, unable to stop the grin which enveloped my face.

Charlie's eyebrows almost met in the middle. "Yeah, why?"

"I just thought..."

God, I felt stupid.

"What, Will? What did you think?" He took a step closer to me and gently took the note from my hand. "I know you saw me in Zar Bar last night and from what you've said I'm guessing you saw me with that blonde hanging off my arm."

"H-how did you know? Why didn't you come and speak to me?"

"Bomber told me this morning that he'd seen you and why didn't you come and speak to me?"

"Because of the blonde," I cried. "I wasn't going to come over while you were with someone. Apart from which, I hated it, seeing you with her. There was no way I was going to come over."

He smiled shyly and looked at me through his lashes.

"You hated seeing me with someone else?"

"Of course I did, you bloody idiot. I didn't want us to split up, it was your sodding idea."

"I know it was, and it was a shit one too." he muttered like a sulky child.

He laughed and I felt my insides go mushy at hearing the sound of it again. One week I'd been without him and it'd felt like a bloody lifetime, yet this here, as we stood in his kitchen chatting, felt so easy; as if we'd never been apart.

"You think it was a shit idea?" I asked as realisation of what he'd said hit me. "You don't think we should split up?"

He shook his head. "No, I don't, I've been a miserable fucking idiot all week."

"But what about the blonde and what about Teresa and Johnny and all the reasons why you ended things in the first place?"

I wrapped my arms around my stomach, unable to believe what he had intimated. I couldn't, because if I did and he told me that although he missed me he still hadn't changed his mind and we had to stay apart, I knew I'd cry and scream like a baby and I had some pride.

"The blonde wouldn't leave me alone, and I had to tell her to fuck off in the end."

"Charlie!" I was shocked but a little bit happy too.

"She wouldn't take no for an answer, trying to put her hands down my trousers, it was disgusting."

"*She did what?*" Now I was bloody furious. "What's her name? She needs to know that only I'm allowed to put my hands down your trousers," I shouted and thrust my hands to my hips.

Charlie grinned. "That's what I told her."

I stopped short and stared at him wide eyed. "You did?"

"Yep. I said no chance, there's only one woman who's allowed to do that and she's the most beautiful and funny woman I've ever met."

"You did not," I replied and rolled my eyes.

"It's what I should have said," he said quietly. "I wish I had. I wish I'd told her that I was an idiot for letting you go and that I'd do anything to get you back. Instead I told her to get her hands off me."

As the sound of my heart thundered in my ears, I studied him. He looked super sexy today, wearing grey sweatpants and a black vest that clung to his chest. His biceps were bulging, his eyes looked sleepy and sexy and his hair was a gorgeous mess. I adored him, I was falling in love with him and I wanted him back too; I'd never wanted to lose him in the first place.

"Johnny and Teresa?" I asked as I took a step closer to him.

"Johnny has agreed to getting a carer and he's going to interview for a night one too, and Teresa," he sighed heavily. "Well, she's gone for now. I'm sure she'll come back at some point and try and get us to let her live here again, but Johnny and I agree that we don't need her in our lives. She drags us down and makes life difficult and I lost the best thing I ever had because of her."

Charlie licked his lips and reached out to pull me to him by the belt of my dress. I placed my palms on his chest and held my breath and wondered whether he was going to kiss me. Slowly he leaned forward and placed one on my forehead.

"I'm so sorry, Will," he whispered, his lips against my skin. "I made the biggest mistake of my life letting you go and hope you can forgive me and let me have another chance."

I tilted my head back and looked up at him to see the sincerity in his eyes and euphoria rushed through my veins.

"I will never begrudge you the time you need to spend with Johnny," I replied. "Because the way you love and care about him is one of the things that makes you so special. I love how you take care of him and nothing that Teresa does would ever make me think any less of you. If we are together, we're in *everything* together and that includes being there for Johnny and facing whatever Teresa puts in front of us."

Charlie nodded and pulled me closer and I was a little shocked to feel he was hard beneath his sweatpants. I jumped and my eyes blinked quickly.

"Sorry," he groaned. "But I've missed you so fucking much and can't get out of my head everything I was going to do to you in that hotel bedroom."

At his words, my own memories flooded back of all the things I was going to let him do to me, as well as the things that I was going to do to him.

"You know I bought some new underwear for that night," I whispered against his ear.

Charlie drew in a shuddering breath and his hard on twitched against my leg.

"Please tell me you're wearing it tonight." His voice was shaky as his arm snaked around my waist to pull me closer. "Because we have a house to ourselves, the locks have been changed so Teresa can't walk in and I need to show you how good I can make you feel, better than you've ever felt before. I need to make you scream."

I was wet, my nipples were hard, and I desperately needed him inside of me. At this point I didn't care if it was quick or he didn't make me come, I only wanted to have sex with the man I was falling in love with – who was I kidding, the man I *was* in love with.

"I'm wearing it," I said as I pushed my chest closer to his and relished in the friction against my sensitive nipples. "I was hoping I might get lucky."

"Oh, you will," he said around a low growl. "No fucking doubt about it.

CHAPTER
40

Did you really think I'd close the door after reading this far?

Willow

Charlie's lips and tongue seductively licked and kissed along my neck, leaving a trail of goose bumps on my sensitive skin.

"Will," he whispered. "I've missed you so fucking much."

"I've missed you, too." The emotion at being back in his arms and hearing his words was almost too much, but I needed to remember every moment of this, because I knew it was going to be epic.

"I'm going to worship you, just like I promised. You're going to know exactly how much I care about you. How much I want you. How much I need you."

I felt myself getting wetter with each word and when Charlie's hand moved down and pulled up my skirt to grab my bum, I thought I might collapse on the spot.

"Fuck," Charlie groaned and walked me backward into the lounge.

I expected him to pull us onto the sofa, but he continued walking, kissing me and undoing each of the chrome buttons on my dress with every step and by the time we'd reached his room, my dress was fully open and the new pink underwear I'd bought was on full display.

"Shit, you look beautiful," Charlie said as his eyes grazed my body. "I can't believe I nearly let you go."

"Well, I'm here now and I'm not going anywhere."

"Wouldn't allow it," he replied as he dropped his mouth to my collar bone and pushed my dress from my shoulders to let it fall to the floor.

My head dropped back as Charlie slowly kissed along to my shoulder and then nipped it gently as he hooked his fingers into my bra strap and pushed it down. Anxious to feel his skin against mine, I dragged his vest up his body, urging him to put his arms up. I missed his fingers whispering against me, but as soon as I'd thrown the vest to one side, he wrapped his arms around me, and his warm body pressed against mine. His hard on pushed against me and strained the fabric of his sweatpants and I was desperate to feel him. Slowly, I trailed my hands down to his tight arse and gently squeezed it relishing in the low moans that it elicited from Charlie. While he continued to kiss my neck, I slipped my hand inside the waistband and moved it to the front, happy to find his cock was hard and bare. I wrapped my fingers around it and gave it a gentle stroke, trailing my nails along it before circling the head.

Charlie groaned and covered my mouth with his, he pushed his tongue inside and kissed me deeply. While he pushed off my other bra strap with one hand, the other unhooked the back. Moving his chest away from mine to let the pink lace fall to the floor, he stooped to take my nipple into his mouth and suck on it, adding his teeth for extra intensity.

The last time we'd been together, Charlie had rushed to reach his orgasm, leaving me frustrated, but now I was desperate for him to throw me on the bed and fuck me into oblivion.

"Charlie," I gasped as he sucked hard on my nipple.

"Tell me what you want?"

"You," I said breathlessly. "I only want you."

He made a low growl and before I knew it, I was being hoisted up, with his hands under my backside. I wrapped my legs tightly around his waist and pulled my hand from his sweatpants so that I could press down on his shoulders, giving him better access to my boobs. When he started to kiss down them and knead my arse, I dropped my head back and moaned with the pleasure that he was giving to me. He carried me over to the bed, and without taking his mouth off me, he put one knee to the mattress and lowered me very gently.

"You are the most beautiful woman in the world," Charlie whispered as he began to kiss down my stomach to my pubic bone, where he then licked along the edge of my knickers.

"I need you to fuck me, Charlie, please," I begged.

"All in good time." He grinned against my skin and then without warning, hooked his fingers into my knickers and whipped them down, pulling them off one leg but leaving them dangling off my red stiletto shoe.

His large hands pushed my legs apart and when I felt the long sweep of his tongue against my clit, I thought I was going to rocket into the sky. Two more licks and then he pushed his tongue inside of me and pumped it in and out in a steady rhythm that his hips might follow, each pump followed by a lick. It felt incredible, it was out of this world mind-blowing, it was everything I had hoped and imagined, and it was only his tongue. I dragged my fingers through his hair, my nails scratching against his scalp, as I felt the waves start to build.

"Oh my God, Charlie, oh my...aaaahhh."

Charlie lifted his mouth from my wet core and kissed my inner thigh before I felt the bed shift. I roused myself just enough to half open my eyes to watch him pull down his sweatpants and step out of them. His cock bobbed against his stomach; big and smooth and I knew I wanted it bare.

"Don't use a condom," I said. "I'm clean, I'm on the pill, and I trust you."

Charlie's face broke into the most beautiful smile, his dimples on full show, and when he walked back to the bed, I couldn't help but marvel at how perfect his body was and how handsome he was. His sleepy eyes had gone, and the fern greens were now vibrant and shining. I had no doubts that coming here and being willing to forgive him for ending things was exactly the right thing to do. He was who I wanted to move forward with, who I wanted to make memories with.

"Charlie," I reached for his hand.

"What is it, Will?" he asked as he took it and moved to kneel beside the bed. "Tell me." He stroked my cheek and then ran a finger down my nose and along to my lips as he traced them gently with a sweet, concerned smile on his face.

"I need to tell you something." He nodded and urged me to go on. "I just...I, well...I love you."

When he didn't immediately answer, I closed my eyes as I didn't want to see the look of fear on his face. I should have kept my mouth shut and not ruined the moment, but the words wanted to spill from my lips. I lay there and wondered what to say to take the sentiment back when he surprised me with a kiss as his hands laced in my hair and then cupped my face. It was so powerful that I had to grip the duvet to ground myself, to be sure that I didn't fall into shattered pieces, because that was the sort of kiss that it was – earth shattering.

"I love you too," Charlie finally whispered. "I know this is quick and that we've had some false starts, but you and me are going to have something amazing, I can feel it."

"You mean it? It's not only because I'm lying here naked and you're worried you won't get any if you don't say it back?'"

Laughing, Charlie climbed back onto the bed and kneeled between my legs and looked down at me with a huge smile – and a huge boner.

"I don't give a shit if I don't get any, but I told you I was going to worship you and make you scream, so that's what I'm going to do."

He dropped down and leaned on his forearms, kissed me again and then pushed inside of me and began a gentle thrust and push. Our eyes locked together, and I wrapped my legs around his waist as he made love to me slowly as he continued his rhythm and built the pressure inside of me up and up and up until I was on the brink. I was almost there when Charlie pulled out and pushed both my knees to my chest. He then pushed back inside of me and continued with his thrusting, this time he was quicker, stronger and harder, with his hips and backside providing the power. Sweat slicked our chests and our fingers squeezed tightly together above our heads as the climax of our pleasure reached its peak, culminating in me screaming, just like he'd promised. Wave upon wave of heated sensation swept through my body as Charlie continued to pump and stretch out my orgasm until I felt him stiffen and cry out as he gave one final, hard thrust.

As his chest heaved, Charlie slowly pulled out of me and placed his hands on my ankles and pulled my legs straight and then gently stroked them back to life as he dropped a gentle kiss to one of them.

"Okay?" he asked as he grinned at me.

I blew my hair out of my eyes and nodded, unable to speak or to find any words which could describe how 'okay' I actually was.

"Good. Now, how about some food?"

Charlie had his back to the headboard, as I straddled him, with a huge dish of cottage pie between us. We tucked in, both of us hungry after our exertion and I didn't think I'd ever felt so content and to put the cherry on the cake, Charlie's playlist for me played in the background on his Bluetooth speaker.

"You've got gravy on your chin," I said as I rubbed at Charlie's square jaw.

"Oh no, you've got gravy on your left tit." He dipped his finger in the pie and wiped it on my boob and then leaned forward to lick it off.

I giggled and shuddered as his tongue tickled against my skin.

"You're bloody insatiable," I said and captured his mouth between my thumb and forefinger and squeezed his lips into a pout which I dropped a kiss to.

"It's you, you make me insatiable. I think I could go all night with you."

I rolled my eyes. "One decent shag and you think you're Superman."

Charlie laughed and tickled my sides making me squeal. When we almost tipped the pie dish over, I gasped and pushed against Charlie's chest.

"Stop, we're going to drop cottage pie all over the bed and then we won't be able to stay in it, because I've got to be honest, I'm liking this bed. It's really comfy."

"Well we'd better move it then, because we're not using Johnny's bed or Teresa's old one and that sofa is a definite no after last time." He picked up the dish and stretched to carefully place it on the floor. "So, apart from the obvious, which give me a half an hour for the pie to go down and I'll be more than happy to oblige, what do you fancy doing. Want to watch a film, or carry on snuggling?"

I thought about it for a few seconds and then a song came on to the playlist that summed up everything about how I felt.

"I'm in the mood for dancing," I said with a huge smile.

"Really? You want to dance?" Charlie shook his head and shrugged. "Okay then, let's do it."

As he started to lift me, I squealed with excitement and clapped my hands as I sprang off the bed without any help.

When my feet hit the floor, I began to jump around, soon joined by Charlie whose grin was just as big as mine. We raised our hands in the air, his cock bounced, and my boobs jiggled as we leaped around to The Nolans singing 'I'm in the Mood for Dancing', and I had one of the best nights of my life.

EPILOGUE

2 Years Later

Love is not about sex, going on fancy dates or showing off. It's about being with a person who makes you happy in a way nobody else can

---

Willow

I looked over at Charlie and let out a little sigh. He was so bloody perfect in every single damn way, and I mean in every way. Things in the bedroom department had continued to get better and better and we hadn't even needed my dad's help. All Charlie needed was to relax and not worry about having to get home to make sure Johnny was okay, or that Teresa wasn't passed out drunk with a cigarette in her mouth. He simply needed some me and him time.

The fact that we had moved into our own house had helped and the fact that Johnny seemed to be pretty loved up with Kristy, a really lovely girl who Charlie had taken on as one of two carers for Johnny; the other being a really nice guy called Pete who did the sleepovers. Not that Johnny thought he needed one carer, never mind two, he was too independent and thought it would be the start of his decline so when he'd stalled about getting one despite his promise, Charlie had taken charge and done the interviews. As soon as Johnny had seen Kristy though, he'd fallen hard for her, but she'd managed to keep him at arm's length for six months before she realised she'd fallen for him too. I believed she spent more time at Johnny's place than her own, often swapping shifts with Pete, so I doubted it would be long before she moved in permanently.

Once we moved into our own home, it wasn't long before Ruben moved into my old room, he'd even kept Hedwig, as Charlie had stridently refused to let me take him. My youngest brother was finally doing what he wanted to do all along, working and not going to Uni and was the manager of a mobile phone shop. He wasn't going to stay there long; he'd made that clear and was already looking for manager posts at larger retail stores. He'd also met a nice guy called Michael who he seemed to really like and who didn't want to hide Ruben or their relationship. We never did get to meet Cane properly, his move from home never happened and he still couldn't tell his parents that he was gay, so ended things with Ruben. I think my brother's heart was a little broken by it all, but now he was with Michael we got to see a lot less scowls and far more smiles these days.

As for Toby, well he was still chasing Polly, who actually seemed to be thawing to him a little bit – she did agree to play spin the bottle with him at our housewarming party and it did end with a long kiss that blew her away. She'd totally stopped talking about Declan and often asked after Toby nowadays so who knew what would happen.

Declan was still dating Barbie dolls and Danny was still loved up with Patsy and planning a wedding, so all in all nothing had changed with the Dixon family. Ivan was still fucking terrible and Maureen was still a pain in all of our arses, but we bloody loved them.

Charlie and I, well, we were happy. Generally, anyway, today though was not a day I was full of joy. In fact, if I could I'd chop his bloody big beautiful dick off, whether it gave me some incredible orgasms or not. It was because of that dick and those orgasms that I was in the position that I was in i.e. flat on my back with my bloody legs in the air with a grey-haired man between them staring at my damn vajajay.

"I think one more push, Willow, and baby will be here."

"Oh my God," I gasped. "I can't, I'm so tired and it hurts so much."

"Hey baby," Charlie cooed. "You can do this; you've done really well so far." He wiped my brow with a wet flannel and then kissed it.

"*Really well?*" I grimaced. "I've been a damn rock star."

He laughed and then must have seen my face because he straightened his mouth into a thin line.

"Yeah, of course you have. You've been brilliant."

"I should bloody think soooohhhh."

"Okay," Graham, the midwife, said a little too brightly for my liking. "Here we go, hold on tight."

"Does he have to sound like we're about to have a ride on the waltzers?" My teeth gritted together as I bared down and pushed with all the energy I had left.

Charlie lowered his head to my ear. "I fucking love you, you know that?"

I nodded, unable to speak and push at the same time, but gripped his hand extra hard just to put my point across, which was 'don't ever come near me with that big beautiful dick ever again!'

When I thought I had nothing left in me, I felt the pressure ease and heard Graham whoop and a shrill new-born cry.

"We have a beautiful boy." Graham lifted the most gorgeous child I'd ever seen.

"He's beautiful," Charlie gasped and leaned down to kiss my temple. "I'm so proud of you."

I drew in a ragged breath, as I looked up at the man who I loved more and more each day and thanked him for the beautiful son that he'd given to me.

"Hey little man, you want to go to Mummy?" Graham asked my crying baby. He then turned to me. "You want to undo your nightgown, my love."

I unbuttoned it and pulled it open, more than ready for the skin on skin with my son.

As soon as Graham placed him on my chest, I burst into tears, the emotion too much to keep in. "Oh my God," I said. "He's gorgeous. He looks like you, he's got your dimples."

Mesmerised, Charlie gazed at us both as he reverently stroked a hand down the baby's back.

"You have a name?" Graham asked as he continued to check over the baby against my chest.

"Dylan Charles," I whispered, not taking my eyes from Dylan.

"Nice name. Now, we need to cut that cord, you want to do it Charlie?"

Charlie nodded and listened carefully to Graham's instructions before finally cutting the cord.

"He's all yours now." Graham smiled down at us, looking so proud as if he'd done all the hard work. "I'll be back in a couple of minutes, and Kaye and I will give him a thorough check over." He looked over to the other midwife who'd been assisting him.

"He's a beauty," she said as she wrote on my chart.

"He's okay though?" I asked as worry enveloped me.

"He seems perfectly fine. We need to check him out that's all."

"You were amazing," Charlie said and kissed me once more. "He's amazing."

"Yeah, I know." I looked up at him and smiled. "I love you."

"I love you more," he sighed. "And I swear I'll be the best father I can be."

"I know, because you're the best man that I've ever known."

Charlie

"Okay," Ivan said as he stripped off his ratty old rugby shirt. "Let me have him."

"Dad, what are you doing?" Willow cried.

We'd had an hour of peace and tranquillity gazing down at the gorgeous baby that we'd created and now it was time to share him. I wasn't sure I ever wanted to let him out of my sight, the first hour of fatherhood had been something beyond anything I'd ever felt before – I felt as though my heart was going to explode with the amount of love I had for one little person who I'd only known a short time. I felt euphoric as I looked up and grinned at everyone as they trooped into Willow's room, while I had my beautiful boy cradled against my chest.

Alongside Ivan and Maureen were all four of Willow's brothers, closely followed by Johnny and Kristy – thankfully Teresa hadn't heard the news and turned up, but I didn't really expect her to. After we threw her out, she came around a couple of times, but each time we stood firm and told her that unless she sobered up, Johnny and I weren't interested in a relationship with her. Needless to say, she hadn't sobered up, so was currently living with her latest boyfriend, or so we'd heard.

"I want to do the skin on skin thing." Ivan stopped in front of me and held out his hands. "Come on Charlie, give."

"You ready for this, Dylan?" I whispered against his blond head.

"Ivan, put your top back on," Maureen hissed and sneaked into my left to take the baby from my outstretched arms. "If he snuggles into that chest hair he'll be lost for days."

"I want to bond with my grandson," he replied with a pout.

"Well you'll have to wait because Nanna has him first, doesn't she, yes she does." As Maureen spoke baby talk to Dylan, he looked up at her with dark blue eyes and lifted his top lip.

"And before you say anything, that's wind," Ivan scoffed and moved to stand next to Maureen and coo over their grandson.

"How was it?" Ruben asked me. "Gory as all fuck?"

"He stayed at the top end," Willow said as she shifted up the bed to make room for Declan and Danny to sit next to her feet.

"Ugh, should think so." Ruben shoved a bunch of flowers at her.

"Got you these and don't let those fuckers make out they contributed, because they didn't."

"Rube, they're lovely. Thank you." Willow took the flowers and immediately burst into tears.

"Oh shit," Ruben muttered as he looked at me. "They're only a bunch of flowers."

"It's okay mate," I whispered. "It's her hormones."

Ruben nodded and went to join his parents to leave space for Johnny to wheel over to me.

"Congratulations big brother. He's fucking amaz-."

"Hey," Declan called. "No swearing, we agreed."

"But Ruben called you a bunch of fu-." He stopped when Kristy poked him in the shoulder. "Okay, okay, but he is an awesome little dude."

Johnny grinned and leaned forward to give me a tight hug.

"Thanks, Johnny. I fucking love him so much already."

"Charlie!" Now it was my turn to be poked, this time by Willow.

"I got you these by the way," Toby said and offered Willow a box of chocolates. "Sorry I ate most of them while we were waiting. You didn't half take a long time."

"Yeah, well sorry," Willow replied, as she peered into the box and pulled out a chocolate, "it was kind of hard work you know, pushing a cantaloupe melon out of my vagina."

Ruben grimaced. "Shit. Too much information, Willow."

"Did you eat the placenta?" Danny asked.

"No, I did not! God, that's disgusting."

"A lot of people do. If we have kids, I might ask Patsy to bring hers home."

"What, like in a takeaway bag?" Johnny asked.

"You could always get it delivered with four poppadum and a free bottle of coke."

"Toby, shut up and carry on eating your body weight in chocolate." Danny turned back to Willow. "Honestly, it's got some seriously good vitamins in it, isn't that right Kristy?"

Kristy shrugged. "I have no idea, I'm a carer not a medical nurse."

"Really?" Toby said as he tilted his head to one side to study her. "I always thought you wore one of those cute little nurse's outfits while you gave Johnny a bed bath."

"She doesn't give me a fu-flipping bed bath. She helps me get into the bath, but now you come to mention it, it is something we could try babe. Weirdly, we haven't tried the nurse and patient role play yet."

Kristy coloured up and slapped a hand over my brother's mouth. "No more. Keep it shut."

We all started to laugh as we realised that they'd both given away one of their sex secrets.

"Anyway," Declan said and rubbed Willow's leg over the top of the blankets. "You've done a brilliant job little sister. He's really handsome and definitely has the Dixon genes."

"What about his willy?" Ivan asked as he started to rummage around in the blanket that Dylan was wrapped in. "Is it little or does he take after the Dixon's for that too."

Maureen slapped his hand away. "Leave his willy alone, Ivan."

"No, he doesn't," Willow stated and took hold of my hand and pulled it to her lap. "He takes after his daddy."

"Oh no," Toby cried. "I always thought Charlie looked like a big dick kind of guy."

"He did get it caught in his zip once," Maureen offered which made all the men in the room wince.

"Ooh yeah, I remember," Johnny said with a shiver. "But that does prove you're pretty well-endowed, bro."

"He is." Willow grinned. "Which is why Dylan's extremely well blessed in that department too."

I rolled my eyes at her and grinned. "I fucking love you, so much," I said and leaned in to kiss her.

"Yeah and I love you too, so bloody much."

As both our crazy families continued to discuss the merits of our son and who he looked like, I watched the woman I loved and thanked every God out there for bringing her to me. There was no one in the world who could hold a candle to her and if I searched for a thousand years, I'd never find anyone more beautiful or funnier. She was everything I'd always wanted and together we would be the family I'd always wanted. Willow Dixon was astounding, and she was all mine.

The End

CHARLIE'S PLAYLIST FOR WILLOW

The Cheesiest Playlist Ever
Oh, Pretty Woman - Roy Orbison
Signed, Sealed, Delivered (I'm Yours) - Stevie Wonder
You Can Get It If You Really Want - Jimmy Cliff
Sylvia's Mother - Dr Hook
Crazy Horses - The Osmonds
20th Century Boy - T Rex
Saturday Night at the Movies - The Drifters
I Only Have Eyes for You - Art Garfunkel
Baby I'm-a Want You - Bread
Good Time Charlie's Got the Blues - Elvis Presley
Grease - Frankie Valley
I'm Every Woman - Chaka Khan
Every 1's A Winner - Hot Chocolate
Never Let Her Slip Away - Andrew Gold
Don't Stop Me Now - Queen
I Wanna Be Sedated - The Ramones
If I Said You Had a Beautiful Body - The Bellamy Brothers
Heart of Glass - Blondie
Girls Talk - Dave Edmunds
Lay Your Love on Me - Racey
The Eton Rifles - The Jam
Since You've Been Gone - Rainbow

Tusk - Fleetwood Mac
Reunited - Peaches & Herb
A Horse with No Name - America
Bye Bye Baby - Bay City Rollers
Tie a Yellow Ribbon - Tony Orlando & Dawn
Save All Your Kisses for Me - Brotherhood of Man
I'm in The Mood for Dancing -The Nolans

https://open.spotify.com/playlist/1oMA2MkTcWvyJQDoRJI7yM?
si=nhzNsxLyTGqiLe_gSd-AwQ

ACKNOWLEDGMENTS

As usual there are many people, I need to thank for helping me with this book and for making it the best story it can be.

Caroline Stainburn for your editing skills. Your attention to detail and ability to spot the words that I use far too much is incredible – I'd say it's amazing, but that's one of those words!

Brooke Bowen Hebert once again for proof-reading for me, even though I sprung it on you last minute.

Tammy Clarke, it's another beautiful cover and a miracle that you understood my usual vague requirements.

To the girls who attended the readers retreat, thanks to you for encouraging me to include Bev and Geoff in the book. Remember girls, next time be prepared to wait three hours for a drink.

Jenn Thompson the dentistry advice and the story were a great help and I hope I didn't get anything drastically wrong.

To all my book family who share, blog, and review thank you, thank you, thank you. It's hard sometimes to get your work out there, so everything you do is appreciated. Special thanks to Claire and Wendy of Bare Naked Words for everything you've done for me on this and other releases. You are awesome and the efforts you go to are immense.

My lovely alpha and beta readers, Donna, Patsy, Laura, Cal and Karen much appreciation to all of you for stroking my ego and telling me how much you loved this book. You know how much I adore Charlie and Willow and you also know it would have upset me if you hadn't, so even *if* you didn't, thank you for telling me you did.

Chloe Walsh, Victoria Johns and Anna Bloom I appreciate you taking time out of your own busy schedules to read The Big Ohhh and give me your feedback – every piece of advice was gladly received especially from such brilliant authors.

As Willow's love of cheesy 70's music is inspired by my own, I feel I need to thank two people who without realising it helped to create this playlist. Helen and Julie, whether it was Abba, Brotherhood of Man or The Jam, it didn't matter because we sang and danced without a care and had the best time ever – oh to be twelve years old again. Love you both more than you will ever know.

Finally, thank you to those who created that music when I was in my formative years. You shaped my world, you guided me through good and bad times, and you prepared me for the 80's. You still have the ability to make me laugh or cry today and I thank you for being with me while I write this book and for helping me to create Willow's personality. It's been a blast.

Printed in Great Britain
by Amazon